A Cloudy Day on the Western Shore

Middle East Literature in Translation

Michael Beard and Adnan Haydar, *Series Editors*

SELECT TITLES IN MIDDLE EAST LITERATURE IN TRANSLATION

All Faces but Mine: The Poetry of Samih Al-Qasim
Abdulwahid Lu'lu'a, trans.

Arabs and the Art of Storytelling: A Strange Familiarity
Abdelfattah Kilito; Mbarek Sryfi and Eric Sellin, trans.

The Candidate: A Novel
Zareh Vorpouni; Jennifer Manoukian and Ishkhan Jinbashian, trans.

The Elusive Fox
Muhammad Zafzaf; Mbarek Sryfi and Roger Allen, trans.

Felâtun Bey and Râkim Efendi: An Ottoman Novel
Ahmet Midhat Efendi; Melih Levi and Monica M. Ringer, trans.

Gilgamesh's Snake and Other Poems
Ghareeb Iskander; John Glenday and Ghareeb Iskander, trans.

Jerusalem Stands Alone
Mahmoud Shukair; Nicole Fares, trans.

The Perception of Meaning
Hisham Bustani; Thoraya El-Rayyes, trans.

A CLOUDY DAY ON THE WESTERN SHORE

Mohamed Mansi Qandil

Translated from the Arabic by Barbara Romaine

SYRACUSE UNIVERSITY PRESS

The translation was supported in part by an award from the National Endowment for the Arts

National
Endowment
for the Arts
arts.gov

Syracuse University Press
Syracuse, New York 13244-5290

First Edition 2018
18 19 20 21 22 23 6 5 4 3 2 1

Originally published in Arabic as *Yawm Ghaa'im fii al-Barr al-Gharbi* (Cairo: Dar El-Shorouk, 2009).

∞ The paper used in this publication meets the minimum requirements of the American National Standard for Information Sciences—Permanence of Paper for Printed Library Materials, ANSI Z39.48-1992.

For a listing of books published and distributed by Syracuse University Press, visit www.SyracuseUniversityPress.syr.edu.

ISBN: 978-0-8156-1109-7 (paperback) 978-0-8156-5462-9 (e-book)

Library of Congress Cataloging-in-Publication Data

Names: Qandīl, Muḥammad al-Mansī, author. | Romaine, Barbara, 1959– translator.

Title: A cloudy day on the Western shore / Mohamed Mansi Qandil ; translated from the Arabic by Barbara Romaine.

Other titles: Yawm ghā'im fī al-barr al-gharbī. English

Description: First edition. | Syracuse : Syracuse University Press, 2018. | Series: Middle East literature in translation

Identifiers: LCCN 2018022452 (print) | LCCN 2018026512 (ebook) | ISBN 9780815654629 (e-book) | ISBN 9780815611097 (pbk. : alk. paper)

Subjects: | GSAFD: Historical fiction

Classification: LCC PJ7858.A53 (ebook) | LCC PJ7858.A53 Y3913 2018 (print) | DDC 892.7/36—dc23

LC record available at https://lccn.loc.gov/2018022452

Manufactured in the United States of America

Contents

A Cloudy Day on the Western Shore

I • Asyout

AT LAST THE RIVER'S EDGE APPEARED: tortuous, overgrown with reed thickets and thorny brambles. The air grew cold and damp. Flocks of white birds hovered and circled in ceaseless patterns. The mother kicked to a stop the donkey she was riding and took in the dark gray ripples of the river.

"There's no one here," she said. "They've sent us to the wrong place."

Aisha advanced a little way on her donkey, and saw a boat moored to a tree trunk, bobbing up and down in the current. She said nothing. She had come all this way, not knowing the reason for the journey, the donkey steadily jogging along and stumbling through the gravel along the way until her own hindquarters ached. She saw a few pigeons huddling against the cold in the hollow of a tree, and wished she, like them, could take refuge far from her mother's grim face.

The mother dismounted, made her way down the slope of the riverbank, and disappeared among the reeds. Aisha heard the sound of panting, and was afraid. Could the wolves have followed her from her distant village all the way to this place? She could never get used to them, no matter how often she saw them, circling her or lurking all night beneath her window. They looked very like huge, dust-colored dogs, with their tongues hanging out, always panting—how could she ever get used to the sight of such creatures?

Her mother emerged from the reeds and beckoned to her. Aisha tied both donkeys to a tree and followed her mother, just as she always did, descending by the narrow path that ran alongside the water, careful to avoid being scratched by the thorns. A hut came into view, constructed of reeds and mud brick. Aisha heard the gurgling of a nargileh and inhaled the smell of sweet tobacco.

"Hey! Ferryman!" the mother called.

There was no answer. Determined, she advanced until she stood before the opening to the hut. There was a lean, dark-skinned man seated languidly inside, holding the nargileh, before a glowing wood fire. It was clear he had deliberately refrained from answering them, not wishing for anyone to disturb his mood or draw him out of his den in such cold weather. He stopped sucking on his pipe and regarded them silently.

"We want to cross the river," said the mother.

He stared wonderingly at them, resting his gaze a bit longer on Aisha, unsettled by her wide eyes and their captivating gleam.

He said, "It would be foolish to try to navigate the river when it's this rough. Come back tomorrow."

"We must cross today," the mother insisted. "We've come a very long way."

"The river's unreliable, ma'am. In weather like this all the spirits of the drowned awaken and come out of the cracks at the bottom. Who knows what could happen?"

Aisha shuddered, imagining these spirits rising out of the water cold, pale, and sorrowful, surrounding her and her mother.

"If you're as skillful as they say you are," said the mother, "you'll pay no attention to such phantoms. That pipe gives you only smoke. I'll give you a sultan's riyal."

But the ferryman was thinking of something else. If the two of them went away now, this young girl would vanish from sight in a moment, and he would miss the chance to contemplate those eyes, to delight in that face at his leisure.

The mother grasped the sleeve of the abaya that cloaked her body, untied a knot in the hem, and from its folds withdrew a silver riyal, clean and shiny. It was rare to come across such a coin in the midst of these isolated villages, most coins here being so coated with rust and dirt it was impossible to know whether they'd been minted in the era of the present sultan or in the time of the great Muhammad Ali. The ferryman reached out his hand, dazzled by the light reflected off the coin. Until then he had only ever seen small brass tokens—and seldom even those. He often took his fee in the form of a few bites of tomato or cucumber, or a single egg. Now he set aside the nargileh, put some wood on the fire to keep it going, and stood up, revealing himself to be tall and broad-shouldered, despite his thinness. He walked toward the tree and tugged on the rope, bringing the boat closer to shore, where it was stabler in the water. The mother turned to Aisha and said firmly, "Get in."

Aisha shrank back, shivering in the chill air, and the ferryman seized the opportunity to reach out and enclose her small, cold hand in his own, his fingers long and coarse. She lifted her feet and stepped into the unsteady boat. He turned to the mother, but she didn't offer him her hand. He held the edge of the boat until she managed to climb aboard as well. He untied the rope, gave the boat a push, and then leapt aboard, water dripping from his trousers. The boat began to rock, adding to Aisha's alarm, and she leaned over the side, prepared to vomit.

"Don't look at the water," the ferryman told her kindly. "Look at the other shore and you'll feel better."

Aisha raised her head. The opposite shore was still far away. There the peak of the western mountain could be seen, although fog had obscured much of its pitiless terrain. Aisha turned toward the ferryman, a melancholy, grateful smile on her face. *Oh, Lord,* he thought to himself, *how did you bring forth such beauty from the belly of this poker-faced woman? I wonder how old she is—twelve? Thirteen? Or older*? Her body was poised on the brink of its ripening and flowering phase; the buds had begun to emerge on her chest. In his heart the ferryman wished he could heave the mother overboard and keep rowing with this young girl, all the way to the river's source.

In the distance a weird howling could be heard, coming from the riverbank. It was none other than the wolf, which had followed her over all this distance and was standing on the shore.

"There are no wolves on this side," said the ferryman, perplexed. "And wolves don't come around like this in the daytime. Lucky for us the river is between him and us."

The boat suddenly shook, and the current began to put it into a spin. The ferryman gripped the oars tightly, a series of whirlpools appearing on the surface of the water.

"Hold onto the edge of the boat," he said. "We should have kept off the river when it's acting up like this. I warned you!"

The boat became an insubstantial thing, something for the current to play with. Aisha's eyes met those of the wolf; she saw its open mouth, its tongue hanging out. The ferryman struck at the water over and over, trying to keep the boat away from the whirlpools.

Alarmed, the mother cried, "You're going to kill us!"

He plied the oars once more, as if he was trying to drive off the spirits that spun with the current. By some miracle the boat stayed upright. A sudden swell pushed it up against a ford composed of water hyacinth, whose roots snaked around the boat and brought it to a stop. Breathing hard, the ferryman thrust his oar into them. “You can get out here,” he said to them.

In disbelief the mother said, “You want to drown us?”

“It’s shallower than you imagine,” he replied. “If we stay in the boat, a whirlpool will open up and swallow us all.”

Aisha stood up. She was afraid, both of the river and of her mother’s grimace. She hopped abruptly into the water and found herself standing on the bottom, which was yielding and slippery. She pushed aside the broad leaves of the plants and began to make her way toward the shore. She heard a splash as her mother jumped in behind her. She went on, pulling her feet out of the mud and setting them down again, holding onto the low-hanging branches of some ancient willows, the trees half in and half out of the water—they were what guided her to the riverbank. Her mother followed her, while the ferryman remained standing where he was, fearful, clutching his oars.

The mother called loudly to him, “You’ll wait for us to come back.”

“And where else would I go?” he replied. “There are whirlpools in the river and wolves on the opposite bank.”

The mother turned to Aisha, who was shivering. In the same peremptory tone she said, “Let’s keep walking. The air will dry our clothes.”

The mountain was close to the shore. They trod the middle of a rocky and desolate path, the journey dragging on until it no longer led anywhere. Aisha’s teeth were chattering. Clutching herself with her arms she discovered that her budding breasts were painful as well. The mother, who went in front, began to quicken their pace. Aisha was amazed—where did she get such stamina? They arrived at a burial ground set into the lap of the mountain, featuring a mixture of rectangular tombstones, crosses, and pillars with shattered capitals. Ground-level openings led to chambers hidden within the mountain. The wind cut through the fissures in the rock with a keening wail.

The mother cast her eyes about, searching for something, some lost thing. A number of meager dwellings appeared, carved out of the rock. She stopped at last before a small house topped by a dome with faded paint, and rapped stoutly upon the wooden door, as if to awaken the dead. Presently, the door opened to reveal a bent old man. He raised his head with difficulty, as though unable to face the light of day. Black soot clung to his beard and his clothing.

"Is it for such a visitation as this," he said wonderingly, "that the weather is so cold? Come in."

Aisha hesitated, feeling as if she was about to enter the very hollow of a tomb. But her mother pushed her once more, and she stepped into a choking gloom, amid the smell of smoke from burning wood and rubbish. Mother and daughter sat beneath the dome, from which thin shafts of light trickled down. The man looked at their damp clothes and the dust that clung to them.

"What a long journey you must have had," he said. "Was there no avoiding it?"

The mother pointed at Aisha and said, "I want you to put a tattoo on her arm."

"Well then," replied the man, "if that's what it's to be, then let me bring a lamp."

He got slowly to his feet, fetched a tin receptacle with a blackened wick sticking out of the top, and lit it with a stick of firewood. It didn't light the place up very much, but lent it a bit of life.

"Why have you come here to the heart of the mountain," he asked, "for the sake of a small tattoo you could simply have got at the Tuesday market?"

"They told us you were the best," was the mother's terse reply, "and now it's up to you to prove it." She turned to the girl. "Hold up your arm." She bit back Aisha's name before speaking it. Aisha still trembled, but she drew back the shawl that covered her head and exposed her arm with its pale and tender skin, unblemished by the sun.

"And what image do you want to put on this little arm?"

"Make it the sign of the holy cross," said the mother, "and beneath it write 'Mary.'"

Aisha gasped and stared at her mother, eyes wide and fearful, but the mother paid her no attention. She went on giving instructions to the tattoo maker:

"I want it to be large and clear, but it must look faded, as if it had been drawn on her skin years ago—practically as if she'd been born with it."

"That will take a great deal of precision, but you've come to the right man. Where are you from?"

"From al-Bayadah," said the mother quickly.

She was lying, as the man certainly knew. He was still examining Aisha's arm, looking for the most suitable place to put the tattoo.

"I know everyone at al-Bayadah," he muttered. "I'm the one who tattooed all the baptismal crosses on their skin. I know everyone from al-Badari, too, and

Deir al-Jabrawi, and even Shatab. Just from your appearance I can tell you two are from Beni Adi or Beni Khalaf—am I right?"

Aisha looked into the man's eyes and found that they resembled those of the wolf that had turned up on the riverbank, eyes that sought to penetrate the abaya concealing her body.

"You ask too many questions, tattoo maker," said the mother. "Get on with your work, and there's your fee."

To Aisha's amazement, her mother once again brought forth a silver coin to work its magic. Where had she got all these glittering coins? The man bit the coin to ascertain with his teeth that it was genuine, then put it carefully into his pocket. From a corner he fetched a packet containing the tools of his trade: pieces of mostly blackened metal, of which only the sharpened points still gleamed. He opened a small jar in which was some dark-colored substance with a penetrating odor, a mixture of zinc and powders extracted from minerals found in the mountain. He alone knew the secret of how to mix them. He took Aisha's arm firmly in his grasp.

Aisha turned to her mother with her eyes full of tears, and for the first time since that morning she cried, "Mother!"

But her mother looked back at her impassively. Aisha felt the needle's bite as it pierced her skin. She neither wept nor cried out, but she wished the man would loosen his hold on her a little.

"Try to relax," he told her. "The more you relax, the less pain you'll feel."

Aisha turned her face away from his foul-smelling breath to gaze at the walls hewn from the veins of the rock, and at the soot that covered them. The pain grew worse, and she tried to free her arm, but his fingers kept hold of her in a powerful grip. Fires of pain ignited throughout her body, and she began to weep quietly. The tattoo maker did not pause, but went right on with the procedure, killing off the living cells with the point of his awl and replacing them with that mixture of zinc and mountain metal. Aisha's arm turned red, and a blue tint began to creep in among the whorled cells of her skin.

All at once Aisha remembered that moment of pain she had felt on meeting her father's fixed, expressionless stare. She had gasped and frozen in place, the men belatedly noticing her presence in the "washing" room, and then pulling her away. The sharp point wielded by the tattoo maker had awoken all the hidden sufferings she had been keeping back: her father's death, the loss of the protective maternal embrace when another man entered her mother's bed.

A kind of paralysis spread through her arm and shoulder, and all of her left side. At last the tattoo maker let go of her arm, but the pain went on and on.

"See for yourself," he said to the mother. "A magnificent cross, with three more crosses at the tips. It will swell a bit, but when the swelling goes down the cross will be there for life."

"We must leave now," was all the mother said.

Her strength gone, Aisha stood up and nearly fell to the floor. She leaned against the wall.

Watching her, the man felt sorry for her. "She needs to rest," he said.

"We haven't time."

The cold wind started up again, freezing their faces. They made slow progress, Aisha's mother supporting her firmly. There was no time for falling down, no opportunity to rest. They passed the rocks and the low openings into the mountain, and then the gray water came in sight once more. Aisha collapsed unconscious upon the ground.

The ferryman rushed to her side. He had managed to drag the boat in and tie it to a willow tree. Beside her child's prostrate form the mother stood striking her cheeks in distress. Not stopping to ask permission, the ferryman knelt, picked up the fragile body, and headed for the boat.

"This is a bitter day, a bitter day for us all."

He studied her face, pale as if she were at death's door, as he lifted her strongly in his arms. Circumstances had granted him an opportunity greater than he had dreamed of. He waded into the water, climbed aboard the boat, and laid her down, wrapped in her shawl. Then he turned accusingly to the mother and found her face bathed in tears. He began rowing swiftly. The wolf, fortunately, had taken itself off, and the whirlpools had abated. He plied the oars vigorously, knowing that the girl's salvation rested upon their achieving as quickly as possible the comfort of the warm hut that was his home.

Disembarking, the ferryman picked Aisha up once more and waded through the water to the door of the hut. The donkeys were waiting patiently, with nothing within reach for them to eat except brambles and wild grass. The mother looked on in silence, not daring to raise any objection. She watched as he laid Aisha down by the fire and covered her. He stoked the fire, careful to direct the smoke away from the girl. He smiled with satisfaction to see the glow of the flames reflected on her pale cheeks, and prepared to go back outside.

"You can't go far with her in this condition, ma'am," he told the mother.

"I wanted to go the rest of the way to Asyout," she said.

"How far from Asyout do you think we are?" the ferryman replied. "You've miscalculated. The railway station is a long way from here—the donkeys won't be able to make it that far."

In the ensuing silence, the mother revised her calculations. The man left her and made a circuit of the beach, looking for dry kindling and some good grass to feed the donkeys. He went wordlessly about his work and avoided meeting the eyes of the mother, who was staring into space. The hut bore the smell of a man on his own; there was a pile of dirty clothes, a clay pot containing the remains of some bread, and the bed of straw upon which Aisha was lying. The ferryman put more wood on the fire and turned to the mother. "There's the sugarcane railway," he said.

The mother came out of her reverie and focused on him. "What?"

"It stops near here. It passes through the sugar cane fields until it reaches el-Hawamdeyya, stopping every so often to take on more bundles of cane. The problem is that it's slow, its cargo is rough and scratchy, and riding it is forbidden."

"Then how can I take it?"

"You're an expert at persuasion. You can come to an understanding with the guards and the driver. The main question is whether you can put up with the hardship of traveling that way."

The mother looked at Aisha's shrouded form. Her eyes were still closed, but that blue pallor had receded from her cheek, and been replaced by a faint blush. Life was stealing softly back into her.

"The train won't come until morning," said the ferryman. "It's late now, and the weather's turned bad. You can stay in the hut—I'll sleep outside."

The mother stared at him, perplexed. She had not expected such an extraordinary gesture of hospitality. Then a shrewd look came into her eye. "I have no more silver," she said.

He didn't reply. He reached under the bed where Aisha lay and brought out a small packet of tea and another of sugar, handling them like valuable treasure. He set the blackened tin kettle on the fire and said, "What you've given me is more than enough, ma'am. Now you're my guests."

Aisha moaned and opened her eyes for a moment. She stared at them in wonder, and then shut her eyes once more. But it was a good sign and restored her mother's peace of mind: a bit of magic, as it seemed, and the ferryman's heartbeat quickened to see it. He handed the mother a cup of strong tea, and made another for himself. The mother tried to rouse Aisha so she could join them, but the girl turned her back. So the two of them sat sipping their tea in silence. Trying to keep his voice down the ferryman said, "I can see that you are people of means. What's the purpose of this punishing journey? You're not running away from something, are you?"

The mother said with a sigh, "It's a complicated matter—more than I can explain to a passing stranger."

"Perhaps it would do you good to unburden yourself to a 'passing stranger.' Who better than a ferryman, who lives always between two shores, with no land of his own, no family to go home to? The water is my country, and the fishes are my family."

The mother sighed again and replied, "I can say only that I'm looking for a safe place, a new life."

She didn't tell him about the canals and irrigation ditches she and Aisha had negotiated, the obscure villages they had avoided, or the mountain passes they had traversed. She said nothing to him of the jewelry she had sold to cover the cost of this journey. She merely set down her empty teacup, leaned back against the wall of the hut, and closed her eyes.

The ferryman observed that, despite the creases that lined her face and the leathery husk of her skin, there was a strong resemblance between mother and daughter. He got up slowly and, keeping his promise, went to sit outside the hut. He contemplated the fading light of day as it sank and dissolved into the waters of the river.

Night in Egypt is darker than anywhere else, especially when the moon hides its pale face. Then the darkness is perpetual, the light an unexpected phenomenon, its dim particles assembled at the edges of the valley over thousands of years: light from reed fires set to repel the hungry crocodile and hippopotamus; from the brick furnaces for baking adobe; from the pottery kilns in which vessels for food and for burial are fired; from the brewery where steam rises off the fermenting hops; from the fragments of rocks quarried and cut to build houses and tombs; from piles of burning quicklime radiating heat night and day; from fires fed by palm fronds and straw for warmth and cooking; from the cane fields set alight to fertilize the earth with the residue of ash; from smoldering temple sacrifices; from burning scented oils, frankincense, and myrrh; and from the fires the builders of the pyramids kept burning throughout the night for twenty years. All these things had coated the earth with their blackness, and the nights with darkness so dense even the winds of the khamsin could not dispel it.

The ferryman sat, a small figure before the chill winds blowing in off the river, contemplating the dark clouds that obscured the moon and stars. He leaned against the trunk of a palm tree, feeling its rough bark dig into his back. A change had come over him—suddenly he was conscious of loneliness and hunger as never before. He was aware of life's passing days, the meanness of the hut in which he lived, the poverty of his meals. It was as if the mere presence of this helpless young girl had altered everything around him. He fingered the silver coin in his pocket. It was his talisman: he would never spend it, for it would remind him always of her lovely face. These thoughts, to his surprise, helped him to endure the cold until morning.

Aisha, the first to wake, saw her sleeping mother and the dying fire. Her arm was aching, and she remembered what had happened the day before. She stood up, reeling with hunger. She went out of the hut and saw the ferryman curled up beneath the palm tree. Sensing her presence, he opened his eyes to find her standing there, silently observing him, her face pale, beautiful, and sad. She didn't know he had carried her in his arms, that he had seized the opportunity to press her to his chest a bit more than necessary, furtively, so that her mother wouldn't see.

"Are you all right?" he asked her. "Did you sleep well?"

She nodded her head and gave him a little smile. Her mother hurried from the hut and said to him, "Which way is the sugarcane railway? Is it far?"

Crestfallen, the ferryman pointed in the direction she needed to go. "It's not far from here—just a little way."

Pointing to the donkeys, the mother said, "I want to leave these animals in your care. Later I'll send someone to bring them back to me."

"My pleasure, ma'am."

She took Aisha's hand, and away they went, the ferryman waving sadly as the wind stirred their black abayas, until they vanished from his sight.

The cane fields were not far from the riverbank. They were exposed, the sugarcane having been cut; its roots still clung to the earth, awaiting the fire that would reduce it to black, salty ash. The ash would then be witness to a small miracle, as new green shoots pushed their heads up through its layers. The harvested cane was divided up and tied in bundles, each one bound by the long, coarse leaves of the plant, which would serve as cords until they dried out and became brittle.

Aisha and her mother seated themselves amid the closely packed bundles. The place was deserted. The narrow iron rails wound a twisting course through the fields and disappeared at the horizon. The guards had not yet awoken. A weak sun shone and there was a bit of warmth. “I’m hungry, Mother,” said Aisha. “I feel dizzy.”

Her mother pulled out one of the sugarcanes and peeled back the leaves that tightly enclosed it. She snapped it into small pieces at the joints, ignoring the little cuts it made in her hands, and extracted the gleaming white marrow, which she offered to Aisha. “What if they see us?” whispered the girl.

Stripping the rind with her teeth, the mother said, “I’ll work something out with them.”

Aisha sucked on the sugarcane, tasting the sweet juice as it ran down her throat and feeling her body revive as if a life-giving potion was flowing through her pores. Nearby, there were stirrings of movement. The mother took hold of the girl’s hand and they hid themselves behind a small thicket. Some transport workers appeared and called to one another as they began hefting bundles of cane and placing them near the tracks. Aisha and her mother stayed where they were, silently watching.

At last a piercing whistle sounded, the still earth rumbled, and a smell of smoke drifted in the air as the train came into view. It was smaller than Aisha had expected. A black locomotive went in front, chugging out a great cloud of smoke bigger than itself and pulling behind it a number of cars, all but the last two loaded with cane. The train came to a stop and the driver jumped down. He talked loudly with the workers, and then the labor of loading the cane commenced. Watching all this, Aisha was alarmed. Could there be room for her amid those prickly bundles?

Gradually the bundles of cane were cleared from the area. The driver was finishing up his noisy exchange with the workers and preparing to remount the locomotive. The whistle sounded, warning everyone to stand back from the tracks. The wheels began to screech on the rusty rails. Aisha looked despairingly at her mother who, on the other hand, was ready to throw caution to the winds.

She took her daughter by the hand and they made their way back toward the last car.

The workers stared at them in astonishment. "What are you doing?" one of them shouted. "Passengers are forbidden on this train!"

A group of men stood in front of them, raising their arms to block the way. At this moment the wolf appeared. No one knew where it came from, but it insinuated itself among the men, weaving between their legs, as if it too wanted to catch up with the train. The men retreated in alarm. Even those who were blocking access to the train leapt out of the way and scattered, while Aisha and her mother ran faster, until they caught hold of the last car. First the mother jumped aboard, then she held out her hand and pulled Aisha up beside her. The coarse leaves buffeted them and scratched their faces. The wolf left the men behind and began running along beside the train, accelerating until it drew even with the driver, who stared fearfully at it and increased his speed. The wolf stopped, its mission accomplished. It stood still with its mouth open and its tongue hanging out, until Aisha came into its line of sight. She stared out at it, meeting its mournful gaze.

The driver made no stops—there were no more loads of cane to collect. The last car rattled along, jouncing its passengers up and down as it went. It was not a comfortable journey, and they were still more fearful each time the train crossed one of the canals or irrigation ditches, when they felt as if they were suspended in empty space, surrounded by nothing that was familiar. Aisha watched in growing alarm as the briny canals passed beneath the train, hoping only that she might not die beneath their choking waters.

When they had gone a long way, the Nile appeared to widen and the mountains to close in. The train was now proceeding through narrow passages amid tilled fields. It picked up speed as it traveled downhill. Mud-brick houses could be seen, as well as stone minarets in the distance. Aisha, at last, breathed freely.

In Asyout the river valley narrows; the mountain—where lawless folk roam the slopes—looms closer. The rocks look alike, rather resembling a spine joining the north to the south. It is not remarkable, then, that the first attempts to unite the two should have been undertaken at Asyout, or that the first seeds of discord should have been sown there, just as the mummies were interred there along with potsherds and the remains of the citadel built by King Menes.

The train did not go all the way to Asyout, but stopped at a depot well outside the city. There, all the bundles of cane, which had originated in various parts of

Upper Egypt, were gathered up to await the arrival of a stronger locomotive that would transport all of them to the sugar-processing plant at el-Hawamdeyya. Amidst the hustle and bustle of loading and unloading, Aisha and her mother were able to slip away, while the driver stayed put, not moving from his seat for fear of the wolf's making another appearance.

The mother moved confidently in the streets of Asyout, but this was the first time Aisha had ever seen such a big and lively city. Her mother, more experienced and streetwise, knew the place she was looking for and made for it unhesitatingly. Despite weariness and fatigue, she seemed to be in a race against time. She walked along, clutching Aisha's arm as if she feared she would lose her in the crush of passersby, shops, flies, and beggars. The streets were dusty, unpaved, and crowded with carts drawn by donkeys and mules, with farmers, Saïdis, miscellaneous foreigners, and khaki-clad British soldiers.

They stopped before an enormous building made of gleaming white stone and surrounded by iron fences, all of this surmounted by a high tower housing a shiny brass bell. It was a church, massive and clean, not like the brick churches on the outskirts of their village. Aisha's mother breathed a sigh of relief. Aisha stood staring at the place—the sight of it took her breath away. There was a sign inscribed in black, but she didn't know how to read or write. Impatient, her mother hurried over to the iron gate, which was closed. She seized it and rattled it, shouting, "Hello? Is anybody here?" There was no reply.

"Is this the end of our journey?" Aisha wondered. "Will we go back?"

Her mother, however, was not about to give up so easily. She circled, looking for a gap she might slip through. In a corner, on the other side of the gate, she spied a rope hanging down. She pushed her hand through the iron bars and pulled it as hard as she could. The chime of a metal bell rang out, resounding through the silence like a cry for help. She pulled and pulled, and the bell kept ringing.

"Mother, that's enough," Aisha pleaded.

"We have to let them know we're here and that we need them."

At last someone appeared, a tall youth with a thick moustache and wearing a small turban. He approached them from the far end of the courtyard, his face betraying irritation. "What do you want?"

"Please," said the mother, "we've come a long way. We only want to meet with the abbess."

"She's busy, and I can't disturb her—impossible. Besides, she never sees anyone without an appointment."

Before Aisha's mother could say another word he turned, moved the bellpull out of reach, and walked away. The mother threw herself at the gate once more and called after him, but without turning or looking behind him he disappeared from sight. The mother protested angrily, striking the gate with her fist.

Aisha was frightened. "Should we leave?" she said.

Through clenched teeth, her mother answered, "Who said anything about leaving? We'll sleep in front of the gate."

They sat on the ground, their backs to the iron bars. Some passersby glanced briefly at them. Aisha kept looking into her mother's face, waiting for her to explain the reason for this arduous journey. The sun climbed high in the sky, then began its descent. Aisha was hungry and thirsty, but dared not complain. The building sat silent, no noise or movement issuing from it.

Then they heard the sound of a door opening. They stood up together. It wasn't the Saïdi youth coming this time, but a slight figure wearing a black abaya and walking with an odd gait. It was a woman, her voluminous robe hanging loose on her body and sweeping the ground. She carried her arms in front of her chest, one hand thrust into the sleeve of the other. She stopped and faced them. Aisha peered at her in surprise—she was a foreigner, dressed in a nun's habit. Her round face was suffused with a modest blush, her blue eyes wide. She looked uneasily out at them through the bars, presumably taking them for a pair of beggars.

She spoke in heavily accented Arabic. "What do you want? We have nothing to offer you."

The mother clutched the bars and entreated her, "We are at your mercy. We've come a long way and we can't go back. Every way back is closed to us. I must meet with the abbess."

"We don't receive transients."

The mother stepped back a little, then pointed to Aisha. "I'm not here for my own sake," she said, "but for the sake of this child." The foreigner turned and looked at Aisha. She could see the traces of exhaustion and hunger and hopelessness written plainly upon her face. "Her life is in danger," continued the mother, "and if you turn us away from your door she will surely die."

With fear in her eyes, the woman said, "Truly?"

"I swear it in the name of the Messiah."

The foreigner hesitated for a moment, then slid her hand into an opening in her robe and drew out a cord attached to a key so large it was hard to imagine it suspended from anyone's neck. She turned it in the lock and the mother pushed on the gate to help her swing it open, then sprang through the gap without waiting for an invitation. With the foreigner in the lead, the mother pulled Aisha along beside her as they approached the immense building, its tower rising above it. They passed through the door into a damp and dimly lit antechamber. Aisha shivered. The foreigner pointed to a wooden bench and said, "Wait here."

Aisha leaned against the back of the bench. The walls were high, with only one window, which was close to the ceiling and had stained-glass panes. This was the only source of light. There were strange images depicted on the walls, people and places and vast ships, all watching over them, impassive and silent. Aisha's mother gripped her shoulders to stop her from shaking.

"Get ahold of yourself, girl," she scolded. "We've reached the end of our journey—don't ruin everything now."

On the point of tears, Aisha said, "I don't know what you're planning to do with me."

"I'll tell you when it's all over."

On hearing the approach of footsteps, she fell silent. The foreigner appeared and beckoned to them. Following her, they crossed a wooden floor, clean and polished to a mirror shine. The walls were faced with gleaming wood as well, and Aisha could see her image reflected back as she passed. The foreigner paused before another closed door and knocked politely. Then she entered, and they followed her. Here, too, there was just one window, an enormous crucifix on the wall, a picture of a woman holding an infant, and an immense desk in the middle of the room, behind which sat an old woman also wearing a nun's habit.

Aisha's mother startled her by letting go of her hand and falling to the floor in a full prostration. Her mother's body, she thought, had betrayed her at last, her self-possession temporary, and now at an end. But then her mother spread her arms, brought her legs together, and lowered her face to the floor, forming the shape of a cross.

Alarmed, the nun behind the desk got to her feet. Standing up, she seemed more imposing. In Arabic distorted by a strange accent she said, "This will not do. Raise your head, stand up."

Without lifting her face from the floor, the mother said, "I cannot, Mistress, not until you grant my request and save my daughter."

"We don't do such things here unless there's a massacre. And no one should prostrate himself before a human being—get up and tell me what it is you want."

The mother raised herself, but remained crouched on the floor with tears pouring down her face. Aisha didn't know where she found them. Pointing at Aisha, her mother said, "I want you to save my daughter's life. Death stalks her."

The woman looked at Aisha, her face like those drawn on mausoleum walls. "Death—how?" she said.

"We are from an old Muslim family, but we converted. We chose the way of Christ."

The nuns, the elder and the younger, gasped, and so didn't hear Aisha's own sharp intake of breath. The mother alone maintained her composure, as she continued her story. "It was a moment of illumination, Mistress," she said. "The Virgin came to me in that state between waking and dreaming, and revealed herself to me. I had no choice but to follow her path."

The old nun looked uneasy. It was a tale too shopworn to be easily believed. The mother knew it, and turned to Aisha. "Show them your arm," she said brusquely.

Her voice had regained something of its commanding tone. Aisha pulled her robe aside, revealing her swollen arm and the points of the cross implanted in her skin. It was ugly and painful-looking, especially on so small an arm.

For the first time, the young nun intervened. She came close to inspect Aisha's inflamed arm and cried, "What is all this swelling and bruising?"

"Our family tried to remove the cross from her skin," said the mother. "If we hadn't run away they would have cut off her arm entirely."

The young nun stepped back in horror and crossed herself. She pressed her hand to her chest and began praying silently, her wide eyes shining with fervor.

Examining the tattoo, the abbess said, "It must have been done by some primitive method, God help us."

The sight of the tattoo made an impression on the nuns that lingered even after Aisha covered her arm once again. Her mother lightly touched the elder nun's knee and said softly, "Save her, Mistress. Accept her into your school. Give her the chance to be educated, and save her life at the same time."

"That is not what we do," said the abbess in some agitation. "We are simply an American school on foreign soil, and we mustn't implicate ourselves in local troubles. We have only girls from Coptic families here—there's no room for fugitives."

The young nun was looking at Aisha, who stood abject and broken before them. She couldn't know that hunger and the cruel journey to which Aisha's mother had subjected her had reduced her to this state. The nun approached the abbess and spoke to her in an unfamiliar language. Aisha's mother looked on in meek submission. The young nun bowed her head humbly and retreated once more to a corner, but the mother sensed that something had changed.

The abbess sighed. Gesturing toward Aisha she said, "What is her name?"

"Call her whatever you please," said the mother quickly. "Her given name won't suit her anymore."

"Don't you have any papers?"

"In our remote village there are no papers. We live and die and no one knows we ever existed."

The abbess cast her eyes about uncertainly. "And have you no luggage or clothing with you?"

"We were running away, Mistress. We would have attracted too much attention had we brought anything with us."

The abbess was silent then, studying the young nun's face, the crucifix on the wall, and the icon of the Virgin. Then she said, "I don't know what to do." She pointed at the young nun, who stood modestly to one side, biting her lower lip. "Sister Margaret says we must offer succor to lost souls, but we came here to help the Christians, and we do not wish to take sides in any unrest or conflict. We have no business with converts or fugitives. We don't want to set the Muslims against us. In our midst this poor child would be a bomb that could demolish our mission here."

"I came in order to save my daughter," said the mother, "not to sow discord. Her presence here is a secret that will go with me to the grave."

"This story you've told me—how many people know about it?"

"Only she and I."

The abbess turned to the younger nun, whom they now knew as Sister Margaret, and spoke to her. Aisha's mother could see that the conversation went on too long for there to be any possibility of retreat or refusal. The abbess sighed. She stood stiffly before the icon, as if waiting for some word or sign. Then she turned to the mother, as though trying to rationalize what she was doing. She said, "Do you swear to keep the secret?"

Aisha's mother replied quickly, "I swear on the Qur—" She stopped and corrected herself. "On the Gospel."

Had the abbess caught her slip of the tongue, or had she already made up her mind? Gazing at the girl's face the abbess said, "In truth she is a sad little flower. She'll take the name of our Lady Mary. May it be a blessing to her."

Now Aisha was genuinely alarmed—at being stripped of her name, in part, but most of all because she was going to stay here in this place, losing her mother and everything that connected her to her old life.

The abbess spoke again. "You may go with Sister Margaret and she'll find you a place in the private residential quarters."

Aisha tried not to breakdown, but could not keep a tremor from her voice. "I want to talk to my mother first."

Her mother spoke quickly to keep her from saying anything more. "We need to say good-bye. God alone knows when it may be possible for me to see her again."

The abbess nodded to Sister Margaret, who led them from the room. They passed once more through the dim and silent antechamber, then into a side passage, which brought them into a small chapel, chilly like the other rooms and so dim that they could scarcely discern the images hung upon the walls. Sister Margaret ushered them to one of the wooden pews, where they sat down side-by-side. The nun then withdrew, leaving them alone.

Aisha held her tongue until the sound of footsteps faded away, then turned to her mother, fighting back tears. Her mother's face was utterly impassive.

"Why are you doing this to me?" said Aisha. "Why would you want to leave me in this place?"

Her mother's reply was resolute and betrayed no sign of weakness or indecision. "What would you have had me do? Was I to abandon you to disgrace and death?"

"I really am disgraced now, with all these lies you've been repeating about me!"

"On the contrary. I saved your life. I removed you from the clutches of that man who was lurking by your bed every night."

"My uncle. He took the place of my father."

"That is not how it was. You were still little when your father died. And then everyone—my relatives, the whole village—pressured me to marry his brother. That's the tradition. But from the first moment my body was resistant to him. I couldn't conceive with him, so you remained my only child. I could have reconciled myself to life with him if it hadn't been for the way he looked at you, the way he tried to touch you. You were too young to understand what he was doing, but it terrified me."

Just then the tolling of the bell could be heard, albeit faintly. Was it just the wind that caused this, or was it time for prayers? Avoiding her mother's eye, Aisha gazed at her surroundings. Now she could make out the walls and the pictures mounted on them: elderly men with long beards and flowing robes, staring straight at her as if they disapproved of her presence here.

She looked back at her mother's face, whose features had softened. It was as if she were somewhere else, absorbed in the memory of a different time and place. All her past sorrows had been stirred to life: when Aisha's father, mysteriously slain, was brought home on the back of a donkey gray as the dust, the village was mute, the mountain colluding in its silence. Her first thought had been to take Aisha and flee with her to Asyout, where she had come from—a decision she delayed for thirteen whole years, unable to summon the courage to leave her house and land. No one knew who had killed Aisha's father—or if they knew they didn't dare say. The elders of the family met and decided that the younger brother should take the place of the slain husband: a decree that struck her like a thunderbolt.

Omran himself was a reprobate: "a raging bull," as his dead brother had called him. There wasn't a woman in the village he hadn't run after, nor a husband who hadn't come to grief with him. His insatiable lust was the subject of the village women's secret gossip, but she hated him, especially after the scandal with the Gypsy girl, whose people had accused him of rape. His family tried to settle the dispute by giving a large sum of money to those drifters; the Gypsies themselves cared little for honor, but the family was angry and the village was disgusted with Omran's behavior. Days later, cast up at the edge of a drainage ditch that traced the borders of the village, they found the girl dead, her body bloated, her mouth crusted with salt and stuffed with waterweeds. No one knew what had happened to her, whether she had slipped and fallen on her own or whether her family had grabbed the money and then killed her and taken themselves off, leaving her to be buried in a potter's field. Be that as it might, Omran, with all that attached to him, would have been the widow's last choice.

Aisha's mother swallowed hard and went on in an undertone, "From the time you were five years old I felt what a menace he was to you. You may even have been younger than that the day I left you sleeping and went out early to the village market. I reckoned I'd be home before you even knew I'd gone out, but when I got back I found you awake, your little body completely naked, like a dove chick newly hatched. Omran was standing there in front of you, pouring water all over your shivering little body—he'd put you into a tin tub and was pretending to give you a bath, but really it was nothing more than an excuse to have the body of a growing girl exposed in front of him. He was laughing with the delight of his power over you, your innocent nakedness, making a sound like some stud bull when it's aroused, pouring the water with his hands, rubbing his hands in your hair, and you sitting there in front of him, cringing in fear. I snatched you up away from him and swaddled you in all the wrappings I could find—you were still so little and slight, so vulnerable to a predator like him. I remembered all the frightening stories that had been repeated about his stalking young girls, and about the Gypsy girl who was found raped and killed in a ditch. He laughed at my terror and said, "How are you going to hide her from me?"

"From that day on, when you slept beside me in my room, I felt for you a dozen times a night to make sure you were still there next to me. I found no pleasure even in food, especially when I noticed your body maturing, your hair growing, your face filling out, and your breasts beginning to swell. I was so overcome by fear I could no longer sleep. Meanwhile, he circled us unceasingly, like a voracious hawk. He paid no attention to me or my threats, he was indifferent to my fear and alarm. He knew I was too weak to stand up to him. In the end the only solution was to run away with you to this place, and to make up this outlandish tale."

Aisha kept silent while her mother, breathing hard, poured out her story. She knew what her mother was talking about. She remembered things her uncle had done, things her mother didn't know about, hadn't seen, his rough touch when he would press up against her body in the enclosure that housed the livestock, when his fingers groped her small chest. There was not much she could do about it—she had tried simply to shrink away from him, to escape with as little damage as possible. She knew her mother was right, but in her helplessness she said, "Must I really renounce my religion, change my name?"

"You're still the same person, by your own name or any other. As for your faith, it's in your heart, my child. No matter where you are you'll go on worshiping the same God."

"What will you tell them back home?"

"Some fib. They won't want to believe it at first, but if I stick to it they'll have to."

"How will I see you?"

"You're part of my heart, Aisha. I'll see you even if you can't see me. The important thing is for you to seize this opportunity and live your life as you deserve to, without shame or dishonor."

Aisha began to cry, feeling how young she was, how lost and hungry. But her mother embraced her, saying, "Don't cry. Smile for my sake. I want to remember you smiling for me, not angry with me or bitter toward me."

Aisha dried her tears and tried to smile. She was overcome with despair, a lump forming in her throat. Her mother stood up and said, "You're safe now."

She kissed Aisha on both cheeks and on her forehead, and Aisha kissed her hands. They heard the sound of the door opening, and Sister Margaret entered. She didn't come toward them but, lightly as a butterfly released from the net, proceeded to the statue of the Virgin and child, and stood before it, her head bowed. Then she went to a small table and lit the two candles that were set upon it. As light filled the room, Aisha and her mother realized that dusk had fallen over them without their having been aware of it. Then the nun got down on her knees and began to pray. Aisha's mother stood up. She didn't look back—she couldn't bear to see Aisha, the forced smile fallen from her lips. She let the door of the small chapel close resoundingly, as if in confirmation of her departure. And it was all over. Aisha felt intensely alone, felt the need of someone, anyone, beside her—even a wolf. She gazed at Sister Margaret's back as the nun continued her silent prayers.

◆ ◆ ◆

"Aoufallah . . . yaa Aoufallah!"

There was a skinny-legged old man dashing up and down the riverbank, shouting these words. Aisha was watching him from the window as she looked out at the river. She couldn't tell whether he was shouting from joy or from fear, but the river was raging, its brassy surface crosshatched with waves, its waters rising to the point of overflowing the banks that contained it. The man would stop every so often, scoop up a handful of the red-tinted water and fling it into the air, then again take up his running and shouting, "Yaa Aoufallah!"

The wind was blowing hot from the western side of the river, out of the foothills of the mountain. Aisha, as was her habit, had woken before all the other girls. She saw the river rising and reddening as daylight came on. The fishing boats were not out, for the fishermen knew that the river in its turbulence would sweep before it red silt, tilapia, and fishing boats alike. The man disappeared in the direction of the city, still shouting. Aisha watched the river birds wheeling in alarm. This was their regular morning itinerary, but at the moment their flight was agitated—something had upset them and was preventing them from flying in their usual arrowhead formation.

The Nile was among the most extraordinary rivers in the world. In the summer, when rivers run dry, the Nile would defy the laws of nature and flood its banks. Beset by winds blowing from north to south, its current runs contrary, flowing north, descending from the highlands of distant Africa, bellowing like a king. Heedless of the dense forests, the vast and scorching desert, it traverses immense boulders, massive and solid, and confronts the resistance of six cataracts. It fills the still forests with its clamorous roar, bubbles with foam, and sends out its spray to create rainbows that never dissolve. It passes among acacia, ebony, willow, and sycamore. It wanders like a sad poet amid the wastes of the desert, undeterred by hills or sand dunes or mountains of granite. It tumbles violently over Camel's Neck Cataract, its waters bubble and froth at Marjan Cataract, and then it slows down to catch its breath before plunging into the cataracts of Beit al-Abd, al-Maʿfour, and Harek. Along its arid track it encounters but little of the dark waters of Atbara River. The sky does not lavish it with rain, nor do the snows melt to refresh it. It is surrounded only by great masses of black stone, which share with it the secrets of eternity; and the river, in turn, takes care not to erase the relics they bear: the inscriptions, the scarab images, the cartouches.

Temperamental, the river rushes on, carrying the mud of first creation, containing something of the Blue Nile's playfulness, something of the White Nile's wisdom. It rises and falls, dividing and spreading at times to lose itself in the swamp beds, only to reassemble in the form of its principal, unified artery. It does not settle down or assume a character of dignified sobriety until it espies the crowns of the palms south of the valley of Egypt. The oldest palm trees known to humankind, they have stood for eons resplendent upon the riverbank, sown by Pharaohs and cultivated by Copts; their dates fed the soldiers of Rome; the Arab conquerors knew the secrets of their seeds and disseminated them.

The waters of the river subside, their power diminishes, but the irrigation systems pursue it, blindfolded bulls ceaselessly turning the waterwheels. Behind each bull there sits a small boy, who holds a stick with a rope tied to it looking much like an ankh, and who urges the bull, calling "Aa! Aa!" The wheel turns, its buckets ascending, bearing magical fountains of river water and depositing them in the canals that branch and branch again across the face of the land, like veins of the body, blood red at the time of the floods, while the earth is black as musk, the crops as green as emerald, the wheat as yellow as jasper stone. Fava beans, corn, barley, lentils, gourds, watermelons, tomatoes, eggplants, and green beans all vie for place in the irrigated fields, while the palms rise up like the arms of the ancient gods, their roots deep in wet soil, their heads well up in the blazing sky.

The river continues its course amid the silence of the valley until the sound of chanting can be heard, and the columns of the temples, the obelisks, the church spires, the minarets appear. Flocks of doves scatter across the sky to feast their eyes upon the sight of the emerald waters before returning each evening to their nests.

Aisha heard the usual morning sounds starting up behind her. The crowded girls' dormitory, with its closely packed beds, had begun to stir, with the sounds of yawning, suppressed squeals, and minor squabbles. The girls made up the beds, whispering about their unfinished dreams and their innermost thoughts. Aisha felt a small hand come to rest on her shoulder, and heard Isis's voice saying mildly to her, "Don't wander too far—morning prayers are still ahead of us."

Aisha turned, and there was Isis with her round, brown face, her coarse hair, which sat atop her head like a tarnished crown, her wide-set eyes, and always on her lips the same friendly smile. Aisha reached out and stroked her cheek. Isis was the only friend she had won since coming to this school. Isis did not try to ask her too many questions, or probe her elliptical replies, nor did she seem surprised by Aisha's never leaving the school or making trips to her hometown during the long vacations. She offered her uncomplicated friendship without restraint or hesitation. Pointing at the sun, which had begun its ascent above the raging river, Isis said, "We should thank the Lord that each day He gives us a new sun."

Aisha smiled and said, "Then shouldn't He vary the routine a little—one day for the sun, one day for the moon?"

"Come along, you little heretic—let's go get ready."

The girls began to line up in rows beside the beds, all dressed in the school uniform: a white shirt with a high collar, a light blue jumper, and shoes with metal buttons. Sister Margaret, however, didn't appear as she normally did each morning to take them to prayers. Instead, the abbess came and stood by the door of the dormitory, fixing them all with a hard stare, impatient for the last of the laggard girls to finish getting ready before scolding them.

Standing next to Aisha, Isis whispered in her ear, "It seems Sister Margaret has thrown us over for her devotions again."

By now they were all accustomed to the ways of Sister Margaret, a wandering spirit in the school corridors. During her happier moments she flitted about everywhere like a butterfly, bestowing greetings and smiles on everyone, and sitting up late by the girls' beds at night to listen patiently to all manner of confessions. But when she was melancholy, when the sparkle in her eye went out—then she would remove herself from their midst and descend to her preferred spot in the cellar, where she would remain without food or drink for long days, during which no one dared approach her. She was a young woman of remarkable beauty, delicacy, and stature. From talk she had overheard, Aisha knew that she was the daughter of one of New York's most eminent families, and that her father had made his fortune as "king" of something or other—whether it was soap, perfume, coffee, or bananas—all that mattered was that he lived in royal opulence. Yet she had renounced all that and fled to this ascetics' retreat. Aisha never forgot that Sister Margaret had been the first to receive her, the first one here to take her part, or that the abbess might not have taken her in but for the sister's urgent appeal.

Isis walked beside Aisha, their fingers entwined. They passed through the dormitory and into the corridor, stopping to wait their turn to go downstairs. The girls' excited hubbub resounded from the worn staircase, where they were all afraid of slipping and falling—they clutched one another, laughing.

Isis said to Aisha, "You're coming home with me to our mansion in Minya. My father will speak to the director here and you'll come as our guest."

"I can't leave here," said Aisha quickly.

"Come now, Mary, it's just a school—you're not a prisoner here. The outside world is passing you by. How are you ever going to see it? And especially my older brother, Menes."

The abbess called out an order for silence, and the girls headed for the small chapel. First they crossed the courtyard, where Rizq stood drawing water from the well in the center. He was a burly man, shabbily dressed, and his was the first face Aisha had seen on coming to this school, but only later had she learned his name. He was the only Saïdi there, and he performed nearly every chore: he was guard, gardener, and attendant, and despite his grubby clothes he kept everything clean. He stood still, holding the rope for the bucket, his head bowed and his eyes cast down until the line of girls had passed by him. It was forbidden for him to look at them, to greet them or address them in any way, as if, where they were concerned, he was not a human being; accordingly, none of the girls could remember having heard his voice at any time—certainly he wasn't deaf, but any speech he uttered fell on ears other than theirs.

Silence descended as the girls took their places in the chapel. As always, Isis was careful to make sure she sat next to Aisha, their knees reassuringly in contact. Father George began to recite the prayers. He always had the Bible in his hand, even though he knew all its verses by heart. All the girls were looking forward to the end of Mass and the beginning of the summer vacation, when everyone went away. Perhaps Father George sensed this, for his sermon dragged on as he talked about "nature's wrath," comparing it to human anger. He had in mind the scene of the raging Nile just outside the school walls at that very moment. Everyone was going away, but Aisha would stay she wouldn't dare go with Isis. She would not stir from this place.

Aisha felt something cold find its way under her feet. With a gasp she lifted them up: it was water creeping across the church floor. The other girls began to shriek. Father George paused uncomprehending, his sermon interrupted; meanwhile, water poured in under the church door and soon the floor was awash. *My God*, thought Aisha, *it's the flood—the river's risen and come all the way here.*

The bells began ringing—no doubt Rizq, apprehending the danger, had begun sounding the alarm. The girls' voices rose in terror as they got up and rushed toward the door and the trickle of water beneath their feet became an inundation. Father George still stood in the pulpit, not yet understanding what was happening. The water had flooded the courtyard as well, coming straight from the river and insinuating itself through the openings in the outer wall.

"Upstairs! *Now*!" cried the abbess.

The girls dashed headlong for the stairs, but Aisha stood rooted in place, staring at the lower staircase. The water was rushing noisily down, taking over, imposing its will, making for the locked door with all speed and no one to stop it. Pointing to the water in the stairwell, Aisha addressed the abbess, shouting, "Sister Margaret is in the cellar!"

Everyone turned in the direction of this new calamity in the making. Father George plunged hastily into the water in his long cassock and descended the stairs leading to the cellar door. First, he tried to open it, and then he pounded on it, shouting, "Open the door, Sister Margaret!"

He kept knocking and calling out, but got no response. The girls stood frozen on the stairs, the water still pouring in—had it overwhelmed and drowned her before she realized what was happening? Some of the girls began to cry, and Isis struck her cheeks in anguish. Father George tried pushing the door, but to no avail. The abbess fell to her knees in the water and prayed.

There was no escape from death, Aisha thought—neither here nor in her village.

All at once Rizq appeared. He began to make his way across the courtyard, roiling the water around him. He descended the stairs in one leap, pushed Father George unceremoniously aside, and threw his shoulder against the door. The wooden slab shook but did not give way. He battered it a second time, and a third—it seemed to Aisha that she could hear his bones breaking, but he gave no sign of feeling any pain. He continued his relentless assault upon the door until he was staggering. Then the hinges tore away. Water burst into the cellar through the gap, but Rizq sprang forward as well, as if he were one with the river's surging current. No one dared follow him. The girls stood trembling on the stairs, while the abbess knelt amid the flood and still the waters of the river spread, overwhelming the courtyard altogether.

At last Rizq emerged, carrying the black-clad form. He was gasping, gulping in air with difficulty, bearing aloft the still and lifeless figure of Sister Margaret. Her wimple had fallen away from her head and exposed her reddish hair, which hung down loose, and on the other side dangled her feet. Because she was unusually tall, it seemed as if there could be no connection between head and feet. She hung limp as death itself, and in the same apparel, the same pallor and silence. There was a collective sob of lamentation, but Rizq pressed forward, looking for a place in the flooded courtyard that was high enough to set her down, finding only the edge of the well. He turned her over in his arms and placed her facedown, then began without hesitation to pound her back vigorously. Her body shook beneath each of his efforts, but he didn't release her from his grasp. Spurts of water turbid with algae and foam gushed from her mouth, as if she were involuntarily emptying herself of the sap of life; she did not appear to be responding to his pummeling, so Rizq turned her on her back once more, grasped her shoulder firmly to keep her from slipping down, and applied pressure to her chest with his palms. The girls inhaled sharply on seeing his hands make contact with her inviolate body, and the abbess closed her eyes, but Father George came forward and held her head, evincing no protest to what Rizq was so boldly doing. Father George raised Sister Margaret's head higher; with his fingers Rizq held her nose to prevent air from escaping and placed his mouth on hers. He covered her lips and began to blow hard. The girls closed their eyes, as Rizq filled her limp body with his own vigorous breath. Her chest began to move slightly, her ribcage responding to the bursts of air being forced into it. Then all at once she rose, struggled for breath, and coughed hard. Some more muddy water gushed from her mouth.

Everyone gasped, hearing the sound of life returning to Sister Margaret, who coughed and coughed. She flailed upward with her arms as if groping for breath from the air around her, Rizq still keeping a secure hold on her to keep her from making any sudden movements. Once more she gulped for air, then reached out and clutched a piece of Rizq's clothing.

"Hallelujah!" cried Father George.

The girls burst out shouting, and the abbess began to weep. They had all witnessed a little miracle. Sister Margaret opened her eyes at last—reddened, but shining—and she gazed into the face of Rizq, who was as close to her as could be. She regarded him with her blue eyes as if seeing him for the first time.

"Could you carry me upstairs?" she pleaded weakly.

Rizq reached under her back and easily lifted her tall, brittle frame. The abbess came out of her reverie and stood up in the middle of the flood.

"Where did you learn all that?" she asked.

Diffidently, Rizq replied, "In the military, ma'am—when I was a soldier."

The abbess sighed and made the sign of the cross. "It is truly a miracle," she said. "Now, let us all go up."

The water kept on rising until it reached her knees; Father George's cassock was saturated. The girls made way for Rizq to mount the stairs carrying Sister Margaret, who had clasped her hands about his neck and surrendered her fragile being to his care. On her pale face was a faint smile. The abbess hurried ahead of them, while the girls waited—they had seen it with their own eyes, this small miracle! Aisha followed the rest up the stairs. They entered the girls' dormitory and Aisha pointed out her own bed, so Rizq went to it and gently laid Sister Margaret down. She, though, kept her arms locked around his neck, not wanting to let go. Aisha heard her say in a feeble appeal, "Don't leave me," while he strove, embarrassed, to free himself from her locked arms.

Later, she told Aisha, "I felt as though he was the Messiah—my own private messiah, come back in the guise of an Egyptian peasant to call forth the life of my body. The resurrection of Lazarus all over again."

Rizq withdrew, his head bowed meekly. It was his first time, and perhaps his last, entering a place in which his presence was forbidden, handling a body he was not even supposed to look at. Outside, the red waters of the river swirled, restive.

The following day, all the streets around the school were submerged. A shimmering lake of dark water surrounded them, with a blazing sun reflected in its surface and a hot wind blowing off the river. Margaret opened her eyes and looked at Aisha. "I'm hungry," she said. Aisha was surprised to hear this word fall from her lips—she habitually ate only enough to keep her alive. There was a rush to get her some food. She began to eat, slowly and meditatively, pausing to look about her as if in search of something. Then, without speaking, she lay down on the bed and fell asleep again, despite the noise the girls were making. She was reclaiming the life-force that had drained away from her.

The school became an island, cut off from everything. The roads connecting it to the city were impassable, while the river swept before it the remains of the things its waters had engulfed: tree branches, fragments of wrecked boats, drowned animals, floating containers. The flood, as overlord, imposed its dominance on the region, demolishing earthen bulwarks and dissolving mud-brick houses. In spite of this, Margaret continued to revive. She stayed on in the girls' dormitory, so as not to be alone in her little room. She ate sparingly, but there was a serious problem with the school's diminishing reserves of food. There were no longer any markets or merchants, nor any traveling food carts. The only people to be seen at all were vagrants who had braved the water in search of such spoils as the flood might yield.

Margaret got out of bed and began drifting about on tiptoe, like a butterfly, smiling, her eyes shining. There was no electricity or telephone service anymore. There was only enough food for one small meal each day, and it was clear that even this would not last much longer. Silently and fearfully, the nuns distributed the remains of the dried foodstuffs. The abbess announced that she would fast until this adversity passed. All creation had been transformed into a lake of reddish water. The mountains of the western shore seemed to belong to a different world.

But Margaret was living her own private happiness. She sat on the bed, opposite Aisha, and said to her, "That angel who saved my life—who is he?"

"That was no angel," said Aisha. "It was just a peasant who's worked here at the school for a long time—how can you not have seen him all this while? His name is Rizq."

"Don't speak of him that way," was Margaret's fretful reply. "He's more than just some peasant—his is a divine gift few others possess. He has the power to restore life. Where do you suppose he is now?"

"He must be downstairs," said Aisha offhandedly.

Now Margaret spoke up in genuine alarm. "Downstairs there's nothing but water, nothing but flooding . . ."

She got up and crossed the floor in her bare feet, leaving the dormitory to peer over the balustrade at the rear courtyard. She found only water and the tops of plants. Aisha started after her and found her clutching the railing in fear, her fingers dug in as if she meant to bore into the wood with them. Her voice shaking, Margaret said, "He's not there. Can he have drowned?"

"Why all this anxiety about him?" said Aisha. "He's strong and can look after himself. He's just like me or any other peasant: accustomed since childhood to these floods. Surely he knows how to keep out of danger."

But Margaret, bewildered, kept turning this way and that, her gaze wandering. When Aisha led her back to bed, she got up again.

The waters went on rising, and there was no longer anything to fill the silence but the lapping of the waves. Now the dried foods were running out as well, as everyone at the school crowded into the girls' dormitory. Aisha had been through this experience more than once in her distant village, but she had never imagined that the river could so isolate a big city like Asyout. With eyes full of dread and anxiety, they kept watch; even Margaret's restoration to life began to lag. She seemed lost, waiting for something that never came.

On the third day the abbess stood up at the front of the dormitory and spoke in a voice audible to everyone. "We must leave here," she said. "We'll brave the water to reach the train station, and from there each of you will go home. We cannot stay on here, under siege, until we die of hunger."

Some of the girls began to weep in subdued voices. They did not know what awaited them downstairs, or whether there were any streets that were safe for passage. But they got up and opened the cupboards where their clothes were stored. Once more the abbess called out, saying, "Take as little as possible—only what you need. We don't want anything weighing us down."

But Margaret clung to her bed, watching the others in dismay. "I won't leave this place!" she cried.

The abbess looked pityingly at her. Gently, as if addressing a small child, she said, "No one knows how long this flooding will last. We may not die by drowning, but die we will. We'll perish from hunger."

Aisha stood in consternation before her own clothes chest. There was nothing in it to bring, nor any place for her to bring it to. Of all of them, she felt the most bereft, with no home, no family, no real name. She had concealed well the deception that surrounded her; now the deeds of the river were about to expose it. She saw tears beginning to form in Margaret's eyes, so she sat beside her on the bed. Margaret smiled wanly and whispered in Aisha's ear, "I don't want to leave this place, because I know he will come."

"Who?"

"My messiah. My savior."

When the abbess bent her stern glance upon them Aisha had no choice but to get up and set about bundling up her old *jilbaab*. Its smell took her by surprise: it was redolent of dust and mud, of the old village. Isis shyly approached and said, "Can you come with me to my father's house? We won't go far—it's in the next city, and I don't think it's in any danger of flooding."

Aisha pressed her hand, on the point of tears. This would not do, either—she couldn't spend all that time wearing her single school outfit. The girls began to form a long line. Margaret rose heavily and stood by the window. There was no movement but that of the churning waters, no sound other than the river's roar, as if life had vanished from the city.

Suddenly, everyone heard a shout coming from below, a voice calling to the abbess and to all of them. Margaret was the first to recognize it. Her eyes shone. "My redeemer," she said joyfully. She was across the room and out the door at a run. Rizq was in the courtyard, up to his chest in the water, carrying on his head a large palm-leaf basket. His face, the color of a husk of wheat, was bathed in sweat, the muscles taut in his bare arms. Once again he mounted the stairs, crossing casually into a forbidden precinct, and placed the basket at Margaret's feet. It was laden with loaves of brown bread, bright red tomatoes, emerald-green cucumbers, and chunks of cottage cheese—a veritable treasure he laid at her feet in the simplest of gestures, as if he were a Pharaoh offering up a sacrifice to his sacred gods. Margaret gazed at him, dazzled. She had believed that her savior must come back to her, perform this ritual for her sake, present her with this gift. The other girls came out of the dormitory, gasping in surprise at the sight of fresh food. They were hungry, but none of them dared to approach until the abbess came. She stared in astonishment at what Rizq had brought. Then she gestured toward the dormitory and said, "Bring these things inside, Rizq."

For the second time, he was permitted to enter the sacrosanct zone. Margaret followed him, smiling radiantly, her spirit replete.

"Where did you get these provisions?" the abbess inquired.

"From the villages on the mountainside," Rizq replied. "The water didn't reach them."

Everyone knew these dusty hamlets, whose lights shone only dimly at night, and from which men descended barefoot and hungry. It would be extraordinary if such villages were now to become their source of sustenance. The abbess questioned Rizq further before allowing any of the girls to touch the food.

"And where did you get the money?"

At this Margaret lifted her eyebrows, puzzled by the question. How could anyone ask such a question of a miracle worker? So it was quite natural for her to answer simply, "God provides."

It was clear that Rizq had spent the few riyals he had, from his monthly earnings at the school. At this moment they all realized that, although he had a part in every task undertaken there, until now he had been invisible to them, and it had never occurred to any of them to find out anything about him.

"We were just getting ready to leave," said the abbess. "Is the road to the station safe?"

"The graves are exposed," he said quickly.

The abbess looked at him strangely. "What do you mean?" she said.

Arranging the bread and cheese before them, he said, "The floodwaters reached the tombs built on the upper hills and laid open the covered graves. We've never seen a flood like this one."

The abbess stared at him a moment longer. Then she signaled to the others to begin eating. Margaret's heart skipped a beat. She joined them, reaching for the food. The cheese tasted of honey.

◆ ◆ ◆

"Come, Mary," Margaret called to her anxiously, "let's go, we'll be late!"

She hurried ahead of Aisha, making her way carelessly amid the remains of the mud and the puddles. Although she didn't know where Margaret was taking her, or what this assignation she was so intent upon might be, the dreamy look in her eyes and the way she walked with her feet scarcely touching the ground made Aisha follow her through the crowds and the uproar of the pottery market.

The earth was still fresh. The imperious river had drawn back after having its way with the land for many days, and the sun now blazed down daily, turning the soft mud to solid earth. Builders and potters set out to gather into baskets the silt left behind when the waters receded. They had been assembling the raw materials for their craft throughout the year. On the other side of the river, farmers commenced the sowing of wheat, barley, and lupine. The earth had feasted on alluvium, a thick layer of matter formed from particles of volcanic rock, which the river carried down from the highlands of Ethiopia and spread over the ancient land, rejuvenating it.

Margaret was wearing the black habit of the nuns, her white skin suffused with a rosy blush as she proceeded amidst a sea of suntanned faces. The potters were lining up the red crockery for which the city was famous, as well as rows of brown pitchers incised with white lines, honey jars with notched patterns and delicate necks, pots for butter and pickled vegetables that were black as night, sculpted planters, cups, mugs, and nargilehs. The fingers of the buyers and sellers rapped repeatedly on the surfaces of the pottery, which gave off a hollow sound, proving its fineness, how well-fired it was. The regular tapping of the pots seemed like the rhythm to a dance melody and Margaret moved in time to it.

"See how beautiful and pure everything looks!" she cried delightedly. "All made from mud, the stuff of first creation, the substance from which humans were formed."

She had obtained permission to leave the school for several hours. The abbess was away on an extended holiday, and the school had emptied, the students having gone to visit their families, all except Margaret and Aisha. Father George hesitated to let them go out, but when Margaret exclaimed that she was suffocating behind the walls, and that she longed to feel the September sun on her skin, he agreed to let her go, on condition that Aisha accompany her so that she wouldn't get lost on the city streets. But it was Margaret who led Aisha through the narrow, interlocking lanes. Aisha was afraid that she wouldn't know the way back to the school, but Margaret knew every inch and had all the routes memorized. They came to a spacious square with a lofty sycamore in the middle of it. Under it stood Rizq, two donkeys beside him.

Aisha stopped short, confused, while Margaret ran to him eagerly and put her hand on his chest, touching him as if to make sure he was really there. He stepped back, however, glancing sharply at Aisha, who said, "I can't believe we've met him like this—is it a coincidence?"

"Of course not," said Margaret, who was euphoric. "It's my doing—I made arrangements with him. Come—here's your donkey. He's going to lead us on a tour."

"In that case, why didn't you come and meet him on your own?"

"Don't be absurd—how could I have gone all the way across the city by myself? Come along—stop wasting time!"

Aisha stood rooted in place. Margaret leaned familiarly on Rizq's shoulder as she tried to climb onto the donkey's back. The long, black garment she wore nearly tripped her, but he kept hold of her until she steadied herself. She laughed joyfully and left her hand on his shoulder, seeming to draw reassurance from him. The two of them began to move forward, leaving Aisha behind. The donkey looked at her with its sad eyes. Where could Rizq be taking Margaret, who had so entrusted herself to him? Aisha considered leaving her and returning alone to the school, but she was responsible for Margaret, and if anything happened to her she wouldn't be able to forgive herself. She took hold of the donkey's bridle and sprang easily onto its back. She kicked it with her heels and started off after the other two.

The road took them downhill to a sandy spot surrounded by ancient trees with peeling bark. Tombstones could be seen in the distance, standing silently in the lap of the mountain with its grim, rocky terrain. Rizq pointed vaguely and said, "There the path to 'Antar's Stable' begins." The mountain obscured the horizon, and nothing was visible. The donkeys began to climb, navigating the rocky steps of the slope. Aisha shivered as she passed among the gravestones. Low openings appeared amid the rocks. Her donkey kept climbing until it stopped before the largest of these openings. Here was the place Rizq had pointed out. From this elevation Asyout looked far away and dazzlingly beautiful: a long line of domes and minarets, surrounded by forests of palm, behind which the river appeared, a gleaming streak at the edge of the horizon.

Delighted, Margaret said, "How happy I am that I've come here at last. I've read a great deal about this place. Hatshepsut used to come here in the guise of a man, to offer sacrifices to her secret gods—the gods of love."

She dismounted quickly from the donkey and hurried, breathless, toward the mouth of the cave. Aisha caught up with her, while Rizq tied the donkeys to a protruding rock and then followed them inside. They made their way through a long passageway hollowed out inside the rock. Its ceiling was covered with a layer of soot, and the corridor was flanked on either side by a pair of misshapen stone statues. The way the figures were posed suggested that they were ancient warriors. The walls were full of paintings in faded colors. Margaret paused, with a deep sigh, before an image of a woman holding a large bouquet of lotus flowers and presenting them to a man. The images were all stiff, and yet they seemed to exude a passionate heat, in their dusty white, dark yellow, and faded green hues. "No doubt she used to meet her lover here," she said, "to sing and dance and make love, and cover his body with lotus blossoms."

They moved on, observed by a broken statue of Anubis, the jackal-headed god of ancient Asyout. Then the corridor opened out into a capacious room, its four corners supported by columns to prevent the stone ceiling from collapsing. Everything was disfigured and broken up, but it bore the traces of bygone splendor. Rizq leaned against one of the pillars, leaving them to wander about and absorb the atmosphere of the place. They gazed at the dozens of inscrutable paintings, hieroglyphs, and cartouches that filled the walls.

"You know," said Margaret, "they've been able to decipher these hieroglyphics and read all these signs."

"And what do they say?" Aisha asked. She was breathing unevenly.

"Maybe they tell about this mysterious queen."

Aisha felt a tremor run through her body. On the wall facing her she saw a painting of a large wolf, incised with deep lines, standing poised upon his four legs. His head was tapered, his ears pricked forward as if he were listening to their uncertain footfalls and the inflections of their voices. Drawn beneath his feet were small representations of Anubis, little messengers awaiting his orders to return to life. Aisha shivered some more under the wolf's silent stare—in her eyes he read all of her buried secrets.

"Why did they make the image of the wolf so large?" she said. "It looks so frightening!"

Margaret caught her breath. "It's another of the gods here," she said. "Maybe, in this city, it was the greatest of the gods of fear and darkness. The remains of dozens of wolves may be buried in this place." She spoke with a wicked simplicity.

Aisha felt suffocated—the air had grown heavy. "I want to leave," she said.

"I need to stay here for a little while," said Margaret. "I want to imprint this place on my memory."

Aisha drew back and leaned against the wall, but her legs wouldn't hold her. She felt as if she had plunged into a network of dead-end passages, the wolf always in pursuit. Rizq was staring at her. Margaret went to her and wiped the perspiration from her brow.

"Mary, what is it?"

"I don't know. I have the feeling a wolf like this one has been chasing me all my life, as if I were bound to all the wolves that come in the night. My mother told me how my story with them began when I was little. I was a very small child when death took my father. So my mother went to join the men who sowed the wheat in our field. She left me asleep in a little hut at the edge of the field, out of the sun's glare. She was distracted for several moments, and when she turned around she found one of those wolves standing by the opening to the hut—just like that, in broad daylight. She was beside herself—she didn't know whether or not it had gone in to where I was sleeping. And had it contented itself with catching my scent, or had it devoured me? She screamed and ran toward the wolf. Hearing her scream, everyone began running behind her. The wolf took fright from the commotion and bounded off. When my mother went in to check on me she found me staring at her, round-eyed and smiling. I was happy, as if I had just been fed, and next to my mouth there was a drop of white liquid. No one believed what had happened—I still don't believe it myself. But the wolves have been following me ever since."

Margaret gently stroked her hair, and put her arms around her trembling shoulders. She looked at Rizq, who stood by stiffly. "We'd better go now," she said.

They went back out into the light. Aisha sat down, and Margaret sat beside her, by the mouth of the cave. Aisha contemplated the sight of Asyout from a distance, and felt a yearning for her village and for her mother's face. Holding onto her to assure her she was not alone, Margaret said, "How beautiful this spot is: the river, the desert, the palms, the domed shrines, the bells, and the minarets—all in one vista. Where can you find such a place?"

Aisha looked into her face. She was no longer the somber nun of old. She was the one who had returned from death a different Margaret, eager for movement, for merriment, for life itself, ready to follow Rizq anywhere he might go. It was plain that matters between them were progressing quickly, but how far could they go? "Why did you bring us here?" Aisha asked her.

Margaret answered unhesitatingly. "This is a sacred place. The desert is all sacred. Our Lady Mary passed this way with the infant Jesus in her arms and Joseph the carpenter leading their donkey. They left their footprints in these sands. Rizq, my own savior, led us here the same way—and my donkey. No doubt the holy family stopped in the same place where we are right now."

Aisha looked toward Rizq, who had untied the two donkeys and was standing with them by the mouth of the cave, ready to descend. She made sure he couldn't hear her before she spoke, saying, "But, Sister Margaret, have you permitted Rizq to touch you?" She was shaking, fearful of Margaret's response, but she laughed.

"And what if he did touch me? He is my own savior, as I told you. He did in fact touch me—he lifted me up, and he kissed me, too, when he breathed life back into my body. Don't you remember? After that, he needs no permission."

Margaret's answer took Aisha aback. She stared at her in astonishment, as Margaret turned in circles, dancing. "It's a miracle," she said. "Time is circular, it never stops turning back on itself. Asyout is truly the city of miracles."

She skipped down over the stones and gave her hand to Rizq, who picked her up lightly under her arms and set her on the donkey's back. Aisha observed that the space between their bodies had diminished to practically nothing. They went in front, Aisha following behind, and all the while Margaret leaned over Rizq, talking with him continuously. The desert was lemon-colored, and the wind blowing across it traced wavy ridges in its surface. The heat of the sun abated, as Aisha witnessed the beginning of a love story that could not be.

At the entrance to the city, Margaret stopped. "We don't want to go back by way of the pottery market," she said to Rizq. "Why don't you find us another route?"

Rizq looked about uncertainly and said, "There is no other way. There's only one other street, and we can't go that way—it's the Greek quarter."

"What of that?" replied Margaret, unconcerned. "I'm hungry. Maybe we can find a place to get some food."

Rizq stood stock-still, though he always obeyed her. Margaret's whims had become too much for him. He looked toward Aisha for help, then said, "I can't take you into this street. The abbess would kill me."

But Margaret actually turned her donkey into the entrance to the street, saying blithely, "The abbess isn't here, and I doubt she has friends in this street who'll betray us to her!"

Her spirit had been liberated from all the old chains, and there were no longer any constraints on her capriciousness. The narrow street that cut through the center of the city was one of many temptations to which she gave way. It seemed calm and well-ordered, above suspicion, with its small shops selling tobacco, groceries, and liquor, and modest doorways screened by curtains of strung shells, bars, wine shops, and little restaurants. Everything was there and waiting.

Aisha was uneasy. "Sister Margaret," she said, "let's go to the school and find something to eat there."

But Margaret was looking eagerly about, sniffing the air with an explorer's instinct. "Why are you in such a hurry to go back behind the walls?" she asked Aisha. "Can't you smell something roasting?"

In fact there was cooking smoke rising from somewhere. Rizq's face was pale as he escorted them. The grocers interrupted their transactions to gape at them as they went by. The black nun's habit drew everyone's attention, inviting curious stares. They stopped at the entrance to a restaurant.

"We can't go in this place," said Aisha. "We'll be expelled from the school."

"Just because we had something to eat? Don't worry about that. You're my only friend, and I'd defend you with my life."

The owner of the restaurant came out and stared at them worriedly. He was Maltese, a short man with a large belly and a thick moustache. For a moment it seemed as though he wanted to bar their entry, but he didn't dare look directly into Margaret's face or at her black vestment. He shoved his hands into his pockets and turned his head the other way. Margaret parted the curtain—beaded with shells, like the others they had seen—and stepped inside. Aisha looked around for help, but Rizq was stupefied, stock-still and clutching the donkeys' bridles, so she saw no alternative but to follow Margaret into the restaurant.

She found Margaret standing stiffly just on the other side of the curtain, her moment of bravado having evaporated. The restaurant was dimly lit, its tables covered with white cloths empty all except for one, at which four women were seated. They stopped talking and laughing as soon as they noticed the nun, abruptly stricken with a kind of panic. They huddled like wet hens. They were wearing heavily embroidered robes, décolleté, their heads adorned with colored feathers. The cigarettes slipped from their fingers, curls of smoke still rising like fine tendrils in the semidarkness. One of them pulled a shawl up over her shoulders, and another made the sign of the cross, murmuring a prayer.

Margaret felt her confidence return, sensing that she had imposed her own will on the surroundings. She moved forward through the utter silence that had descended; there was no sound but her footfalls and the rustle of her clothing. Aisha caught up with her after nearly stumbling over one of the tables. She hastened to sit beside Margaret, attaching herself to her. The women's expressions changed from anxiety to perplexity. Rizq was still outside, standing next to the donkeys, but presently he overcame his hesitation and went cautiously inside. On seeing the four women, he was about to turn around and run back out in consternation, but Margaret beckoned to him to come and sit across from her and Aisha at the table. His presence changed the atmosphere of wariness and fear that had prevailed at first. The women began whispering, for the sight of the three of them was incongruous, giving rise to numerous speculations. One of the women laughed in a low voice.

The air was thick with the aroma of something roasting, which came from the back of the restaurant. It mixed with the reek of alcohol rising from the cellar, in addition to the four women's perfume and the odor of their perspiration.

The Maltese proprietor was still outside, certain that the newcomers would soon leave, and that there was no point in asking them what they wanted.

One of the women got up—the one who had laughed a few moments before—put her hand on her hip, and stared quizzically at Margaret, Aisha, and Rizq. She cast a contemptuous glance at Rizq and ignored Aisha, focusing her attention on Margaret. "Excuse me, Sister," she said, "but are you actually a nun? Or are you new to this place and wearing a costume to attract customers?"

Margaret flushed a deep red. She opened and closed her mouth several times, then finally spoke. "We're all children of the Lord," she said.

The woman turned toward her comrades, momentarily at a loss. Then she spoke again. "You really blushed," she said. "I must have drawn the wrong conclusion. You actually are a nun, then. Pardon me, but if what you have in mind is to save our souls, you've come to the wrong place."

Margaret found her voice at last. "We just want a meal," she said. "That's all."

The woman drew herself up and clapped her hands impatiently, bringing the proprietor at a run. She pointed to Margaret and said, "See what the daughter of our Lord wants."

She went back to her table, and the rest of the women stood up to leave, feeling that their presence in the same room with that black habit was insupportable. Margaret asked the proprietor, who had resigned himself to the circumstances, to tell them what was available, and he ran down the list of dishes as if the information were a burden and he wanted it off his chest.

When the food was set before them, they felt very hungry indeed. As they began to eat, the proprietor stood by, seething with anger, thinking they were enjoying having brought his business to a halt, for the defection of the four women meant that other customers would desert him as well.

Margaret laughed. "They thought we were here to compete with them," she said.

Aisha blushed, and Margaret laughed again, full of mischief. She looked at Rizq, who was eating his food with rapid bites, scarcely bothering to chew it. "Lord," said Margaret, "I love the way you eat—it's primitive, actually, but it makes food seem like both a necessity and a pleasure."

They chatted as they ate, and even Rizq joined the conversation, in his peculiar Saïdi idiom. They forgot the differences among them, and the stern rules of the school vanished. No one remembered Father George, who was waiting for them. Meanwhile, the Maltese proprietor was ready to lose his mind. A number of customers had entered the restaurant—local landowners, farmers, and Europeans—but at the sight of a nun they hurried back out.

At last Margaret brought out a few coins and placed them on the table. Outside the restaurant a small group of effendis, peasants, and policemen had gathered to watch for the nun and her companions to emerge. A hum of voices arose as soon as they appeared. One of the peasants approached, and Rizq tensed, thinking he intended to block their path. But the man stared into Aisha's face and said, "Aren't you Aisha, daughter of the late Mohammed Abu al-Ainayn?"

The color drained from Aisha's face and a tremor went through her. She had never imagined that her past could loom up so suddenly before her. She tried to hide behind Margaret, but the man kept on staring at her, waiting for an answer. Rizq stepped in front of them. "Get out of our way!" he shouted. "I assure you she's a Christian girl. So stop bothering us."

But the man was too curious to relent. "I'm sure," he persisted, "that this is the same girl. She disappeared from our village three years ago, but I know her very well. I was a friend of her father's."

At a loss, Rizq looked at Aisha, who managed at last to speak. "He's lying," she said. "I don't know him."

"Get out of our way," said Rizq.

Resigned, the man threw up his hands and stepped aside. The three went their way, back to the school. On taking Aisha's hand, Margaret found that she was trembling violently. The tremors continued even after she went up to bed and buried herself beneath the covers.

Several days went by before Margaret brought up the subject with her, although she talked constantly about other things. Even in bed at night, she mostly talked about Rizq. She wanted to know every detail of his earlier life, but there were no details.

Aisha and Sister Margaret were both sleeping in the empty dormitory, while Rizq slept always in the small room next to the outer gate. Most of the time Father George was preoccupied either with prayer or with a revision of the New Testament that he was writing. He had traveled a great deal between Egypt, Palestine, and Syria, and he was concerned with the question of bringing geographical descriptions in the New Testament into conformity with the actual topography of the land. So he was always hard at work in his room, which was full of maps and globes.

Aisha woke in the middle of the night. The window was open, the full moon lighting up one side of the dormitory. Margaret, also awake, was perched on the windowsill. Sitting with her knees drawn up and her chin resting on them, the moonlight shining in her long, unbound hair, she seemed a pallid specter, worn out with thinking. The sight of her made Aisha anxious, and she sat up in bed.

Margaret turned her head slowly in Aisha's direction and said in a soft voice, "How are prayers performed in your religion?" Aisha made no reply to this, but her heart beat harder. "I'm just wondering," said Margaret. "I want to imagine Rizq when he's performing his prayers."

Saying nothing, Aisha gazed at the shadow Margaret cast with the moonlight shining off of her. She couldn't see her face clearly. At last she said in a choked voice, "Are you going to report me?"

Margaret got down off of the windowsill and knelt beside Aisha on the bed. "No, I won't," she said. "Heaven doesn't like lies, but earth always needs its little fibs. I don't want to know what troubles you've been through, but I have no doubt they were terribly cruel, for you to have done what you did."

Aisha found that tears were streaming down her cheeks. She was afraid, and Margaret's gentle words only made her more so. Sitting next to her on the bed, Margaret put her hand on Aisha's shoulder and pulled her in close. "Religion doesn't divide people—stupidity does. Tonight we'll share a bed."

As Aisha acquiesced, Margaret lay down on the bed, and all at once Aisha felt a warmth she hadn't experienced since she stopped sleeping beside her mother. She smelled the fragrance of Margaret's hair as it spread out on the pillow, and the child-like scent of her body. She closed her eyes, feeling Margaret's breath against her face.

She didn't know how long she had slept, but she awoke feeling cold. The bed beside her was empty. She looked about for Margaret, finding the rest of the beds in the dormitory likewise vacant. Not daring to leave the room, she stood beside the window. The shadows dissolved and gray streaks began to appear beyond the river. The street was empty, but the wolf was there, standing beneath the window. She went back to bed and wrapped herself in the blanket. Cold, loneliness, fear . . . what if Margaret hadn't pardoned her deceit, and had deserted her?

She felt a hand on her shoulder and sat up in alarm, startled to see Margaret sitting on the edge of the bed. Her face was flushed and her eyes shone with an unearthly gleam. She was a different person from the one who had lain beside Aisha earlier that night.

"I've fulfilled my vow," said Margaret. "I've surrendered to him, body and soul!"

Aisha gasped. She knew at once what Margaret had done, unthinkable though it was. Margaret hastily put her hand over Aisha's mouth. Her fingers were both cool and warm. "This was my promise from the beginning," she went on, "to give my body only to our Lord and savior, and that's what I've done. I gave it to my own messiah, my personal savior . . ."

Pulling Margaret's hand away from her mouth, Aisha spoke between clenched teeth. "How dare he touch you?"

"He had to," Margaret replied. "I was the one who insisted—I went to his bed. This was the first time for us. I never knew any man before him, and he had never touched a woman—just the way it ought to be. We were innocent, just as we should have been. It was as if we were swimming in an endlessly flowing river, or dancing a never-ending dance. At that moment I knew it couldn't be wrong. And that is just as it ought to be."

She squeezed in beside Aisha in the bed. Her body was warm, having known fulfillment at last. She tucked her hand under her head and murmured sleepily. "What's done is done. I regret nothing."

◆ ◆ ◆

One of the cleaning women alerted Aisha to what was happening. There was a large crew of cleaners busy in every part of the school, tidying it and preparing it for the start of the new school year. One of them came to Aisha, who was absorbed in a book, and said, "The police have surrounded the school."

Aisha got up and tried to cross the room to see what was happening, but the dormitory floor was slippery, awash in soapy water. So she climbed onto one of the beds, and began leaping from one to another. At the door she found the other cleaning women in a group, talking fearfully in whispers. She was surprised also to find the abbess standing in the outer corridor, watching events unfold in the courtyard below. Her hands were tucked into her wide sleeves, her features set in a harsh grimace. On her return from her extended journey her face had looked even sterner than before. Now Father George was standing beside her. Aisha hesitated, on the point of going back inside, but the commotion coming from below drew her forward.

Policemen were pouring in through the school's outer gate and making straight for the little room in which Rizq resided, carrying truncheons and chains. There were more of them than the room could contain. From inside it rose the sounds of shouts and blows. Aisha's heart quaked to hear Rizq's voice as he cried out for help. They all came out, dragging him along the ground, his face covered in blood. He was still resisting them, but the troops surrounded him and rained blows on him from every side. They tried to drag him toward the school gate. He looked up in an appeal for help from anyone, but found only the grim face of the abbess. A young officer approached on horseback and gestured to the troops to put a choke collar on him, to stop him struggling. They tightened their formation around him, some holding his arms, and tried to get the metal ring about his neck, while he snarled and shouted. He was barefoot, and there was nothing to cover his body except a torn undershirt and a pair of dirty trousers.

The abbess turned toward Aisha, who was quietly weeping, and bent her implacable glare upon her. Down below, the battle continued, with no sign of Margaret—where had she gone? Had the abbess locked her up in the cellar? How had she found out so quickly what was going on? Rizq could take no more beating. He fell to the ground. They bound his wrists with a rope, which, at a sign from the officer, they tied to the horse's saddle. The officer drew the reins taut and spurred the horse into motion. Rizq's face was ground between the dust and the gravel; his head, as the horse gathered speed, was battered by the stones in the road, until the horse disappeared from sight.

Aisha sat huddled on the floor, staring at the dust rising up in the wake of the struggle. She was incapable of speech. The abbess turned and stared at her for a long time, then withdrew without a word. The door to Rizq's room was shattered and there were traces of his blood on the ground. All the plants he had tended were trampled.

During the night the school was transformed, as the silence of a tomb descended upon it. A scant moon appeared in the sky, its light too faint to dispel the gloom. Aisha sat up, slipped from her bed, and left the dormitory. She descended to the courtyard and then to the stairs that led to the cellar. She knocked on the door, calling, "Open the door, Sister Margaret—it's Mary. I need to talk to you."

She didn't hear a sound from within, but she was afraid to raise her voice any more, for fear of rousing those upstairs. She sat on the stairs, and felt the cold night air invade her body. Was Margaret sleeping? Had something happened to her? Had she seen what took place in the courtyard? Aisha felt despair and guilt as a party to all that had occurred—and yet everything seemed fated, inescapable.

She heard the door shifting on its hinges and raised her head to find Margaret standing before her, clad in a thin white gown, scarcely adequate to keep off the nighttime chill. She was spectrally pale. Aisha stood up and embraced her. Her body was thin and cold, and she was shivering. She sat down with Aisha on the stone steps and whispered, trying to contain her tears, "Have the Romans taken him?" Her wide eyes shone brightly, dark though the night was.

"The police took him," said Aisha, "a big gang of them, and an officer on horseback."

"Did they put the cross on his back and make him climb the hill? Did they kill him on account of me, to complete the cycle?"

Aisha peered anxiously into Margaret's face. She was speaking in a hollow voice, as if it came from some other realm. Her eyes looked cloudy and vague. It angered Aisha that Margaret had chosen this of all times to retreat from the world. "Wake up, Margaret!" she cried. The police came, they beat him with unimaginable cruelty—why did you not intervene? Why didn't you try to stop them?"

On the point of tears, Margaret replied, "I couldn't. I was lying there helpless, I couldn't move—everything that was happening was taking place in another world. The abbess carried out her threats in spite of all my pleas."

"How did she find out?"

"She saw me leaving his room in the middle of the night. This morning she took me to a doctor and found out that I'm pregnant."

"*What*?"

"It's a holy child, Aisha—there's no sin or scandal, whatever she may say. She only wants to take revenge on me. She didn't know I was the Magdalena and that the story of the crucifixion would come full circle."

She went up into the courtyard and circumambulated the well. Then she went into Rizq's demolished room. She ran her hand across the rough bed, which still bore his scent. She inhaled, filling her lungs with it, then knelt upon the floor. She picked up a handful of dust, in which were traces of his blood, smearing her head and face with it. Aisha watched her, wide-eyed with astonishment. Margaret looked up at her and said, "Come with me—let's go away from this accursed place."

She went to the iron gate, tugged at the metal chain that secured it, and the chain gave way to her fingers. She soundlessly opened the gate—it seemed as though some extraordinary power enabled her to do all these things. Her white garment billowed around her, exposing her pale legs, and the breeze stirred her hair. They walked through the streets, empty not only of people but of mud and filth as well. Margaret made her way, lightly and quickly, in the direction of the river. Its waters were quiet and tranquil, dark except for the faint light of the moon. There was only the soughing of the willows at each breath of wind. Farther away, the flank of the mountain appeared like a black shadow with a serrated edge. Margaret proceeded down the embankment, indifferent to the brambles and the stones.

"Be careful!" Aisha cried. "You could drown!"

Margaret stopped and looked back to face Aisha. "I drowned already—remember?"

She turned a circle, knelt upon the ground, and dug her knees into the mud, wracked with weeping. Aisha went to her, placed her hand over her heart, and said, "Calm yourself, Margaret. Let's go back to the school. There's been enough trouble already."

"What's happened is only the beginning," said Margaret. "I've been bleeding since yesterday. I've bled out every drop of blood in my body. I knew they were crucifying him outside, and even so I was too weak to go out to him and stand up for him. My body is completely dried up, and I've lost the last trace of life he left inside me, the last memories of my own messiah."

She rose and took off her gown. Aisha drew a sharp breath at the sight of her nakedness, but before she could make any move Margaret had plunged into the water. The mud clinging to the shore must have yielded, for the stark-white body sank suddenly into the river's black depths. "Margaret," Aisha cried, "where are you?" She threw herself in after her. The water engulfed her, its chill penetrating her bones. Casting about, she found no trace of Margaret. Again she screamed and called, flailing desperately at the water. She dived beneath the surface with her eyes open and discerned a shape of livid white, sinking, surrendering to the motion of the current. Aisha thrashed about under the surface until she got hold of Margaret's hair, reeled her in, and pushed her upward toward the surface. "Hold onto me!" she cried. "I'll get you out!"

"I don't want to," Margaret sobbed, trying to free herself, but Aisha held on fiercely to her hair and pushed her anguished face above the surface of the water. She was light, as if her body had been emptied out, left hollow. Gasping, Aisha propelled her forward, until they both were mired in the mud. Margaret seemed too weak to attempt any resistance. Aisha dragged her by the hair until her face was well out of the water, and then began to weep.

"Margaret," she begged, "please, don't make me keep pulling you by your hair. Promise me you won't go back into the water!" Margaret's naked white form was half-exposed, the other half submerged in the mud. She had tried death by drowning for the second time.

Suddenly Margaret spoke, struggling for breath. "What is your other name?" she said. "Your Muslim name."

"Aisha."

"In the name of your God, Aisha, let me find peace in the depths of this cold river. This is my resting place."

Her hand still clutching strands of Margaret's hair, Aisha wept. "Don't do this to me," she pleaded.

They stayed like that, half-immersed in the cold water, half-exposed to the chill of the night. It was dark and gloomy, and the waves slapped peevishly at the shore. Together Aisha and Margaret grew still, Margaret's body going slack. Her spirit was slipping away, with no one to prevent it.

Then in the distance Aisha heard, faintly at first, a sound—a continuous hum that grew louder as it approached—one of the automobiles so seldom seen in Asyout at all, much less on the river road at this time of night. Any passerby who could help would serve Aisha's need, and she thought of going to the middle of the road to flag down the vehicle, but she stayed where she was, clutching Margaret's sodden tresses, not daring to let go of her, for fear she might slip away into the river in a matter of seconds. Feeling herself on the point of freezing from the cold and the damp, Aisha called out for help.

"I don't want anyone to see me naked like this," Margaret moaned feebly.

But it was too late for that. Aisha heard the car come to a sudden stop, its wheels skidding in the dust and gravel. Then came the sound of footsteps approaching. She shouted again, and when she looked around she saw Father George, who gave a sigh of relief.

"Praise the Lord," he said. "They're here." He raised his voice and called out, "Here they are!"

At that moment three other men arrived. The abbess was not with them. They were three foreigners, unusually tall, and formally dressed. They moved in quickly, and saw Margaret's body half-sunk in the mud. "The naked girl—is she the one?" said one of them, addressing himself to Father George, who nodded, turning his face the other way. The one who had spoken now said, pointing to Aisha, "And who is this?"

"Just a student from the school," Father George replied.

No one paid any attention to her. One of them took off his coat as the other two moved forward and released Margaret's hair from Aisha's cramped fingers. As they pulled Margaret out of the mud, Aisha retreated and sat huddled out of the way. The one who had removed his coat covered Margaret's nakedness with it, and then felt her throat. "She's still alive," he told the others.

He tucked the coat around her to warm her. "Sister Margaret," he said, "we're from the American embassy, and we've come to fetch you."

She made no reply. One of them picked her up easily in his arms. Strands of her wet hair dangled, and her body hung limp. Though her eyes were closed, Aisha waved a hand at her as they carried her to the car, which was waiting above the river. After a moment, Aisha heard the sound of the engine fading in the distance, and then silence fell, leaving nothing but the cold and the dark of night. No one had seen her or taken any notice of her, and yet she was happy that Margaret was still alive, and that someone had come to her rescue. But who was there that could come to the aid of Rizq? Was he even still alive?

She got up, shivering, clutched her chest with her arms, and went unsteadily through the streets, which were still empty. Dogs barked in the distance. The sky was very black, and what little moon there had been was now gone. The school looked dark, devoid of life. But the iron gate was open, just as it had been when she left it. She stepped inside, and was startled to find the abbess standing in the middle of the courtyard, looking grimly in her direction. Aisha stopped, trembling. She wanted to tell everything, all her secrets and Margaret's, all the burdens that weighed upon her slight frame and her tender age. Her story had become too complicated—she couldn't take another step without unburdening her inmost heart.

But she heard the abbess's voice. "There is no longer a place for you at this school," she said.

Aisha gasped. "I'll tell you everything, Mother Superior," she said.

"If you talked from now until morning," said the abbess, as coldly as before, "it wouldn't change a thing."

"I have no place to go for shelter," said Aisha. "And in all that's happened I've done nothing wrong. I can—"

"I don't wish to hear it," said the abbess. "I'll stay here until you gather up your things and get out. From this moment, I don't want you here."

There was nothing more to be said. Aisha climbed the stairs and turned on the light in the dormitory. She was struck by the whiteness of the empty beds. On the walls were words, and hearts drawn with arrows, which the cleaning compounds had been unable to remove. The room was permeated with an air of desolate abandonment. Her bed was the only one unmade, the only one bearing any trace of life. She opened her clothes chest. Her clothes were few—a handful of undergarments belonging to the school and the black *jilbaab* in which she had first arrived from the village of Beni Khalaf. She took off her wet clothes, leaving them on the floor. She picked up the old *jilbaab* and pulled it on. It was all she had to warm and protect her body. She looked at the garments lying sodden on the floor, and those in the chest that were dry. There was nothing else that belonged to her. All her efforts had come to naught.

When she went downstairs the courtyard was empty. The gate stood open, waiting for her to leave, and the streets were silent—even the dogs had stopped barking. The shops were closed; in the recesses of the alleyways homeless children slept and street peddlers passed the night on their carts. The only way open to her was to go to the railway station. The station was dark as well, a series of wooden shelters erected in the middle of an arid expanse. She curled up on one of the wooden benches, clasping her knees with her arms. She saw the wolf circling her at a distance as she sat waiting for morning to come, and with it the train. Where was she to go?

2 • Minya

"YOU CAN'T STAY HIDDEN IN MY ROOM ALL THE TIME, MARY—what will my mother say? And my father? You've got to come out and get to know them."

Was she being evicted? Had Isis tired of her being there? Aisha was sitting in a corner of the room, still wearing her old peasant dress. She had no idea what to do, how she should behave. She had taken the train here without thinking anything through carefully. And when she found herself ensconced in the mansion she felt she had made a mistake. She would have to go back to the village of Beni Khalaf, come what might.

She had taken a desperate chance in coming to this palace set on the banks of the Nile, hidden amid acacias and regal palm trees. The servants had refused to let her set foot over the threshold. Surveying her dusty clothing and disheveled appearance, they took her for a beggar. She pleaded with them, but to no avail; it was Menes, Isis's brother, who came to her rescue. He had seen her on several occasions when he had taken his sister to school. It was he who admitted her, albeit with a puzzled expression on his face and a gasp of surprise from Isis at the sight of her—Isis had stared, scarcely recognizing her. Then she made haste to take her to her room, not wanting anyone to see her in the state she was in. Aisha passed through the mansion, awestruck by the gleaming white marble, brilliantly colored carpets, crystal chandeliers suspended from high ceilings, and portraits in heavy gilt frames from which glowered men with curling moustaches. Feeling she had no right to enter such a place, she sequestered herself in Isis's room.

Several days passed in which she was unable to come to any decision. She wanted to leave and continue her journey—no matter where. Isis, however, held fast to her, refusing to let her go. Aisha told her an abridged version of what had happened at the school, and saw tears come to her eyes on hearing of Margaret's fate, but she didn't like to let her go her way without first discussing matters with her father and asking for help. Aisha, though, kept to her confinement in the bedroom. She didn't dare go out and face the others in the household. "Please, Isis," she said in a shaky voice, "I don't want anything. Let me be. A few more days, and I'll go back to my village."

"You're not going anywhere, and you're not attending the party dressed like that."

"Party? What party?"

"The party my father's giving tonight. All the country's most important people will be there—you'll see. Unfortunately, most of them are old. The young people will be scarce, as usual."

Aisha watched her skipping happily about the room like someone who belonged to a different world. "Isis, please," she begged, "I've never been to a party in my life, and I'll spoil everything, the way I always do. I only came here for a temporary haven. If you want me to go now, I will."

"In the house of Wasfi Pasha," Isis replied firmly, "you must do as Wasfi Pasha's family does."

"But I haven't anything to wear."

Isis ran to open a closetful of clothes for her. In all her life, Aisha had never seen clothes so beautiful or so costly. She stood there, transfixed.

"My clothes are all yours to choose from, Mary. Pick out whatever you'd like."

"Please—I couldn't . . ."

"The Pasha—my father—won't help you with anything unless you impress him by showing yourself to him at your finest."

A regiment of servants entered the room—young girls dressed in jet black. They waited for a sign from Isis, then pounced on Aisha. They took her to the bath, removed all her old clothes, tossed them into a trash bin, and began dousing her with endless jugs of hot water. They scrubbed her all over with soap and fragrant oil, and wrapped her in thick cotton towels. Isis laughed to see her fluttering in their hands like a wet sparrow. She went on resisting, but bowed her head before the hairdresser, who came expressly to style the women's hair at the mansion. She trimmed Aisha's hair and expressed her indignation that such beautiful hair had never been cared for until now. She applied a mixture of henna and scented oils, buffed and varnished Aisha's fingernails, then rubbed powder on her face and lipstick on her lips. Aisha was transformed in spite of herself. In the mirror she saw an unfamiliar face, bearing no resemblance to the old Aisha.

Isis pulled an armful of dresses from the closet and spread them on the bed. They were of gleaming silk and chiffon, with dentelle trim. Isis held them up in front of her, turning them this way and that. She held them under Aisha's nose and from them wafted Isis's own perfume, which it seemed she never varied. Dazzled, Aisha took one of them from her, a sleeveless dress with a wide scoop neck. She imagined herself in it, décolleté, arms smooth and bare. Abashed, she said, "I would be embarrassed to wear anything like this!"

"These are special party dresses," said Isis. "Inside houses and salons, you can't be seen by any of those peasants outside. The only ones who'll see you are the scions of wealth, and they're used to these things."

"I can't."

"Don't be difficult. Or what's the point in your having studied at that wretched school?"

Standing before the mirror, Aisha was mortified at the sight of her exposed neck and the shape of her breasts. She reached for the hem of the dress, about to take it off, but Isis cried, "Silly girl! That dress is yours—from now on I won't wear it anymore."

A woman came into the room. Feeling at first as though she was looking at a picture from one of the glossy American magazines they had at the school, Aisha was riveted. The woman was tall, dressed in a simple sheath. Her hair was waved and styled close to her head in front, braided in back. In her hand was a holder with a lit cigarette at the end of it. She leaned against the door and said languidly, "Girls, girls—what is all this commotion?"

Isis stood up straight and said, "Mama, this is Mary, my friend from school."

The woman looked at Aisha with a faint smile on her lips. She didn't greet her, but her face bore no expression of distaste. She crossed herself as if to dispel fears she harbored within, and said, "You look lovely in that dress."

Thank God, Aisha thought, that this woman had not seen her in her dirty peasant dress. She ducked her head shyly, but the woman had already turned to leave, saying, "Try not to be late to the party, and do try not to spoil it!"

With the same languorous steps, she walked away, Aisha staring after her in wonder—although she didn't know whether her words had expressed displeasure or caution. But Isis turned to Aisha with a smile. "Eveline Hanim. The one and only."

The chandeliers were all lit up, and the crystals cast all the colors of the rainbow. Aisha knew that in the cellar there was a remarkable machine for generating electricity, which the Pasha had brought back specially from England, and which was running full blast on this particular night to drive off the darkness that cloaked the village, the mountain, and the river. Dozens of torches had also been lit, and were flickering in the wind. They formed two rows along the driveway connecting the mansion to the road that passed through the farmlands, and two more rows flanking the stairway from the house to the river landing.

As the evening's events commenced, the guests began to assemble at the mansion. Aisha stood next to Isis at her bedroom window, watching the horse-drawn carriages pull up, dispensing, along with the ostrich feathers that emerged from within them, whiffs of lavender and face powder: the women were beautiful. They carried themselves just the way Eveline Hanim did, and doubtless talked like her, too. The men seemed well pleased with themselves: a mix of Egyptians, foreigners, and British officers. Servants kept coming, bowing to each guest, while the drivers descended from the carriages and set baskets of fodder before the horses.

An old carriage arrived, rattling on its four wheels, which looked as though they were about to fall off. It stopped in front of the door, and several men got out of the back seat, carrying musical instruments. An older man, tall and extremely thin and wearing a scarlet tarbush, got out of the front seat. Isis's brother, Menes, came forward quickly to receive him and help him up the stairs to the house. Behind them came a youth, of slight build despite his height, and dressed exactly like the old man, as if their clothes had been cut from the same fabric.

"The artist has arrived," said Isis excitedly, "the evening's star entertainment! Master Saleh Abdel Hayy and his ensemble. He is the maestro who performs for kings and sultans. The young man following him is his son Sameh. They say his voice is beautiful, too, like his father's."

But Aisha was too distracted to pay attention to Sameh. Before she could stop herself she said, "Your brother, Menes . . . how handsome and elegant he looks tonight!"

"He's all yours," said Isis offhandedly. "Just leave me the rest of the young men at the party!"

The servants conducted the artist off to one side, away from his group. He and his son entered by the front door, while the servants led the rest of the ensemble to a side door.

"They'll serve dinner to the ensemble first," Isis explained. "But the maestro will sit at the table with the other guests. Ah—it's time for us to go down."

This was the moment Aisha had been dreading. Again she begged to be allowed to stay upstairs, but Isis, with childlike obstinacy, was determined that Aisha should accompany her. Together they descended the first few steps leading to the main room, now full of people. Feeling herself about to trip, Aisha clutched the banister, trying to hide behind Isis.

Eveline Hanim was the first to notice them. She muttered between her teeth, "I don't know why Isis has insisted on bringing this peasant girl with her!"

But Menes stared in wonder at Aisha, unable to believe her transformation—she resembled a Coptic princess of old, just like those whose pictures he had seen in the monasteries at Fayoum: wide-open eyes, head held high, an expectant gaze. He moved toward the staircase. Isis gave him a little smile, thinking he was approaching on her account, but in a disconcerting move he took Aisha by the hand and drew her forward.

"Come this way," he said. "Say hello to the Pasha."

She allowed herself to be towed behind him, struggling to keep her balance. He led her to a group of men who were talking and laughing, in the midst of whom was a man who looked exactly like Menes, apart from his grey hair and his curled moustache.

"Father," said Menes, "this is Mary, Isis's school friend and classmate."

The Pasha turned to her and studied her, a slight smile on his lips. "You've graced our party, young lady!" he said.

Isis came over and kissed her father, then adroitly steered Aisha over to where the women were sitting. Eveline Hanim was smoldering with irritation. Isis sat beside Aisha as if to protect her, Aisha herself sitting in the chair at the end of the row. She listened to the women's chatter—they were speaking English and French, with only a smattering of Arabic thrown in here and there for fun. They talked about Cairo and the khedive Abbas and the endless parties that had taken over Cairo with the advent, in force, of the Europeans. Aisha noted with pleasure that Menes had not stopped staring at her.

The Pasha, on the other hand, looked anxious. He kept going every few minutes to stare out from the balcony that opened onto the Nile, before returning to his guests.

The musical ensemble took its place in the center of the large room and the musicians began tuning their instruments, while the maestro sat on a chair drinking a cup of deep yellow aniseed tea.

Voices rose suddenly, and the Pasha hurried to the balcony along with a number of the guests. Aisha craned her neck and saw the dahabeah all lit up and gliding across the surface of the Nile. Isis stood up, took her by the hand, and led her to another part of the room, away from the crowd. The Pasha held out his hand to Eveline Hanim, who got up and took it, gathering up the train of her dress with her free hand. Together they quickly left the room and descended the stairs leading to the river, followed by a great many of the guests and British officers.

"He's the guest of honor tonight," Isis said, animated. "Lord Cromer." Aisha looked at her questioningly, and Isis went on in a whisper, "He's the British high commissioner, the actual leader—sultan above the sultan himself. Every winter he goes to Luxor—he and his second wife, Lady Katherine—and it's understood he'll stop in with us. My father is very proud of their friendship."

The rituals of another world were being enacted before Aisha's eyes. The servants brought torches and went down to the landing at the embankment. The ladies congregated on one side and the men on the other, all eyes fastened upon the dahabeah as its mooring lines were cast upon the shore. The crew set out wooden planks to form a gangway. Aisha held her breath, seeing Lord Cromer appear in the ship's doorway, beside him a tall lady wearing a fur coat and a large hat, which concealed her face. The sight of them evoked a wave of excitement among all the onlookers standing onshore. Some clapped enthusiastically, while the British officers raised their glasses and cheered. The stately old man advanced with dignity and self-assurance, proceeding through the applause that greeted him until at last he achieved the shore. The Pasha shook hands with him and the lady extended her hand for him to kiss. Eveline Hanim ducked her head and curtseyed, and then she and her husband stepped aside so that Lord Cromer and his wife could precede them up the steps, everyone else following in their wake.

The crowd returned once more to the grand room in which the party was taking place. Not all of them shook hands with Lord Cromer—there were only a few who dared to approach him, few who were favored with the honor of shaking his hand. He himself chose whose hand he would take, and whom he would ignore. He stood in the middle of the room beneath the enormous chandelier, casting a cold eye upon the assembled guests, gazing out at them from some other realm. At last he sat down in the midst of the gathering, and Aisha was able to get a look at his elongated face, thick moustache, and silver hair, as well as the medals displayed upon his chest. Lady Katherine had removed her coat and revealed her shimmering black dress. Her face was very pale, its expression one of extreme ill humor, of irritation with everything about the surrounding atmosphere—it was as if she went about holding her nose. She sat next to Eveline Hanim, who shrank perceptibly.

Aisha got as far away from all of them as she could. She wished she might find a way to go upstairs and disappear into Isis's room. She kept to a corner, cowering there and hoping no one would notice her.

In another corner of the room Master Abdel Hayy stood up, having finished his aniseed tea, and sat down at the front of the musical ensemble. The musicians seated behind him were tense, uneasily watching this gathering of Pashas and foreigners. When Lord Cromer stopped conversing with those around him, Isis's father hurriedly signaled to the ensemble. The maestro cleared his throat as if he was coughing up the dust from the road, and the musicians began tuning their instruments. When he signed to them with his finger held aloft, they began to play. Each time they finished a piece he nodded, and they applied themselves to their instruments once more. He allowed himself time to compose his voice and prepare to perform. All at once his song rang out, in the sorrow of one abandoned and sleepless. His voice was husky at first, but then it gradually cleared, as if he were drawing his breath from deep caverns. The faces of the musicians in the ensemble reddened with the exertion of playing. Then the musicians, among them the boy, began repeating the maestro's refrains after him.

Aisha glanced at Lord Cromer's face, and found that it too was flushed. He placed a hand on his shirt collar, as if in an effort to loosen a necktie that was choking him, and a look of dismay crossed Lady Katherine's face. She fixed her gaze upon the maestro's throat as his voice rose. Among the guests, the Egyptians swayed, under the spell of the music, but the foreigners, baffled, were motionless.

Suddenly Lord Cromer stood up and shouted in English, "Oh, do be still! This wailing, it's unbearable."

The room fell abruptly silent, and the maestro came all at once to himself, out of his reverie. "Honorable Lord!" he cried beseechingly.

Alarmed, the Pasha hurried over to Lord Cromer; Eveline Hanim was in a swoon.

"Sir," said the Pasha, "what is it?"

"Dismiss him at once," said Lord Cromer, gesturing toward the artist. "I can't take any more of this lugubrious moaning. Have you no one else?"

The artist understood little of what was said, but his face had gone pale with humiliation. The members of the ensemble began packing up their instruments, although no one had instructed them to do so, while the artist stood rooted in place, his face quivering with a mixture of emotions, as if he might weep. The boy went and attached himself to his father.

The Pasha hurried over, took the artist's arm, and gently pulled him away. "Please come with me," he said. Master Abdel Hayy was breathing with difficulty, but he left the room with the Pasha. The musicians struggled with their instruments as they strove to get away; the boy seemed about to cry, and all the while Lord Cromer stood erect like a victorious general observing the remnants of his routed enemy.

"My God," he said. "What a nightmare. I thought I was going to faint."

Soon there rose a murmur of subdued laughter among the foreigners. Eveline Hanim came to herself and glanced about, bewildered. The Egyptian guests held their peace at first, then joined in with the rest in low, uneasy laughter. Aisha felt very sorry for the artist, whose husky voice had moved her to the core, putting her in mind of Margaret's sorrows. She looked about for Isis. Isis was seated beside her mother, dabbing at her face with a small handkerchief.

Aisha was startled to find someone staring fixedly at her—indeed, he could scarcely take his eyes off her. It was a young Englishman, in his late twenties, with a narrow, melancholy face and a thin moustache the color of straw. She looked the other way, but she could tell he was still watching her.

The Pasha returned, speechless with embarrassment. But Lord Cromer, with all the modesty of a conqueror, clapped a hand on his shoulder and said, "Nevermind, Pasha. Your choice of entertainer was unfortunate, but you did well in your choice of guests. I'll bring this evening's party to life."

With that, he strode manfully to the ebony piano in the corner, on which Isis took her lessons from a French music teacher. Chuckling as he raised the lid he said, "Lucky for me it's clean—dust would have interfered with my playing."

Everyone laughed raucously. He applied himself smoothly to the keys, abruptly filling the room with their music. Eveline Hanım revived, and the pallor faded from the Pasha's face as the tension eased and the foreigners murmured admiringly. The Egyptians kept their resentment to themselves: another defeat—what did it matter?

Aisha looked about anxiously. However proficient the playing, she felt oppressed. She slid warily along the wall, hoping no one would see her or hear the rustle of her skirt. Lord Cromer had reached a climax in his performance, so Aisha managed to slip out onto to the wide balcony, well away from all of them. She shivered at the touch of the night breeze on her face and shoulders. She saw the blazing torches illuminating the drive that stretched away from the entrance to the mansion, and beyond them the darkness that blanketed the adjacent hamlet. The sound of the piano reached her, mixed with that of the crickets and frogs.

She drew a deep breath. Down below she saw the musical ensemble leaving the mansion, the men with heads bowed, as two of them supported the artist. They went haltingly with the old man, pausing every couple of steps, and then proceeding, eyes cast down. None of them dared raise his head except the boy, who turned and looked at the mansion, his face wet and shining with tears. Would the old man even be able to make it to Cairo in this condition? Would he ever sing again? They supported him until, with difficulty, he got into the carriage, which in turn began its difficult progress.

"Are you sorry for him?"

She heard the voice coming from behind her and started up in alarm. The question was put to her in English. It was the young Englishman who had been staring at her all the while. He approached now with a drink in his hand, his face quite flushed—perhaps he was already slightly drunk. Aisha moved to put some distance between herself and him. Still, he continued, saying simply, "It's the same with me—I'm not happy about what that conceited peacock did. Listen to that dreadful performance of his—he fancies himself another Chopin, no less."

Aisha smiled. The carriage bearing the musicians faded into the mist rising off of the fields, while the performance went on inside. The young man seemed not to expect her to say much. Extending his hand to her, he said. "I forgot to introduce myself. I'm Howard Carter."

There was nothing for it but to offer him her trembling fingers, hoping he wouldn't notice how cold they were. Maybe he did notice, though, for he held onto them a moment, possibly to steady them. He smiled, looking directly into her face again. "Perhaps you haven't heard of me, but I know you—I've seen you more than once."

"Me?" exclaimed Aisha, astonished. She felt the blood rising in her veins. "It's the first time I've ever attended an event like this," she said. She was about to add that for years she had never left the school, but she remembered Margaret and the men from the embassy, and she pressed her lips shut.

Inside, the guests applauded. Guessing that the party must be over, she moved to go back in the house, but Carter stood in her path—he hadn't yet finished with what he had to say, and he didn't want to miss this chance to be alone with her. The piano playing resumed, and the wind picked up, carrying with it the scent of the burning torches.

"Excuse me," said Carter, "but I have seen you many times . . . at Beni Hassan al-Ghuroub . . . Beni Abid . . . Fayoum . . . Deir al-Bahri in Luxor . . ."

In mounting discomfiture, Aisha said, "You must be mistaken, sir. I'm a classmate of the Pasha's daughter, Isis, at a private school. I've hardly ever left the school."

But the young man held fast to his conviction. Perhaps drink was to blame for this.

"Many times I've made paintings from reliefs of your face," he said, "its features in all their details: this rather proud nose, the wide hazel eyes, the magnificent high forehead, these blue-black tresses, the complexion tinted brown by the sun and red by the Nile."

"Sir!" cried Aisha.

"I can show you the evidence," he said. "I've got it here with me—if you'll give me a chance, I'll bring it to you from the carriage."

Aisha didn't know what to do. He stood eagerly before her, the glass in his hand, breathing hard with the force of his emotions, hollow-eyed and with a burning stare.

She bowed her head. "Are you sure I'm the one?" she said. "To foreigners, all Egyptian faces look alike. And you, too, to us . . ."

"Yes, yes," said Carter, "it was like that in the beginning. When I first came to Egypt. But after so many years I can distinguish all the faces. Yours in particular."

"You're confusing me, sir."

"I work now for the preservation of antiquities, but I was originally an artist, and I'll always be an artist. The job was a chance that came my way in life. My mission is to familiarize myself with the faces and memorize their features the way a poet memorizes his verses."

Carter stepped forward and placed the glass he was holding on the parapet. "Wait here," he said. "Don't move; don't go anywhere—now I'll prove to you everything I've been saying."

He hurriedly left the balcony, oblivious to Lord Cromer, who was still absorbed in his playing and possessed indeed by the spirit of Chopin. The eyes of the guests were upon him as he crossed the room, his brisk footsteps loud enough that Cromer's fingers fumbled at the piano keys, though he didn't look in Carter's direction. The Pasha observed with alarm his departure from the house, and looked toward the balcony—perhaps there he could discover the reason for what had happened. He knew Carter was one of the most prestigious of those commissioned to work in Upper Egypt, for he was the director in charge of the Egyptian Antiquities Service, and his authority extended from Asyout all the way to the Sudanese border. He was sought after every year by all the lords and important state visitors, including Lord Cromer himself. His departure in such a manner was another scandal the Pasha didn't need. He glanced at Eveline Hanim, who was also upset and once more looking faint. He didn't dare get up and go after Carter, with Lord Cromer at the peak of his performance, his fingers gathering speed on the keyboard and his breath coming fast. He finished with a resounding chord.

Lord Cromer, out of breath, stilled his hands and let his arms fall to his sides, getting his wind back on the conclusion of his contest with the keyboard. Everyone stood up and began to applaud wildly, Lord Cromer dipping his head, offering barely perceptible nods in acknowledgment of their enthusiasm.

Out on the balcony, Aisha was watching Carter as he dashed out of the house and hurried across the open space illuminated by the flickering torches, heading for a horse-drawn carriage that stood in a corner. "This is madness," she said to herself. "This Englishman will get me mixed up in some scandal." She mustn't stay longer on the balcony, especially while she could hear the applause inside—she must steal quietly inside and mingle with the crowd, so as to belie any connection between herself and this Englishman.

She entered the room on tiptoe. Lord Cromer was the center of attention—everyone stood around him shaking hands with him once more. He had won a twofold victory: first over the elderly artist, and then a second time by proving his musical aptitude. Aisha was hoping to pass unseen, but Eveline Hanim spotted her, and threw her a vicious glance, concluding that she was the reason for the lunatic Englishman's untoward exit. Eveline Hanim would wait until after the party to settle accounts with Aisha.

In the midst of this commotion, the wild-eyed Englishman reappeared, coming in from outside and holding in his arms a bundle of paper scrolls. It was clear he had snatched them up at random from among a larger collection of scrolls. Lord Cromer craned his neck, ignoring all those who surrounded him. He regarded Carter with a sneer. The others all turned toward Carter as well, as Cromer spoke. "Mr. Carter," he said, "I see you didn't care for my playing."

Carter stopped. He dropped one of the scrolls, and as he knelt quickly to pick it up the rest of them fell to the floor. He began hastily gathering them up, muttering unintelligible words. No one moved to assist him—even the hosts, the Pasha and his wife, were unable to move. They knew he had angered Lord Cromer to a degree that precluded anyone's stepping forward to help him. At last he gave up his attempt to collect the scrolls. He said, finally, "I beg your pardon for this disruption. I wanted to show you . . . that is, to show her, something."

He pointed toward Aisha, who was standing against the wall. They all turned to her, including Lord Cromer, and she wished she could vanish from their sight. But here they all were, seeing her for the first time all night, registering her presence. Isis looked at her sympathetically, and smiled. As the blood drained from Aisha's face, Carter quickly began to pick up the scrolls and spread them on the floor, looking about for heavy objects to secure them. It was Menes, finally, who came to his aid, bringing small articles of glassware and setting them on the edges. The papers began to reveal their contents: watercolor paintings done in delicate lines and subtle hues, the design nevertheless clear and unambiguous. They were all of Egyptian faces—or rather, of one face in particular: portraits in profile showing a proud nose, wide eyes tapered at the corners by the application of kohl, flowing locks of hair and, arranged on the forehead, jewels whose designs alternated between flower patterns, serpent heads, and sun discs. The designs differed from one painting to the next—the dress, the hairstyle, the cosmetics, and the jewels—but the face was the same. The assembled crowd could not but turn and study the paintings with interest. Even Lord Cromer himself stood still and examined them.

Breathing audibly, Carter said, "I made these paintings from different tombs, from the various pharaonic dynasties. I've done hundreds of paintings—I copied them from the stone surfaces of the walls. But this face always leapt out at me and animated my sketches to form these features on the page—it was as if this face was pursuing me. At first I thought I had lost my reason, imagining there was a wandering spirit that had left its tomb thousands of years ago and now taken to following me—and I a foreigner, come from across the seas."

Carter paused for a moment to catch his breath, and looked at Aisha to see her reaction. But she, along with the rest, was staring at the paintings in amazement. The guests kept quiet, so Carter resumed, "I began to gather these faces together—I didn't send them to the Archaeological Society in London as I did with the rest of the paintings. I felt they were something that belonged specially to me—this face that revealed itself only to me. I've kept these scrolls with me and never left them. It's a strange coincidence that I brought them with me tonight—I never imagined that I'd come across this face here."

He stopped, out of steam. He looked at Aisha, but she didn't return his gaze. She didn't dare lift her face to meet his eye. The crowd studied her features for a moment, then went back to the paintings spread out on the floor, and a murmur rose as they began circling the paintings, viewing them from different angles, then looking back at her, while she clung closer and closer to the wall.

"Mary," said Carter, "be good enough to raise your head a little."

"He's not talking to me," thought Aisha. "He must mean someone else, not me."

And Eveline Hanim thought to herself, *If that girl doesn't raise her head I'll evict her.*

But Lord Cromer came resolutely forward, reached out with a finger and tilted her chin, lifting her face. He gazed at her and said, "I thought perhaps Carter was exaggerating, as is his wont, but no—the resemblance is clear. She could be a fugitive princess from the age of the Pharaohs."

In spite of herself, Aisha felt tears starting from her eyes. Everyone applauded—because of Lord Cromer's courtliness, of course, and the verdict he had pronounced. He let go her chin and walked away from her, the rest of the crowd following in his wake. That concluded her role in this night's party, and there was nothing in her way except Carter the madman, and between them the pictures spread upon the floor. She dabbed at her tears and tried to look at the paintings. She remembered her long journey, fleeing from her village, the wolf that stalked her, the life she was living under a false name and identity. But the pictures, in spite of everything, bore something of her, as if he had not copied them from ancient lines incised in rough stone, but from a lucid mirror in which, when he sat before it, he could see through to her soul. She kept asking herself, *Is that truly me*?

"I was certain," said Carter, "that you were present and alive, from the number of reliefs depicting your face that I saw on the walls and columns and obelisks. And now I've seen for myself that you actually do exist."

Aisha reached out for one of the paintings and picked it up. It showed her face in profile, wide eyes filled with sorrow. "It's me and it's not me," she said. "I'm far more unhappy than this picture. There's more life in the colors of this painting than there is in my body."

Carter went to her and put his hand on her shoulder. She didn't shy away from him—on the contrary, she took comfort from his gesture. "Could you sit for me one day?" he said. "I'd like to paint you from life, after painting you from stone. I may not be a brilliant painter, but I feel that your face will lend me the inspiration I've been looking for."

On the point of tears, Aisha replied, "Please—enough! I don't know what will become of me tomorrow. I live day to day, moment to moment. I have no real home. I always feel like an outcast. Even wolves pursue me."

"I, too, am pursued by wolves. Perhaps the same wolf stalks us both."

They looked at each other. He wished he could embrace her, but he did not dare.

3 • The Tombs at Beni Hassan

YES INDEED, MY LITTLE PRINCESS—our life is a chase that never ends, breathless and relentless. And the wolves are not the only hunters. The wolves show their faces occasionally, but are hidden behind masks most of the time.

I had gone to great lengths to escape, to get far away, to hide, even before I encountered the wolf for the first time. By the time I saw it standing there, watchfully, beside the entrance to the tomb, I had already trembled to hear it howling in the silence of the night. It had banished sleep and robbed me of my peace of mind. But when it stood before me I was calm, as if I had come to know it and to expect its arrival. It gazed at me with luminous eyes and open mouth. Startled, I stared at it: a dusty wild dog, only bigger and sleeker than a dog, with a tapered muzzle and prominent fangs. It stared back at me, surprised by my youth and small stature, and the harshness of my isolation. It didn't seem capable of mauling me, at least in that moment, as I sat beside the blazing campfire, which I had fed with enough firewood to keep it burning all night. This was the reason the wolf was watching me from outside the tomb, without setting foot inside.

Newberry had warned me about the danger of spending the night in that place. He was my oldest and most experienced leader, and he knew the secrets of this primitive region. He wanted me to work only in the daytime, then take the ferry and return to the eastern shore, but I was bewitched by the place, its sullen rocks whose fissures sprout thorns, and those black crevasses intersecting with the ridges of the mountain. He said, "I don't mean to underestimate your abilities, but I hadn't imagined they would send me a youth of eighteen years."

I didn't feel slighted by his words, for I was still a few months shy of that age. I didn't tell him that I had actually embarked upon my first sexual experiences, here upon the hot sands of this strange country, but I felt that this tomb in which I was to work was my gateway to the adult world. The wind was still hot, even after midnight, the river opaque as a riddle, the sky close and rich with stars. I had never before seen a sky packed with so many stars, and I was intoxicated with the space and the silence—until that wolf turned up. He stretched his paws, then sat near the opening of the tomb. I didn't know whether he was there to guard me from attack by the other wolves or whether he was waiting for the fire to die down so as to launch an attack himself. I rose cautiously, gathered up all the bits of kindling and tree limbs that I had, and began tossing them onto the flames. My only hope was for the fire not to die out before daybreak—and when would that be?

Nothing broke the silence but the crackling of the wood fire—could it be that this was where the hunt would come to an end? It was Newberry who had brought me from Cairo to Minya onboard an old sailing vessel. I preferred to travel by water, so that bad luck would lose my trail; the ship traveled against the current, and the water bore particles of dark-colored mud. I had spent my childhood at the edge of a dark-green river full of algae and bits of melting ice. I contemplated the flat green expanse that covered the bank on the east side, while the west side was hemmed in by desolate hills, and the desert was as close as could be.

We disembarked together and joined the crowd at Minya. The colors of the faces, the suntanned complexions, amazed me. We rested for one night at the only hotel in the station square, and the next morning crossed to the opposite bank thanks to an old and very small boat. We climbed the arid hills to the tombs of Beni Hassan.

There were deep trenches amidst the rocks. Newberry pointed to one of them and said, "Here is your palace, the one you've been seeking."

I noted the veiled sarcasm, but I was busy exploring the place, studying the walls of the first tomb I entered. Its paintings were faded, covered with a layer of fine dust, but they were real and authentic, full of ancient spirits in their natural abode, no embellishments or artificial gloss. Although pale, as if about to fade away altogether, they were protected from the effects of time by this patina of dust. They were not stiff or mummified, the way I had seen them for the first time at Lord Amherst's mansion. I wanted to reach out and touch them, but I was afraid they would vanish like a dream.

"Our team is made up of two others," said Newberry. "You'll meet them in the morning. Mr. Fraser and Mr. Blackden. They have undertaken to copy the paintings in the other tombs. We shall all cooperate in finishing up this area."

"Where are they now?" I asked.

“They’ll turn up in good time. The important thing is for you to know the scope of your work, so that you don’t interfere with theirs.”

I arranged my things—my small case, scrolls of paper, colored pencils, and a little food. I did this in such a deliberate way as to suggest that the place had become my own, and that I was staying here.

“You’re not in Swaffham, you know,” Newberry cautioned me. “This place is full of vipers and wolves and hyenas. It’s not a picnic.”

The wolf got to his feet and turned in a circle, sensing, perhaps, that the blaze had subsided. I grasped a flaming stick and brandished it, making a loud noise. I wanted him to move off a bit, but he saw through my childish ploy. He kept staring at me with his piercing eyes, and then he began to howl. His voice split the silence of the mountain, and from afar dozens of other voices responded. Was he summoning them? Or was it a farewell? He wagged his tail and threw me a final glance before he left. I was sure he would return some other night, when there was no fire lit.

I commenced work in the morning, even though I was tired from my night’s vigil, and from the stifling weather. A small dinghy came, and in it were some supplies which an elderly boatman named Idris brought. I didn’t go to the other tombs to make the acquaintance of those who worked there. I wanted to be alone for a while, to contemplate these cryptic paintings and try to decode their messages. I paused for a long time before a depiction of a bird. It was standing on the branch of a tree that was not visible in the picture, folding one wing and spreading the other, as if it were half-still, while the other half was poised to take flight. I stood there unable to believe what I saw. I expected it to come to life and burst from the shadowy tomb. I opened my case with a trembling hand and drew from it my papers and watercolors. There was a small table with a low chair, at which I seated myself and got to work at once. I felt as though it was essential that I rescue this bird from its silent death, to shower it with my watercolors and infuse it with a new spirit—perhaps it would find its way to the other world.

I remembered the first time I stood before these paintings, the shiver that ran all through me as with my eyes I traced their details—a shiver of fear and amazement, and a strange kind of hunger. I was young, but the chase had begun. Yes indeed . . . it started years ago, elsewhere, on a rainy night in Kensington, our first home, when we all left, fleeing the darkness: seven siblings, seven hungry mouths, and in our mother’s arms the eighth, who was still suckling. My father was in flight from his creditors and the announcement of his ruin. We left our old house and most of our clothes and other belongings, each of us taking only what he could carry. We took shelter from the pouring rain under the station roof, until morning came, and with it the first train that would carry us to another town, far from all the memories of childhood, of brick houses and cobblestone streets. The train didn't tarry: it raced across the fogbound flat countryside, severing us from everything that had any connection with the past. My mother cried, and so did the baby. She tried to quiet it by offering it her breast, but that didn't seem to satisfy it. For many a long day this feeling would cling to all of us: there was never enough food to fill all those stomachs. My father was puffing on his pipe, pretending nothing had happened. At that moment his smoke was turning our stomachs, nauseating us. Next to his seat was a small number of his things, which he had been determined to bring along and keep by him: a roll of canvases, a bundle of different-sized brushes, and a quantity of half-empty paint tubes. My father was seeking a new start, and we had no choice but to go to the old family home in Swaffham—to my paternal aunt, who most particularly hated my mother.

We crowded into the basement of the small house, the mice having fled on our account. My elder brother soon left us to seek his fortune in London. My aunt tried to get me to attend the school that was affiliated with her church, but my father refused; she persisted in her efforts to give me spelling lessons through the use of the New Testament. For the first time my father took me with him to look for work at the nearby estates, for he was afraid to face rejection on his own. Together we rode in a hay wagon that jogged along monotonously. He had brought examples of his paintings: short-tailed dogs, wide-eyed cats, and stray foxes—paintings our fugitive state had prevented him from finishing.

"Of course," he was telling me as we rode along, "I prefer to paint animals. They are sincere—they don't know how to dissimulate. Likewise they have no objection to their own looks, as can be plainly seen in my paintings."

Our destination was the stately homes of the nobility, those accursed Englishmen who loved their spoiled pets more than they loved their wives, according to my father. Together we climbed Didlington Hill, where Lord Amherst's estate was: an old fortress with moss growing upon its stones, ivy and fern surrounding the window frames. The butler looked us over haughtily, but he admitted us into the presence of Lady Amherst. The dim corridors exuded the scent of wood varnish and old spices. We trod upon carpeting so soft it seemed to me that if I should trip and fall I would get lost in its dense pile. We entered a hall whose walls were covered in portraits of glowering faces and uniforms adorned with medals—lords, generals, and captains. My father looked at me, feeling diminished and wishing he could retreat. But the lady came, carrying a blindingly white Persian cat. My father talked to her about how he specialized in painting domestic animals, and had gone into a number of stately homes and painted all the creatures they housed, from birds to dogs and cats to racehorses, even snakes, and animals that had been stuffed and mounted. It appeared that despite all this the lady did not need his services, especially since his Lordship, her husband, was away on a long hunting trip. But then the Persian cat, taking her unawares, leapt onto my lap, where it subsided in a heap, settling itself comfortably. The lady looked at me in amazement. She agreed to have my father begin painting her cat and to bring me along whenever he came. At last we smiled at each other, he and I. We'd see some bread and butter and eggs on our table; perhaps we could have a little peace of mind and a fresh start.

It would be absurd to say that the cat's leap changed my life—it wasn't so random as all that. The incident was no more than a chance occurrence, but it was the reason behind our regular trips to Didlington. My aunt was angry, exasperated with my father for not giving her a chance to instruct me.

The animals began to change as new portrait subjects were introduced, and the paintings were replaced, one for another. The lady owned a menagerie of tame beasts in her back garden—monkeys from Africa, small Bengal tigers, colorful equatorial birds. I, too, brought a small tablet and some pencils. I would follow his brushstrokes and perhaps the course of his life, as a wandering artist passing through estates and manors to paint the animals they housed. Surely I would be like him.

One day my father was painting an ill-mannered monkey. It would eat the fruit of a banana and fling the peel, while the lady smiled and my father tried to feign pleasure in this teasing. It was a foolish scene. I pulled out my chair and wandered away from them, through the long corridor, over the plush carpet. I saw the mirrors, the paintings, the carpets, and the elaborate silver candlesticks, as well as the swords, daggers, and hunting rifles.

Eventually the corridor took me to a dimly lit hall, with faint light filtering in through narrow openings in lowered blinds. The air was stale—there was neither a source of heat nor any ventilation. When my eyes had adjusted to the shadows, I discerned wondrous things such as I had never seen before. There was a statue of black stone: a slender woman, her nose broken but still held high, her full lips pressed together, her eyes wide and deep set; in her hand she held what looked like a flower bending forward on its stem and resting on her fingers, and she stood as if she was just about to step out of the shadows. In the middle of the hall was a massive stone sarcophagus, with exotic figures incised and painted on it, including an image of the flower that the woman held. Next to this was an old wooden box whose colors deeply penetrated its texture—outlandish images, such as staring eyes, open hands, serpent heads and jackals, strange faces decorated with jewelry that was stranger still. Everything was oddly positioned. There was another statue representing a cat standing poised on its hind legs for a savage attack, possessing nothing of the docility of the animals my father painted. Next to this was a glass case, under which were many ancient artifacts, some of them broken and incomplete—pieces of stone, wood, and greenish brass; huge vessels of pottery, marble, and granite, with extraordinary designs etched upon them; paintings hung upon the walls. There were fragments of ancient linen, worn and frayed, resting behind panes of glass. There was a picture of a warrior holding a bow and nocking an arrow as he stood upon a two-wheeled horse-drawn chariot. The hall was filled with remarkable pictures of brown-faced people with wide eyes and long, curling lashes—they belonged to another world, a different era. I knew nothing about them, and yet I moved among them, feverish, wanting to reach out my hand and touch them, to make sure they were really there. I was afraid, though—they looked like talismans for wizards, followers of Merlin.

Could I draw these, rather than the cats and other pets? Could I get at the life behind the faded, stiff façade? They must be connected in some obscure way to this peripatetic lord, to those foreign countries he frequented. They were not to be found in our world, that much was certain. No one in Kensington or Swaffham, or even London, could fashion such totems.

I retreated to a corner of the room, breathing hard, trying to regain my composure. I opened my tablet and began to sketch what I saw onto the paper. I tried to solve the riddle of the faint smiles and fixed stares. The heavy atmosphere of the hall began to constrict my breath and enter my bones, arousing in me awe and fear and pain. I kept sketching until the light faded and darkness descended.

No one saw me pass through the corridor. My father was still seated before the unfinished painting of the monkey, banana peels strewn all around him. He looked at me, puzzled, and said, "Where did you run off to?"

"I don't like monkeys," I said ambiguously.

We went down the hill together, but found no wagon to take us to the house, so we walked a long way under squalls of fine drizzle. In the basement, after everyone had gone to sleep, I lit a small candle and turned over the pages I had filled with sketches. Where could these things have come from? And what did they stand for?

The following day I was already waiting for my father before he awoke. I pilfered another of his tablets and stuffed more pencils into my pocket. I saw my aunt clutching her Gospel, but I hid behind my father. I rode the hay wagon with him.

He sat before the monkey, trying to persuade it to hold still. I waited a little, until he was preoccupied, then crept off to the dim hall. I raised the blinds a bit, to admit more light, then began tremblingly to draw. I had acquainted myself somewhat with these strange forms, and I could tell that if I continued drawing like this the moment would come in which they would disclose all their secrets to me.

Was it the largest statue talking to me? Had it been transformed into this enormous man blocking my light and wearing an impressive uniform and holding a pair of gloves in his hand, which he slapped impatiently against the other hand? Frightened, I got to my feet, the papers and pencils falling from my lap. I darted away in front of him, my feet scarcely touching the floor as I made for the door. I heard his voice behind me as he bellowed, "Wait, you little thief!"

I ran into the butler as he passed through the corridor. My father was sitting, irritably eating a banana, while the monkey watched him in amazement. I was already sprinting over the lawn and heading down the hill as black clouds began to gather. I heard angry rumblings, but I didn't know whether they came from the house or from the sky. I looked behind me, but saw no hunting dogs—maybe they couldn't pursue me yet, or perhaps they were taking my father hostage in my stead.

I didn't go to the table to partake of our dinner of potatoes. I stayed by myself, quaking, down in the basement, listening to the sounds of their utensils clattering against the plates. I didn't know whether my father had come home or not. Then I heard the sound of his heavy footsteps coming down the stairs. I couldn't lock the door from the inside. He was extraordinarily angry. I realized that he had lost his job at the manor, and perhaps he would not be able to get work at the nearby estates, either. Through clenched teeth he said. "I'd like to break your neck—but not tonight, because Lord Amherst wants to see you in the morning."

I didn't sleep at all that night. I was sure he would drag me into the manor's cellar and leave me to rot. But there was no escape—I had to go. The following day we climbed the hill, while I repeated the words of apology that my father dictated to me. I must confirm my guilt, then apologize fervently and sincerely, and then retreat, but without turning my back to anyone. But at the door the butler made a clear sign to my father, saying, "You wait outside."

I looked at him pleadingly, but my father hastily withdrew. The butler pushed me, and I went along in front of him. The corridor seemed silent, and gloomier than usual. I closed my eyes, but the scent of the old hall was slowly taking possession of me. The butler stopped and left me to go in by myself. It was crowded as ever with all its artifacts. My interrogators awaited me—they fell silent on seeing me. The lady turned a kind face to me. A tiny shaft of light fell upon her features, making them appear to radiate more good will than those of the others. Lord Amherst was sitting beside the black basalt statue. He wasn't angry or agitated, the way he had appeared the day before. Beside the coffin embellished with paintings was a third person—a man, sitting stiffly upright, elegant, with sheets of paper spread out upon his knees. I could tell from the first, swift glance that they were the pages that bore my drawings. I continued to stand there in silence; I had forgotten all the words of apology. They kept staring at me in amazement—I didn't know why.

The lady said languidly, "Come forward, Howard. Let Sir Percy Newberry have a good look at you."

I took a small step forward, so that I was in the middle of a patch of light. I was uneasy. The man raised his head and studied me. He was slender, with piercing eyes, an aquiline nose, and a thick moustache that covered his upper lip entirely. He drew a sharp breath and said, "Good Lord! He's younger than I expected—skinnier and hungrier, too."

I didn't know what game it was these gentlemen were playing. He raised the hand that held my drawing sheets, and peered at them once more. Then he stared at me superciliously, and said, "Are you sure you're the one who made these drawings?"

I couldn't keep silent. "Indeed, sir," I said.

Sir Percy turned to address Lord Amherst, who had caught me yesterday. "My dear Amherst," he said, "he doesn't merely replicate all the details precisely, he invests them with new life. How did you manage to infuse life into these exanimate artifacts?"

He directed the latter question to me, but I didn't know how to respond. I didn't know what he meant, but he wasn't waiting for an answer from me, either. He went back to examining the drawings. He spoke to me again. "Do you know where these things came from—the paintings and statues and sarcophagi and other relics that fill this hall?"

My throat was dry. The situation was becoming increasingly awkward for me. I shook my head. Trying to take the measure of me, he asked, "And how far have you got with your instruction?"

"Not far," I said.

Her Ladyship spoke again, as languidly as before. "The dear boy!" she said. "His talent's inborn!"

Newberry said, "They are from Egypt—it is a small piece of our vast empire, but it is packed with these objects."

I couldn't keep still. I didn't believe it possible that such objects as these could exist somewhere in profusion. I wanted to sit down, or lean against something. I said in astonishment, "Other things like these? I can't imagine it!"

"What may be found there surpasses anything you could imagine: dozens of temples, hundreds of statues and obelisks, the walls of the crypts decked out with paintings. Don't bother to look around you—the things that are here are nothing by comparison with what is in Egypt. The astonishing thing is that the peasants who live amidst these splendid objects don't know their worth."

At last Lord Amherst raised his voice in protest. "But, my dear Newberry, this collection was chosen with immense care."

I couldn't understand what the discussion was about. I said breathlessly, "But if Egypt is a small part of our empire, why do we leave all these beautiful things to them? Why don't we bring them all here?"

All three of them glanced at one another and then burst out laughing. Even the scowling Lord Amherst joined in the hilarity. I looked on in confusion. I was certain of only one thing: that I was not going to be punished, and there was no need for me to recite those apologies.

"It's a fine idea, really," said Lord Newberry. "But it's impossible to carry out. Those people didn't grasp the value of what they had—it was we who informed them of it—and now it has become difficult to appropriate the objects from them. This is in addition to there being a number of things it would be impossible to transport."

In an attempt to be more serious than the others, her Ladyship fixed her gaze upon me, making me aware of her radiant beauty. She said, "Would you like to go to Egypt, my dear Howard?"

"Would my father go with me?" I said foolishly.

Lord Newberry turned himself altogether toward me. He made no reference to my stupidity, but spoke seriously. "No," he said, "of course not. Your father can't go with you everywhere. This is employment—a job—at which you will earn money, while at the same time drawing the objects you love. There is funding from the British Society for the Preservation of Egyptian Antiquities. You will go to the important sites and record all that you see. Then, even if some disaster should occur, natural or unnatural—an earthquake, flooding, a fire—and all these things should be lost, your pictures will remain; you will be the eyewitness who surveyed and saw and recorded them."

I didn't understand a word of what was being said. I didn't know why they were trying to send me to this distant land, instead of locking me up in the cellar. To rescue me from my confusion, her Ladyship said, "There is no need to answer right away, Howard. Go and talk it over with your father. Take your time."

◆ ◆ ◆

How distant this moment seems, as if it belonged to some other realm. And how strange my father's face seems, like the face of a relief carved in the wall—stiff and sad, yet unable to refuse an offer that would relieve him of one of those hungry mouths.

At noon, I felt a man's shadow fall on me as I was absorbed in my drawing. I thought it was Idris, bringing the day's provisions, but it was Newberry himself, dressed in khaki. He wore short pants and on his head was an enormous hat. He was staring red-faced at my work.

"For Christ's sake!" he exclaimed. "What do you think you're doing?"

Before I could utter a syllable, he had snatched the drawing I had before me and held it up to examine it more closely. He looked at the wall to see how well my handiwork conformed to the original. Then he stared at me in consternation and said angrily, "This is certainly not what you came here for. I thought Fraser and Blackden had explained to you the procedure you are to follow for this job!"

I had not yet met those two men, nor had it felt to me, during the preceding days, as though there was anyone but me in these tombs. But he went to a corner, picked up the roll of tracing paper and a bundle of black pencils he found there, and held them up. "What do you suppose these are for?" he said.

"I don't know," I said.

"The point is that you can see through them to the painting on the wall, so as to trace it exactly, retaining the same proportions and all the details. You must place the tracing paper over it and trace it directly. This is what we do with all the artwork, whatever the surface—whether concave or convex, smooth or grainy, colored or not. The important thing is to replicate them just as they are."

What he wanted was entirely different from what I had thought. Rapidly folding up a sheet of tracing paper, he continued, "Then we fold the paper like this before sending it to London. There they will undertake to sketch the paintings in ink and prepare them for printing. What is crucial is that your tracings be exact."

Listening to him, I was astounded. I had not imagined that these paintings would be handled in such a primitive fashion, or that someone I'd never seen would be inking them in—someone who hadn't touched their soul. Why had they brought me here, then? This work didn't require talent or passion.

Newberry must have noted the look of despair on my face. "No need to feel disappointed," he said. "We have before us a tremendous labor. This tomb is one of dozens that have been discovered and are yet to be discovered. We must complete them all, and if one of us were to sit here all day drawing a single bird, we'd need more than a century to finish the job."

Knowing discussion was futile, I said, "But at least we'd attain something of the beauty found on these walls."

"You're still young and inexperienced. It is financial considerations that constrain our activities. We must complete this task before the grant money runs out. Those funds were specially earmarked for us to gather all these paintings into special volumes and preserve them within the Egypt Exploration Society. We are in a race against time, my boy."

I didn't know at the time that he was a man of antiquated ideas, or that it was he who had devised this method, managed to persuade the London office, and on this basis selected all those who would work with him. He wasn't about to let an upstart like me overturn all his convictions. He wanted to finish, in only five years, the recording of all the paintings to be found far and wide throughout Egypt, and to impress this scheme of his upon everyone with the utmost rigor.

He left me and went to check on the other tombs, but I was hamstrung. My colored bird lay where it had been tossed upon the floor, and I felt it was worthless. I took some sheets of tracing paper, affixed them to the wall, and began outlining the paintings strictly, stripping them of life. And the dream I had cherished and for whose sake I had come to this desolate place became a nightmare.

Working away bitterly, I was unaware of time passing. Whenever I finished with one of the tracing sheets I hung another in its place. I wanted to get this over with as quickly as possible, so that I might have time left over to do what I loved. I stopped only when I heard the sound of raucous laughter coming from the entrance to the tomb. Two men were standing there, smoking and gesticulating in my direction. I knew them at once: George Willoughby Fraser and Marcus Blackden, my two colleagues, whose acquaintance I was late in making. I stood up from my work. They tossed their cigarettes outside the tomb, laughing. They were rather large men. The sun had burned their faces and lent them a reddish tan. They offered their rough hands for a handshake.

Fraser, the taller and bulkier of the two, pointed to the tracing paper sheets full of sketches and said, "Evidently Newberry's lecture made a great impression on you—you keep working even after the light fades. Do you want to lose your eyesight just to satisfy him?"

Blackden put his hand on my shoulder and drew me outside the tomb. I must have looked like a hollow reed under his arm. The two of them sat me down between them on the riverbank amid the wild esparto plants. Blackden said, "You mustn't waste this enchanted moment when the colors of the river change with the sunset—a thing of life and beauty in this dead place. Come, let's enjoy it together, before the dreary darkness descends upon the land."

From his pocket he extracted a metal box full of tobacco and began rolling some into slender cigarettes. He did this quickly and adroitly, then offered one to me, but I politely shook my head. The sun began to sink behind the mountain upon whose flank we were sitting, and the water changed color, taking on a faint yellow tint, then the reddish purple of the cherries in Swaffham Wood, and finally a grayish hue crept in upon it. The birds, ever present above the river, soared in arrowhead formation, and on the other bank clouds of fine mist rose up among the crowns of the palm trees. I was enraptured by the sight, but I heard Fraser mutter as he puffed on his hand-rolled cigarette, "We deserve a better fate than this. We all came here to escape personal misfortunes we couldn't endure. Each of us was dreaming of great discoveries—and look where we've fetched up."

I didn't know how to reply. It had been a crushing day, and these words added to my despondency. The sun set quickly among the rocks, and the river lost its splendid colors.

"Enough of this self-pity," Blackden cried. "We'll take the young man with us and go spend the evening on the other side of the river. We'll go to Saft al-Khamar."

I said in a subdued voice, "I'm accustomed to spending the night in this place."

"Nonsense. You'll end up being eaten by wolves, or losing your mind. These walls aren't going anywhere—they've been here for thousands of years, and they're staying put."

It was no use putting up resistance. They were overpowering, seething with boredom. I felt, too, that a part of my spirit had been torn away. They brought me down to where Idris sat waiting for them. He calmly guided the boat over the dark ripples as the wind grew cooler. The night was less oppressive on the other shore, the mud-brick houses and the little shops illuminated by torches and lamps, and the farmers returning from the fields with their beasts in tow, weariness in their faces and their feet conspicuously bare. They stared at us without resentment, but they took care at all times to keep well out of our way. The darkness of the place was alleviated by a bonfire from which emanated the smell of manure. Children circled the fire, shouting, and women concealed their faces behind veils or velvety shawls. My companions knew their way; they must have traversed it every night.

We proceeded to a square filled with sugarcane merchants. A row of donkeys were eating the coarse leaves. The two wandered for a long time among the unassuming creatures, until they came across three strong ones. I despaired as a young muleteer helped me climb onto the donkey he had selected for me.

We followed Fraser's lead as he hurried along in front. The muleteer panted with the effort to keep up with him. We set ourselves upon a route that wound through damp fields, from which rose the croaking of frogs mixed with the noise of dogs. The sky receded a little, but still teemed with stars. I was breathing hard, as if heading out on a journey with no return. All at once Blackden began to sing, an Egyptian song, surely, for its words had no meaning and its rhythm was strange. We crossed a worn wooden bridge over one of the canals, and entered fields full of cornstalks, the rustle of whose leaves sounded like hoarse muttering. I had given up, having lost my confidence since leaving the tomb. It was strange that it was the tomb I longed for, not my home so far away.

A stand of palm trees came once more into view, from which we could deduce that a town or village must lie beneath them. "At last," Blackden exclaimed joyfully, "Saft al-Khamar!" He was pleased, giddy as if all his happy memories reposed in this shadowy place. We didn't enter the village streets; we steered the donkeys around them via a network of canals and ditches that surrounded them. The village didn't detect our presence—even its dogs stayed quiet. Then, gradually, noise could be heard, increasing in volume. A stone structure appeared, light emanating from its wooden shutters. The voices kept getting louder as we got down off our donkeys. The muleteer made haste to tie them to a stake and sit down beside them.

Blackden pushed me toward the entrance of the building, exhorting me, "Go ahead, boy. You'll be the first to venture into Christo's tavern tonight."

The place was more crowded than I had expected, brimming with the odors of tobacco, alcohol, and urine. The crowd was a peculiar assortment, transformed by the dimness into an indistinguishable mass, despite their various origins: Europeans, city folk in tarbushes, thick-bodied farmers different from those I had seen outside, Gypsy women with coal-black hair and full lips, women flushed or pale, all of them hiding their faces behind masks of heavy cosmetics. In the middle of all this an obese woman gyrated while everyone clapped.

From behind the bar a fat Greek man called out, waving the bottles he was holding, "Welcome, my best customers! I've been waiting for you!"

Feeling suffocated, I wanted to escape, but Blackden had his hand on my back and pushed me until I was face-to-face with the corpulent Greek. "We have here," Blackden said loudly, "a fresh virgin. We need you to help him forget about this country's pitiless nights."

The Greek bared his crooked teeth. "God bless the foreigners, the wretches, and the virgins!" he said. "You've brought him to the right place."

I only just moistened my lips with the glass of wine he handed to me, but my stomach contracted immediately. The other two drained their glasses in one go.

The Greek kept refilling them. The others shouted as the dancing woman jiggled her belly and swung her hips.

Fraser said, "The only way you'll be able to stand Newberry is if you come here every night."

In one respect, he was right. Newberry had let me down, and no doubt he had let them down as well. "He promised us," Fraser continued, "that we'd have a part in the excavations and the archaeological discoveries that would get all the newspapers in Europe talking about us. And here we are instead, copyists of wall art in some remote, desolate tomb."

Surprised, I said, "I thought the excavations were taking place far to the south."

"You really are green," he said. "Just a few miles from here is Tel al-Amarna. That's where the madman Petrie is searching for Akhenaten's tomb. Every day Newberry creeps along behind him to eavesdrop on his findings. It wouldn't surprise me if one day he killed the man before he could achieve any results."

They went on drinking, and I saw that I had no alternative but to stay and be a spectator. I moistened my lips some more with the nasty wine—perhaps I'd get used to the taste. By listening to other people's conversations, I slowly familiarized myself with the mixture of faces that filled the room. There were regional administrators, government employees, cotton magnates, and mayors of nearby villages. How did this portly Greek manage to bring them all together here in this dim cavern so far from the city, and immerse them in rural nightlife?

"He's the king in these parts," said Blackden. "Every farmer in this village and the surrounding villages owes him money, and no matter how good their harvest, it's never enough to pay off their debts. But there's another, more important reason he can get them all to come here . . ."

Suddenly the place fell silent. From some obscure part of the establishment came a beautiful young girl. Her face was not masked with cosmetics, unlike the others. All eyes turned toward her as she calmly and self-assuredly made her way among them. The Greek smiled, observing the reaction to her appearance, like a breath of fresh air in the stifling fug of the tavern.

I stared at her in amazement. This wasn't a fit place for her, but Fraser raised his glass to her and said, "She's come at last, Helen of Troy, whose honor the Greeks took more trouble to defend than she herself did."

She merely smiled, and sat down by the bar, while the crowd formed a semicircle around her and stared. I could see that she was the real attraction that drew all those customers to this godforsaken place.

"My precious girl is pleased with you tonight," said the Greek with relish, "and she's going to sing for you."

I looked at Blackden. He was staring mutely at her, enchanted, while her gaze wandered the room without fixing upon anyone in particular. She began to sing, her melodious voice issuing from her throat to fill the space and enliven it a little. I didn't understand the words, but the modulations of her voice took me back to the flat country I had left behind, the undulating sea beneath my feet, the faces of my seven siblings, crowding around me and vying to carry my case as I prepared to set out, my mother's tears, and my father's expression, set and impassive.

Then I remembered the fragrance of the first body I had known.

The ship that bore me from Liverpool had covered many miles, and when the city called Alexandria came into view, the ship grew feeble as an old woman. I was holding onto the iron rail, as the city and its white buildings drew ever nearer to me, an African bird sitting on an egg, breathing out heat. There was no fog to muddy my view of it, nor did the sun seem to hide from it. I stepped onto the quay and was overwhelmed by the crowds and the cacophony on all sides. I was surrounded by brown faces indistinguishable from one another, all shouting to one another at close range, gesticulating, and moving in all directions. Their clothing looked more like rags than garments; flies and dust swirled around them. Was it possible that these were the people who had fashioned the objects preserved in Lord Amherst's hall?

Bewildered, I stood still, not knowing where to go. An elderly porter went past, his back bent, carrying a wooden box. I saw his face for a brief instant, wide-eyed with a large nose and prominent cheekbones. He was one of them, one of the faces carved in the worn wooden panel in Lord Amherst's hall. I made my way very slowly through the crowd, and discovered that these were the selfsame beings, that they had climbed down from the temple walls, had stepped from their paintings and the illumined papyrus sheets. They were the ones, the very same, but they were more wretched, not so dignified, all of them milling about aimlessly, uncertainly, under this burning sun, as if they were living in a time not their own. I stopped abruptly, transfixed.

All the passengers who had accompanied me on the ship's passage had gone their way. I turned to see whether anyone was waiting for me, but found no one: I was alone and forlorn, not even eighteen years old, in short pants, with my case of reinforced cardboard, and tweed cap. I was not supposed to linger in this place—from what they had told me I had assumed that someone from the Department of Antiquities would be waiting for me, to help me board the train for Cairo, so that I might present myself to the director, Gaston Maspero. But after a long wait I realized that no one would come.

There was nothing for it but to leave the port on my own and use the few Egyptian liras I had with me to find my way to the railway station. At the entrance, a guard inspected my passport, and on determining that I was British he raised his hands in salute, snapping his heels on the ground. I perceived that, despite my youth, I enjoyed all the benefits of the empire. The street outside the port was crowded with people and carts drawn by horses and donkeys. On the other side stood a number of military trucks draped with the British flag. I felt secure, for there were people who would take it upon themselves to look after me on this strange turf. An elderly porter pressed upon me his offer to take my case and conduct me to one of the hotels. I signaled my refusal. He was of lowly appearance and spoke broken English. I wanted to walk until I was tired, for after long days of traveling by ship I was longing for the solidity of dry land.

"One piaster," the man said desperately. "I'm at your service."

I didn't answer him. I walked along Gomruk Street, among shops, warehouses, agencies. There were people wearing dusty cloths on their heads—where had those come from? And why had they substituted them for the striped head coverings that appeared in the paintings? What were these garments? Where was the cloth they used to wrap around their waists, showing off the beauty of their bare chests? Why did they now show themselves in such ugly trappings? What happened to the wide eyes of the women, outlined in shades of kohl? Perhaps this was a temporary phenomenon, for ports always draw mixtures of all kinds of people. Inside, perhaps, they were still as they had always been, beneath all this dust.

I heard hoofbeats right behind me, so I stepped aside to allow the horse to pass, but the vehicle the beast was pulling stopped beside me. There was a black carriage—later I learned that it was called a *hantour*—drawn by a skinny horse. The driver sat erect, with a long switch in his hand.

I heard a hoarse voice calling to me, "Hey—you! Foreign boy!"

The voice was calling to me in halting English. Seated within the carriage was an unveiled woman, wrapped in a black abaya, a little older than I was, wide-eyed with curling eyelashes, her nose a little prominent, lips painted a vivid red that went well with her copper complexion. On her head was a kerchief in similarly bold colors, looking a little like the head cloths found in the paintings. Surely I had seen her before, in a carving or a picture, or in one of Lord Amherst's books. I stood stock-still, while she went on whispering her broken phrases.

"Come—get in quickly."

I stood frozen in place, but she held out her hand and pulled me toward her. She didn't need much strength to prevail over me: I was dazzled, in shock, incapable of resistance. She seated me beside her, and signaled to the driver to proceed, so he flicked his switch over the back of the skinny horse. The carriage rolled on, leaving behind the port and its dun-colored establishments. I saw a sign shaped like an arrow, bearing the words "To the city center," but she didn't go in that direction. She did not speak, but merely held onto my arm, as if she was afraid I might hop out and escape. The wind grew a little less hot. I was going back toward the sea, but from a different direction. I didn't look at her, but her body kept bumping against mine with each lurch of the carriage. Suddenly the sorry buildings disappeared, and the sea came into view, green and open and sparkling with whitecaps.

The carriage came to a stop, and the girl leapt down gracefully. She beckoned me to get out. Seeing my fearfulness, she said, "Don't be afraid. I won't eat you!"

I picked up my suitcase and joined her. The carriage drew away all at once, and I stood there listening to the horse's hoofbeats until they faded away, leaving only the murmur of the surf. She took off the wooden shoes she was wearing, drew the black garment about her, and walked barefoot in the sand. I felt drained, and a sensation of seasickness upset my stomach, but I followed her. A wooden structure appeared before us, a small dilapidated building. It was amazing that the hut could withstand all that wind. She pushed open the door and went in, while I stood outside, irresolute. She extended her hand once more and pulled me inside. I smelled the aroma of wood permeated with salt and iodine. There was nothing in the hut but a small bed woven from palm fronds and a window giving onto a faded sky in which there was only a single bird. She seated me on the edge of the bed and took off her head covering. Then she sat before me and gazed intently into my face.

"How young you look!" she said. "Your moustache is nothing but yellow fuzz, like a chick's down."

She fell silent for a bit, then reached out and wiped the perspiration from my brow. She spoke again. "Tell me the truth. Have you ever touched a woman?"

"My mother," I said.

Laughing, she said, "I know that, silly! I don't mean that kind of touching. I mean touching an actual woman, who can really give you something—something that's not like what you get from your mother."

She knelt upon the ground and unfastened the straps of my sandals. Examining my reddened toes, she exclaimed, "What rosy little toes you have, just like goldfish. Are you a soldier? But no, you're too young and mild-mannered. What do you do?"

I found my voice and managed to say, "I'm an artist."

"Are you really?" she said. "Do you do portraits of children or of adults? It doesn't matter. You must have money. Isn't that right?"

I was barefoot, inside a tumbledown shack, with an exceedingly bold woman, and I didn't know what awaited me outside. I took out all the liras in my pocket and showed them to her: twenty pounds, an advance sum I had obtained in Liverpool, before I boarded the ship. I had wanted to give some of it to my father, but I'd had no opportunity. She looked at me, and at the picture of King George V depicted on the coins.

"That's a lot of money," she exclaimed in surprise. "I won't take more than I'm entitled to."

She took exactly five pounds. She could have taken the entire sum, but she returned the rest to my pocket. Then she got up and began to undress. Her copper-colored body seemed warm and familiar.

"If you're an artist," she said, "then why not begin with me? Do you like my body?"

But artwork would come later. Meanwhile, I was shy and didn't know what to do. She had me stretch out on my back, and then she took over completely. The heat of her body transmitted itself to mine, which had known only the coolness of childhood. Her movements matched the rhythms of the surf, the flow tide filled with desire, the ebb tide a respite in which to catch the breath. Prodding me, she said, "You're as shy and tender as a girl. Don't close your eyes—this is your first time, and you must experience it fully, in every way." I tried to do as she said. Her face had changed color and seemed alien, but it was the rest of her that was doing all the work. I found myself trembling, quivering in every cell of my being. A part of my soul left me and inhabited her body.

She fell deeply asleep, still pressed up against me. Her face resumed its normal color and she appeared much younger than I had thought. Feeling warm and languorous and sad, I lay staring at the ceiling, whose timbers seemed about to scatter with the wind. It was as if the world had suddenly changed, and everything I undertook upon this strange terrain would be different. I clung to her.

When she stirred, I asked her about her mother. She laughed and said, "What do you think? Cleopatra, of course." I couldn't tell whether she was joking or serious. Then I slept.

I woke in alarm. There had been a knock upon the door, and at first I imagined it was my father, or my aunt with her Gospel in her hand, or Lord Amherst himself. But the girl covered herself, her coppery skin, and sprang nimbly from the bed. My back was hurting, and the palm fronds had left marks on my skin. The girl, though, went out through the door, closing it behind her so that no one would see me. I heard the sound of her talking to some man, their voices rising and falling. The man's was rough, but hers was strong and commanding. I thought they must be quarreling. I heard her make a harsh, hawking noise in her throat, and then all was still. It seemed that the man had gone away. The door of the shack opened and she appeared, holding a huge silvery fish still fighting for its life.

She smiled and said, "That was a fisherman, bringing us this fish—you must be dying of hunger."

She went to a corner of the hut, where there was a tin receptacle filled with ash, on which were laid some sticks of firewood. She did no more than to drag it outside and light a fire in it, blowing on it a little and then leaving the rest to the sea breeze. I got up and watched her as she washed the fish in seawater, then sat down on the beach. With her hand she scraped together some moist sand and, with some salt, heaped it up all around the fish, as if she was performing an ancient rite, in which the fish was no more or less than a small sacrifice. The wind could just about have plucked off the light robe with which she cloaked her body;

even this nakedness was part of the ritual. As gulls began to circle around her like a nimbus, she placed the fish, with the wet sand encasing it, upon the crackling fire. A trail of smoke rose, and she blew resolutely on the fire until little tongues of flame issued forth once more. She pushed aside strands of her hair each time they fell and got in her way. What was happening around me was unreal—I was walking in a dream. I opened my small case, took out my tablet and pencils, and began to sketch upon the white paper, making a drawing of the first pharaonic ritual I had seen. I stopped after a little while. Her face was flushed and she was out of breath. She came over to me and studied my sketch.

"You're drawing me," she said. "What did you see in me that you liked?"

"Go back!" I cried. "Keep blowing on the fire!"

Laughing, she went back to the fire. "You like fish Alexandrian style, then!" she said.

The fish was done before I had finished the picture. She picked it up carelessly, hot as it was, and split it open. The exposed white belly divided in two, the spine extended like an Eastern landscape. She reached over and began feeding me the still-hot pieces, while I kept working on the picture. Her image was imprinted on my mind, so that I had no need to ask her to resume blowing on the fire. I was surprised by the flavor of the fish. I had come from the island of fish—it was the staple diet—and yet I had never tasted such delicious fish as this. Together we finished it off, leaving the spiny bones scattered on the ground beside us while we made love for the second time, this time gently and slowly. She whispered to me that I was a quick learner.

"Day is almost done," she said. "We'd better go out for a little so that we don't get bored with each other too soon."

We bathed in the sea, put on our clothes, and walked through the sand. We rode a small, colorful wooden cart with an awning, drawn by a mule. The water took on a violet color, the sun crimson: a world painted in watercolors, which had not yet lost the imprint of the divine. The tracks left in the sand by the mule were the only thing in creation that had just been born. The cart stopped before a vast stone building—an old fortress, half-collapsed, its stones dark with a dusty coating of gunpowder. A great portion of the stones had been torn away and lay broken and scattered about the ruined walls. All that remained standing were turrets riddled with gaps, also ringed with gunpowder. The whole place gave off an odor of conflagration and death.

"What is this?" I asked, dismayed. "Was there an explosion here?"

"It's one of the fortresses that were demolished," she said gloomily. "There were about thirty of them, all of them razed to the ground. None but this one remained to bear witness to what happened."

I circled the fort, and saw the moss and other creeping plants that grew upon its walls, the remains of rusted-out cannons, in which birds had built their nests.

"Who did all this?" I asked.

"Infidels," she replied. "Infidels from your country—perhaps your father was among them."

"My father wasn't a soldier," I said defensively, "just a painter of tame animals."

I sensed that she had suddenly grown angry with me. All at once the traces our bodies bore of our earlier passion dissipated.

I moved away from her and busied myself with walking among the remaining stones. The sun continued on its course, dropping behind the edge of the horizon. It seemed that darkness would fall more quickly than I had imagined. They had sent me from Swaffham to paint this country's antiquities and preserve them. Why, then, had they treated them with such savagery—assuming this girl spoke the truth? The winds grew colder, finding their way in among the ruins. She muttered angrily, sitting and shivering on one of the stones. I was afraid to touch her. All that was between us had been dispelled in an instant.

I heard her say in a quavering voice, "I was young, eleven years old. So everything is burned into my memory. We had a little house in Mex, and a small boat in which my father went out to fish. I thought the sun hid inside this fort, which was close by, because every night it disappeared into its turrets. My mother was one month pregnant, and she wanted some fish to eat. My father couldn't go out in his boat—he was afraid of the huge ships that filled the horizon, afraid of their monstrous cannons pointed at the city, at our houses. We were all trembling. I heard my father talking to the other fishermen. The British commander of these ships had issued a warning for the city to surrender all its forts and guns and matériel, or else they would destroy them with their mighty cannons. We were quaking with fear, but we didn't realize that we were poised on the brink of a catastrophe. My mother and I went to the nearby market, but there was not a fish or a piece of fruit to be found—the place was deserted. Those who were able had fled in a panic.

"The hours until the deadline slipped away like grains of sand. No one knew the real reason behind all this agitation, or why all these ships had congregated off the coast. There was a big fight in which people had died—a foreigner from a distant island had killed an Egyptian at the donkey market, and this had set off the dispute between the two sides: something that could happen in any city. But the infidels' ships had seized the opportunity and had come. Maybe they had been there already, concealed just over the horizon.

"At midday all hell broke loose. The first missile landed in the heart of our house in Mex and killed my father instantly. He was the first to pay the price in the city's downfall. We had nothing to do with this al-Makari who had died or the foreigner who had killed him, but the whole city was in flames. The few cannons in the forts were trying to return fire, but their missiles were weak and fell into the sea before reaching the ships. The forts began to fall, one after another, and all the people took to their heels. But we wanted to go back to our burning house, where my father's body was. We stayed on, sitting terrified amid the desolation of a city in flames and waiting for the missile that would release us from this calamity, but it never came. The whole city raised its white flags, and the fires raged on.

"We buried what remained of my father's bones. We lived in this shack on the beach, until my mother also left me, and went to join my father."

She allowed me to support her and help her to walk. The mule-drawn cart proceeded slowly; there was no light, but we found our way to where the shack stood. I lay down beside her—we felt a killing cold, and clung together seeking heat, but I didn't dare make love to her. I wish I had—perhaps that would have alleviated our feelings of bitterness. In the morning, I had to continue my journey. She wasn't angry with me. I was simply an experience for her, unrelated to the war. I felt melancholy.

At the railway station, which looked like a Roman structure, I found the train waiting for me.

◆ ◆ ◆

Helen sang on, while I lived in those moments that seemed so distant, there on the beach at Alexandria. Helen's voice was unfamiliar and fresh, and it seemed inappropriate that it should be released into the air of this corrupt establishment, amid these bleary faces. Her musical phrases entered my very depths, reminding me of that brief relationship with an ephemeral young woman, which seemed destined never to be repeated.

While we were riding back on our donkeys, Blackden exclaimed confidently, "She was singing for me." Perhaps it was so, or perhaps she was singing for herself, and not for anyone else in the room. I despaired—all I wanted was to get back to the tomb . . . but that was impossible in such darkness, and with wolves about.

I got up early, before the others. I had had a troubled sleep in the archaeologists' rest house. I couldn't stand to wait until my companions awoke; even Idris was sleeping. He got up in an ill humor and took me across the water to the tomb. I got started immediately on finishing up the required tracings. I was hoping to get them out of the way as quickly as possible, so that I would still have time to create a record with my own drawings as well, without Newberry looking over my shoulder. I was unconscious of time passing, but at noon he came and stood, with his towering height, at the entrance to the tomb. I rolled up the sheets of tracing paper and presented them to him, but he was angry.

"You went with those two to the tavern at Saft al-Khamar!" he exclaimed. "Did you not?"

I felt guilty. He reminded me of my father when he scolded me. Abject, I hung my head meekly. He shouted once more, "They'll destroy you—they're a pair of useless scoundrels. Copying the paintings from these walls is the most they can manage, but you—you're still young, and this country is uncharted, it lies open before you. You can explore it if you wish, rather than waste yourself in it."

I didn't entirely understand the purport of his words, but I felt that he quite reciprocated their dislike of him. There was some tacit struggle being waged among the three of them, which I could sense, without knowing the reasons for it.

I wasn't aware that the Christmas season had arrived until I received a letter from my father. No snowflakes had fallen, no evergreens had been set up, and no caroling voices had been heard: Christmas was dusty and hot, and even the few churches that lay in our vicinity observed the festival on a different date. Fraser and Blackden were preparing to go to Minya. They were invited to a huge party at the home of the irrigation supervisor, who was a willful Irishman with twin daughters who could dance and play the piano very well. I wanted to go along, but Newberry gave me an exasperated look, so I excused myself from accompanying the two others.

Fraser looked at us suspiciously. "What folly is this?" he demanded. "You two are going to spend Christmas Eve in the darkness of this tomb?"

He got no answer from us, so he left us and went down to the river with his friend. Midday passed in silence, both of us pretending to work, but Newberry would frequently go off and leave me. He would stand contemplating the Nile, smoking distractedly. Some unnatural air hung over him, and in the end he found it necessary to break his silence.

"Gather your things," he called brusquely to me. "We're going."

"To the irrigation supervisor's party?" I answered in surprise.

"Don't be ridiculous," he said. "We're going rather a longer way than that. We're going to Tel al-Amarna."

I hadn't imagined that he himself would take me to the excavation site, where Petrie was—Petrie, about whom I had heard so much. I organized my rucksack, careful to put my art supplies in it. Newberry was waiting for me at the entrance to the tomb. It was clear that he had arranged everything so as to be rid of the other two; that he preferred, rather, to take me with him. This would be a remarkable Christmas indeed.

We crossed the river and took a mule-drawn cart, which jostled us up and down. We traveled such a long way it seemed to me that my bottom wore out. The dig was some distance from the village in which the farmers dwelt, but it was certain that the subterranean city here extended beneath their houses. We approached the site slowly; I held my breath. Newberry gestured toward a white-bearded man who stood haughtily upright, and I realized that I was looking at Sir William Petrie. His physical stature matched his reputation, earned by his dozens of discoveries, his learned papers, and the scholarly posts he had held. We went to him, Newberry shook his hand, and they exchanged a few words. It seemed Petrie hadn't noticed me—I was there by chance, between these two great men.

"I've come to congratulate you," declared Newberry hoarsely, "on your new discovery."

Petrie was unable to conceal his irritation. With a sigh, he replied, "We've not nearly completed it. I'm surprised the news has got out so quickly."

He himself conducted us to a place above the excavation on which he was working, where the outlines of the buried city were clearly visible, as if they were borne of the sand and pebbles. He thought that these were the remains of the city whose construction the Pharaoh Akhenaten had ordered when he became angry with his old capital, Thebes, and defected from it. The new city flourished for about twenty years, until the Pharaoh died, and then its inhabitants left it to return once more to Thebes. We saw the remains of small houses crowded together, looking more like sunken pits, with mud-brick walls missing their roofs.

"This is where the workers lived," said Petrie, "the ones who built this city. They erected the temples and palaces and grand houses and the tombs of the nobles, while they occupied these cramped rooms—the way it's always been."

Fragments of statues appeared, as well as a fallen obelisk, rendered impotent by the surrounding debris, unable to stand erect. In the middle of the city was a high hill of sand. Here Petrie stopped and fingered his beard. He stood meditatively for a moment, then said in a low voice, "It's the eternal hill—the ancient Egyptians always built one. Out of this the form of the pyramids evolved. This was an attempt on their part to stand up in the face of the void, for creation is a bottomless sea, and this hill is what would remain after the floodwaters of the Nile receded. It embodies the resurrection after death. Here dwells the god."

Newberry was shaking, lifting his feet from the ground only with difficulty, as if expecting the worst. I didn't know what it was that frightened him and made him so very hesitant. Perhaps this was the reason he hadn't dared to come by himself. When Petrie had asked him how he knew about the discovery, he'd offered no plausible explanation. Did he have a pair of eyes inside the site? Petrie didn't make much of this, nor had he any will to prevent Newberry from paying the visit for which he'd come.

We all descended into the vast hole. Columns of dust were still rising—it seemed as if the earth was breathing, now its shoulders had been relieved of this load. One of the men brought a blazing torch, and we entered a tomb that was situated behind the hill. The greater part of it was roofed; the paintings, the faded colors, were gradually revealed before us. Once more the magic manifested itself and a new surprise was unveiled to me.

I don't know from what depths these outlines emerged, what visions had hung in the mind as they took shape upon this wall. How had it been possible to distill all those customs and rituals into these small, ordered pictures? I stood contemplating them until the light faded. I felt that I was memorizing these outlines and storing them in my mind, knowing what the ancient artist would do in his next painting—I was thinking according to the same method as he. I understood how he would make his transition smoothly to the next image: farmers carrying sheaves of wheat heavy with grain; fishermen hauling up fish with the water still dripping from them; young girls clad in diaphanous robes, playing music and dancing; all watched over from on high by the disc of the sun, its rays transformed into outstretched hands. There were no cartouches displaying illustrious names, nor references to venerable kings or sacred gods. I was dazzled, following the glow of the torch upon the wall, on the point of weeping.

Newberry reached out and with his fingers delicately brushed away some of the dust. Breathing hard, he gazed for a long time at the figure that appeared. He was standing at his full height, altogether silent, like an ancient god. He drew a sharp breath, then burst out all at once in a voice from which he was unable to eliminate traces of schadenfreude, "This is not a royal tomb!"

"I am aware of that," Petrie replied.

Newberry gave a sigh of relief, and his breathing at last grew regular. It was not the discovery he had feared it was. At once the atmosphere of the tomb was full of tension, and I felt afraid. Petrie gave us a nasty look—he seemed to wish most urgently to evict us from the tomb as quickly as possible, but Newberry took the torch from the man who was holding it and began almost to skip about, elated, exclaiming insincerely, "splendid," and "magnificent," and "astonishing."

We left the tomb together, all of us perspiring heavily. "Thank you, sir," Newberry said in a rush. "We should have liked to stay longer, but we have an engagement."

We had no such thing, but Petrie didn't press us. We walked through the desolation surrounding the site. Newberry was silent, but still stepping lightly as a little child. The mud-brick houses of the village came into view, and voices rose, belonging to sellers of cane and grapes, and men with donkeys for hire.

In a faint voice I asked, "Are we going to return to the tombs of Beni Hassan?"

"By no means," he exclaimed merrily. "We deserve to celebrate. I shall take you to an amazing place."

I stopped walking. I was tired of his vagueness and his treating me as if I was a small child. "Sir," I said, "I need to know what is going on. You can't keep dragging me about blindfolded."

"Have you still not understood?" he cried, exultant. "Petrie hasn't found the tomb of whose discovery he has been dreaming, the tomb of the king I was afraid he would reach before I did."

We found ourselves once more in the middle of the donkey market. Newberry examined the animals for hire, repeating his indistinct mutters, then stopped in front of two strong mules. He turned to me and said, "I think these two will do."

I protested again. "I still don't understand."

Leaping astride one of the beasts, he gestured to me. "Come along, let's be off. Enough stalling. We've got a long road ahead of us, and I shall explain all."

I saw nothing for it but to climb astride the other mule. Newberry leaned over to speak to the muleteer. "I wish you to take us to Dayr al-Barsha," he said.

The man tried to haggle, although he was already preparing to mount his own beast. "Sir," he said, "the road there is rugged, and we'll have to cross the Yousefi River."

"Do try not to drown us in it," replied Newberry calmly.

The man went ahead of us. We entered a warren-like vortex of mud houses, and proceeded to cross canals, using whatever there was in the way of rickety bridges. The Yousefi River stretched before us like a glittering knife, slicing the green fields. Its current was swift, and flowed more strongly than the other more ordinary rivers, as if its waters felt choked between its two banks. The muleteer searched until he found a dilapidated bridge, full of gaps. At every moment I was afraid the mule's foot might slip into one of these. In front of us the man proceeded on a tortuous trajectory with his little donkey, navigating a labyrinth of treacherous holes. I was terrified, hearing the sound of the rushing water beneath me.

"This current," Newberry remarked conversationally, "carries the largest number of drowned bodies in Egypt. The ancient tales tell of Joseph, that prophet of the Old Testament—you know him, of course. They say that it was he who carved out this river in only a thousand days: *alf-i-youm* in Arabic. Thus he undertook to breathe life into the arid oasis known as al-Fayoum, and the name of this oasis was inspired by those thousand days."

I was too frightened to listen very closely to his words. At last we reached the other side. All at once our field of vision admitted a vast desert; I hadn't thought it was so close. We now took an old, sandy path. On the far horizon a chain of pale blue mountains appeared, seemingly unattainable. I heard Newberry speaking in a strained voice.

"I was afraid when I came here," he said. "I feared that he would discover before I did what I always dreamed of finding, the burial site of Akhenaten, the heretic king. His tomb is located in this region, perhaps in the center of Tel al-Amarna, or perhaps beneath the sand upon which we are now treading. It's a strange country, not subject to any order that we know of. When you live in it it torments you, and yet suddenly it will bestow upon you an undreamed-of opportunity. I am certain that after all this perseverance I will receive my bounty, and discover the location of this tomb."

I stared at him, amazed. I had thought making a record of the paintings on all of Egypt's ancient walls was the extent of his ambition, whereas explorers were people of an altogether different sort, possessing hidden powers that enabled them to burrow down through the earth's layers and read its secrets.

"Why is it," I questioned him, "that this heretic king seems so important?"

"There was no one like him," he said, bemused, as if the dust of the desert had rendered the ghost of Akhenaten incarnate before us, and we were pursuing it. "No one else did as he did, renouncing all the ancient deities and choosing a single god. Why did he do that? It's still a mystery. He rebelled against the priesthood of old, and conceived a religion that was simple and clear, in the form of sun worship: no need for the temples with their gloomy interiors, or the priests with their arcana—rather a god you can see plainly as he shines upon you each morning. At a stroke he did away with mysteries and rituals and those who claimed ownership of the gods' secrets. Can you imagine such a deed?"

I was much struck by the words I was hearing. I understood at last why the paintings were different in this place from what I had seen elsewhere: in these paintings the gods had been thrown over, the priests had gone into hiding, and the kings and other leaders had disappeared; ordinary people had instead risen and become visible, people to whom no one had paid any attention. "But can we possibly discover a tomb of such importance?" I said. "We are merely artists!"

"This is the key to our strength," Newberry replied. "We can read the paintings, discern the signs, and follow the guideposts. Believe me, my boy, I've worked with these people for a long time—Petrie being perhaps the most knowledgeable of them. They've been digging and digging, but in the end they are led by blind chance. This earth has been keeping its secrets for thousands of years—do you think a handful of Europeans can properly explore it in just a few years?"

He fell silent, trying to catch his breath, while the mules kept struggling onward, the soft sand slipping beneath their hooves. Then a bell pealed. The sound gripped the desert and echoed across the silent blankness. More bells began to ring, and Newberry said confidently, "They've seen us."

"Who?" I asked, startled.

"The monks at the monastery. They keep constant watch over the desert from their high tower. When they see any travelers they ring the bell for them, fearing that perhaps they are lost in the desert, or are about to be."

The walls of the monastery appeared suddenly, like something wrought from the landscape, solid and impregnable, absorbing the violence of the sandstorms, its stones bonded by the action of the sun's heat. The pealing of the bells grew more impressive the closer we came to its source.

"This is Dayr al-Barsha," said Newberry, "one of the oldest monasteries in the world. The monks built it upon the footprints left by Christ when he passed through here fleeing from Palestine."

This land! Everyone had passed through here. Again Newberry had mentioned a prophet, a second one, and perhaps Akhenaten was a third, of a different sort. Why had God placed our island at such a remove?

We dismounted before the vast gate. The muleteer was to leave with his beasts and come back for us at the end of the following day, according to Newberry's request. The man agreed, demanding no payment.

The monastery gate was fashioned out of the trunks of palm trees, which still retained their natural shape, having simply been split down the middle. An iron ring hung from it, on which ancient crosses were incised. Before Newberry could lift it the gate opened, its rusty hinges squeaking shrilly. From behind it a gray-haired monk emerged and went to him, greeting him by name. A reddish beard encircled his pale jaw. His features didn't look Egyptian in the least—perhaps his long sojourn within the dark cells had given him this sallow complexion.

We followed him inside, and he turned to welcome me, saying, "I am Brother George." Newberry insisted upon maintaining his air of mystery, but I was overcome by the place. I followed the two of them without a word, studying the domed structures that surrounded the courtyard and the doves that had alighted in the center and were plucking their food from the sand. We arrived at a long corridor, on either side of which were low doors leading to small rooms. I learned later that they were the cells in which the monks lived, but that some of them were designated for guests of the monastery.

"You'll spend the night with us," said the monk. "Our beds are rough and our food is humble, but we have good wine."

My cell was small, with nothing in it but a modest bed, a huge cross hanging on the wall, and a window overlooking the expanse of desert. I stared at the sand dunes, which spread out before me as far as the eye could see. I wondered how Jesus found his way through such a maze. Darkness fell, and the bells rang for evening prayers. I stayed in my room until prayers were over, and no one pressed us. We sat with the monks at a long wooden table, eating bread, cheese, and dates, and I drank a little of the wine. They spoke Arabic, English, Greek, and other languages, moving about the hall in their black cassocks. They drank a lot of wine; no doubt the cellars of the monastery were well stocked with it. Newberry was also imbibing with less than his usual restraint. Brother George put his hand upon his arm. "Don't worry," he said reassuringly, "They'll be here tomorrow." I didn't care to ask what he meant—I wouldn't get a straight answer in any case.

I spent the night half-awake—the wind never stopped stirring the bells; I missed the sound of the river and the wolves' desolation. At dawn I saw lines of monks, who had spread out all about the desert that surrounded the monastery, gathering firewood and looking for the heads of mushrooms buried in the sand. I went out into the courtyard. Monks were at work there as well, cleaning, making bread in a small oven, and tending the little farm adjacent to the monastery. They put as much energy into performing their tasks as they did into drinking wine.

Newberry had awoken as well. He was standing and talking to Brother George, seeming anxious and tense. The higher the sun rose in the sky, the more uneasy he grew.

The bells rang, and I realized that other travelers had appeared on the horizon. Newberry went with Brother George to the gate—it seemed as if they were waiting to identify the visitors. The rusty hinges creaked and the gate swung open. There were three Bedouins astride their camels, leading an additional camel with no rider.

Turning to Newberry, Brother George said, "Didn't I tell you? They've come on time."

They stood before the gate, shaking their legs pointedly; obediently, the camels folded their own legs and settled on the ground. The three men leapt from their backs and approached the entrance to the monastery, led by an old sheikh with a white turban and a thick beard, and clad in a heavy abaya of sheep's wool in various shades. He shook hands with no one, merely placing his hand on each of our shoulders—it wasn't a greeting so much as a demonstration of his good intentions. The other two stood respectfully behind him.

"Welcome," said Brother George. "Welcome, Sheikh Qindil. Welcome, men. Allow me to introduce my English friends."

He went ahead of all of us to a little hall in a corner of the courtyard. It was furnished with mats, and scattered to one side of these were small cushions in glowing desert colors. He began pouring tea into tiny pottery cups. I studied the face of the sheikh, who looked as though he had just stepped out of the Bible. He spoke a strong dialect of Arabic, answering Newberry's persistent questions. Brother George kept reminding them of the agreement that had been contracted between them. I didn't grasp the terminology very well, but I knew that they were talking about an undiscovered tomb in an unknown place. The more they talked, the more Newberry's face brightened. At last Sheikh Qindil stood up. He looked at Brother George and said, "We'll go now. We must get there before the daylight is gone."

Indicating us, Brother George said, "You are responsible for their welfare, Sheikh Qindil."

The sheikh put his hand upon his own neck and inclined his head, responding with a few rapid words. Brother George shook hands with the men, clapped me amiably on the shoulder, and bade me visit him again. We went out of the monastery gate. The camels were still crouched upon the ground, their jaws moving lazily. They gazed at us with their sad eyes. Newberry took me by the arm. Pointing to one of the beasts, he said, "You'll ride this camel, Howard."

I took a step back in alarm. I had never before ridden such a strange animal. It seemed wild and untrustworthy. "Never fear," said Newberry reassuringly. "In the desert children ride camels from the time they're born.

In a strained voice I replied, "I was not born in the desert."

"Riding a camel doesn't require practice the way riding horseback does. Horses move their front legs and then their hind legs, and they go very quickly. Camels don't do that. They put one foot forward, then follow it with the hind foot. Only one leg at a time is in motion, and they don't have hooves—their feet are soft, which makes them proceed with a slow and measured gait across the sand. Believe me, camels don't sway a great deal, or give anyone much opportunity to fall off of them."

This exchange was conducted in English, but the Bedouins were smiling, as if they were following the gist of it. I wasn't convinced, and each time the camels moved their jaws I felt more afraid. "First of all," I insisted, "I want to know where we are going."

"Perhaps," said Newberry, "to the greatest discovery of my life and yours. Come along; climb aboard, before the day is lost."

He went over to the other camel, raised his leg, and confidently straddled the creature's raised back. The camel extended a foreleg and then a hind leg, and leaned a little to one side. It seemed to me that Newberry would roll off onto the ground on the other side, but the camel quickly stood up, lifting him high up on its back. Newberry stroked his thick beard and gestured silently to me that I should do as he had done. My heart was in my mouth as the camel lifted me up. I felt as though I was hanging suspended all alone in space. The Bedouin men laughed and pointed at me. From the monastery gate, Brother George called out, "May God bless all of you!"

The camel began to walk slowly, while I rocked back and forth on it until my spine was all but dislocated. I needed to loosen my tensed muscles a little, and hold onto the wooden halter in front of me. Sheikh Qindil was leading us on the back of his own camel. The wind filled his abaya as if he was about to take flight. My clenched stomach began to relax, and the camel proceeded smoothly as if it was floating above the sand. I felt as though we might continue on a never-ending journey. A distant chain of mountains appeared and blocked the horizon, its colors shifting as we drew closer and closer. There were odd-looking rocks scattered about us, round and white, as if laid in this spot by immense birds. How could Newberry communicate with these men without Petrie finding out—or, indeed, without Fraser and Blackden finding out? It was clear all this had been arranged with the help of that mysterious monk.

The desert changed color and became whiter, as if it had been covered with salt. We began to see limestone formations, and soon the earth was devoid of all forms of plant life. The camels' pace slowed. We were surrounded on all sides by mountains, and grains of sand carried by the wind beat upon our faces.

We stopped, finally, by the slope of a high mountain, and the camels lowered us, so at last I could jump down from mine and touch the earth once more. I felt dizzy, as if my feet were not firmly placed upon the ground, but I proceeded to climb the rocks behind the others. It was not a constant ascent; at intervals we descended and had to circle around all the rocks blocking the way. I was panting and Newberry was breathing hard, but that didn't stop him from springing over the rocks, following the old Bedouin, who stopped at last, pointing at the hollowed-out rock.

"This is the place," he said.

We gathered and all looked down. There was a low corridor in the heart of the mountain, carved into the rock by sharp pickaxes. Newberry didn't wait for any further explanation from the sheikh. He hurried down toward the dim cavern. I hastened after him. We were in a low passageway, its walls smooth and polished: a mountain of marble, quiet and waiting. I felt the walls, which were coated with fine dust, behind which were bas-reliefs. Newberry kept going deeper, but I stood mesmerized before the walls at the entrance. The Bedouin sheikh stopped and regarded us, smiling as if we were two children amusing ourselves. One of the Bedouin who served him brought an unlit torch, which gave off a scent of pitch. We went a bit farther into the dark passageway. The man ignited the torch, and the place lit up. The carving on the wall showed clearly, a low relief with no colors. I brushed away the dust, holding my breath, my heartbeat coming faster. I asked him to bring the torch closer.

An important personage was seated upon his chair, watching the crowded scene that was taking place before him. There was a king's body in its shroud, arms crossed upon the chest, clutching the scepter in one hand and a lotus flower in the other. On his head was the double crown, for the two realms: Upper and Lower Egypt. There were hundreds, maybe thousands, of men pulling him with ropes. Not a living king, then; no living king would be pulled by ropes, and certainly no living king so immense that the men beneath him would look like a swarm of ants. What everyone in this splendid scene was pulling must have been an enormous statue.

The panel was full of details, dozens of them. It was difficult to read all the symbols in them by the flickering light. Was this a statue of the apostate king, Akhenaten? The face was indistinct; the image was chipped, and many features had come away from the body. On the lower part of the wall there were piles of marble fragments. I took out some paper and began to sketch the contours of the panel with trembling fingers. All at once, however, Newberry returned. He snatched the torch from the Bedouin's hand and dashed back into the passageway.

Darkness enveloped me, and I could no longer make out any details. Was it possible that discovering a tomb could be this easy?

I tried to follow the light source; the passage grew narrower, and there were more piles of rock. Newberry was standing before the last pile, which blocked everything else. In a strained voice he said, "I have a feeling it lies behind these rocks." I turned and studied the walls, looking for any kind of sign. Impassive, they gave nothing away.

"We have to go now," said Newberry. "But first this Bedouin must swear to tell no one."

He hurried off, and I turned to follow him. He stopped at the front of the passage and entered into an uneasy exchange with the Bedouin sheikh. Newberry got out some money and they proceeded to negotiate. I took this as an opportunity to go back and work on my drawing. By the time they concluded their discussion I had completed the basic outlines. I would have to come back another time in order to finish the work, but now Newberry was very ill at ease.

"Draw a detailed map of this place," he commanded me as we stood at the entrance. "I don't want us to lose our way when we come back here."

This time he let me catch my breath as I went over the layout of the site. It would be necessary for me to be able to distinguish this mountain from all the rest, to ascertain where the opening was located, and to set down a visual representation of the path that would lead us through this desert.

We commenced the journey back. The air had grown cold as the sun began to set behind the mountain, and the sand took on a somber cast, a pale reddish hue. Newberry, lost in thought, did not speak the whole way. "How can he be so certain?" I wondered.

We found the mules awaiting us by the monastery wall. The Bedouins gestured their farewells to us, placing their hands upon their chests and bowing their heads. They took their camels and went back into the desert. We had to complete the rest of our journey in the dark. The muleteer led us as we made our way through the shadows. We were very close to one another. Newberry was breathing a little more easily now. I said to him, "But how could such a king be buried in that isolated place?"

"He was buried in secret," replied Newberry with conviction. "His followers chose this distant place so that his enemies wouldn't go there and desecrate his body."

"What are we going to do?"

"We must find a patron who finances these excavations. I shall contact Lord Amherst at once. First of all, we must make sure . . ."

His voice began to fade from my hearing. I no longer heard anything but the hum of the insects buzzing about my head, stinging me—I hadn't got used to this yet. My day had been long and tiring. Feeling the cold air from the fields penetrate my bones, I shivered from head to toe. I don't know how we arrived, or how I managed to get down off the mule, or how I rode in the mule-drawn cart. I heard Newberry say, "We shall go at once to Minya. I must find a way to get a message out of the country, even if it means sending Amherst a long telegram."

"I want to go back to Beni Hassan," I said feebly.

"Don't be absurd," he said. "It's the Christmas holidays. We shall rejoice in the occasion together."

"I'm exhausted. I want nothing more than to return to the tomb—it's the only secure place for me."

He snorted. "I don't wish to go back tonight. I want to arrange my communiqués."

"I'll go back on my own."

It was odd to find Idris sleeping in his boat, as if he were waiting for me, and to hear the sound of the wolf howling on the opposite bank, greeting me. By now Idris was used to my peculiar behavior, and had no objection to going out on the water at night. I was shivering, my face drenched in sweat. Idris supported my trembling frame, climbing the rocky slope with me and settling me on my rough bed. He also started a fire, as various images obtruded upon my vision. I no longer knew where I was. I cried out, trying to ask for help from my mother or father, or even my aunt, but there was no one to reach out a helping hand to me. I heard Idris's voice saying, "You're feverish, my young foreigner."

I was swamped in a sea of perspiration. I could no longer see or hear anyone. Everything had gone dark. I don't know how much time went by, but when I opened my eyes it was day, and a red-faced doctor was in attendance. He must have been angry, since he had been obliged to come from the other side of the river. "You've got malaria," he announced. "Take this medicine and keep to your bed. Your temperature will rise, and you'll be feverish. It will go down a bit in the daytime, but it will come back at night. Whatever possesses you, to stay in a place like this?"

I subsided once again into a miasma of heat and delirium. I opened my eyes to find Idris attempting to press the pills into my mouth. Once more I sank into darkness. The night was long, the tomb was full of smoke, and the wolf was watching me with its glowing eyes. Perhaps it had entered the tomb and run its tongue over my face—my features were drenched in its saliva, and its odor filled the place.

I opened my eyes and tried to get up. I saw the faces of Fraser and Blackden staring at me. "Where did you and Newberry go?" demanded one of them sharply. "Don't try to lie."

I closed my eyes and the darkness swiftly returned. I tried to push away the things that were pressing on my chest. Fraser was gripping the collar of my shirt and shaking me roughly. No, it was the heat, making me shiver—that and the nightmares that closed in on me, causing the world to come down around me. But the paintings on the wall of the tombs, those remained fixed and immutable, the only reality standing between me and death and the void.

I don't know how long it was that I lay suspended between consciousness and delirium, but I came to myself feeling terribly thirsty. The fire was dying and Idris was asleep on the ground. The gray lights of dawn came in through the entrance of the tomb. I got up with difficulty. The earth swayed beneath my feet, but I kept walking. The waters of the river had begun to recede, revealing a number of green islands. I sniffed the air. I saw the birds, which had begun their morning sorties, and I knew that I had been given a second chance at life.

Idris was happy when he saw me. He insisted he was going to prepare some onion soup for me. I laughed, but he swore he had learned the recipe from foreigners—from Englishmen—and that he was very good at making it, even though he didn't care for the taste of it.

I sat by the entrance to the tomb until the sun rose and bestowed its warmth upon my body. There was no one but me on the western bank. Idris said, "The foreign gentleman, the high-ranking one, still hasn't turned up, and the other two have been gone for two days."

No one came until after midday. Then Newberry arrived, stood facing me, and took in my wasted body. Speaking through his moustache he said, "You really are ill. I met with the doctor at Minya and he informed me."

He didn't wait for me to answer, but launched straight into talk of the steps he had taken for his project. He had sent Amherst a long telegram and obtained from him a provisional agreement to fund the project. Lord Amherst wanted to visit Egypt with his daughter—he wished to see the site for himself. He was wildly enthusiastic, his expectations running high.

Weakly, I asked, "Can the thing really be so simple? Couldn't we be mistaken?"

He looked at me in disbelief. "What do you mean?" he cried. You saw for yourself the paintings at the entrance to the passage!"

"Indeed. Thousands of slaves dragging an enormous statue, but they were heading out of the tomb with it, not into it. By no means are these burial rites."

I didn't know why I said it, why I wanted to dampen his enthusiasm. I was alarmed by this zeal of his.

"Where is that painting? I wish to see it."

I went inside, opened my case, and looked for the papers that had been with me—the map I had drawn, the wall panel I had sketched in its basic details, and the notes and instructions I had recorded, so that we might refer to them later on returning to the spot. But there was nothing. Everything had disappeared.

I shouted at Idris, "Where have my papers gone? What happened while I was delirious?" He looked at me, mystified. He didn't know why I was shouting.

Newberry advanced swiftly and stood before me in alarm. "What do you mean?" he cried.

Crushed, I sat down. I felt guilty. It seemed as though my fever was about to come back. "I was ill and feverish," I said. "I didn't know what was going on around me."

Abruptly Newberry advanced on Idris with rapid steps and seized him by the neck. The man got to his feet, terrified. He cried out for help and tried to free himself from Newberry's grip. Newberry shoved him up against the stone wall. "Who took the papers?" he demanded.

Idris was choking. I tried to get up to come to his rescue, but Newberry shouted at me to keep my distance. Struggling for breath, Idris said, "I swear I didn't see anyone. I didn't invite any stranger to approach this place. There were only the two foreign beys who work here."

Newberry stopped pushing him. He released his grip on Idris's neck. Idris picked himself up and scurried away, making hastily for the outside of the tomb. He must have gotten into his boat and gone back to the other side of the river.

Newberry looked at me and I looked back at him, both of us dismayed, unable to utter a word. At last he said, "Did you tell them?"

I hung my head, unable to deny it. Had I in fact done so? Had they listened to me when I was raving, and learned the secret of our journey? I couldn't endure his accusing looks. He felt betrayed—by me, by Fraser and Blackden. He walked out of the tomb. I couldn't go after him. There would have been no point in trying to make the best of things.

The two of them didn't come until sunset. Tucked under their arms were a number of folded papers and a case filled with drawings. They headed in our direction, as cheerful as if they were enjoying a particularly triumphant moment. Newberry was watching them, eyes narrowed. They stopped and faced him defiantly. Blackden got out the folded papers, waved them right in his face, and said, "We went there and spent two whole days."

"What do you mean 'there'?" Newberry asked in a choked voice.

Fraser stepped forward and tossed the map down in front of him, the map they had stolen from my case. "That cave you were thinking was Akhenaten's tomb was nothing but a quarry for the high-quality marble they used to make statues of kings."

With an effort, Newberry swallowed. He clutched at his thick moustache as if clinging to it. "You're lying," he said. "You're both lying, no doubt about it."

Fraser challenged him. "The supervisor of that quarry was Hatnup—he was the man sitting on his seat at the entrance, watching the workers as they labored to pull the statue. We found his name recorded in five different places."

Trying to maintain his composure, Newberry said, "You had no right to go there without my permission. And you have no right to steal my maps and interfere with my discovery."

"The truth is," Blackden retorted disdainfully, "you ought to thank us. We saved you from the hazard of falling prey to the Bedouins' deception, and from wasting money on a search for more rocks . . ."

Newberry made off in the direction of the Nile. He wasn't listening to them; he was preoccupied with getting to some air he could breathe. Adamantly he kept repeating the same words: "You had no right . . . no right . . ."

I was angry with them, but incapable of taking any action. Pointing to Newberry, Fraser said coldly, "He's become an old man. He doesn't accept defeat easily."

I felt that it was our defeat, all of us—the end of us as a team. We would not be able to stay here together after this. These barren rocks, the harsh environment—had they brought out the worst in us, or had we all come to this primitive place already freighted with these small, petty feelings?

4 • Doubara Palace

THE PASHA GESTURED TO AISHA, inviting her to sit down opposite him, but she stood until he took his own seat. The wheels of the train began to squeal, the palm trees swayed, and a gust of wind blew, full of dust. The compartment in which they were sitting was opulent, with luxurious seats upholstered in green leather, walls decorated with pictures, framed under glass, of the old temples and of boats floating on the Nile. The Pasha rested his chin on the head of his cane and studied her, making sure she was comfortable.

She was not comfortable. She clamped her knees together and laced her fingers, wondering whether the Pasha had recognized the dress she was wearing or realized that it belonged to his daughter Isis. But he was absorbed, gazing at her face. Her skin was the color of a husk of wheat ripe for harvesting. She had fine, symmetrical features, wide eyes, shining brightly—he had not imagined that peasants could possess such grace. She seemed resigned to her fate; she had no other recourse. He felt rather like a priest, taking her as a fresh sacrifice to an old god in order to gain his favor. The idea disturbed him, so he tried to put it out of his mind.

He said—simply in order to say something—"Don't be so downcast. You're going to live in the most important place in Egypt. You won't be a servant—certainly not. You'll be a companion to Lady Katherine, the wife of the honorable Lord Cromer. She is even more important than the wife of the khedive—perhaps more important than the khedive himself!"

He tried to be cheerful, and to ease the burden of the long journey for her. She nodded compliantly and looked fixedly into his face, afraid to lower her gaze, in case that would be felt as an insult. The last ranks of palm trees disappeared, as if they had finished bidding her farewell. The edge of a mountain appeared; a faint, uneasy line.

"It may be," the Pasha resumed, "that Lord Cromer is a little strange—stern, and not very kind—but he has to be that way to govern a chaotic country like ours. What can we expect? But it was he who selected you, by the way, and designated you as a companion for his wife—in all these months that have passed since our party, he hasn't forgotten you."

It didn't matter what he said. She was afraid of Cromer. After what he'd done to the artist, Master Saleh Abdel Hayy, could she be safe with him? But there was no alternative. She had wished she might be given the chance to return to her little village and spend a few moments in her mother's embrace. But she couldn't go back—she was forever compelled to keep moving northward, always northward.

There was a knock at the glass door and the conductor appeared—a thin man in a yellow uniform. Before he could speak, the Pasha threw him a hard look that made him retreat, apologizing profusely. The train stopped at some station, and vendors crying their wares appeared outside the windows. On went the train, stopping and starting, stopping and starting. Aisha grew bored, and gave up reading the names of the stations. On her right a small river appeared—it seemed familiar to her. The riverbank receded into the distance from time to time, then resumed its place running right alongside the train, the shimmering surface of the water clearly visible. Finally, after innumerable hours, the train chuffed its last exhalation and the wheels screeched along the tracks, bringing the engine to a halt at a vast, crowded station.

The Pasha disembarked; Aisha picked up her bundle of clothing and stepped down behind him. The roof of the station was exceedingly high, the ground beneath it covered with crisscrossing iron rails. In front of the station was a broad square, thronged with carts and vendors. Darkness began to fall upon the place, and lamps were aglow with a faint silvery light. A black carriage trimmed with gleaming brass pulled up and stopped before them. The Pasha climbed aboard, and she settled on the small seat opposite him. He rapped with his cane on the floor of the carriage, saying in an imperious tone, "Take us to Doubara Palace." The driver snapped to attention and the horse stirred, both having realized that they had an important man onboard. The driver cracked the whip in the air, and the horse set off at a trot.

Aisha opened her eyes wide, staring at the street that opened up before them: two neat rows of trees with lofty houses behind them, lampposts surmounted by gas lamps, people walking freely and fearlessly along the sidewalks, the road full of carriages pulled by horses, and even a few cars. She saw the horse-drawn tramways as they moved forward, bells clanging. For the first time, Aisha laughed. She felt strangely elated, seeing how far the city extended, and the neat appearance of its inhabitants. The street ended at a wide square filled with people, plants, and lights.

"This is Ismaïliyya Square," said the Pasha. "It is the most important place in the city. We are close to Doubara Palace now, where Lord Cromer resides."

She saw a row of white palaces scattered along the shoreline of the river. The Nile was different from what she had seen before, lively and flowing vigorously, covered in lights reflecting off its surface. The carriage moved along an avenue whose trees towered over it. Still the palaces appeared, one after another on both sides of the street. At last the carriage stopped before the largest and grandest of them, which resembled a brilliantly white animal reclining upon the shore, the river slipping deferentially along before it. Aisha alighted breathlessly. There were two English guards, one on either side of the door, their posture erect, their faces ruddy, clad in short pants and red caps, and gripping rifles equipped with sharpened bayonets. The Pasha moved toward a smaller side door and spoke to a man who sat behind a modest desk.

"I wish to meet with his Lordship," he said. "My name is Paulos Pasha, and he . . ."

The man noted his name on a piece of paper and indifferently passed it along to another guard, who left them standing there. Then the guard returned and said, speaking severely, "Lord Cromer does not receive Egyptians after five o'clock in the evening. Why don't you come early tomorrow morning and announce yourself then?"

Mortified, the Pasha explained, "I'm not asking for anything. I've brought something that personally concerns Lord Cromer. I ask only that you inform him as to who I am."

The guard exhaled sharply, his patience at an end. Egyptians of this type irritated him. "Come back in the morning," he barked.

"I cannot," pleaded the Pasha. "This girl is with me, and it is essential that I myself turn her over to his Lordship. I won't take much of his time. He is apprised of the matter."

Noticing her for the first time, the guard looked at her, and curled his lip—the gift did not warrant disturbing his Lordship. But who was he to decide? Aisha was amazed at the abject tone of the Pasha's words. He had lost his dignity and authority. The guard addressed him once more. "What did you say your name was?"

For the third time, the Pasha humbly repeated what he had said. Aisha felt sorry for him, wishing he would take her and let them leave this place. The guard left them standing there yet again and was gone a long time. The palace windows, brightly lit, appeared between the trees. The Pasha didn't dare look at her. Then came the sound of a telephone ringing. The guard behind the desk picked up the receiver, and then ushered them inside.

They crossed a long corridor in a capacious garden paved with stones, and climbed the stairs leading to the palace. The sound of a melody being played on the piano reached them, a slow and gentle air, which did not at all accord with the nervous atmosphere. They entered a grand hall crowded with furniture: European sofas, Indian weavings, Chinese urns, and pieces of pharaonic sculpture. They remained standing, while Lord Cromer sat at the piano, absorbed in his playing, oblivious to the world and unaware of their presence. There was no one to listen to him—he was playing for himself, for his own private enjoyment. The piece, which was at its climax, began to subside into a gradual decrescendo, until it concluded, and he heaved a sigh of exhaustion.

The Pasha clapped appreciatively, and Lord Cromer turned, startled, as if he had forgotten he'd granted them entry. He closed the lid of the piano and rose to his feet, revealing his flushed face, white moustache, barrel chest, and middling height. Not forgetting his imperious military bearing, he looked at the Pasha as if he was an alien creature with no right to encroach upon these grounds. He appeared not to have noticed Aisha.

"May God bring your Lordship a pleasant evening," said the Pasha ingratiatingly. "I apologize for disturbing your leisure hours, but I've brought the girl whom you requested."

Lord Cromer let out his breath in exasperation. What he was obliged to put up with from these Egyptians and their tactlessness! But he said, "You've gone to a great deal of trouble, Pasha. I doubt Lady Katherine remembers this business."

Then he turned politely to where Aisha was standing. A baffled look came over his face, but he didn't move from his spot. "I believe," he said, "that this is the young girl who was at the party—the one at which Mr. Carter made such a scene about her."

The Pasha's face, at last, glowed with pleasure. He hastened to point out the worth of what he was offering.

"Indeed, honorable Lord," he said. "He thought she was an ancient pharaonic deity."

"This stubborn fellow called Carter . . . he won't leave off making difficulties. Ouf—I had no wish to remember him on a calm night such as this."

He drew a bit closer and, for the second time, with his fingers lifted Aisha's chin and raised her face to his scrutiny. She felt she might die of embarrassment.

"Who knows?" he said. "Perhaps her presence will offer Lady Katherine some diversion."

He went to the small table in the middle of the room, picked up a little silver bell, and shook it gently. A Nubian servant, tall and thin, appeared. "Take this girl to the servants' quarters," said Lord Cromer. "Tidy her up and prepare a place for her."

Aisha stood fearfully in her place. With dread, she registered the words *servants' quarters*. The Pasha signaled to her encouragingly, indicating that she should go. A look of relief had appeared on his face once Lord Cromer accepted his gift, but as she went out the door of the hall she heard Cromer's voice, which had resumed its coldness. "I shouldn't like to delay any further your return to Minya, Pasha."

◆ ◆ ◆

It was only after three full days that Aisha encountered Lady Katherine. She had spent the interval in the small building across the garden; it was crowded with an assortment of servants—Irish, Scots, Armenian, Indian, and Nubian. Straightaway, one of them—clearly the one in charge—shouted at her, "You've got a dreadful stink about you—her Ladyship will be able to smell you from ten meters off!" Aisha was mortified. All the odors of this long day clung to her body: her sweat, the dust, other travelers, the flies, the fields, the manure.

The women stripped off her clothes and thrust her into a tub filled with hot water and soap bubbles. They loosened her braids and scrubbed her scalp. They took her old clothes and put them into a receptacle from which flames leapt, until they were burnt to cinders. "No need for fleas in this house!" said the imperious one: Mistress Julia, as Aisha would later learn. She was an old woman, but of robust physique; her skin was stretched taut on her bones and her blue eyes were protuberant. They gave Aisha a clean set of clothes resembling the ones they wore, and assigned her a cramped room just wide enough for a bed and, beside it, a small table that held two books, the first of which was the Bible. The second was a book of poetry with tiny English print, entitled *Paraphrases and Translations from the Greek*, which Aisha found, to her astonishment, was by none other than Lord Cromer.

After several days, Julia herself conducted her to the main building. This morning the first floor was alive with activity, crowded with employees and visitors. Julia led her up by a back staircase directly to the second floor. They ascended gleaming white marble stairs and proceeded down a long hallway filled with a great many paintings, which hung upon the walls—scenes from India, Greece, and Egypt—the same traditional arrangement that was to be found throughout the house.

Lady Katherine was sitting on a balcony looking directly onto the Nile. She held a fan, with which she was dully fanning her face. Aware of their entrance, she did not turn, but said loudly, "This place is unbearable. Everything smells—the streets, the people, the food—even the stench of this river is intolerable."

Julia stepped forward. "My Lady," she said.

Her Ladyship turned then, and Aisha saw that her belly, white and exposed, was distended. She looked at Aisha and said, "Who are you, then?"

Julia tried to explain to her, but she didn't know why this Egyptian peasant girl was here, either. Bored, Lady Katherine waved her fan. Then, all at once, she remembered. "Ouf," she said. "Go away."

Aisha turned to go, and Julia smiled maliciously. But then her Ladyship said, pointing with the fan, "No one ever understands my orders. *You* go. *You* stay."

Julia turned and left quickly. Lady Katherine gestured for Aisha to sit on a mat on the floor, close to her feet. Aisha gazed at the Lady's belly—her delicate skin stretched to the point where the traceries of veins were clearly visible. She was petite and beautiful, much smaller than the powerful Lord Cromer. The Pasha had informed Aisha that this was the second wife, whom Cromer had married a few years after the death of his first wife, Lady Ethel, who had suffered a long battle with kidney disease. Lord Cromer had loved her devotedly—but men so quickly forget.

The silence was broken when her Ladyship spoke peevishly. "This strange Turkish princess is coming," she said. "She never stops prattling away in Turkish and Arabic—even French—but never a single word of English. Ouf! If it were up to me we would not receive her. How can one find anything to say to such people?"

Aisha kept silent, and Lady Katherine turned to her, saying, "You can translate, can you not?"

Aisha nodded, pleased—only now did she understand her role. She wasn't a servant—she would have nothing to do with cleaning or serving food. Her Ladyship fanned herself rapidly in hopes of a cool breeze. Then she spoke again. "Don't let her give me a headache. Just translate the essential parts. My God, I wish I could go somewhere far away from here!"

Aisha listened in silence, scarcely breathing, holding as still as possible. She was afraid this world-weary lady would send her away on her first day. There they sat, her Ladyship complaining all the while, Aisha listening, until they heard a knock at the door. Lady Katherine covered her stomach and gestured to Aisha to open the door.

The visitor was an Englishman, rather young, but stern-faced. "Inform her Ladyship," he said, "that Mr. Harry Buell, secretary of the Orient, wishes to see her."

Before Aisha could stir from her place, Lady Katherine cried, "Come in, Harry, and for God's sake let us have no more of these irritating formalities."

Harry took a few steps into the room, and inclined his head as he stood before her. She gave him her hand, but he didn't kiss it. He retained his somber expression, as if performing the most irksome of tasks. "Princess Nazli Fazil has arrived," he said. "She is downstairs."

Her Ladyship groaned, expressing her reluctance. He seemed to have been expecting this. "She is a woman of some importance to us," he continued. "After all, she is the khedive Ismaïl's niece, and practically the aunt of the present ruler, Khedive Abbas. She is the link between us and those Turks who run this country. His Excellency the Lord Cromer wishes you to be patient, and lend her your ear for a little while."

Moving the fan back and forth in front of her nose, Lady Katherine said, "Has she put on that oil of cloves? I can't abide the smell of it. It would nauseate even a child."

"Please, your Ladyship, she is waiting. We'll open all the windows on the ground floor."

Was he in earnest, or were his words tinged with sarcasm at her Ladyship's excessive affectations? The man left; Aisha remained, standing on tiptoe, watching Lady Katherine as, grumbling all the while, she slowly prepared to go down to her guest. From moment to moment she would stop, irresolute, as if about to change her mind, but at last she left the room and, with exaggerated caution, descended the staircase.

Princess Nazli was seated in a corner of the spacious salon, and indeed she did give off the scent of cloves. She rose when she saw Lady Katherine coming. She was a statuesque figure, draped in a green silk abaya stitched with pearls. She also wore a gauzy Turkish veil, but she lifted it when Lady Katherine approached, revealing a few strands of hair the color of roasted coffee beans. She stood, and each reticently touched the fingertips of the other. They sat down facing each other, her Ladyship fanning her nose all the while as if to fend off the smell of cloves. The princess cast a questioning glance toward Aisha, but Lady Katherine saw no reason to introduce her. Her Ladyship's face looked childish and vulnerable.

"Princess," she said, "what is it? Why did you so urgently wish to see me?"

Aisha began translating. The princess's features relaxed, once she recognized the position of the new girl, and knew that at last every word she spoke would be understood. She pulled the filmy veil off her face altogether. All ten of her fingers were bedecked with rings. When she adjusted her robe, the smell of cloves intensified, and Lady Katherine's face grew pink.

"Respected lady," said the princess in Arabic, "you know that I am among the greatest supporters of the British presence in our country. You have brought civilization across the sea, introducing electricity. At every council meeting I sing your praises—yours and his Lordship's."

Lady Katherine endeavored to conceal a yawn behind the edge of her fan. The princess now turned to Aisha, who perhaps would manage to convey the import of her words. She waited a few moments, then resumed. "This is what has induced me to come to you with the request I hope you will communicate to his Lordship."

All at once Lady Katherine spoke, making no attempt to conceal her irritation. "Why don't you petition his Lordship directly?"

"I did consider it," said the princess, "and might have done so were it not that there is a humanitarian consideration, which is perhaps more readily grasped by a woman than by a man. I've come on behalf of the Orabiites. They've been punished, they've paid their penalty—the suffering they've endured in exile is enough!"

Aisha translated her words carefully, and saw Lady Katherine's eyes grow wide, shock registering on her face. "What do you mean, 'Orabiites'?" she said.

"Orabi and the officers who followed him. Orabi has become an old man, and is powerless now."

Lady Katherine sat up, suddenly attentive. "The leader of the insurgents!" she cried. "How dare you bring up this subject?" She rose to her feet and nervously agitated the fan.

"It's hot," she said, "and the smell is unbearable. Ouf! Wasn't Orabi the man who tried to bring down that relative of yours . . . I don't know his name . . . ? Since when do you take the part of the peasantry? You hold them in greater contempt than we do—of that I'm certain!"

The princess turned to Aisha as if appealing for help from her. Then she said, half in supplication, "All that is in the past, your Ladyship."

Thoroughly worked up now, Lady Katherine said, "This country is full of graves. And yet nothing here ever dies."

At this moment Lord Cromer appeared. The light was coming from behind him, so his face looked dark, his features obscure, but his tone was sharp. "What is going on here?" he exclaimed. "What is all this noise?"

Lady Katherine turned, breathing hard, her face flushed, as if she was about to burst a vein. "The smell of cloves is unendurable, and likewise the demands of this princess."

Lord Cromer turned and cast a harsh glance upon them all, fixing his gaze upon Aisha more than the rest, because she hadn't managed to protect his wife. He didn't approach the princess or greet her. He did no more than cautiously incline his head, saying, "I beg your pardon. We have an important appointment with the doctor, and I must accompany my wife there. Please make yourself at home."

He gave his hand to Lady Katherine, who took his arm and away they went, out the door of the salon. The princess stood rooted in place. Then she sank once more onto her seat. She seemed pitiable, stripped of power. She had built great hopes upon the granting of her request. She looked at Aisha, who also stood there, head bowed. She was sorry for the insult that the princess had received—she could see how unhappy it made her.

In a low voice, the princess said, "Perhaps you find it strange that I came here to defend the enemies of my family—how absurd that I believe in them to such an extent. I thought Orabi and his partisans could change everything, even the color of my skin and eyes, but they failed me. They were routed by those English.

"The Orabiites were a passing dream, a brief moment out of the vastness of time, during which the peasantry could breach the wall of their isolation and find the voice that had been struck dumb. They had been confined within their narrow valley, behind mud-brick walls and a maze of canals and ditches. They suffered the curse of a silence that had lasted thousands of years, during which they had forgotten the vocabulary of grievance and the cadences of protest. They had given themselves up to a state of abasement, battered by every class above them, the world over—all those who lorded it over them and consigned them to the lowest caste, who utterly humiliated them, never giving them a chance to pick up a sword or fire a shot. They could possess no more than an axe with which to till the ungiving earth beyond the reach of the replenishing flood of the Nile, and a plow behind which to toil. They were remembered only when wars broke out and demanded a price the upper classes were unwilling to pay. At such times the bodies of the peasantry would be transformed into kindling with which to feed a conflagration that could never be sated. The moment it was over, they were relieved of any spoils they had gained, stripped of all badges of honor, and sent back to their villages of silence to dig the great canals and waterways that would connect one continent to another. This is what the khedive Ismaïl did when there were too many wars in which he had to be involved—in Greece, in Africa, and Mexico. He summoned them from their villages and thrust them into the furnace of war. Those who must die died, those who must be lost were lost, but some of them stayed in the army, carrying weapons rather than plowshares. From the living flesh of those peasants rose the Orabiites. They stood up to the khedive and cried in a voice of outrage, 'When did you take it upon yourself to enslave people who were born free?' This was the voice of their leader, Ahmed Orabi, a rare example of eloquence among the peasantry—he had acquired his fluency after prolonged silence, humiliation, and oppression. But scarcely had he raised his clarion call before it was silenced, drowned out by the roar of British cannon fire with the treacherous collusion of the khedive. They destroyed the Orabiites' forts in Alexandria and slaughtered their peasant fighters at Tel al-Kabir. The villagers shook their heads sadly, saying, 'Wolseley has beaten Orabi.' And with that they lapsed once more into silence."

Aisha did not know what to say. She simply stood there before her, wishing she would get up and go away, and this scene would end. The princess, however, remained seated. She rummaged in her bag and brought out a piece of paper, which she spread in front of her to reveal lines of writing in black ink. The Arabic letters were elongated, as if they had been written by a professional calligrapher.

"This," she said, "is a poem one of them sent me, from exile, far away in the Indian Ocean. His name was el-Baroudy . . . Mahmoud Sami el-Baroudy. He was Circassian but, like me, he had believed in them, and so had joined them and been defeated with them. From exile, he wrote this poem for me. It's not a love poem—it's full of misery. Although he didn't say so outright, I know he was suffering terribly. How sad that they banish poets to such brutal places."

Aisha didn't know exactly what the princess was talking about. It seemed she ought to say something to soothe her distress. The scent of cloves had dissipated and been replaced by an air of sorrow. "Perhaps he'll return . . ."

The princess stood up at last, with a sigh. "It's the second defeat for me," she said. "I won't dare come back here again—I've tried everything in my power with the English: I repeated their words, and rationalized the things they did, even after the incident at Dinshaway, all in order to win their favor, so that I might bring forward this one request. And all my efforts are gone to waste."

She folded up the poem carefully and put it back into her bag. She turned toward the door, but she had gone only a few steps before she stopped and turned once more to Aisha. "What is your name, girl?" she asked.

Forgetting her borrowed name, she said, "Aisha."

"I've always liked the names of the peasantry."

She went her way, vanishing from Aisha's sight, but something of the melancholy scent of cloves remained behind.

Aisha's days working at the governor's mansion blended one into another. At first, she didn't know the meaning of any of what went on in front of her. She walked in Lady Katherine's shadow, observing her belly, which continued to expand. In spite of this, her Ladyship went on attending parties and receptions. She got into the habit of repairing to a corner, where she could watch everyone without being seen, awaiting an opportunity for Aisha to make her way unobtrusively in among the guests. Lady Katherine would attach herself to Aisha and whisper her demand that she translate for her everything that was said about her behind her back. Aisha was unhappy with this role.

She realized gradually that the governor's mansion was the axis upon which the world turned: everyone hoped to gain admittance through its gates and to stay, even if for only a few moments, beneath its roof. First thing every morning it was packed with swaggering British soldiers, elegantly dressed consuls, princes, Pashas—perhaps even the khedive himself came in disguise. At noon would come village administrators and mayors, sheikhs in turbans, those seeking mediation, and those with illusory projects in mind. All these Lord Cromer greeted with penetrating looks combining arrogance and disdain, including Aisha herself. Familiarity and habituation to her presence did not change this look of his—it was of a piece with the particularities of his job—perhaps it was the greatest and most important qualification by which the empire chose its staff.

By what unfathomable means had this lord—who hadn't been a lord to begin with—ascended to his exalted rank? He had been a lazy, refractory, and dull-witted boy, who didn't do well in any regular school. Only military schools cared to accept him, since they demanded less intelligence, and more obedience to all the mindless orders. Their only condition was that their students be scions of the aristocracy, distinguished by cruelty, coldness, and love of fox hunting. Graduates of these schools assumed posts serving the empire overseas, and continued to advance through the ranks according to a rigid hierarchical system by which such assignments were completely beyond the reach of the lower classes.

As a result, the lazy student—who continued to detest scholarship throughout his life—found before him a vast and open swath of land, from the sunny islands of the Mediterranean all the way to the mysterious heart of Asia. He ascended the venerable ladder of the empire, whose weak spots no one had yet discovered. He went to the Greek island of Corfu, where he produced an illegitimate daughter, and contracted an advantageous marriage with a child of the aristocracy, who was the reason he qualified for a grander post in India. In that country's steamy, humid climes he lived, witnessing its bouts of terrible famine with a cold heart, while merchant vessels dumped shipments of rice into the Ganges to keep the price from dropping.

When he went to Egypt as high commissioner, he thought he was a prophet, a reformer, and an emissary for Western civilization amid the subhuman peasants and Muslims. He believed that the occupation of Egypt must be permanent: how could such a country be left to itself—a country located at the center of the world, having jurisdiction over a crucial artery connecting the seas to one another, and commanding a fortune in cotton that bloomed brilliantly, resplendently white? When he listened to the Egyptians' wishes for better education and independent rule, his contempt only increased. "What odd ideas these people have," he would mutter to those around him. "Isn't it enough that I safeguarded them against thirst and drowning when I built the dam for them at Aswan?"

In spite of everything, it was necessary for a certain closeness to develop between Aisha and gravid Lady Katherine, who suffered from persistent feelings of loneliness and alienation. The two of them would cautiously descend the marble staircases that led to the Nile, where they would board a felucca to take them to Dahab Island. Sometimes they would ride in the horse-drawn wagon, and cross the Kasr al-Nil Bridge to the Gezira Club. Members of Cairo's high society became accustomed to seeing them together: the white lady and the wheat-brown girl who tagged along behind her. Despite the heaviness of her Ladyship's movements, she was very active, and when Lord Cromer traveled on one of his missions she did not see fit to keep to the house.

"The house," she said, aggrieved, "is full of ghosts. It is occupied by the spirit of his first wife, Lady Ethel. I'll show you her room . . ."

And she took Aisha to the room, which was always locked. They went in, entering an atmosphere laden with dust and the remnants of a musty scent. Dust motes hung in the air, the closets were full of old clothes and disintegrating furs, and there were empty glass bottles on the tables from which all vestiges of perfume had evaporated.

Lady Katherine was haunted by the ghost of the other woman. Gasping for breath, she said, "She was an angel. She forgave my lord things even God could not have forgiven. I was nothing but the unfortunate woman who came after her."

The heavy curtains were drawn, and it seemed to Aisha that the smell of the dead wife was stored up here, that Lord Cromer had done everything in his power to preserve it. Pictures of her, in little ornate silver frames, were everywhere, her submissive features gazing out at them with her expression of readiness to accept everything.

"He still calls me by her name in moments of intimacy," said Lady Katherine.

There was an invisible crack, Aisha now began to see, in the deceptive calm that lay over the house.

"How I long to leave!" said Lady Katherine. "I want to give birth to my son far away from this place."

But she could not have her way. She gained more weight, and her movements grew more lethargic. The house filled with visitors and petitioners. Her Ladyship did put her foot down, however, when unexpected visitors came to the palace.

Aisha awoke to the sound of some sort of commotion, and loud cries. The noises were not coming from within the palace, but from outside the walls. She crept from her room and went up to the roof of the servants' quarters. Through the trees that surrounded the palace she saw them all: a group of young men wearing bright red tarbushes and blue uniforms, close in age and alike in appearance. They had come from one place, perhaps from a school, and they carried a sign bearing the words, "Down with Cromer, the Dinshaway murderer!" On their shoulders rode a youth who was their age, but much thinner, and with a louder voice. He was waving his fist in the air and shouting, "Down with the murderer of Dinshaway! Murderers, get out of our country!"

Aisha was frightened, not understanding what was happening, or why they were so angry. Nor was the affair confined to those young effendis—others came as well: turbaned sheikhs and men in gallabiya. More signs were added to the demonstration—one depicting a soldier lashing a peasant with a whip, and another showing a gallows from which the dead body of a peasant hung.

British soldiers began to pour in from somewhere. They surrounded the house, weapons at the ready. The tumult and the uproar intensified. Aisha hastily went back downstairs—doubtless by now the noise had woken Lady Katherine, who would need her to explain what was happening. She dashed across the garden, to be surprised by Lord Cromer himself, in the center of the reception hall. He was talking animatedly to a group of officers.

"They'll get tired of barking," he declared, "and they'll leave. But I don't want a single one of them to get near the door of the house!"

It was strange to hear this highborn man called a murderer, strange for those angry protesters to come to the palace instead of the usual sycophants. Aisha hurried up to Lady Katherine's room. She found her awake and anxious. She would watch the crowd from her window for a little while, then hastily return to the balcony overlooking the Nile, to catch her breath.

"Do you smell their stench?" she cried to Aisha. "They are polluting the air with their spittle. Why have they come here? Why don't they go to their useless khedive and leave us alone?"

Aisha stood silent, her heart beating rapidly. She could see the square in front of the house better now. The protesters had not tired or gone away. There were more of them, including many women who had joined, clad in black abayas, their faces covered with white veils. The shouting became a continuous roar, as dozens of signs were raised, demanding Lord Cromer's departure or his trial. The mob crept into the vicinity of the house, and Lady Katherine could no longer bear to sit in her room. She went down to the reception hall, Aisha behind her. Lord Cromer was agitated; the household staff were mingling confusedly with the soldiers.

"I don't want our soldiers to get involved unless it's absolutely necessary," Lord Cromer spluttered. "No killings in front of the house. It's quite enough, what the newspapers are doing to us already."

Harry Buell was standing beside him, a great many telegrams in his hand, which he was rapidly leafing through. "It is Mustafa Kamil," he announced decisively to Lord Cromer. "He is the one who is stirring up the world against us, with his articles—they're being published not just here, but in Paris and London. It is he who brought the students from the law school out into the streets and led them here."

Lord Cromer's face flushed still more deeply. Through clenched teeth he said, "He is an agent of the khedive and the Turkish sultan, damn them all! Summon the Egyptian police—let them deal with their own rabble."

The police did not come right away. In the meantime, Aisha repaired to an out-of-the-way corner, fearful that they would discover the color of her skin, her face drained of blood. They were all of them roused, their aspects dark; captive lions in their cages.

Lady Katherine was helpless to find a breath of fresh air. She withdrew to a secluded room and sat down beside the wall, hugging her knees to her chest and trembling. Aisha searched until she found a window giving directly onto the seething mass of people. She listened to them carefully. They had been joined by peasants from Dinshaway—no one knew how they had got there, or who had informed them of the time and place. They were relatives of the victims and eyewitnesses to what had happened. Elements of the tragedy began to assemble in Aisha's mind as she hid behind the window. Each person added a small piece, a bleak detail in a dark picture. The voices of the effendis subsided and that of the peasants rose, resonant with grief and sorrow, old wounds reopened once more by Dinshaway.

A little while before, no one in the world had known that a little village called Dinshaway existed. It was an anonymous point surrounded by dozens of villages in the Nile Delta, dry and hot, and full of dovecotes. It was for this last that the British soldiers left their camp in the nearby village of Kamshish, and went to shoot the pigeons of Dinshaway. They thought the pigeons were wild, not anyone's property—fair game, just like the land they occupied. They picked a bad day—a hot one in the month of June, and an hour that was even worse—precisely midday, and they chose the most impoverished of villages. They didn't find any pigeons along the way, as they'd expected to, but they found them pecking grain from the threshing floors within the village. They fired repeatedly, the pigeons falling one after another, until their fire ignited tongues of flame in the dry stalks. And one of the village women fell, wounded. The villagers were enraged, and drove out the soldiers, one of whom shot yet another villager, this time killing him, before they ran off, back to their encampment. But the sun accomplished what the villagers had not been able to do, felling one of the Englishmen, who died.

Then the soldiers, angered, emerged from their camp, and headed back toward the hapless village. They avenged themselves viciously on the villagers, as if it had been the villagers who were directly responsible for what their scorching sun had done. They imprisoned all the men in the village mosque, then dispatched more than fifty of them to prison. The aristocrat Lord Cromer considered the incident an insult to the British Army, and a show trial was organized, blind retaliation its object. Even the lawyer who was appointed to defend the farmers betrayed them, turning on them and inciting the court against them. Four of the farmers were put to death by hanging, thirty-six were whipped, and the rest sentenced to life in prison. All the sentences were carried out in front of the stunned inhabitants of the village. In the hearts of those who had been suffering from oppression and defeat, Dinshaway evoked feelings of implacable fury.

The Egyptian police arrived, and a hellish scene of violence and mayhem was enacted outside the house. The chants turned to screams. Up to this point, they had done no more than repeat their angry words—they had not cast a single stone at the house. They were nonviolent, just like the residents of Dinshaway before the hunters arrived, but when the demonstrators felt the viciousness of the truncheons they began to pick up stones from the street and hurl them at the palace. Stones bombarded the house, and some windows broke. Cudgels were brought down upon the heads of all and sundry, and a choking smell of blood rose up.

Her Ladyship could not find a breath of air. The English guards prudently retreated indoors, leaving the Egyptians outside to take their fury and cruelty out upon one another. A fire engine came and directed its hoses upon the demonstrators, who by this time were surrounded, and even those who tried to retreat could find no way out.

Aisha felt as if the blows landed upon her own head. Meanwhile, Lord Cromer's face was still dark, and Lady Katherine had fainted. The battle raged on until, at last, evening fell.

When the fight was over, the house seemed changed. It was not just that the windows had broken, but that the splendor of the place had dissipated, its power neutralized. The furnishings and objets d'art had been removed from their regular places, and the rooms had acquired an air of randomness—the glossy paint dulled, spots of dirt on the white marble.

Everyone was soundlessly busy with activity in the grand rooms of the house. Lord Cromer had shed his habitual coldness and become an exhausted old man. Lady Katherine had stopped moaning and pleading for air that was free of "the stench." She didn't try to elicit from Aisha any explanation of what had happened—there was no need for explanations. When Lord Cromer came to check on her, she said succinctly, "I want to go away. I do not want to give birth to my son amidst all this hysteria."

"I'll arrange it," said Lord Cromer.

It was a long night. No one slept. A surprising strength pervaded Lady Katherine's bloated body, and she forgot the day's travails. She opened her closets, and servants brought cases of various sorts. Her Ladyship went to and fro, giving orders to all of them, as little by little the closets emptied of clothes, shoes, hats, and jewelry cases. She was taking almost everything that belonged to her, as if she did not intend to come back. This house was no longer hers—in any case, it belonged to Lady Ethel: it bore her imprint and the scent of her body. Lady Katherine had always felt that she was a transient guest.

The following morning a great many sweepers came, and began to clean up the square in front of the palace, under police supervision. They removed what was left of the signs, washed away traces of blood, and replaced the stones that had been pulled up. When the horse-drawn carriages arrived, the English guards stepped forward, dismissed the Egyptian police, and began organizing the conveyance of the cases and their arrangement in the carriages. Aisha stood well out of the way, watching Lady Katherine descend the stairs, her face at last radiant with happiness. She was leaning on her husband's arm, but she seemed unaware of his presence—of anyone's presence. She made her way to the carriage at the front of the line. The train was waiting at the station, and would not dare move before her Ladyship's arrival. It would take her to Alexandria, and from there she would board a steamer that would carry her to her distant homeland.

Aisha found herself suddenly unemployed, since with Lady Katherine's departure she had lost her rationale for being in the house. She went to her room to pack her case, and discovered that the clothes Lady Katherine had purchased for her seemed unsuitable beyond the confines of the house. She could not walk in the streets wearing them, or take them back to her village.

She sat on the edge of the bed, overcome by the thought: where could she go, when there was no place for her? Everywhere she sought cover she was left exposed and naked. Should she go back to her village, to her helpless mother and her uncle who lay in ambush? How long would she be able to keep him off her? How long would she be able to bear life in that isolated village, now that the world had opened up before her? How would she ever be able to set down roots in the soil, and endure the wounds inflicted by its thorny brambles? But what alternative did she have?

On the first day she did not leave her room. On the second day the servants looked at her pityingly, and no one asked her to leave. They were waiting for Lord Cromer to return from Alexandria, for he was the only one who could settle her affairs. She lingered diffidently in the servants' quarters, not daring to cross the garden or go to the main house. They might forget about her, and she might stay forever inside this shell.

But Lord Cromer returned once the mistress had set sail, and life in the household returned to normal. Visitors and petitioners began once more to flock to the house, and the square fronting the governor's mansion was restored to cleanliness. Aisha began to wilt in her silence, contemplating her packed case and awaiting the order for her departure at any moment.

The moment came during one of the evenings she spent in anxious apprehension, when Julia came to her and said coldly, "His Lordship wishes to see you. He is taking five-o'clock tea in the garden."

He hadn't forgotten about her, then. She considered taking her case with her when she went to him, so as to proceed in one direction only, and not be forced to retrace her steps under everyone's gaze, but she went to him empty-handed. She crossed the garden, trembling. He was sitting beneath a little pavilion illuminated by electric lamps. Flowers grew around it, and tendrils of hyacinth bean climbed its posts. She stood before him. He was dressed all in white, as was his habit, and in front of him were cups of tea and biscuits, as always. She stood there silently with her head bowed.

She heard him murmur in a low voice, "I didn't reckon that I would have any need of you—I never thought I would need anyone—and indeed Mr. Harry Buell had arranged what was owing to you on termination of your service. But I wish to know what these people are saying about me." He gestured toward the folded newspapers piled in front of him on the table beside the tea service. Aisha didn't understand exactly what he wanted, nor did she believe her eyes when he indicated that she should sit in the chair opposite him. She hesitated, but he gestured again, insistently. She sat, holding her breath. He pushed the pile of papers toward her, and resumed speaking. "Master Nicola, the official translator for the palace, has gone to Lebanon, and may not return. I didn't care for those bloody dry translations of his, anyway. I want you to tell me what these newspapers are saying about me—don't omit a single letter, and don't try to appease me, the way Nicola did. Translate every damned word for me!"

Hearing for the first time such words of revilement coming from his mouth, Aisha knew that the demonstration and subsequent defection of her Ladyship had rattled him.

She swallowed, then reached out and picked up the first newspaper, entitled *al-Liwa*. Doubtless whoever had arranged the newspapers had put that one on top. Its first headline read, "Get out, murderer of Dinshaway!" This was printed in small letters, and beneath it in slightly larger letters was "Mustafa Kamil," the same name that had been repeated throughout the demonstration. She read it silently to begin with—the words were savage and accusatory. He watched her shifting expressions with a piercing and steady eye. When she hesitated for too long, he scolded her, "I'm not a little child. I can bear it."

She began to translate the words in stumbling phrases, but she gained a little courage when she saw how calm he was. She translated the harshest lines without his commenting or becoming upset, although occasionally he would break his silence with a sarcastic laugh, or he would shake his head in perplexity. When she read him a piece in one of the papers about how Khedive Abbas had issued a decision that all those incarcerated in connection with the Dinshaway incident were to be released, Lord Cromer waved his hand in dismissal, saying, "That damned Turk—he wants to be a hero at my expense."

This was her first day in her new position. Days of work followed after that, as the newspapers piled up. There were newspapers that owed their continued existence to him, and these praised his works in Egypt, but he pushed them aside, as if he sought only what would cause him pain. He directed her to pause before an article bearing the headline "Abominations of British Justice." He attended for a little while, and then when he learned the name of the author he sat upright in his chair and picked up his teacup with trembling fingers. When it was empty, he cried in a hoarse voice, "Wilfrid Blunt. I thought he was my friend."

Seeing that he was distressed, Aisha stopped reading, but he composed himself and indicated that she should continue. The writer was openly calling for the British authorities to recall him, on the grounds that he was no longer fit to govern Egypt, that he had obstructed justice and the law, replacing them with the rule of barbarism and revenge. Aisha paused for breath. She didn't see how he could endure all of this. He made no effort to urge her to read more, but sat lost in silence, except that he was breathing hard. She didn't dare move or try to get up.

After a little while he spoke. "Are there other articles taken from the British newspapers?"

She quickly turned over the yellowish pages. There was indeed one more article, and oddly enough she knew the name of the author. She had seen his name on the cover of a number of books in the library at her old school in Asyout. He was a great writer—she would not have imagined he might take an interest in a faraway event in a distant land. She was afraid to mention it to him after what had happened with the first article.

She said lamely, "There is another article, but the name of the author isn't clearly legible."

He snorted. "Girl," he told her, "I'm stronger than you suppose. What is his name?"

Directly she said, "George Bernard Shaw. It's not actually an article. It's the introduction to a play called *John Bull's Other Island*."

"They're mocking me even on stage, then?" he sneered.

The writer asked the play's audience to imagine that a group of Chinese had descended on a placid English village and begun shooting its ducks and geese and turkeys on the pretext that as far as they knew these were wildfowl. What sort of feelings could the English villagers possibly have but anger and hatred toward such intruders?

Lord Cromer lifted his hand. "That will do," he said. "It's bad enough already."

She stopped reading. He sat silent, as if trying to comprehend all he had heard. In a low voice he said, "This is a strange country. I don't know why they hate me. I freed them from the arbitrary cruelty of the Turks, but even so no one stands with me, and no one grasps the meaning of my reforms. I built the Aswan Dam for them, and defeated the rebels in Sudan. This land is fit only for the dead!"

He was speaking to her, trying in his bewilderment to find an answer in her face, as if she represented all the peasants whom he had struggled for so long to understand. He stood up. "This," he said, "is a squalid and ungrateful place!"

Leaving her sitting there, he walked slowly away until he vanished into the darkness of the garden.

Their sessions occurred frequently. It was easier to get along with him than with Lady Katherine: he wasn't put off by other people's odors—perhaps he couldn't even smell them—and his angry tone in response to the newspaper articles softened, but there was always something to remind him of this incident. She began to avoid such topics, and he did not try very hard to press her. He became more at ease in her company. What he wanted to know was how others saw him, and how they saw the world he had undertaken to construct. Aisha had thought him recovered from the reverberations of Dinshaway—but it was not so.

One night Aisha dreamed of her mother. She saw her features clearly. She wasn't complaining or aggrieved. She was encircled by a glow of tenderness and longing. Aisha dreamed that she went back and inhaled the fragrance of her body, wandering about her village, and breathing in the smell of mud and crops and manure. But suddenly she felt Omran's fingers crawling on her flesh: cold, skinny, trembling fingers. She opened her eyes in fright. The little room was dark—illuminated by only a faint light coming from the kitchen. It was enough for her to discern Lord Cromer's face. She started up and drew back from him in alarm, gathering the covers over her chest. She could smell his breath, a mixture of tobacco and wine. His breathing was labored, as if there was no air in the room, and his eyes glittered as if they were full of tears. Aisha did not cry out—in truth she wasn't afraid of him, for he was in a pitiable condition.

Looking at her like a guilty child, he said, "They're here."

Aisha shrank back against the wall. "Who?" she said.

"Those peasants from Dinshaway," he said. "I don't know how they sneaked in past the wall . . . they're in the garden now—I could smell their sweat, I saw their ghosts through the trees."

"There are guards everywhere—how could they sneak in without being seen? Perhaps it was your imagination, sir."

"They've come to get revenge! I'm not afraid of them, but I don't know why they've come to me. Why don't they go to the judge who sentenced them, or the lawyer who betrayed them?" He was shaking. He gripped the edge of the little bed, which also began to shake. She was seriously frightened now.

"Why didn't you summon the guards?" she said. "Why have you come to me?"

Trying to master himself, he said, "Go to them. Talk to them. You are the only one here who can do that. I wish to know what it is they want of me."

"Perhaps we should just wait until they go away."

"They won't leave before sunrise. Or maybe they won't leave at all. I can't have any peace with them in the garden of my house."

His tremors were contagious and communicated themselves to Aisha, as did his fear. She was too young to be drawn into Lord Cromer's private nightmares, but there was nothing for her to do but get up and find her slippers. She clutched her robe about her, and proceeded, while he followed behind. He was like a child who doesn't want to let his mother out of his sight, but he let her go out, without following her. He stayed behind, taking refuge inside: he did not dare cross the threshold.

The air in the garden struck her, cold and damp, and the stars seemed far away, hiding behind the trees. She didn't know which way to go, but the wind pierced her through and through, while the grass soaked her feet. She wanted to walk around for a bit, then go back to him and assure him that the garden was empty, that he had been imagining things, but in fact she sensed something hovering in the air, lost and wretched souls. All at once the wind filled with voices and faint murmurs. Her heart quaked, and she felt a kind of overwhelming sorrow. Suddenly she knew which way to go. The voices were coming from behind a stand of small trees. They were there, seated all together on the ground, seeking concealment among the interlacing branches. They were not ghosts. There were three of them, two men and a woman, and they were not peasants, nor were they from Dinshaway. Their black skin, bathed in sweat, shone beneath the light of the stars. They clung to one another, shivering, staring at her with terror in their eyes.

"Who are you?" said Aisha. "Where have you come from?"

They continued to stare at her. They had been expecting someone else, not a brown-skinned adolescent girl. One of them spoke. "We are slaves," he said. "We escaped from the Pasha's house and came here."

"What Pasha?" said Aisha, bewildered.

"The great Pasha. There is no place in Egypt that will give us asylum from him but here."

Aisha couldn't believe her ears. She looked at their emaciated bodies, their protruding bones. "But how did you manage to sneak past the wall?" she said.

The woman said, "We are slaves, child. While we live we are constantly hunted. Escaping, leaping over obstacles, stealth—these are skills essential for us to stay alive."

Lord Cromer was incredulous when she told him what she had discovered. He was still fearful and hesitant to follow her into the garden. Then the blood returned to his face and the furrows in his brow vanished. He stood up to his full height and reclaimed his self-assurance, crossing the garden behind her. The slaves were in the same place as before, just as frightened and starved. He stood before them and Aisha took up her role as translator.

No sooner had they pronounced the name of the Pasha from whose palace they had fled than Lord Cromer exclaimed with delight, "Mustafa Fahmi Pasha, the chief minister—what a piece of luck!"

He was transformed into a little child, irrepressibly animated as he listened to Aisha translating for him the words of the three slaves. The slavers had brought them from the Sudan and taken them on the Forty Days Road—a route across rugged desert and along tracks where no one could offer directions except the camel herders who drove their animals from the south to the north—a journey that took a full forty days. The souls of those who came out alive at the other end were impervious to fear and hunger ever after. The three slaves were passed from hand to hand among the slavers and brokers until they fetched up at the Pasha's palace. Life within the palace was not too bad, especially for the woman, who more than once found her way into the Pasha's bed. But they dreamed of freedom, and they had no recourse but this in all of Egypt. Lord Cromer was the only one who could oppose the Pasha and give them this freedom.

The lights went on all over the palace—even Lady Katherine's room was lit up. The slaves were transferred to the reception hall. Julia herself undertook to offer them food and water; Harry Buell arrived yawning, but as soon as he realized what was going on he promptly came fully awake. He began composing telegrams to Britain's Ministry of Foreign Affairs, and sending delegates to all the Egyptian and foreign newspapers. He requested from them, by order of the honorable Lord Cromer, to send journalists and photographers to the administrative palace, starting early in the morning, as there was stunning news awaiting them: the most serious violation ever committed by a high-ranking Egyptian authority against the law prohibiting slavery, which had been implemented in every part of the British Empire some hundred years earlier.

In the morning, the house filled up with packs of journalists, correspondents, and the merely curious. The three slaves were placed in a corner—they did not understand all the commotion, and were alarmed, fearing that they would once again be turned over to the authorities. Cameras milled about in the courtyard, popping and flashing with each picture taken. The journalists would listen briefly to the slaves, then focus their main attention on Lord Cromer and his statements concerning his decision to take the prime minister of Egypt to court. Aisha was standing beside him as his interpreter. He had grown strong, self-assured, no longer fearful of any ghosts, certain that he would answer all those who accused him of savagery and cruelty. He was now once more on the side of civilized values in this barbarous country ruled by barbarians!

Into the middle of this crowd came Harry Buell. He addressed Lord Cromer in an undertone, but Aisha could hear the words. "It's *al-Liwa*," he said. "We refused any dealings with them, but they sent one of theirs anyway. He's called Abdel Rahman al-Rafiy."

"Let him in, of course," Lord Cromer replied cheerfully. "This is an unusual opportunity. I was expecting them particularly."

Aisha accompanied the man as he entered. Unlike the other correspondents, he wasn't a youth. He was of short stature, tending toward corpulence. The expression in his eyes was meditative and sad. He didn't have a paper and pencil like the rest, nor did he rush as they did to join the throng encircling Lord

Cromer. He stood in a corner of the hall studying all that was happening as if committing it to memory. He kept quiet, not wishing to call attention to himself. But Lord Cromer, carried away though he was, began to find the man's presence unsettling, and kept glancing at him from the corner of his eye, fearful that he might abruptly accost him with questions about Dinshaway. The man did no such thing, but went on listening to the exclamations and admonitions of Lord Cromer, the pitch of whose voice had risen.

All at once the short, heavyset man spoke up. Without moving from his place, he said, "But why are you doing this to the Pasha, when he's one of your closest friends, and was among the first and most eager to cooperate with you?"

Naturally, Lord Cromer had expected no less than this sort of poisonous question from the man. Holding his head up confidently he replied, "Mustafa Fahmi Pasha is still a friend of mine, but the law is my closest friend."

The words rang out, and Lord Cromer felt proud and pleased with himself for having given the best possible answer to the newspaper that had been insulting him for so long. Nodding his head, he added, "And now, gentlemen, I have much work to do. The translator will stay with you in case you need to question these unfortunate fugitives." And with that, he turned and hurried into his office, followed by Harry Buell.

Aisha stayed behind, lost in the crowd, hoping the event would come to a close. But many of those who had entered this house for the first time were reluctant to leave it so soon, and so they stayed, wandering about, gazing at the portraits hung upon the walls and the statue busts, asking Aisha about whatever came into their heads. She was thinking of slipping away, when she heard his voice calling to her. "What are you doing here?" he said. "Don't you see what a liar this man is?"

She turned. It was the man from *al-Liwa* who was speaking to her. He looked searchingly at her. His name, she recalled, was Rafiy. "I work here," she said. "I'm merely the translator—the substance of what is said is no concern of mine."

But he wasn't willing to let her get away so easily. "He's trying to evade the issue of what he did at Dinshaway, and to that end he's throwing away the most important ally the English have here."

"Sir," said Aisha firmly, "you could have brought this up with Lord Cromer."

He shut his lips tightly, having no reply at first, but then he hung his head and said, "You're right. I'm sorry to have troubled you."

He took a step backward, away from her, and she felt remorseful for having dealt so sharply with him, and because despite his anger he had maintained his courteous demeanor. He cast a glance around, looking as if he wanted to talk to the slaves, but it was clear he had no wish to stay long in this place. He turned and left, ahead of all the others.

As usual, Lord Cromer emerged the victor. When Aisha sat with him in the garden some days later, a pile of newspapers before them, the Dinshaway affair had retreated into the shadows, and in the spotlight was a discussion of the prime minister's trial: would Lord Cromer pardon him or let him fall prey to the rigors of the law? Aisha was more comfortable translating for him the things that he liked to hear and that confirmed him in his opinions. Their sessions came to be one of the staples of Lord Cromer's daily labor, far preferable to the humdrum quotidian reports that Harry Buell placed on his desk each day. But Aisha couldn't feel at ease—the question put to her by the man named Rafiy kept reverberating in her ears: "What are you doing here?" She realized how very much she had distanced herself from her real world, that she was connected only to people outside these walls. She was living under a name not her own, hiding inside a skin that wasn't hers. She must retrieve all her forgotten history and go to see her mother, if she was still alive—Aisha didn't even know. She must go to her village and endure some part of what her mother had endured—but when would that moment come? When would she manage to make up her mind?

Not until she saw Howard Carter for the second time did Aisha know that the moment had in fact arrived.

She and Lord Cromer were sitting in the garden when she saw him coming toward them. In spite of the dusk, which had begun to settle upon the trees, Aisha recognized him immediately. She saw how he carried himself, noticing that he looked thinner and taller than before. He stopped directly in front of them, and she saw his face clearly, the dusty straw color of his hair, the paleness of his skin, the hollows of his temples. He had lost the sparkle Aisha had seen in him the first time. He was fatigued, his clothes wrinkled, and on his shoulders were remnants of dust he hadn't stopped to brush off.

He inclined his head toward them without a word, making no attempt to excuse himself for his abrupt arrival. Lord Cromer turned and studied him for a while, as if trying to remember who he was. He could see at once that he was looking at an exhausted man who was struggling to maintain his composure. For all that, Carter turned to Aisha and dipped his head, a faint smile on his lips. Lord Cromer took this as an opportunity to say sarcastically, "Mr. Carter—you surprise me with this visit. Do the gods still reveal themselves to you?"

In a subdued voice, Carter replied, "No indeed, your Lordship. I see nothing anymore but nightmares."

"What a pity," said Lord Cromer. "You ought to consult the doctor."

"I know what my malady is, sir."

He fell silent. He didn't know whether he ought to speak in front of Aisha, or whether he should wait until she withdrew. She did in fact rise to her feet, but Lord Cromer gestured to her to stay, and cast a cold eye upon Carter, not inviting him to sit. Carter's was a losing proposition from the outset, but he couldn't hold back from speaking his mind.

"I have been torn from my world, sir, and what I came to Egypt for has been lost. I've been moved from the Valley of the Kings to Tanta, where there's nothing but a handful of mosques and cramped neighborhoods and weary peasants. You've punished me, although I'm innocent—punished me merely for having preserved the relics of which I was in charge, and protected the people who worked under my authority."

"You damaged my work," said Lord Cromer coldly. "Your conduct was implicated in an international incident between us and France, whose consul general you insulted, and then you refused to apologize. I don't take such errors lightly, Mr. Carter. I did not dismiss you from your work, although that is what you deserved. I let it go at transferring you to a different site."

"You transferred me to a void, a backwater—you've ruined my career."

"Mind how you go, then. This country has plenty of trackless desert—I could move you to a place still more remote."

"You can do no such thing, sir."

Aisha was following this exchanged openmouthed—it would never have occurred to her that she might witness such a heated clash of wills in which neither party stopped addressing the other with formal titles or even raised his voice against the other.

Howard reached into his pocket and drew from it a folded paper. He advanced until he could place it upon the table right before Lord Cromer's eyes. "Here is my resignation, sir," he said. "You won't be able to move me anywhere now."

Lord Cromer sat unmoving, not even extending his hand to take the paper. Carter turned to Aisha, dipped his head slightly, then turned and took his leave, disappearing among the shadows of the trees. Aisha got to her feet. She felt that she could remain silent no longer. It struck her suddenly that this place, too, was exile, and that it would strip her of the power to do or say anything, change her into a dead thing.

Lord Cromer looked at her in disbelief. "I haven't yet given you permission to leave," he said.

In a strangled voice she said, "I want to talk to him."

"He is worthless. There is no point in talking to him."

But she had already begun to walk away from Lord Cromer, and soon she, too, disappeared into the shadows of the trees.

5 • The Valley of Thebes

TIME MARCHES FORWARD, and the dream does not last. And so here I stand, my princess, at the edge of the void, a stranger with no safe place to go. My arid paradise was lost to me; little had I known there was a snake watching from behind its rocks. It was my paradise, or so I thought, there in the desolate wastes of the western shore of the Nile. Luxor was this strange, ancient city, burning like hell, stifling like thwarted hopes. When I first set foot upon its other bank, I was engulfed by the accumulation of the ages, and the spirits that could find for themselves no resting place. The Valley of the Kings was full of boulders, black caverns, dusty columns, broken statues, and fathomless abysses. Although it revealed none of its buried secrets, its name didn't suit it—or so it seemed to me at that moment. Its rocks glowered, tumbled against one another along the Nile and yet rising in the shape of a pyramid, leaning forward and forming a stony peak tilted toward the surface of the river as if suffering from unquenchable thirst. To this valley I came, my princess, where the bodies of the ancient kings lay awaiting eternal glory. But they were plundered and rent asunder before they could achieve the moment of immortality or the blessing of redemption.

When I crossed the line between the valley and the desert, I heard the eerie voices that issued from the two massive statues of Amenhotep III. The wind filled the crevices in the statues, which emitted a fearful, keening sound. The Greeks thought that the spirit of their great leader Agamemnon inhabited the statues, and that he was stricken with both unending sorrow for his daughter Iphigenia—whom he had sacrificed in order to raise the winds of war—and anger toward his wife, Clytemnestra, who betrayed him, and then killed him on the day of his triumphant return. But I felt that these voices spoke particularly to me, warning me not to enter the world of the dead. They were all that occupied this holy silence, but I didn't listen to them. I crossed all the boundaries in the hope of winning for myself something of that silence for which I longed.

As was my habit, I did not seek accommodation in lodgings or a rest house. I settled where I found the reliefs and paintings at which I never tired of looking.

I found a place for myself within Deir al-Bahri. The rocky outcropping in whose embrace the temple had been erected shielded me from the vast and empty desert. I awoke each morning to smell the residual fragrance of Hatshepsut's perfume (Hatshepsut, whose trees came from the distant land of Punt: the wood had turned to stone, but its essence remained). Then I would spend the whole day reproducing the paintings with which the walls were covered: of women in diaphanous robes bearing offerings, of the sacred mysteries of childbirth, and the ritual sacrifices to the gods. At night, when I fell exhausted into slumber, Queen Hatshepsut came to me unclothed, wearing nothing but her false beard.

Every day time stole away a piece of my life—I was passing beyond my twentieth year, and the filament binding me to the world of the living had been severed. Ever since I left Beni Hassan and took up the work of excavating and searching for antiquities, swallowing great quantities of dust, I had dwelt in the silence and chill of Deir al-Bahri. I had become more solitary and withdrawn, but I realized this only when I met Rosalind Paget, or Rosa, as she insisted I call her.

One day at noon, I stood rapt before a wall—it was at this time of day that the light was best diffused throughout the temple halls. The mural that now drew me was filled with paintings of ships and sails and oarsmen wielding dozens of oars as they plied the waters of the Red Sea: paintings depicting one of the great journeys of discovery to the land of Punt in the interior of ancient Africa. Many details had been effaced—a not infrequent occurrence among fractious dynasties. I was trying to fill in the missing parts of the panel in my imagination—I saw it as if I were living the moment in which the artists completed it, and then I saw a shadow fall across the wall in front of me. At first I supposed that Abdel Rasul had come to bring me my daily provisions of food and drink, and I didn't bother to turn toward him—he was used to my long silences, and accustomed to leaving the supplies next to one of the columns and taking his leave.

But now I heard a woman's voice. "You are very much taken with this panel," the woman said, "are you not?"

Startled, I turned to her. I found her standing before me, tall and slender as a reed, dressed in khaki, like a man, holding a straw hat in one hand and in the other a portfolio full of papers. Her hair was cut boyishly short; she had attractive, delicate features and a pale complexion touched by the sun, which had lent a rosy blush to her cheeks. She held me in her blue-eyed gaze, surprised and perplexed.

Taking a step toward me, she said, "They told me a great deal about you, but I hadn't imagined that you were so countrified and removed."

I didn't understand what she meant, but she didn't seem alarmed by me. She took another step forward and contemplated the lines I was still sketching. She turned over my papers without troubling to ask my permission. She was so close to me that her perfume filled my nostrils. She was absorbed in her scrutiny of my work. All at once she turned and gave me a delighted smile. Extending her hand, she said, "I'm Rosa. And you, I believe, are Mr. Howard Carter."

Her hand was small and soft. Afterward I saw traces of color on her fingers. She wasn't an ordinary tourist as I had at first assumed. She opened her portfolio and showed me the paintings it contained: strange sketches inspired by the Temple of Dendera, and Edfu, and even the temples at Philae, which were submerged most of the year. Her paintings were not representative—there was much in them that was spontaneous and of her own invention. She put something of herself into all the old pictures—her work was not staid, like mine. She was a free spirit who thought little of traditional constraints—perhaps she had never had occasion to encounter Percy Newberry and receive his stern instructions, which had not troubled me until now.

Brushing some tendrils of hair out of her eyes, she said to me, "I was one of Professor Petrie's students at London University. All the while I was hoping to come to Egypt to dig with him, but when at last I managed to get here I found him packing up his tools. He had completed his task. He was angry because he couldn't finish his excavations at Thebes. Now I'm working at Dr. Edouard Naville's site. He's the one who recommended I come find you."

I had worked with Petrie on his excavation after I left the tombs at Beni Hassan. He thought he was the only true scholar of antiquities, that the rest—including Naville himself—were merely scavengers, relying upon hazard and strokes of luck. I wanted to tell her that I liked Naville, despite Petrie's opinion of him. He was Swiss, a large man full of life and the spirit of adventure. He received support and ample monetary gifts from a French tramway company, without which he wouldn't have been able to carry on his work for so many years, removing thousands of tons of rock from in front of the Bahri temple, until he exposed its façade. He had paved the way for me to gain access to the place in which I now lived.

Just then, however, all words escaped me. My heart began to pound furiously, while she talked on, simply and naturally. I had grown used to protracted silence, and sustained speech was no longer possible for me. This was the first time I had stood before an unaccompanied woman who worked in this field.

"How can you live here?" I said to her. "I mean, encamped among all those men?"

Laughing, she replied, "It's never been a problem as far as I'm concerned—I don't care much for women in any case."

We wandered together through the halls of the temple, as if Hatshepsut had transcended time and come to walk with me, without the artificial beard this time. I told Rosa that this temple had been built for love—Hatshepsut used to meet her lover, Senenmut, here. We stopped in the inner sanctum before a picture of the goddess Hathor made with deeply incised lines. The goddess of joy, love, and beauty, she originated as a divine cow, and she retained her large ears. The custom was to depict her on the walls of the mausoleums for the sake of those interred there, in the hope of easing their return to life. At her feet was a jug of wine, life-giving to all who drained it to the dregs.

I made no reply to Rosa. All the words gathered inside me, without emerging. It was she who talked, disturbing the silence in which thousands of years had passed, and filling it with an irrepressible liveliness, which dispelled the chill that pervaded the passageways. We concluded our tour, proceeding along the great corridor leading down from the temple gate, toward the Nile.

"What a magnificent place," she said. "But how do you endure such silence and solitude? You remind me of a story being put about in the American newspapers lately about a man who lived alone in the forest. The difference is that you live in the desert."

I pointed out to her the Theban Nile River plain extending before us. "This is no desert," I said. "A civilization was born here."

In the beginning there was a beam of light, a gust of wind, and particles of dust. This valley was no more than a lake, its waters full of pondweed, reaching all the way to the horizon. Then came the goddess Hathor to set about drying it, but she quickly grew bored with this operation, creating nothing more than a small piece of dry land, upon which she laid the world, like an egg. To begin with she had pictured it in her imagination, generating the first pulse beat of creation, and setting the cosmos upon its course. The sun emerged from a lotus flower, and into the silence the flamingo uttered its first cry. The first man was born from a bull's semen and the first woman from a dewdrop.

I didn't say all that to her, of course, although the words I had stored up in my breast were on the point of bursting out. I went on listening to her talk. She said she had seen some books published in London that contained my depictions of the tombs at Beni Hassan and Deir al-Bahri. She knew more of me than I did of her. She was waiting for me to say more, but I couldn't. The capacity for speech came to me only when I caught sight of the towering figure of Abdel Rasul astride a donkey, kicking his legs to make the beast go faster as he brought my daily food supplies.

"Stay for lunch with me," I said to Rosa.

She realized then that the time had passed more quickly than she'd imagined. "Thank you," she said, "but I promised Naville I would have lunch with him."

She went away, Abdel Rasul watching her from the back of his donkey. With an obscure smile on his face, he placed the food before me. I ate a little, then discovered I had no appetite for it. The silence in the tomb became more than I could bear, and I went to the edge of the river, where white birds dipping their bills in the water looked at me in surprise, and then flew away on lazily flapping wings. I found the reflection of my face in the surface of the water strange—I hadn't seen it for so many days that I had forgotten its features: the untidy beard, dusty moustache, sunken eyes, and the whole covered with a mask-like suntan. This wasn't me—it was as if a strange figure had taken me over. I took off my clothes and plunged into the river. The water embraced me and sent a shiver through my body. I searched among the plants along the shore until I found some stalks of wild basil, and I scrubbed myself with its green leaves. The sun went down faster than usual, darkness fell, and I was more alone than ever.

She didn't come the following day. She hadn't made me any promises, and I didn't want to sit about waiting for her, so I went ahead with my daily agenda. But in spite of myself I was watching for her arrival. I remembered the sparkle in her eyes when she looked at the paintings inside the temple, and I felt sure she would be unable to resist their magic, she would have to return to them. And yet she had, no doubt, been annoyed by my silence—she must have been disappointed in me.

Two days later I went to the site of the excavations on which Naville was working. The place looked like a beehive, thronged with dozens of workers, ceaselessly digging and heaping up their finds. Naville employed more workers than anyone, and paid them better than anyone else did. He was famous among the fellahin of al-Qurna, who lived on the western shore, for paying workers three piasters a day, and they provided an inexhaustible workforce. I saw him standing by himself at the edge of a wide trench, watching the workers removing sand from potsherds. He was massive and bare-chested, robust as if he had drunk all the goats' milk to be found in the Alps. His thick moustache curled up at the ends and his forehead shone with sweat. He wore no hat, and seemed untroubled by the blazing sun. I turned my back on him—I wanted to see her first of all, and make sure that whoever it was that had visited me at Deir al-Bahri wasn't some will-o'-the-wisp. I made my way among the workers as they applied themselves to their digging, gathering into woven baskets whatever was left behind. I went down into the outermost trench, and spied her sitting on the ground, holding a small brush with which she was removing dirt from a little pot of red-tinged marble. I stood watching her slow movements as she revealed the details of a funerary urn. So she really did exist. She sat there absorbed in her work, clad in the same khaki garb, with the same short hair, and the same fine features. As I stood there all the pretexts I had prepared by way of explaining my presence at the excavation site flew out of my head. It seemed imperative to advance and say directly to her, "Why didn't you come back to me?" But I didn't.

I felt a hand come to rest on my shoulder. When I turned, there behind me stood Naville, with his massive frame. "At last," he cried, "you've come out of your hermitage! I dare say the Benedictine monks of the Middle Ages were not so cloistered as you."

Rosa looked up and glanced in our direction, the ghost of a smile upon her features, but she didn't move from her position. I was at a loss, thinking Naville must have known the real reason I was there. He spoke again. "It's for the best that you've come," he said. "I was going to send for you in any case."

I was hoping he would leave me to gather my courage and approach Rosa, but he put his hand on my shoulder once more and drew me aside. "Have you not heard," he asked, "that the dahabeah belonging to the American millionaire Theodore Davis has arrived? All Luxor is talking about him and the reception parties he's been hosting. He has become the point upon which visiting dignitaries converge—the other day he entertained the crown prince of Austria. He wishes to invite you."

I had not heard anything about him, but this was not surprising, for winter was the high season for social activity in this remote city, and dozens of upper-class Europeans descended upon it every year. I would see them on their visits to the temple, as they passed by me in their wanderings about the site. Most of them didn't see me, and for my part I grew accustomed to taking no notice of them, so it was quite natural for me to say to Naville that I was not interested, but Naville was not the sort of man to take no for an answer very readily.

"You can't refuse," he said. "He wants to see some of your work. He's mad about Egyptology and has donated a great many rare pieces to the Metropolitan Museum. Come—you'll enjoy yourself . . . and Miss Paget shall be with us, of course."

I looked at Rosa, and she returned my glance, nodding her head. Was she inviting me to go with them? Or was she too distracted? I was annoyed, for Naville spoke in the manner of one who has his own way in everything. I hurried away without uttering a single word to Rosa, but the next day I shaved my face and changed my clothes. I was precisely on time, and we crossed by felucca to the eastern shore, where the three of us together boarded the dahabeah that was moored by the bank, flying the American flag.

I had put on my best clothes and made meticulous use of European cologne, but I looked altogether like a beggar in this exalted milieu crowding the ship's deck: men and women all wearing fine clothes in subtle colors, stepping lightly with their glasses of bubbling champagne. They laughed softly and spoke in low whispers. Feeling out of place, I began to cast about for a means of escape, but Rosa gave me a small encouraging smile—even though we had made the crossing together, it seemed as though now she was noting my presence for the first time. I would need a little something to drink, so as to acclimate myself to this environment. Theodore Davis approached, a towering figure clad in a jacket of brilliant white—the same shade as his moustache—with a straw hat on his head.

"We'll sit together," he said, firmly shaking my hand, "and then I'll look carefully at your paintings. In all this hubbub I can't concentrate on anything."

Taking my arm, he led me away to a woman younger than he but of similar height. She wore a low-cut gown studded with pearls.

"This is my assistant, Emilia Andrews," he said. "I rely upon her for everything. She shall take charge of you this evening."

And in her turn, Emilia took me by the arm as if I was a small child. I turned to look for Rosa, but she had vanished from my sight. How had all these people so suddenly entered this world: scions of wealth, aristocrats, diplomats, so many great names? Some of them shook my hand, others settling for a nod of the head. I made a complete circuit of the ship's deck. I saw Naville clutching a glass of champagne, in the laughing company of a small group of important people. Beside him stood Rosa, head cast down. I stood gazing at her in confusion—what was the mystery of this girl? Why did she seem so distant? I had eyes only for her, but did she actually see me?

When it was time for lunch, we all sat down at a long table. Emilia took my hand and seated me beside her. Rosa sat across from me beside Naville, who drank and talked ceaselessly. Our eyes met and she smiled at me once more. There were many varieties of food, but everyone was sated already. They ate a little of each dish, scarcely tasting anything, before the plate was taken away and replaced by another in its stead. Dish after dish was set down and then removed.

"My dear Howard," said Emilia, "why is it that you seem so puzzled and distracted? I've been talking to you all this while!"

After lunch, I was as eager as Davis was for him to take me to his stateroom in the bowels of the dahabeah. He gave himself over to attentive scrutiny of my paintings. I had brought him my own personal collection, the colored ones I kept well apart from the daily labor at which I was employed. These were my true self. He was avid to know the times and places in which I had devoted myself to their creation.

"I shall buy them," he said all at once.

I had not imagined that deals could be made so easily, nor had I intended that these paintings, which had absorbed a part of my life, should be for sale. That they should be published in this man's books was unthinkable—they would remain in my possession one way or another—that anyone else should take them over seemed not merely bizarre but altogether impossible. Davis looked astonished at my refusal—he was used to getting whatever he wanted. He stared at me, bewildered, and evidently embarrassed. But Emilia caressed his forehead, gave him a quick kiss on the lips, and asked him to leave us alone. I was tense, sensing that I had fallen into a trap, here in this swaying stateroom.

"My dear Howard," said Emilia, "you're in love with this girl, Rosa . . . aren't you?"

For the first time, my voice rose in protest. "Certainly not."

"That's as may be," said Emilia calmly, "but at the very least you are interested in her. I saw how you looked at her all during the reception. During lunch you never took your eyes off her, but alas she was looking in another direction. She can't see you in your position."

I was aware of a lump in my throat, a constriction in my chest. She, however, regarded me with a determined air—it was only too obvious that she was a mature and experienced woman, while I was still stumbling about in my twenties, not knowing how to embark upon my first experiences in the world of women.

"What do you mean?" I said in a choked voice.

"Clearly you have taken yourself well away from the world, my dear," she said. "You don't wear suitable clothes, and you don't know the proper way to eat at table. Moreover, you are always silent—how can you get her attention like that? You must make her look at you, change your appearance, become more receptive to life—and money was invented to serve these ends. I don't know how much you earn each month from your work, but I'm sure it is a negligible sum."

My wages did not exceed five pounds a month, but I dared not admit this to her. It was enough for me—or at least I thought it sufficient.

"These paintings you guard so closely," Emilia resumed, "will not for long be in Mr. Davis's hands. He will most likely donate them to a museum, and thus will their glory redound to you. No one will remember who bought them from you. Take the money, my dear—you need it. And let me teach you some skills that will enable you to win over this young lady."

When I left the berth at last, the sun was about to set. So enchanting was the view of the river that a hush had fallen upon the crowd. They were all standing at the ship's rail, gazing at the water as it changed color—there was no other river that performed such wonders. Rosa was standing on her own, while Naville sat upon a chair, evidently immobilized from too much drink. I approached and stood beside her, the boldest step I had taken in all the twenty years of my life. We stood there in silence. A great deal had happened to me on this day.

"Why haven't you come back to visit Deir al-Bahri?" I asked her at last. "I thought that I . . . what I mean is . . . I thought you were interested in the paintings there."

She turned toward me, surprised. "I thought you found my being there annoying," she said. "You kept so silent all the time, and you didn't press me to stay."

Her reply shocked me. I realized all at once that everything Miss Emilia had said to me in the stateroom was true. Rosa stood near me, her hand clutching the ship's rail close to mine. I wanted to place my fingers on hers, but I lacked the courage. I glanced behind me. Naville sat overcome by sleep. She looked at him, amused. How could such a powerful man be vanquished by drink?

"I'd like you to come back," I said at last. "There are beautiful paintings you haven't seen yet. It would be my pleasure to show them to you."

She placed her hand over mine and smiled at me.

She didn't come the following day, either. Davis came, as well as a great many of the guests who had attended his party. They were mounted upon donkeys, whose backs they warmed with blows from their switches, stirring up the sand and making a great din amid the silence of the dead. The peasants and the muleteers held the edges of their garments between their teeth and tried in vain to keep up. I could only smile, seeing Davis jump down before me, eager as a child. The weather was hot, but it was apparent that the residue of the previous evening's libations had not yet evaporated from all of their heads. They milled around me, turning over my papers, then dispersed themselves about the temple. Emilia kissed me on the cheek as was her manner, and presented me with a carefully tied parcel.

"This is for you," she said. "For the pretty young lady. Don't open it until after we leave."

I was downcast, feeling sadly neglected by Rosa. I accompanied them into the various chambers, reading the inscriptions and interpreting the paintings, disparate fragments of the life of a queen whose abysmal luck had decreed that she should be female.

"For twenty years—the length of her reign—her body oppressed her," I explained. "She strove to delude herself and everyone else that she was actually a man, merely born with the wrong traits. Her real tragedy was in not finding a man who was her equal. Her father, Thutmose I, had left her with an illegitimate brother whom she was forced to marry, despite her contempt for the bond that united them. She was not granted a suitable position on the throne by his side, or a warm place in his bed. He persistently marginalized her, putting his favorites above her, and he repeated what his father had done, producing with another woman an illegitimate son whom he undertook to raise as the heir to his throne.

"Hatshepsut, though a mild and bashful girl, could not bear being defrauded and ignored. She grew up unobserved behind the scenes. Her body matured and was convulsed with longing; her mind was open to all tactical options, but what happened thereafter was mysterious. A young man, an architect and a genius, came into her life—that was Senenmut, who eventually built this temple for her. Did he come to know her early on, and did this relationship grant her the strength and the impetus to rid herself of her husband, or did Senenmut make his appearance later, the recompense destined for a solitary widow whose bed was cold, her body long forsaken?

"Hatshepsut bestowed upon this architect eighty honorific titles, and charged him with the care of her only daughter. She would make love with him only in a boat set upon the waters on moonlit nights. In love she was passionate, as a ruler powerful. Not only did she wear a false beard, but she was the first woman in history who wore gloves in order to conceal the fragility of her fingers.

"She built one of the strongest fleets in the ancient world. Her ships went first to the country of Punt, in Africa, whence they fetched wood and perfumes. From the wood they constructed another fleet, grander and more vast, capable of traversing the Sea of Shadows. But destiny was to turn back upon itself. Her husband's illegitimate son lay always in ambush, hiding in the shadows of the palace, waiting to find the right moment to avenge his father's death. No doubt the priests helped him to seize his opportunity and pounce upon her—her and her lover the architect—in one fell swoop. The outcome of these events is obscure, but death did not divide them for long. There was a passageway connecting her tomb to his, so that they could meet again at world's end."

I stopped speaking and turned to see whether there were any questions. There stood Rosa, leaning against a column surmounted by a capital. She was gazing at me, her eyes shining. The group withdrew, but she came up to me and said, "I thought you had forgotten how to speak. I didn't know you were so good at relating tales of love."

All the others waved good-bye to me as they mounted their donkeys in preparation for departure. Emilia turned and embraced Rosa. She kissed her and whispered a few words in her ear, and they laughed together like mischievous girls. Then at last we were left alone. We sat together before the wall, upon which were depicted women presenting offerings to the god Amun. She took out her papers and began to sketch rapidly. I wanted to tell her how many things had changed for me, to tell her about my sudden feeling that I had reached a point at which I must stop and make a life-changing decision. But the words accumulated in my chest, too weak to come out. I forgot all the advice Emilia had given me as I contemplated Rosa's profile, while she sat there beside me with her shoulder nearly touching mine. She resembled one of those young girls who were presenting the offerings—but to which god? I didn't know.

"Don't stare at me so much," she said, "or my features will get mixed up with the outlines of your paintings!"

She was smiling, but I was embarrassed, feeling myself wanting in courtesy. She did not object, though, when I took her hand. We went out to the balcony outside the sanctuary. Abdel Rasul was headed toward us, bearing my food supplies, and together we contemplated his mysterious smile. She took a little food with me, and I, my tongue loosed at last, recounted to her something of my experiences in Egypt. Suddenly I remembered the day when I had met Fraser, when he had stood upon the stony perimeter of the tombs at Beni Hassan and said, "We've all come to this place to escape our personal afflictions." Why had a pretty girl like Rosa come to such a place? Was there someone she was running away from? What sort of trouble would drive a girl like this to bed down in such a desolate place, in an encampment inhabited exclusively by men covered in dust? I dared not ask her.

At sunset, I walked with her to Naville's encampment. The desert was hot, the ruins imposingly silent. The waters of the Nile were unsettled, like a troubled heart. We paused for a moment, far from the eyes of others. Ought I to kiss her at this moment, or settle for foolishly squeezing her hand?

In the days that followed I saw her, and we continued with our paintings, our conversation, our strolls among the columns of the temples and the flocks of migrating birds at the river's edge. I inhaled her mild fragrance at leisure and my heart let go of the loneliness in which I had dwelt for so long. I came to know her shifting facial expressions: serious as an old woman, mischievous as a child, alluring as an unattainable ancient goddess. She allowed me to clean the paint off of her fingers and tuck her hair back behind her ears for her. One day while sitting beside me she stopped painting, stood up, and moved a little way off. Then she seated herself before me. She set her papers in her lap and said with a smile, "I'm tired of copying these stiff figures. I'm going to do your portrait instead."

She began sketching with animated strokes, as if the lines on the paper had been held prisoner inside her fingers for a long time. She would raise her head every so often to take in my features, gazing for a long time into my eyes, as if she wanted to penetrate my mind. I was trembling, no longer finding it easy to make eye contact with her. So I spread out my papers as well, and began to work on her portrait. We laughed together in conspiratorial delight, as we rapidly plied our brushes. We finished at the same moment.

We sat side by side, each of us attuned to the proximity of the other's body. She had portrayed me with my hair unkempt; my eyes were shining, but their expression was faraway and sad; she had drawn my nose larger than life, my moustache as scarcely more than an accumulation of fuzz.

She gazed for a long time at her own portrait, then looked at me quizzically. Could it be that she had read between the lines, and did she know what an anguished spirit was behind the image? I had done no more in my portrayal of her than to bedeck her with crowns and scarabs and ankhs.

The season was almost over, with everyone preparing to leave, in dread of Luxor's scorching summer. In just a few days the dahabeah and the grand ships would slip their moorings and head north with the tide of departures. Would Rosa go with them?

Emilia had brought me a parcel of new clothes, which enabled me better to keep up appearances before Rosa. I had accepted the gift because Emilia reminded me of my aunt, my father's sister, who taught me English by means of the Bible.

I, too, was drawing near to the end of my special season, and I had realized that there was no need for me to stay on alone in this place. The decisive moment for me with Rosa came at sunset. We were standing together on the bank of the Nile, the fields stretching out before us lushly verdant. I reached out, rested my hand on her shoulder, then kissed her on the cheek, which was soft and warm. She stared at me in surprise; I put my arm about her waist and kissed her on the lips. Her lips were cool. She didn't pull away, but neither did she return my kiss. My whole body was perturbed, and I said in an unsteady voice, "I'm going to change my life—I shan't remain in this profession any longer. I've sold some of my paintings, and received a large sum in exchange. I'll give up this wretched job and be free to do my own painting—I'll be able to earn plenty to set up a house worthy of you."

She did not reply. I tried to take her in my arms once more—the first kiss, I thought, had not expressed my true feelings. But she withdrew her hand and held me off, preventing me from making a move. On her face was a resolute frown.

"I'm in love with Naville," she said. "I came here for his sake."

My mouth fell open in astonishment. I wanted to speak, to interrogate, to object, to comprehend—or at the very least to point out to her that Naville was married and had no right to make her fall in love with him and abandon me for his sake. But all at once she had become cold and distant, and all power of speech left me. The most I got from her was a brief, pitying glance; she had no attachment to me, and she owed me no explanation.

"I think I shall go now," she said. "I'm quite sure I can find my own way."

Late that same night, Abdel Rasul visited me unexpectedly. I heard his approaching footsteps. He stood erect before me, planting his staff in the sand. On his head was an enormous turban; he was barefoot. "Foreigner," he said, "I saw the light coming from your camp—this is not your custom. You go to bed early, and rise with the dawn."

Startled, I said to him, "I didn't know you roamed about at night, too."

"This is my land," he replied, "I wander it at all times. For me, night is like day. I know the terrain well—I don't need light."

"Perhaps you were looking for artifacts to steal!" I said sardonically.

Without losing his temper, he answered, "No one plunders his own land, foreigner. Whatever is here, buried or out in the open, we have a right to. You are temporary guests—the Turks and Circassians were here before you. But it is we who remain."

I kept quiet for a bit. I felt much of what he was saying was uncalled-for, but there were other things I wanted to talk about with him. What happened in the valley did not much concern me; I knew they all stole things: the farmers, the diggers, the explorers, the museum curators, the consuls, and those who called themselves Egyptologists. All of them vied for the spoils buried in this arid patch of ground. I was weary and brokenhearted, and I couldn't tell whether Abdel Rasul's arrival was mere happenstance or whether in some mysterious way he knew about what had happened to me that day.

"That girl," I found myself saying to him, "the artist who used to come here—did you know that she was romantically involved with Naville?"

"You mean the young foreign woman?" he replied. "She is his mistress—everyone knows that. They're getting ready to travel to Cairo together."

It was as simple as that—quite clear. How could I have been the only one who didn't see it? How could I have been so gullible, carried away by an illusion?

Abdel Rasul stared wordlessly at me. Then he spoke. "Don't let these things distress you, foreigner," he said. "Everyone here is just passing through, and all their liaisons are temporary as well. When the season ends, everyone heads north and all promises expire. That's always been the way of it."

The following day I went to Luxor and sent a telegram to the Egyptian Antiquities Service in London, informing them of my resignation. I stopped by the Winter Palace Hotel, where Emilia was packing in preparation for her own departure. She kissed me sadly, seeing the look of despair on my face.

"You knew she was his mistress," I said to her, "and yet you still insisted that I pursue my relationship with her."

She sighed. "That little fool," she replied. "I wanted to give her the opportunity for a normal romance."

"You should have told me what was going on, that it was serious between them . . ."

"My dear, this sort of thing happens every day. Such is the game of love and deception. You'll grow up one day and become a part of it, too. Come . . . you must have a glass with us before we go. How unfortunate that I met you too late, my poor young friend."

There was nothing natural about what was happening, but the season was ending all the same. They all went away, and I stayed on, alone. I too should have gone, but it was a long way to my village of Swaffham, and I didn't think the journey would bring me any consolation.

I took to exploring the dusty streets of the city, which wound between close-set houses of mud brick. I bumped up against passersby but avoided the water buffaloes and donkey-drawn carts. I didn't notice that I had entered the slave district situated on the outskirts of the city until I found myself in the very heart of it.

Little barefoot children surrounded me, showing their white teeth, entwining their small fingers with mine. They clustered around me, compelling me to go where they wanted me to go. I stumbled over stones and dirty puddles, but they kept pulling me along. This neighborhood was where enslaved Africans congregated, having escaped over the borders and evaded their masters; here also were fugitives from the law, as well as those fearful of revenge from blood feuds, among others—outcasts all. The houses were small—shacks, rather—with bamboo walls and roofs thatched with palm fronds. Seated before them were African women clad in colorful garments, their hair bound up in small turbans. Lamplight flickered before every house. The women called out to the children, encouraging them to continue pulling me. I did not resist; the glasses of wine I had drunk were turning my stomach.

The children led me to a capacious building with a large gate made from the trunks of palm trees. They pushed me inside, and the gate closed behind me. I stood in an exposed courtyard, an African temple constructed of palm fronds interwoven with tree branches. Coming toward me was a massive woman, whose colorful clothing was barely secured above the swell of her ample bosom. She drew me by the hand, as if my presence was nothing out of the ordinary, leading me across the open space. We entered a dimly lit sorcerer's maze consisting of innumerable corridors and chambers.

The air in the hall was thick with a suffocating cloud of smoke, and closely packed with bodies white and black. In the center was a lit brazier from which rose a dense column of smoke. They were burning a large chunk of West African hashish: the lot of them were inhaling nothing but hashish fumes. A sense of warmth and torpor pervaded my limbs—I was exhausted, I needed to rest. I was handed along to another woman, an alluring black girl, slimmer and younger than the first, her hair arranged in tiny, beaded braids. I gave myself up to her, disappearing into her. Some men came in carrying frame drums. They gathered around the fire, beating the drums loudly, while in their midst a woman, entirely naked, executed a sinuous dance. The black girl clung to me, running her hands over my body. Opposite me I saw a white woman sitting sandwiched between two black men, their legs entwined, their hands clutching at her breasts.

I felt a strangulating anxiety; the black girl took me out to the long corridor and brought me to a narrow room in which there was nothing but a straw mat and a worn pillow. She removed her clothing and flung herself upon me. On the point of weeping, I tried to extricate myself from beneath her weight. I wanted Rosa, with all her delicacy, despite her frivolity and shortsightedness. "What's the matter with you, the lot of you?" the girl shouted full in my face. "Why do you come to me with all your complications and your squeamishness?" Before I could make a move, she sank her nails into my face. The corpulent woman I'd encountered earlier intervened, pulling the girl off of me and wiping traces of blood from my face.

In a confiding tone she said to me, "If you'd rather have a boy, just say so. It's all on offer." All I wanted was to get away from this place. The black girl spat at me, and crouched naked in a corner of the room. I gave the big woman all the money I had in my pocket, and an even larger black man appeared, lifted me up onto his shoulders, and tossed me outside.

I stayed no longer in Deir al-Bahri, but took up residence in the village of al-Qurna, leaving the world of the Europeans on the other side of the river. I had learned to speak Arabic fluently, so there was no impediment to my communication with the peasants in the village, and by degrees I penetrated their society. I saw the ones who surreptitiously dug for treasure, and those who counterfeited the statues and other antiquities, or made imitation papyrus fragments. They formed a hidden world, to which it was no easy matter for foreigners to gain access. But once I submitted my resignation they began to trust me a little more. I continued to frequent the temples scattered about the area—Medinet Habu, the Ramesseum, and Deir al-Bahri. I visited gravesites replete with magnificent paintings, such as the tomb of Seti I, featuring the most extraordinary paintings I've seen in all my life, and the tomb of Amenophis II, where the mummies of kings who could not achieve immortality are laid in rows. I made my paintings, and I saw the world I had for so long been unable to see as I had wished.

The Nile kept rising until it covered the broad expanse of flat land, and swarms of mosquitoes expanded with it. We took to immersing ourselves in the water every day, but we could no longer reach the other shore—our connection to the rest of the world had been severed. The image of the god Hapi, who gave the Egyptians the yearly flood, was incised upon the walls on the Island of Philae. His features combine masculine ruggedness with feminine delicacy. He wears a crown woven from palm fronds, and his arms are weighed down with the abundance of gifts he carries.

The world no longer mattered to me in any case. Abdel Rasul told me he was preparing to provide me with a boat that would take me to the other shore, and from there to Cairo, the countryside not being a fit place now for anyone but its native inhabitants. But I was ill and exhausted, and had given myself up, under assault by the fevers of malaria each night. I had no thought even of crossing the river to see one of the doctors. I swallowed some of the tablets that were among my possessions, and spent my nights in feverish dreams of the rains of Swaffham and the wolves of Beni Hassan. When I saw the pitying expression in Abdel Rasul's eyes, I realized that I was too weak for there to be any other world for me.

The fever diminished, the waters receded from the plain, and the oppressive heat faded, especially in the evening. I wanted to go out and move about, and to resume my artwork, but Abdel Rasul shook his head: I was too frail to go out in the blazing heat of day, but when I kept insisting he at last agreed to take me along on his nocturnal peregrinations. Together we made our way under the moonlight, which made the tombs appear less desolate, while the wolves called to one another from afar. We went to the Ramesseum, breathing the fragrance of the green fields. Before us rose the trunks of the ancient palm trees, which had been bred and had multiplied for ages upon ages. I observed the tracks of Abdel Rasul's large, unshod feet in the soft sand; it was as if he left his imprint everywhere he went. We heard the sound of the water wheels irrigating the soil by night, long after the heat of the day and well away from the eyes of the irrigation inspectors. The water buffaloes and the blindfolded bulls rotated them in never-ending circles. Everything appeared unreal. The scoops drew up the water from the bottom of the well and dumped it into the canals leading to the field, the wheel's axle always turning within a vast hollow stone cut from basalt, shining with moisture and reflecting the moonbeams.

"That piece of granite," said Abdel Rasul, gesturing toward it, "before it became the axle of this waterwheel, was a pillar for the house of al-Qurna's mayor, which stood close to the banks of the Nile. A depraved man he was. He bedded only the daughters of Gypsies. After he died we used bulls to drag all these stones here; it took three nights, working until dawn, to move every stone.

"Before the mayor lived in the house, it served as a barracks for the French soldiers, who spent some time here while artists recorded these ruins. When the house was destroyed, British soldiers took it over and set up camp within its walls on their way to do battle with the armies of the Mahdi. I myself saw their campfires, as they smoked their pipes and cleaned the bayonets on their rifles. The honorable Mahdi was a hero but, like Orabi, he was unlucky.

"Before that these stones were the foundation of the little mosque until it succumbed to the floods that submerged the valley. Those who built the mosque had taken the stones from a Mamluk fortress of al-Zahir Baybars, when the sanjaks came to this land. And they say that the Mamluks took it from an old Coptic stronghold enclosing a church and monastic cells, and that the Copts had effaced all traces of the ancient pharaonic inscriptions the stones had borne, replacing them with images of the cross, which remain to this day."

In this solemn place, his voice seemed to draw its subject-matter from the echoes of long bygone eras. "How do you know all these things?" I asked him.

"This is what they say," he replied cryptically. "There are many tales. Each stone here has its tale to tell."

We walked a long way, and I felt the night air fill me with great energy. I wanted to work; I wasn't thinking of sitting for many hours amid temples so long silent, but it was essential that I prepare myself for the coming season. Having arranged matters so that my paintbrush should be my livelihood, I didn't dare tell my father that, in spite of myself, I had been transformed, cast in his image.

The season was still some weeks off; the excavations would not begin for at least another two months, but Naville came to me, catching me by surprise when he entered my residence amidst the houses of al-Qurna. I was stretched out upon my bed, which I had sprinkled with cold water. He stood beside me, towering over me, his thick moustache curled up at the ends until it connected with his muttonchops. As he looked down at me a smile I could not read played about his lips. Had he come to gloat, to mock me? Had Rosa told him, perhaps in one of their moments of shared sensual bliss, about the ill-fated offer I had made her? Had they paused to jeer at me and then resumed their lovemaking once more? It seemed as though he must not know anything about the truth of my feelings or the secret hatred I bore him.

He sat down before me and said simply, "You've given me a run for my money—I'm quite worn out from looking for you. I nearly gave up—are you in hiding from some legal judgment?" He was back to teasing me. "I've come early," he continued, "before the start of the season, expressly so as to seek you out!"

"I didn't think you needed anyone," I replied tightly.

"Now then, don't be cross," he said jovially. "There's nothing between us to warrant any of that. I've come to offer you a good job."

"I've submitted my resignation, as a matter of fact."

"Forget about that trifling job—it practically paralyzed you. I've come to offer you grander employment, perhaps the greatest occupation in southern Egypt. You're still young, but I think you're the best man for the job."

In spite of myself, I began to attend to his words. He started telling me about the Egyptian Department of Antiquities, the first agency of its kind in the world, founded in 1858 by the scholar Auguste Mariette, the man who composed the scenario for the opera *Aida*. He wished to preserve the artifacts from those who would plunder them, but the agency was unable to assume its role as guardian of Egypt's antiquities—it remained weak, for want of funding support. Its mission was to conserve the existing artifacts, to grant permission for excavations that set out to unearth more, and to take its share of the discoveries. This goal was not adequately fulfilled, and this displeased the current head of operations, who wanted greater authority for the administration, with more control over the vast wealth to be had. So he undertook to divide Egypt into two regions: one extending from Cairo to the city of Qus, and the other from Qus southward as far as the first cataract. Naville had decided that I should be the inspector for the antiquities of the southernmost territory. All these sprawling archaeological sites covering more than five hundred kilometers would be under my jurisdiction, and my salary would be four hundred pounds a year—which is to say that my modest wages as a copyist of ancient art would suddenly increase sevenfold.

I sincerely hated the man, but he had come to me offering the opportunity of a lifetime. In spite of myself, I would have to go with him to Cairo to meet Gaston Maspero, one of the most famous scholars of Egyptian antiquities, to whom everyone referred with reverence and respect. I had not yet recovered sufficient strength for such a long journey, but the offer was very tempting. I wondered, was I truly in love with Rosa, or had I attached myself to her because she represented the only possibility open to me in this fierce desert? Abdel Rasul brought us cups of mint tea, helped me pack my case, and insisted upon taking us in his boat across the river to the east bank.

The ship, which served Cook's Tours, was nearly empty. The only passengers onboard were employees, and some tourists fleeing the heat; Egyptians were not permitted to travel on this ship unless they were servants or cleaners. There was a long journey ahead of us, with much time to be spent in each other's company. The Nile was still dyed red from the floods. We did not speak seriously, Naville and I, until we had traveled together for some time. The ship turned with the Nile before Qena, and there were the peaks of the mountains, appearing to stop the flow of the river, the course of the currents, for the ship had reversed direction, as if to make its way back southward again. We were standing at the ship's rail, gazing at the rows of palm and Jerusalem thorn and sycamore. He drew a metal flask from his back pocket, curved so as to fit easily into that part of his trousers. He drank from it thirstily, wiping his moustache and belching in between gulps. He offered me the flask, but I declined. I wanted to keep my wits about me until I knew what sort of game he was playing with me.

All at once I heard him say, "We've split up. My wife found out about us and raised a great fuss. She had to go away, and my wife decided to accompany me from now on, for as long as the excavations continue."

I said, barely able to get the words out, "Were the two of you making fun of me?"

Waving the flask, he replied, "You mustn't think that. She was in love with you as well. She wished she had met you under other circumstances. But what was between us was passionate. I myself am not yet over losing her."

"Is that why you've designated me for this position—as some kind of compensation?"

"Don't be absurd. I don't owe you anything. You'll be a great help to me, and you'll facilitate the excavation works that fall within my remit—that's all there is to it. All I want is for you to provide me with some protection against theft and other such inconveniences; I shall take care of the rest."

My only mistake had been in not knowing he was in the way. How could I have stood any chance against him in a contest for her affections?

My meeting with Gaston Maspero went well—or at least I managed to sign a contract for employment according to the conditions Naville had conveyed to me. Maspero was surprised at how young I was, but even more so by the energy I had demonstrated and the experience I had acquired in the course of those few years. I was to preserve the opened tombs, as well as those that were targets for looters on a daily basis, and I was to sort out the work among the diggers, who were all vying to be assigned to the excavation at Thebes. I was, moreover, to take on all the thieves, be they peasants or museum curators or the specious scholars who hung about on the eastern bank, awaiting their chance.

"You've just become king of the city of the dead. You have your private palace within the halls of Medinet Habu, as well as your own private zoo."

So spoke Emilia Andrews when she visited me in my new house. The dahabeah that brought her and the other wealthy Americans had returned to Luxor with the start of the new season. I had no palace, just a modestly furnished government rest house, overlooked by the columns of the ancient temple, which lent it a certain grandeur. There was no zoo, but there was a small open space in front of the house that was filled with flowers; there was also a racehorse called Sultan, a donkey called San Aten, and a small gazelle. It was Abdel Rasul, who had become my preferred assistant, who had caught the gazelle in his net and brought it back to the house.

Was this a satisfactory solution? Had I returned victorious to Thebes? Abdel Rasul always prodded me with such questions when he brought me my mint tea with sugar every morning. Was this the paradise I had dreamt of? Each day I pondered the winged serpent incised on the front of the gate to Habu, wondering where, in my paradise, the serpent lay hidden. My heart was still tender; I had to reestablish Naville's friendship once more; I had to treat myself as a person of importance, an essential part of wealthy society—those who frequented the region for their own pleasure in its warm winters and its vivid legends. I chose my garments well, partook of my meals in a civilized manner, and spoke engagingly to matrons and young ladies. I shed the skin of the solitary rustic, and became once again an English gentleman who enjoyed his position and the privileges of his race.

My task, however, was more difficult than I had foreseen. The areas were vast, the tombs exposed, the temples unprotected, and the watchmen who undertook to guard them few and often in league with the thieves. It was my objective to erect iron fences around the temples and at the doorways to the tombs, to oversee the diggers who were doing the excavations at each site, and to inspect the sacks of manure transported by the donkeys to ensure that none contained smuggled goods. The place was rich—indeed, bloated—with treasure, but quite desperately deprived of all means of protection.

I rode my horse, Sultan, galloping in every direction, and I traveled by boat to the temples dispersed around Luxor, but I sometimes felt as if the business was beyond my capabilities. Old friends I reckoned had forgotten I existed descended upon me. Newberry turned up, carrying a permit to dig. He was able to make an excavation at one of the outermost sections of the valley, where he stumbled across four rare gold plates with the Apis bull inscribed upon them. The agreement was that he should take half—two plates only—and that the other two plates should go to the Egyptian Museum, but as he was an old friend I trusted him more than I should have, and deceit was part and parcel with the game of hunting for artifacts. I was enraged, but there was nothing I could do.

I knew a number of immensely wealthy swindlers, who invited me to their parties, such as Theodore Davis, whose assistant, Emilia, had secret connections to smugglers and thieves. How great was my astonishment when he offered a donation toward installing the iron gates to fortify some of the tombs; but my surprise dissipated when I realized that he, too, had got a license to dig in the Valley of Thebes.

Even Lord Amherst himself, my erstwhile benefactor—his daughter came by herself from England to try her hand on a dig; she had inherited from her father an infatuation with Egyptian relics, and she wanted to have her own private collection. I advised her to get well away from the already congested Valley of Thebes. She went south to dig for relics and, at Qubbat al-Hawa, near Aswan, she happened upon some rare papyrus manuscripts. They could not be divided, and she was an upright woman, who would not stoop to maneuvering behind my back. I gave her a statue that had been discovered at the Ramesseum, taking in exchange for it the rare papyri. I promised her I would draw up a copy of the originals for her.

Not everyone, however, was as conscientious as this lady. I was not equal to all those high-and-mighty types—it would have required more energy than I possessed to oppose them. All I could do was to apprehend some of the peasants, who would hide little figurines and scarabs inside the loads of manure they were transporting on the backs of their donkeys. I turned them over to the police and the courts, but the courts did no more than fine them a mere fifteen piasters. They were the least of the problem, and they were the only ones to meet with punishment, though the penalties were inconsequential. The law, however, was weaker than all of them, and the thieves were everywhere, all around me, closer to me than they had any business being.

I was at Edfu when I heard that the tomb of Amenophis II had been looted. A telegram bearing the news reached me swiftly. I had to return as quickly as possible to the Valley of the Kings. I spent the whole day shifting from one mode of transportation to another. When I arrived on the western shore I headed at once to the tomb. I descended its broken stairs into the depths, holding onto ropes for support, clutching a blazing torch. This was the most capacious of the tombs, used to inter a number of kings. The mummies had remained within it until recently, until Maspero asked me to move them to the museum in Cairo. I had in fact transferred all of them, with the exception of King Amenophis himself, whom I judged it unseemly to remove from his house.

I raised the torch to see. The mummy of the king was there all right, but it was mutilated, the head separated from the body, the forearms from the upper arms. The thief who had done this knew what he was doing—he was looking for any trinkets with which the mummy might be adorned; whether he found any or not I don't know. He hadn't dared to lift the fragments of linen packed with pitch to see whether anything might be hidden underneath, in the center of the mummy.

I turned around to see whether there was anything else besides the damage to the mummy. I didn't find the model of the sailing boat that had been in one of the corners. The kings had taken care that there should be such a boat amongst the goods closed within their tombs, for at a time when the wheel was unknown boats were the only means of transportation in life, as well as the way in which souls were conveyed to the afterlife. Once again, the thief had known what he was doing.

I was suffocating with the heat in that place, and beside myself with agitation. I extinguished the torch I was carrying and began stumbling toward the exit, feeling my way along. The watchmen, looking at me with indifference, responded lazily to my questions; as usual, they had seen nothing, they had heard nothing—they too were collaborators; indeed, it may have been one of them who arranged the theft. I turned my attention to the area surrounding the tomb, hoping to find some traces. At the entrance to the chamber I found two footprints, which had left their impression in the moist sand at the time of the robbery; the sands had dried beneath the sun, and the tracks had stayed as they were.

I knew whose footprint this was: the deep-sunk heel that seemed as if it was separated from the sole; the broad toes, each pointing in its own direction. This firm print, which seemed designed to show that the land belonged to none but the owner of that foot, the way an old wolf might mark its territory with its urine.

My first and most essential skill woke within me. I brought my papers and pencils and began sketching a picture of the foot. I drew it to scale and in the minutest detail, shading in around it as necessary to render it clear and unmistakable. Then I took it to the police. I had irrefutable evidence—no one could deny it.

The evening of that very day, policemen descended upon Abdel Rasul's house, having crossed in force from the eastern shore. The officer in charge, who was English, had responded to my urgent request, and my insistence upon the enormity of the offense. They turned the house upside down, but found nothing. They knocked upon the walls and dug beneath them in search of a secret cache, but again to no avail. They did not leave Abdel Rasul alone, however. They beat him and cut off his moustache; they unwrapped his turban and used it to bind his hands behind his back. Then they drove him before them amidst the villagers, who watched what was happening and trembled. I was standing close to the river as they propelled him toward the ferry. He looked directly at me, breathing hard. He was angry, feeling the insult. Ignoring the hands of his captors belaboring the back of his head, he focused his gaze on me. Each of us felt betrayed by the other.

"If I were English like you," his eyes said to me, "would you have treated me this way?"

They drove him past me. He had played me false; never had I imagined that he would take advantage of my absence and plunder my tombs. But were the tombs mine . . . or his?

He remained in prison for a number of weeks, but the judge paid no heed to the evidence I had submitted, not taking it seriously. Late into the night I heard the sound of drums and *mizmars* celebrating the safe return of Abdel Rasul to the village. The viper depicted upon the gates of Habu had stirred, and paradise was no longer safe.

Abdel Rasul did not come near me after that, but I saw his footprints everywhere, his constant effort to remind me that I was living upon his land. In fact, however, he was the least of my enemies. The most dangerous of them lived on the other shore: the innumerable dealers in antiquities, foreigners who got them for next to nothing from the peasants and sold them in fantastic quantities to the museums of Europe.

The most notorious of these was the German dealer Ansinger, who supplied the Berlin Museum with smuggled artifacts. He was active and strong, and the law protecting foreigners prevented me from getting anywhere near him or even thinking of laying a hand on him. I knew he had got his hands on an important artifact, perhaps the most significant archaeological find yet uncovered—namely, a colored statue or bust of a queen—something of this nature, at any rate. He was keeping it somewhere, waiting for the right moment to smuggle it out to the Berlin Museum. So Emilia whispered to me, pointing him out to me at a party.

"He's the most prodigious of all the thieves around here," she told me. "Look how sure of himself he is. He's happened upon things no one else ever has."

Winter society in Luxor was full of gossip and rumors, but Emilia spoke wrathfully of Ansinger, and I was even more enraged than she. But I did not have the authority to search his lodgings—he was a truly formidable enemy. The only thing I could do was prevent him from crossing to the western shore.

He didn't forgive me for it—since I took up this employment no one had forgiven me anything. He wrote an article for one of the French newspapers published in Alexandria that was a savage attack on me. He wrote in French, so as to get the immediate attention of Gaston Maspero, saying that I did not deserve this position, being nothing but a copyist, uneducated and unqualified; that from the time I assumed the responsibility for the valley there had been one disaster after another, with tomb robberies increasing—as if he himself were not one of those thieves; that the roof of King Seti's tomb had collapsed and Amenophis's tomb had been plundered; that there had been no end of catastrophes. What truly saddened me, though, was what happened on a certain October morning.

It was a warm morning, and for the first time in a long while I dreamed about Rosa. She was standing before me in the same place where we had been accustomed to watch the sun set behind the temple walls. She was asking for my forgiveness, hoping for another chance with me. I woke longing to visit my flower garden, but I found the gazelle dead. It lay there stiff-legged, its ears strained as if to listen, its glassy eyes vacant, and its body cold. I cried out in anguish and turned about fearfully, only to find another corpse: my donkey, San Atun, lay dead as well. The valley of the dead was indeed full of the dead, and they were meant for me. I hurried to my charger; him I found, fortunately, still standing. Some miracle must have kept him alive—or perhaps his turn had not yet come.

Furious, I spurred him forward, plunging into the streets of al-Qurna, which were empty. I knew everyone rose with the dawn to go to the fields or to cross to the other side of the river, where work was to be had serving the tourists. I pounded my fist upon his door and shouted, "Come out here, Abdel Rasul!"

I thought he must have done his deed and fled to the other side of the river, but out he came. He was wearing only his undershirt and long under-trousers. His moustache was awry, his head bare, and his feet unshod. His appearance did not deceive me—I knew he had not slept that night—that he had been lurking about my house, looking for an opportunity.

"You vile traitor!" I shouted at him. "You've killed my animals—I've no doubt you set out poison for them!"

He gazed at me steadily. "Why," he said, "would I do such a thing to helpless beasts? If I wanted to poison anyone it would be you, yourself."

His reply infuriated me all the more. I was shaking, and my stallion, Sultan, stamped his hooves uneasily. "You couldn't get to me," I said, "and so you killed them."

"Our beasts also die," he said. "Where do you think you're living? This is the valley of the dead—the place is full of snakes and scorpions, wolves and jackals. Give thanks to your English god that you wake each morning and find yourself still alive!"

He didn't retreat, but stood there with his chest thrust out. I remembered his humiliation, when he was being shoved here and there by the police; now, at this moment, he was stronger than I was. He could take revenge, and not for himself alone; rather, he had gained the power to threaten me. I jerked the stallion's reins and departed; there was no point in turning to the police; this was his land, in the end, and he was surrounded by kith and kin, while I was but a passing stranger, as he had said to me on more than one occasion.

I dug a big hole behind the house and buried the gazelle and the donkey in it. While I was heaping dirt upon their still bodies, I realized all at once that I no longer had a place in this valley. When Maspero's telegram reached me, informing me of my transfer from the Valley of the Kings to the northern district, I understood that everything was preordained, and that I must leave this hot and savage place just when I had taken my first steps in the realm of archaeological excavation, having learned—thanks to a great many scholars, amateurs, and thieves—how I might discover the secrets of that strange parcel of earth.

After protracted delays and postponements, excuses made on myriad pretexts, I at last took my leave. I crossed the river on a felucca. I hadn't told anyone when I was going, but I found Abdel Rasul standing on the shore. This was the moment of his final triumph over me, and I expected him to greet me with smug satisfaction and derision, but he did no such thing.

"I've come to bid you farewell," he said. "I bear you no grudge. If you should return to Thebes, you will be my guest."

He said nothing of what had come to pass between us, neither his betrayal of me nor my treachery toward him. He was noble in his way, despite his abject poverty. He was at any rate more honorable than the robbers operating on the other side of the river.

As the boat began its northward journey, all the temples, obelisks, and lofty columns passed before my eyes in a silent farewell. I understood that this place would be ever in my heart, and that I would return to it someday—but when? I didn't know.

I received my assignment as director of antiquities, specifically as director of Lower Egypt. I sensed that Maspero still trusted me and didn't want to leave me in the lurch—merely to lessen the volume of criticism directed at him and his men. He exchanged me for a Mr. Arthur Weigall, assigning each of us to the position formerly held by the other: a straightforward trade, as he told me in all simplicity; to me, however, it meant exchanging one world for another—exchanging a land I knew and loved, whose details I had memorized and dreamed about at night, for an alien realm about which I knew nothing. I was no longer that callow youth who had disembarked at Alexandria thirteen years earlier. I had changed: I knew Arabic well, I had encountered many kinds of dishonesty and treachery, and I had grown skilled at working in the field of excavation and exposing what was real and what was false in the world of antiquities. But Cairo was not my domain. The raucous society of foreigners alarmed me; I would have to seek out my own cave, my private cell.

I decided to live at Saqqara, at the midpoint between two worlds, close to the dividing line between Upper Egypt and the Delta. It was a primitive region, full of promises yet to be unearthed. I had been there in the company of Flinders Petrie after he moved there from Tel al-Amarna. Here was ancient Memphis, which had been the capital of Egypt for thousands of years, after the Pharaohs discovered that Thebes was too remote to rule over such a vast empire. The area was enchanted and wretched at one and the same time: full of royal tombs and mastabas, small pyramids and the huge stepped pyramid that was the only one of its kind, funerary temples, and even Coptic monasteries. It was a veritable complex of interconnecting ancient remains, but subject to ruin on an alarming scale.

Perhaps, I persuaded myself, I was getting closer to the dream of discovering Akhenaten's tomb, waiting for me somewhere in this area. Even with the sadness that weighed upon my heart, I was confident that matters would improve. In spite of myself, I was pervaded by the dream that had possessed Newberry, who had now left Egypt and settled in London. I had heard about the discovery of the walls of ancient Troy, in Turkey, as well as that of the Labyrinth on the isle of Crete, and I dreamed of making a comparable discovery—a discovery so significant it would raise my status from that of a mere copyist to that of an explorer whose name would be remembered in books and encyclopedias. I was certain, just as Newberry had been, that the tomb of the heretic king was waiting for me somewhere!

But then some Frenchmen, those frogeaters, got in the way and spoiled everything.

There were only fifteen of them: a number of men, as well as two women and two children. They arrived on a Saturday at midday—a cold January day. It was clear that Saqqara was the last stop on their crazy expedition. They were exceedingly drunk and boisterous, and they filled this silent realm of ancient ruins with their brouhaha. They were looking for a place to rest, and all they could find was Mariette Pasha House, where Petrie and his wife were staying. It was a government house established by the head director, Mariette, who had founded the Egyptian Department of Antiquities. As long as Petrie was there stopping the area from being utterly ruined, Maspero gave him the right to live there.

The Frenchmen invaded the house; fortunately, Petrie's wife was not there—the house was empty but for a single watchman armed only with a cudgel, which he dared not raise against the Frenchmen. He fled from his post and went to the other watchmen stationed in the area, but they were likewise fearful of taking them on. Europeans claimed a deadly inviolability in a country they had assiduously humiliated for years upon years. There was nothing Raïs Khalifa, the chief watchman, could do.

"I'll go and fetch the foreigner, Carter," was all he said.

I was away at the edge of the desert, and with me were a number of guests whom Maspero had sent from Cairo. As soon as I heard what had happened I decided to return at once, but matters in Saqqara deteriorated faster than I could get there. The Frenchmen had become still more inebriated, and decided to go into the Serapeum, a complex of passageways and mausoleums and funerary temples surrounding the pyramid. The watchmen were still just as fearful as before. The guard told them they could not enter without paying the admission fee and purchasing tickets. Then Mr. Mohammed Effendi came and asserted his authority, amid the clamor of objections and protests. In the end they gave in, but they bought only eleven tickets. They wanted to enter all at once, but the guard stopped them. He wanted each of them to show his ticket, but they broke down the flimsy door and entered in spite of him. They dispersed through the corridors; not one of them knew anything about the character of the place, and no guide dared approach them when they were so riled up. Off they went, and then they came back again.

"It's too dark in there," they shouted at the watchman. "We want candles."

The guard had nothing of the kind; such was not the custom. They grew more enraged. One of them punched him in the nose, laying him out on the ground. Then they demanded their money back from Mr. Mohammed Effendi, but the man couldn't do it. The tickets had already been processed, and a refund would come out of his salary, which was small to begin with—he would lose every piaster of it and more. Once more, they set upon him. They snatched his tarbush, the symbol of his status relative to the other workers, threw it on the ground, and trampled upon it. They took all the money he had on his person, then returned once more to Mariette Pasha House to carry on with their wild debauch.

When I got there I found all my workers in a bad way, beaten and insulted. The doors to the house had been pulled off their hinges and there were wine bottles everywhere. I would not have imagined that these people could imbibe such quantities. They stared at me in perplexity when I entered the house—perhaps they hadn't expected any other Europeans here, only the humble peasants.

"You gentlemen," I said to them, "have destroyed private property. You have no right to be here, and you must leave at once."

They all burst out talking at once. They were speaking French and, as is usual with the French, the women spoke loudest. One of the women came forward. She spoke a bit of English, and recounted to me in halting speech what my men had already told me outside. I said to her, "You have no right to take back the money, nor any right to be here, and if you don't leave immediately I shall evict you by force."

One of the men stepped forward then and brought his fist toward my face; I was able to get hold of his arm and push it away. I turned to Raïs Khalifa and asked him to assemble the watchmen who were at hand. I was being threatened, and there was no retreat. The Frenchmen, though, as soon as they saw the watchmen coming to attack them armed with sticks and chairs and whatever was to hand, delivered a painful blow to Raïs Khalifa's head. He looked at me and asked what to do.

"Defend yourselves," I told them firmly.

And, for the first time, the watchmen took courage and raised their sticks and clubs and laid into the Frenchmen, delivering blows to their heads and bodies—it was the first time Egyptians, since the defeat of their leader Orabi, had dared to raise weapons against Europeans. They drove them out of the house, so the Frenchmen began to pelt us with stones, but the clubs overtook them until they all took flight and cleared off. Some of my men were wounded, and many of the furnishings had been demolished. I saw to the men first, and then went to submit a procès-verbal of the incident at the al-Badrashayn police station—but I found that the Frenchmen had arrived there before me.

Things quickly got out of hand. The newspapers broadcast the incident each from its own perspective. The French papers offered up peaceable French tourists whose only fault was to have asked for their money back, whereupon they were set upon by a wicked gang of Bedouins led by a conniving Englishman; the English papers, meanwhile, attempted to defend me, but their account of the events was vague. Mine was one voice against fifteen French voices, and the peasants had no voice at all. I wrote dozens of reports and procès-verbaux and went to a number of precincts for questioning, and each time everyone's questions were settled, but the situation remained tense, until Lord Cromer himself summoned me to his office.

I did not like to go and see this man. I felt that he treated me as if I were an Englishman fashioned from different clay. He sat there with his grimly set features, his expression haughty as he faced me. From the corner of my eye I glimpsed an immense file with my name on it, stuffed with papers and newspaper clippings. He looked weary and impatient. He listened to my brief report of the incident without interrupting or questioning me.

At last he spoke. "You will go to Monsieur de la Pollinaire," he said, "the French consul general, and apologize to him for what has happened."

"What is the sense of that?" I cried, stunned.

Abruptly, out of patience, he replied, "It is the only way to close such a sticky case. We don't want any more tension between ourselves and the French. Go and apologize, and let that be the end of it."

I inclined my head and withdrew. I had no intention of apologizing—this was the final humiliation for me: I was not about to abase myself before a bunch of drunken louts, no matter who they were, high-status employees or not. It was no concern of mine if one of them was the director of the gas company and another was the sister of the French consul and still another the comptroller for the Bureau of Finance. I was convinced I had done the right thing: I had defended myself and my men.

I told no one of my intention, but everyone knew it when, as the days passed, I did not go to meet the consul. A great many people sent me letters entreating me to apologize, to relinquish my pride and thus avert a crisis. The news had reached Paris—the Ministry of Foreign Affairs was putting pressure on the consul, the consul was leaning on Lord Cromer, and he was leaning on me. But I was fed up, sick of it all. I had had enough of disappointments, and I had no wish to surrender what was left of my dignity.

◆ ◆ ◆

"And so," said Aisha, "you didn't apologize—is that right?" They were sitting on the edge of a wooden bench in the middle of a garden in Ismaïliyya Square. The vendors offering lupine-seed snacks and roasted corn had begun lighting torches; the area between the square and the bank of the Nile had filled entirely with splashes of light.

"In spite of all the pressure everyone was putting on me," he said, "I found that I couldn't . . . nor did I want to apologize. Lord Cromer wouldn't forgive me for that. He ordered my transfer to Tanta, far from everything I knew and cherished. The nature of the excavations I worked on changed—now it was all digging in silt, not the dry desert sand. And I uncovered nothing but the remains of animals, rather than of kings. I was all but suffocating, I felt like death every day. Lord Cromer had put my back to the wall, leaving me no alternative, as far as I could see, but to tender my resignation."

Silence fell between them. The street vendors still circled them in vain. Aisha felt how lost he was, and how lost she herself was as well: the two of them with no longer a piece of solid ground to stand upon. "What will you do now?" she asked.

"I don't know. I'll wander about, and look and search—perhaps there will be another opportunity. I don't want to return in defeat to my country in the north. I still have a dream . . ."

"What dream is that?"

"I'll find someone to help me discover Akhenaten's tomb. He is the greatest king of ancient times. Like me, he refused to allow others to determine his fate. He refused to submit to the gods that decreed the fate of humankind. He chose one lucid god: the light. He sought to find his own lost soul just as each of us must do."

Aisha was returning home alone by night, heading toward the high commissioner's palace, while he set off in another direction. They didn't know whether or not they would ever meet again, but she was thinking about him, and about that strange king of whom he had told her. The guards set about questioning her before allowing her to enter, but her mind was on other things—she was thinking that she was much in need of someone who could guide her and tell her what to do. She was in need of someone like Akhenaten.

6 • Sayyida Zaynab

THE DRIVER PULLED UP THE REINS. The horse stopped and whinnied softly. Aisha was jostled inside the carriage. She clutched her bag so as not to drop it—it contained all she had in the world: a few gold sovereigns she had snatched from the high commissioner's palace. In her other hand she held a copy of the newspaper *al-Liwa*. Pointing out the building, the driver said, "This is the place, miss."

She hesitated before stepping down. She felt she had not yet sufficiently collected her wits, and she didn't know how she was to conduct herself. She found herself in front of a black sign which, in gleaming white script, bore the words *al-Liwa Publishing*. The driver grumbled at the delay; it seemed she had no choice but to disembark and approach the entrance. She mounted the worn steps, which led only to a single door. She didn't need to obtain permission to enter, for the door was open. She went in and found herself in a vast room full of men in European dress, all intent upon their work behind small desks stacked with papers. In the corner stood a little machine making a ceaseless racket. High up on the wall was a great sign reading, "He who lives for himself alone did not deserve to be born." She read it aloud in an undertone, not noticing that everyone had stopped working and sat staring at her. Clearly it was the first time a woman had ventured into this place. One of the effendis approached her.

"May I help you?" he asked. "Have you a complaint?"

She was wearing an abaya, which covered her body, and she wore a small hat, but she had not put on a veil. Her face was showing, brown, delicate-featured, alluring. She hesitated a moment, then burst out with, "I want to speak to the Pasha."

He looked at her, smiling, not put off by her boldness.

"We have only one Pasha," he told her, "namely, the Leader, Mustafa Kamil, who isn't here at the moment. In any case, you'd need an appointment to see him."

Flustered, Aisha cast about helplessly. Neither of them said anything for a moment. Then the man took pity on her and spoke again. "The director of the paper, Abdel Rahman Effendi al-Rafiy, is here," he said. "You can meet with him."

She followed him to a narrow corridor and from there to a dimly lit interior office, from which emanated an odor of rancid ink. He gestured toward a man who could scarcely be seen behind the papers that covered his desk. But as soon as he shifted position his round face appeared, and Aisha knew him at once: he was the journalist who had spoken with her at Lord Cromer's house. He stared back at her, trying to remember her.

"Why, it's you!" he said. "Didn't we meet at that alarming house, with that overbearing, arrogant man?"

She nodded her head, smiling—she liked the way he revealed his surprise, and his apt description of Lord Cromer. The other man sensed that he was no longer needed; he gave a nod, and left. Al-Rafiy gestured to her to sit in one of the chairs. She pushed aside the papers lying on it and sat down with difficulty. He stood in front of her.

"Did Lord Cromer send you to spy on us?" he asked.

She laughed merrily. "He sent me," she said, "to spy on the Pasha himself. Would it be possible for me to meet with him?"

"We prefer to call him 'the Leader,' he said. "Meeting him is no problem, but he's a difficult man. I can easily give you all the information you want . . . what exactly *do* you want?"

"I want to work here with all of you," she replied gravely. "I'm fluent in English and I know French as well. And . . ."

His expression was one of astonishment. "What do you mean by 'work with' us?" he said.

"I've left Lord Cromer's house," she said, "and I won't go back to work there. Have you got a job for me?"

He didn't answer her. He left her there, hurrying from the room. Everyone saw him go into the Leader's office, seize a big black telephone, turn the crank rapidly, and tap the instrument repeatedly. He asked to be connected right away to the number he requested. Aisha had no idea what was happening, or what had made him so uneasy when just a moment ago he had been so jocular.

He came back out of breath, and spoke hurriedly. "The Leader will be here shortly," he said. "You must wait for him—we'll give you some tea and water . . . something to eat as well, if you like."

This sudden solicitude surprised her. Al-Rafiy made a show of appearing busy at his work, and the other men kept getting up from their desks, pretending to move papers about, all the while throwing quizzical glances her way. She took nothing but a glass of water.

The Leader was there in about half an hour. He was a man of short stature, and young despite his frail appearance. Supporting himself on a cane, he was dressed in a thick coat and a tarbush was jammed upon his head in such a way that only a bit of his face could be seen. When al-Rafiy brought Aisha to him, she found him standing in the middle of the room, leaning upon his cane. He raised his head and studied her. Aisha was startled by the brightness of his eyes, which blazed in spite of his pallor, as if he had channeled all the life-force from his body and poured it into his eyes. He took in the brownness of her complexion, her attenuated peasant stature. A slight smile appeared upon his face.

"You're young," he said, "to work in a place like this. Can you tell me about Lord Cromer—what he's up to in his house, what he thinks of us as Egyptians?"

She didn't know what he meant. "Sir," she said, "please forgive me. I came to look for work, not to talk about Lord Cromer!"

The Leader seemed ill at ease, and al-Rafiy intervened.

"The matter of a job is already settled—in fact, you're to be appointed translator for *al-Liwa*. What the Pasha means is . . ."

The Leader held up his hand, silencing him, and bent his piercing gaze upon Aisha once more. "I don't wish to know anything about Cromer's personal life," he said. "That doesn't concern me. But he is an enemy of our nationalist movement, the man standing in the way of Egypt's independence. I want to know what he thinks of us, the Egyptians—does it occur to him that we deserve our freedom?"

She didn't know what to say. She was too embarrassed to speak to him of the contempt Lord Cromer and his wife harbored toward Egyptians, Cromer's perception of them as an anonymous, undifferentiated mob of rabble-rousers. She tried to remember something specific. "He read *al-Liwa* every day," she said. "I myself translated some of the articles for him, especially after what happened at Dinshaway."

The Leader's face brightened, and al-Rafiy rubbed his hands together delightedly, the two of them feeling that they had not been working in vain, and that their heated arguments and protests had reached their greatest enemy. "And what," said the Leader, "did he do then?"

Aisha thought for a moment. Then she said, "He saw ghosts."

"What?!"

"He saw the ghosts of the farmers from Dinshaway and imagined that they'd been able to steal into his garden, that they'd come to settle accounts with him."

A strange thing happened then. The Pasha suddenly cast aside his cane and stood up straight, as if all at once his health had been restored to him. He began to caper about with joy, and al-Rafiy did likewise. They became two overgrown children, raising their voices and shouting. The men in the big room got up from their desks and flocked to the office door.

"Listen to this, all of you!" cried the Leader. "Lord Cromer has started seeing ghosts! He's begun to take leave of his senses!"

A jubilant atmosphere took over, everyone feeling that some sort of victory, however small, had been achieved. Laughing, the Pasha turned to Aisha. Taking note of her dark complexion and her pharaonic appearance, he asked her, "What sort of wage has al-Rafiy set for your employment?"

"He didn't mention wages," she replied.

"You are hired," said the Leader, "at a rate of five pounds flat."

This time it was Aisha's turn to exult—she had not supposed that her good luck could extend so far. But now, from the back of the crowd of men, one surprised voice arose. "What exactly is going on?" it demanded. "Is this a demonstration?"

Everyone turned toward the entrance, where a rather tall young man was standing. He was brown skinned, and broad shouldered despite his slight frame. In his hand he held a bundle of folded papers. He stared in wonder, taking in the festive mood, so alien to the air of seriousness that prevailed in the house of *al-Liwa*. He came forward and extended his hand, with its long fingers, toward the Leader.

"Greetings, Pasha," he said.

No one noticed that the Leader's euphoria had diminished slightly. He shook the young man's hand, trying to smile at him. "Greetings, artist—you've come at the right moment. We are celebrating the arrival in our midst of the youngest and first female editor at *al-Liwa*. With her commences the Egyptian woman's awakening and entry into the field of journalism. Is this not a moment worthy of your brush?"

The youth turned to her and bent his clear-eyed gaze upon her. He had a long, narrow face and a comically small beard. He ducked his head shyly and looked away. The rest all began to go back to their tasks, and Aisha, not knowing what else to do, drew back until she was against the wall. Al-Rafiy, meanwhile, observed the exchange in silence.

The Leader, reaching for the young man's bundle of papers, said, "This, Aisha, is Mahmoud Mukhtar, one of Egypt's talented young artists. What have you brought us today, Mukhtar?"

The other sighed with fatigue—clearly he'd had no sleep. "What have I brought you, Pasha?" he said. "Drawings and more drawings."

He spread the papers on the desk. The Leader stood back to look at them. The artist's strokes were brutal, thick and black, as if they had been etched into the paper: pharaonic forms well-known to Aisha. She had seen their like when she went about with Sister Margaret, but here they were different, as if they had taken on a new quality—cruel in some way. For some moments the Leader was absorbed in contemplation of them, and the youth seized the opportunity to turn to Aisha, his expression warm, as if he knew her from somewhere. A smile was all she could manage. It was pleasant to look upon his features.

The Leader spoke. "Splendid, Mukhtar," he said. "We'll publish these drawings on the front page. It is important to remind the people that they have an ancient civilization—this will bolster their self-respect and their desire for freedom."

"Thank you, Pasha," said Mukhtar, smiling. "I wanted to draw something that would help us endure the present."

The Pasha once more studied the drawings. Then he fixed his gaze upon Mukhtar. "But," he said meaningfully, "where is Islam, Mukhtar? The civilization to which we are all connected? Have you forgotten that we are affiliated with the Ottoman state, be it ever so hateful to the English?"

Mukhtar looked at him in surprise. "I haven't forgotten," he said, "but the civilization of the Pharaohs is the thing that always distinguishes us—that is what makes Egypt unique and unparalleled. Islamic civilization, on the other hand, is something we share with many others."

"And who ever said that we wished to stand alone? Why should Egypt face by herself the British Empire in all its might?"

"I am not a leader or a hero, Pasha. I merely depict what I feel . . ."

Mukhtar got to his feet as if about to take his leave, but the Pasha gestured for him to wait. He was breathing hard, like one readying himself for an even more difficult confrontation. "And is it," he said, "this obscure feeling of

'Egyptian-ness' that sent you to that other newspaper—*al-Siyaasa*—and made you contribute a drawing to their pages? Don't you know that they are partisans of the English?"

Mukhtar's face colored. He stepped forward and began gathering up his papers. "What I know," he said, "is that they are a liberal political party, and that Lutfi el-Sayed is a nationalist, seeking freedom just like the rest of us."

"What freedom? The freedom belonging to vassals of the English?"

The tension had escalated suddenly. Al-Rafiy, who had remained silent all the while, now stepped in. "I think," he said, "that the two of you need to sit down and come to an understanding. Let's go, Aisha—let me show you around this place where you'll be working."

He took her by the arm and left the room. They passed through another corridor. Her heart quailed as the voices rose in the exchange still taking place inside the office. But now al-Rafiy was pointing out to her a small desk jammed into a corner. He tried to smile. "We need someone who can translate the Leader's speeches and letters into English. We had another translator who sat here, but he left us and went over to *al-Siyaasa*."

Nodding her head toward the other room, Aisha said, "The paper that the Leader is arguing with him about?"

"Just so," said al-Rafiy. "I'm not angry with that paper the way the Pasha is . . . Lutfi Pasha is a great man. His only fault is that he doesn't hate the English enough."

He laughed easily, picked up a sheaf of newspapers from the corner, and set them before her. Dust particles floated up from them, and Aisha began to cough. Al-Rafiy laughed again and said, "See how everything that comes from the English stirs up trouble?"

Thus began her first day at work: far from the house of Lord Cromer, facing life's wide-open prospects. She couldn't believe she'd got a job so easily; she had chosen the right place. She resolved to finish all her tasks today, so as to prove to them how capable she was. She heard the Leader's voice as he left, the others calling out their good-byes. Then the voices began gradually to fade, while she pursued her work, absorbed. But when she looked up after some time had passed, she discovered that she was almost entirely alone. The effendis' desks had been vacated, but the machine in the corner of the hall never stopped humming. There was no one but a single cleaner, who stood leaning against the door, patiently waiting for her to finish. She would have to gather up her things and go—but where? She had abandoned the only place that had sheltered her in this city, with no other alternative to fall back on. She sat frozen in place, while the cleaner stared at her uncomprehendingly. Then he withdrew, leaving her sitting there in the room, overwhelmed by her fear and loneliness.

A few minutes later, however, she found al-Rafiy standing before her, smiling kindly at her, though he looked exhausted. He gathered up the papers she had finished, shaking his head as he leafed through them. He looked her in the eye and said, "You've had a full day. But you're not going to spend the night at this desk, are you?"

The color rose in Aisha's cheeks and she lowered her head. "I haven't any place to go," she said.

"That is a problem," he replied. "Why didn't you say something when it was still light outside?"

He thought for a bit and shook his head in perplexity. Then he spoke. "Wait here," he said. "I'll be right back."

She picked up her bag and tried to arrange the papers cluttering her desk, to move them away from the older piles. Al-Rafiy returned, wearing his coat, and made ready to leave. As they descended the stairs, he told her in a merry tone, "I can't take you to my house—my wife would evict me. We'll sort something out."

She walked with him along Noubar Street, which stretched before them, while the sky darkened and the streetlights were illuminated slowly, as if they were waking up. He asked her where she had learned English. When she told him it was in Asyout, he exclaimed with a laugh, "Good heavens—in the midst of all those Saïdis?"

He knew the city well, and he knew where her former school was, too. He had practiced law in Asyout immediately after graduating from law school. He spent a full year in the offices of Alouba Bey, the most famous attorney in Upper Egypt, but when the Leader, Mustafa Kamil, founded *al-Liwa*, he invited al-Rafiy to serve as its editorial director, and since he had been a dedicated member of the Nationalist Party from the time of its inception, he left his legal post and with it the city of Asyout, and went straight to Cairo. He could not disappoint his leader, but he did disappoint his father, who had wanted to see him follow in his footsteps and become a judge. He feared for his son, subject to the capricious winds of politics. Al-Rafiy, however, had no regrets about leaving the legal profession behind—he was confident that he would return to it one day, for the commoners all around him were too ignorant to know their rights, and would be in need of someone to guide and instruct them in these matters. He would write a book on the subject, but only after he had rested a bit from the exertions of the nationalist cause.

They stopped before a small building with glass doors. "The owner of this hotel," he said, "is Greek, and he has a good reputation. You won't run into any trouble if you spend the night here."

The Greek peered at her, puzzled. It was rare for a young Egyptian woman to come to the hotel alone. Al-Rafiy talked to him, assuring him that he was responsible for her, and that he would look after her. All around her in the hotel lobby she could see residents of various nationalities, none of them Egyptian, and she was afraid the owner of the place would not receive her, but at last he nodded his assent. Al-Rafiy turned to her, and drew a whole sovereign from his pocket. Aisha shook her head no, but al-Rafiy insisted she take it. "It's part of your salary," he said, adding, "Consider it an advance. I'll come back in the morning and take you to a housing agent who can help you find lodgings."

At last she was alone, sitting in her hotel room, which was small and clean, presided over by a large picture of the Acropolis, which crowned the hills of Athens. She locked the door securely behind her, but the voices coming from the corridor and the adjacent rooms still unsettled her. She was hungry, having eaten nothing all day, but she didn't dare leave the room. She sighed, stretched out upon the bed, and lifted her feet high in the air—the sense of liberty that possessed her was stronger than her hunger. She had reclaimed her name and hidden the sign of the cross beneath her clothing. Thus began a new life in a new city, and yet she felt at this moment the most pressing need of her mother. Here in such a vast city the two of them might hide together. Surely Aisha would one day find some means of contacting her mother—but first she must find a place to live, and settle down.

The following day, however, was an exhausting one for her. Al-Rafiy came by for her in the morning, punctual as the clock. He took her to a housing agent's office, but he hadn't time to stay with her; he left her with the agent and went to the newspaper office. The search began by winding through the tortuous streets and alleyways. She was ill at ease with the agent, who gestured with his hands, and spoke in a loud voice, cursing everyone. Her only option, though, was to follow him meekly. On the other hand, this did not sit well with the landlords she met, who looked askance at her, plainly suspicious, and shook their heads in flat refusal. They knew that a young girl alone, dwelling amidst families, would turn men's heads and arouse the ire of their wives, stirring up gossip.

She went with the agent to the boardinghouses and apartment blocks in the neighborhood that were reserved for unmarried women, but the rent was high, nearly equivalent to her salary, and all of them were full of Greek or Jewish women. These were shopgirls, waitresses, and entertainers: independent women who enjoyed their unmarried lives. They had no use for a prim Egyptian girl, imposing herself upon their world. He took her to the rooftops of the great houses, where the smell of soap and carbolic acid wafted from every corner, and the washing lines, laden with clean linens, obscured the sky. Here were servant girls, house cleaners, doormen, and unemployed country folk, who alarmed her. He descended with her to the basements, small, foul-smelling rooms squashed in among the old cheese factories and cheap wine presses, the tailors' and cobblers' workshops. Suddenly, the city loomed large before her—she could no longer face it on her own.

"Why don't you just marry someone, anyone," the agent said to her, "and solve the problem of where to live?"

She didn't answer him. She was tired and overcome, and there was no time to go to the newspaper. At the end of the day she returned, with an effort, to the hotel. The Greek eyed her doubtfully as she requested a second night. As she had done the previous night, she locked the door to her room and confined herself there until morning.

The accommodations proposed by the agent today were even worse than those of the day before. He conducted Aisha on a series of frenzied expeditions through the city, while her lungs filled with dust and her chest contracted in the isolated rooms into which no sunlight penetrated. She was upset by the leering doormen and the servant girls' obscene gestures. The locales shifted, the streets growing narrow and dusty, the houses more squalid and crowded. She was assaulted by the odor of feces, the remains of pickled vegetables, and bodily decay. Aisha begged the agent to take her away from this nightmare.

She couldn't believe her eyes when Noubar Street appeared before her once more, and she saw the sign bearing the legend *al-Liwa Publishing*—it was like a life ring. She was worn out and in despair. "No more," she said to the agent, and with that she turned and left him.

"But miss," he called after her, "I want my fee!"

She didn't turn around—she was afraid she might burst into tears. She didn't know where she would go. She went quickly through the door of the building, then stopped. She couldn't let them see her in such an abysmal state. She sank down upon the stairs and took off her shoes. What if the Leader should see her in this condition? She sat on all the same, paralyzed with exhaustion.

Then she heard a voice calling to her. "Why are you sitting there like that? Are you all right?"

She drew her bare feet back hastily and hid them under her skirts. She brushed the traces of tears from her eyes and lifted her face to him. It wasn't the Leader—it was the tall, brown-skinned young man with the small beard and the familiar eyes. In his hand he held some folded papers. He continued down the stairs until he was next to her, and smiled as though he hadn't noticed her disheveled appearance.

"I was asking after you today," he said simply. "They said you'd been gone since yesterday."

She felt the blood rise to her face. "Why?" she exclaimed.

All at once he was at a loss, as if he hadn't expected such a question. At last he said, "I wanted to explain what happened between me and the Pasha. I haven't abandoned my principles. *Al-Siyaasa* is not so bad as he imagines."

He knew, and of course she knew as well, that he was trying to find a pretext for talking to her. That was all right. "I'm happy to listen," she said. "I'm very good at listening—only I'm so tired just now."

"So I see," he replied. "You look as if you'd been lost in all the streets of the city."

He had noticed her discarded shoes and her bare feet, and she was mortified. "I'm a stranger to this city," she said. "I was looking for a place to live, but so far I've failed."

His face lit up. "So that's how it is," he said. "You're spent from making the rounds of the city—you must be hungry as well. I'll take you straightaway to al-Rakib's shop, and then to Umm Abbas, who can rent you a room. Once you've had enough to eat all your problems will be solved."

There was something so compelling in his manner that she could not object—perhaps it was the charming simplicity with which he spoke, or perhaps his mysterious promise that all her problems would be solved was what overcame her shyness and her fatigue. She stood up to join him, and he waited for her, smiling, as she put her shoes back on.

They walked together in the street, which was thronged with people. He was taller than she was and she had to strain to hear clearly what he was saying, observing his little black beard wagging as he spoke. He had a long stride, and she was out of breath with trying to keep up with him. He waved his long-fingered hands in the air, emphasizing his words—he was determined to explain to her his passing dispute with the Leader. Thanks to the time she had spent in the high commissioner's palace, she knew that Egyptian Pashas quarreled with one another constantly, and that many who declared their hostility toward the English went furtively to meet with Lord Cromer and inform him of their fealty, trying to assert their own rights with him over those of others, but she was certain that the Leader had done no such thing.

They entered al-Rakib's restaurant in Sayyida Zaynab Square. She had let Mukhtar take the lead—there was nothing for it but to trust him. The proprietor seated them behind a wooden partition, to prevent men from stealing furtive glances at her. Aisha felt at ease: after the period of exile and rootlessness she had endured, things could now settle down a little. The broth was hot, and as they let it sit for a while a layer of fat formed on the surface, keeping it warm. She burned her tongue a few times, Mukhtar laughing out loud when he saw her confusion. The restaurant was filled with diners, and the Sayyida Zaynab Mosque, which was opposite, was filled with supplicant worshippers.

"Who is this Umm Abbas?" asked Aisha.

"She is the proprietress of the house where I live, in Gamamiz Lane. Since she was willing to accommodate a nuisance of an artist like me, a man with a hammer and chisel in his hand day and night, surely she'll look after a girl on her own, like you."

He didn't ask her about herself, or inquire as to the reasons she found herself alone as she was in the streets of Cairo. He kept talking about everything else, all the while devouring chunks of meat and breaking a loaf of bread into large pieces as if he hadn't eaten in years. Aisha remembered Rizq's manner of eating, and felt a lump in her throat. She studied Mukhtar's narrow face and his foolish beard. He wasn't much older than she was, and yet he talked as if he were the master of all creation.

She had never heard of the village of Tanbara, from which he came. Perhaps it resembled her own distant hamlet, now lost to her, with its houses of mud brick and straw, its sprawling fields and thriving crops, the berry bushes and sycamore and willow trees, its intersecting irrigation canals and heaps of manure, waterwheels that never stopped turning, and frogs that strained their voices with their croaking. His father was the mayor of his village, a man of dignity, whose status derived from his ascetic and God-fearing ancestors, who had come from the distant lands of the Maghreb. They had been on their way to perform the hajj in the house of God, but they had settled in the rural heart of the Delta.

Mukhtar was born the only son of the mayor's second wife. His mother was pretty and delicate, unsuited to the harshness of life in the village. What made that life the more difficult for the two of them was the hostility of the mayor's older sons, from his first wife, who saw in the new baby a rival for their father's fortune. They hated him from the first moment, and declared their enmity to him before he was even weaned. His helpless mother was unable to take them on. She feared for him while he was still a tender little parcel of flesh and blood. She removed him from his father's house, taking him to the home of her brothers in a nearby town. He came to feel lonely and wretched, his father ignoring his existence, while his mother's visits became few and far between. He spent his days sitting quietly by the edge of the canal.

"One day I was playing in the mud as usual, when all at once the clay in my hands spoke to me, yielding to my fingers and taking shape. It assumed the form of the animals in the village: the lowly donkey, the water buffalo incessantly chewing its cud, and the bull, staring into space. The clay spoke, addressing itself to me and revealing the secrets of creation. The children of the village left their games and gathered around me. A little girl cried, staring at the figures of ducks and geese, for she had expected them to come to life."

Al-Rakib placed before them small dishes containing varieties of organ meats—tongue and lungs and spleen. She ate little, still listening to him. His words were more delectable than the food.

"My mother returned to her brothers' village after my father died. She came back to me—I was her sole remaining comfort. She tried to get me to attend the *kuttab*, to learn the Qur'an, but the sheikh of the *kuttab* was hard and cruel, and in her absence I had changed—I had become a free spirit that could not bear sitting in an enclosed space. I would run off into the fields and make for the banks of the canals, where the clay was. When I grew up a bit, I discovered that the village was no longer a fit place to live in, for clay was all it had—that, and one kind uncle, as well as a great many hateful ones. It was necessary for my mother and me to move to Cairo, and in this city I began to be educated, and to draw and to make my way."

They left the restaurant and crossed the square to the Sayyida Zaynab Mosque. They recited al-Fatiha, then plunged into the tangled neighborhoods behind the mosque. She was dazzled by the rows of little shops—the merchants selling colorful clothing and turbans, the saddlers, hatters, sellers of pickled vegetables, fava beans, and cereal—all beneath the blazing lights of the gas lamps, familiar and soft; it was as if their proximity to the mosque bestowed upon them an air of unreality. Mukhtar never stopped talking. He wanted to pursue an education, to study the fundamentals of sculpture in Europe, but this was beyond his reach. He pointed to a building with a high wall, which looked different from the other structures in the vicinity. Workers were still painting it and cleaning it at this late hour.

"This," he said, "is the building I dream about: the school I'm waiting to see open its doors."

She looked at the long, white wall in puzzlement. It bore no sign, but workers were toiling hard at it.

"What school is this?" she said.

"The School of Fine Arts," he replied. "French and Italian professors will come to teach here—so said Prince Yusuf Kamal, who's overseeing its construction. It will be a home for the arts, and it will take me in, which will be a bit of solace for the fact that I can't go to Europe."

Aisha smiled. "What makes you think they'll accept you?" she said.

"As soon as I meet the director of the school," said Mukhtar, "I'll make him a clay statue, and he'll admit me on the spot."

They walked through the alleyways, which had grown dark, apart from the dim light of the oil lamps that were set upon the doorsteps of the houses. The house bore the number five. Meeting Umm Abbas was the most difficult moment. They mounted the steps and knocked on the door of the second-floor apartment. They waited for some time, and then an enormous woman appeared; clearly it was only with difficulty that she was able to move about. She stared doubtfully at Aisha, trying to guess who she might be and from where she had come.

"She is a relative of mine," Mukhtar lied, "a distant one."

Umm Abbas did not appear to believe this. She fixed Aisha with a shrewd eye and said, "Where are your people, girl?"

Aisha swallowed hard, then spoke with the conviction of one who had expected such a question. "They all died in the flooding of the Nile two years ago."

Startled, Umm Abbas now spoke a little more gently. "How will you pay the rent?" she asked. "Is your kinsman here going to support you? He can scarcely pay his own way."

Aisha responded decisively. She took out the note al-Rafiy had given her and presented it to Umm Abbas. "This is the first of my wages from my job."

Umm Abbas's mouth fell open in surprise. "God almighty!" she said. "A whole pound in one go . . . where do you work?"

"At *al-Liwa*—with the Leader, Mustafa Kamil."

Aisha was full of surprises. "Merciful God!" the woman burst out, overcome with astonishment. "Do you see him?"

"Of course I see him," Aisha replied. "His office is next to mine."

Taken unawares, Umm Abbas was capable of no further sarcasm or resistance against Aisha's all-out offensive. She looked at the two of them, perplexed, then said slowly, "Girl, you are as pretty as can be, and that's what worries me. I've lived my whole life as a paragon of honor—no one's ever said a word about my house, and I won't have that change after you come to live here. I'll get a room ready for you in my own apartment—you'll have nothing to do with the basement where your kinsman lives. Don't go down the stairs that lead to it or go into his room. Understand? The eyes of the neighborhood here are open and they don't miss a thing. If you consent, then you're welcome here."

Aisha didn't dare tell her that she hadn't known Mukhtar until today. She nodded her head compliantly, the color high in her cheeks.

"Now then," said the woman, "get along with you, Mr. Mukhtar—good-bye. We'd like to prepare the girl's room."

◆ ◆ ◆

In the morning, Aisha awoke in her little bed. She now had her own private room, her private life. She had slept well, and she felt safe, although her heart beat faster than usual. She heard children's voices—they were playing hopscotch. She looked out her window onto the cramped neighborhood. She saw street vendors selling fava beans, bread, and tomatoes. There, too, were the women who were her neighbors, wringing the washing before hanging it out to dry. They stared at her, surprised and curious. They knew it was only a matter of time before they would find out all about her from Umm Abbas. When she went down, preparing to leave for work, she found Mukhtar waiting for her downstairs. He accompanied her on the walk to the paper. He was amazingly bold, imposing his presence at her side from the first day, in the sight of all and in broad daylight. The residents of the quarter all regarded him with awe—they realized that he was a person of distinction who would not stay long in these basement lodgings, but that his place was with the illustrious inhabitants of Helmiya al-Gadida. She walked along, feeling safe at his side. He didn't beset her with questions about her past life or overstep the bounds of propriety with her. He maintained an air of gentle courtesy, awaiting the moment when she would trust him completely and open her heart to him.

The terrain between Sayyida Zaynab and Noubar Street came to be among the most beautiful in her eyes: narrow alleyways like lines in the palm of the hand, fountains offering fragrant rosewater, deranged men circling the Sayyida's shrine with their censers, the ill and the crippled converging on the shrine from everywhere and clinging to the close-set iron bars surrounding it. Prayerful entreaties and requests for pardon emanated from atop the minaret of Sheikh Hanafi, and dhikrs were recited every Thursday.

Oh, Mother, thought Aisha, *I wish you could be with me. I would introduce you to Mukhtar, and tell you about the plans taking shape within me, about the way my heart pounds when I see him waiting for me, this tremor that seizes my body whenever our hands accidentally touch. I'd like you to meet Umm Abbas, who can't sleep now until she's made sure I've come home, and who doesn't have her breakfast until after I wake up.* Al-Rakib's soup was always hot; doves roosted gently upon the shacks belonging to traders in antiquarian books in the middle of the square; every Tuesday the peasant women arranged eggs and balls of butter in gleaming pyramids; and licorice sellers banged on their trays, crying, "Sweet licorice for sale!"

As the day approached on which the School of Fine Arts was to open its doors, Mukhtar's agitation grew, especially when he heard an announcement by the French director of the school that there would be rigorous exams for every student—each would have to submit an original example of his work, expressive of his character. This dreadful project distracted Mukhtar from his attentions to Aisha. Little did he know that all the fibers of her being were fraying and breaking and struggling to reassemble themselves, especially as he began to distance himself from her a little. He didn't abandon his morning routine with her, but he no longer awaited her on the way back. She would hear the sound of his hammer and chisel in the middle of the night, but none of the neighbors complained, nor did Umm Abbas object—it was Aisha who was shocked on the morning she went downstairs and did not find him waiting for her. The door to his room was locked and silent. She had heard his voice as he worked through the night—now he must be deeply asleep. She cast about and discovered that no one was paying any attention to her, so she descended the few steps and rapped on the door. She waited for him to rouse himself in haste and answer her knock, but still there was silence at the door. At a loss, she left the house, her head bowed. She wished she could disappear, so that no one would see her making her way alone, like someone walking naked and unprotected. The city was transformed into a nightmarish thing. She climbed the stairs to *al-Liwa* and immersed herself in her work. There were the Leader's letters, which he would dispatch to the House of Commons in Britain, and an article he wished to send to the London *Times*, criticizing Lord Cromer's policy on education. While busy with her translations, she saw al-Rafiy coming and going; the men in the pressroom chatted and exchanged pleasantries with her to which she replied distractedly, waiting and waiting for the workday to end.

When she left *al-Liwa*, once more she failed to find him awaiting her at the bottom of the stairs, so again she made her way alone and wretched through the straitened quarters of Sayyida Zaynab. She heard the greetings of the vendors and the neighbors, but she was unsure whether or not they were mocking her. She approached the house; there was no one looking out of the windows, so she went down the three steps leading to the basement. She trembled, approaching the forbidden realm against which Umm Abbas had warned her, but she saw no alternative. She heard movement within: the sound of a hammer striking stone, and intermittent conversation, so she knew he was inside and that there was someone talking to him. She knocked angrily at the door. The tapping of the hammer stopped and she heard some commotion, then the sound of the bolt being drawn back. The door opened, but it wasn't Mukhtar who appeared—it was a woman, no less—statuesque, voluptuous, her hair uncovered, loose and tumbled. She wore a robe open at the top, revealing the contours of her breasts; it gaped open as far down as her belly. On seeing Aisha the woman made an attempt to button up the robe, her mouth moving as if she were chewing on something. She stared indifferently at Aisha, who felt the blood rising to her head and the earth spinning beneath her feet.

"Who are you?" she cried.

Leaning against the door with her soft, bare arm, the woman said, "That's the question we should be asking, you, love. You're the one who knocked on the door, so first of all you tell me—who are *you*?"

Aisha was on the point of toppling over from shock, but she got hold of herself, although she was ready to burst into tears.

"I'm looking for Mukhtar," she said.

"He's busy just now."

But before Aisha could faint, Mukhtar came out from within the apartment, holding a small chisel in his hand and covered in flecks of white dust. He stepped forward slowly, as if exhausted from lack of sleep, his hair rumpled as usual, bits of the white dust clinging to his little beard. He stared at her as if he was seeing her for the first time, and said simply, "Oh . . . Aisha. I forgot to escort you. I've been preoccupied—honestly."

That was how it was, then. The towering woman moved aside slightly, leaning against the door, her prominent chest still interposing itself between Aisha and Mukhtar.

"So you two know each other," she said. "Her body doesn't look like it's up to the job."

Aisha shouted with all the fury she'd been holding in, "*Who is this woman, Mukhtar*?"

She was imploring him to say something to rescue her, take away this pain and confusion. Mukhtar raised the hammer and gestured vaguely toward the interior.

"Now then, love," said the woman, "is there anyone who doesn't know me? I'm Nabawiyya al-Mustahiya. I'm well-known already, but they'll repeat my name in times to come as well. Show him the statue you've made of me, Master Mukhtar."

The woman made way for Aisha to enter as if daring her to cross the forbidden threshold. Aisha looked to Mukhtar for help, but he was distracted, striking the hammer against his palm. The woman regarded her with a mocking smile. Aisha took a breath and held it, then stepped into the room. The interior was dim, a faint glow emanating from a gas lamp which cast more shadows than light.

All around it were small statues, most of them unfinished, and paintings were propped against the walls, as well as fragments of torn-up drawings and piles of rubble from clay and stone. A bed was tucked away in one corner, and there was a table laden with dirty dishes. Aisha looked at the woman, who pointed firmly at the center of the room. There stood a block of stone, too large for the space it occupied. From within it the body of a woman, in all its mature femininity, seemed about to burst forth, as if ready to rise from its inert state and spring to life, emerging from the silence of the stone. Despite the feelings of rage Aisha harbored, she sensed the life that emanated from the stone. The woman's features were finished, and she strove to lift up her head, but locks of her hair were still embedded in the block; her shoulders were raised as if she were leaning upon her elbows but they were also obscured within the carved-out hollow of stone. The most striking part of the statue was the woman's breasts. They were bare and fully formed, the nipples prominently erect—how could he have sculpted them like that? How could he feel such lust for her?

Aisha turned her face away, finding it difficult to catch her breath—she was in turmoil, beset by feelings of jealousy and wrath. Nabawiyya al-Mustahiya grew surer, more self-satisfied. The statue's features corresponded closely to her own, but it had graced her with a kind of magnificence she could not match: Mukhtar had managed to draw this quality from within his own depths. Unable to endure his silence or his air of indifference, Aisha turned her back on him and left the room. She climbed the dark staircase, stumbling and falling. She knocked at the door of the flat upstairs, forgetting for a moment that she had the key and that Umm Abbas moved laboriously. She opened the door and burst inside, to find Umm Abbas seated in the middle of the salon and staring at her in alarm. Aisha flung herself weeping into her lap and told her what had happened—the feelings that had engulfed her, the woman she had found Mukhtar's room, and the statue that burst from within the stone like some debauched creature.

The lady of the house began rocking her gently. "You've been led astray, child," she said. "You've fallen madly in love with him, perhaps more than he has with you. You shouldn't have made such a mistake."

"What?" cried Aisha, distraught. "Doesn't he care about me? Is there something between him and that woman?"

"Of course not," said Umm Abbas. "I've known her since she was just a girl living in the neighborhood. She changed after that. Now she works at a house in the red-light district, God help the faithful. Mukhtar knows this, but I'm sure Mukhtar is not one of those men—he's not that kind."

"Then what is she doing with him in the basement?"

"She's helping him. She stands before him and does as he tells her. He pays her a fee for this—he discussed the matter with me before he brought her here. That is all there is to it. Look at it from that angle, and don't let yourself be consumed by jealousy."

But she burned with it all night long. She was unable to sleep, thinking about the statue: that woman rising from within the stone as if emerging from Mukhtar's embrace, sated and replete. She resembled Margaret, coming back from Rizq's room with her hair unbound.

At last morning came. Aisha went downstairs, wobbly legged and unseeing. But there stood Mukhtar, waiting for her, utterly calm and clear-eyed. He walked beside her. She waited until they had emerged from the tortuous alleyways into the square, far from any ears that might eavesdrop on their conversation.

Then she demanded of him, "Have you slept with that woman?"

"Of course not," he said simply.

"But she lay naked in front of you. I saw her body completely exposed. Obviously you must have done so!"

"If I were to do that with her it would ruin everything—I'd lose my creative drive. I put all the desire I feel into the hammer and chisel. If I had done otherwise the statue would have come out lifeless, with no energy. It pleases me that you sensed the energy radiating from it."

He didn't justify himself or attempt to ease her anguish, even though he could see from her eyes that she had not slept. All he did was offer her a cold explanation she only dimly understood.

"But," cried Aisha, "she is a disreputable woman!"

"I know," he said, "but that's the kind of woman who is willing to model for me—me and my fellow-artists. If I had asked you to take off your clothes in front of me, would you have been willing?"

"Damn you!" she said. "You and Nabawiyya al-Mustahiya and the School of Fine Arts!"

But they walked on together all the way to *al-Liwa*, and he was waiting for her when it was time to go home. Nabawiyya did not set foot in the house after that; Mukhtar relied upon his memory to finish the statue.

By the day of the school's opening, Mukhtar's anxiety had reached a fever pitch. Aisha did not go to the paper, and Umm Abbas looked out of her window, as did the rest of the neighbors. A wagon drawn by two horses arrived and several porters went down into the basement, collected the statue, and brought it back up the stairs, Mukhtar following them and issuing cautionary instructions. Embarrassed that everyone should see the statue in such a state of nakedness, Aisha brought a white sheet and covered the sculpture, warning the porters by no means to raise the sheet. The porters rode beside the statue to keep it from tipping, while Mukhtar and Aisha walked through the streets adjacent to Gamamiz Lane. He was anxiously wringing his hands, while she tugged encouragingly on his arm.

"They'll surely admit you to the school," she said. "It's a magnificent statue."

She hated it, though, and she meant to demolish it if she ever got the chance. The whitewashed wall of the school appeared, and a sign bearing the words *School of Fine Arts* had been raised on high above the gate. A group of students stood by the door, each one carrying the project he was to present: shrouded paintings, rolls of paper, plaster statues, pieces formed out of metal, wooden carvings, figures made up of interlocking glass pieces, and works of hammered brass, but Mukhtar's stone statue was the largest and most impressive of them.

As he prepared to go inside, Aisha said to him, "I'll stay here and wait for you."

So he went inside, the porters behind him carrying the statue. She wished the statue were of her, wished he had asked her to do this thing, for she would have done anything for his sake, to help him fulfill his dream of crossing this whitewashed barrier. She leaned against the wall facing the door, and watched the other students as they passed through it carrying their objects. The forecourt emptied—only she remained, waiting, all alone. She pictured Mukhtar standing before the admissions board. He would be nervous, and would not speak well; the statue, though, would speak better than he could. But did Nabawiyya al-Mustahiya's body have to be the means to his success? At this point, she had no option but to pray to God for his success. She closed her eyes, then heard a voice calling out to her.

"I can see you're finally happy with the statue and its creator!"

Aisha knew the voice immediately, although its owner had covered her face with a flimsy veil, and tried to conceal her outrageous body inside a black abaya. So ended Aisha's moments of serenity; now she was once more overcome by rage.

"What have you come here for?" she demanded of the woman.

"Have you forgotten that I'm the subject of the statue, love?" said Nabawiyya al-Mustahiya. "I'm a partner in this young man's future—they'll accept him solely on the basis of his good taste in choosing a model to pose for his statue."

It was no use quarreling with her—Aisha would be the loser. She glared at her with repressed fury as she leaned against the wall beside her. Was this woman so close to Mukhtar, then? Should she believe Mukhtar when he said he had never gone near her body, or had there been something deeper than that between them? She wanted to know, and there was no way to find out except to continue the conversation with her.

"Why are you wearing these clothes and covering your face?" she asked.

"Because I'm bashful, my dear," she said. "I'm famous for that—some customers prefer me for my shyness, although this is not what I would choose."

She paused a moment and looked searchingly at Aisha. "I assume," she continued, "that by now you know quite a lot about me?"

She put the question innocently. Aisha found within herself the courage to ask, "This house where you work . . . does Mukhtar go there?"

"Of course he does, dearie, but not for the reason you've got into your head. He came once to look for someone who could help him with his project. I accepted—even though he's got very little money—because, love, I like art. Mukhtar isn't the type to be one of our customers. The ones who visit the house regularly are the English and the successful merchants. What would a penniless student like Mukhtar do with us?"

Much to Aisha's surprise, their conversation continued. Her alarm subsided, and she found herself listening to some of the particulars Nabawiyya had to relate—at first in disbelief, and then in astonishment, which gave way to enjoyment. Nabawiyya talked about the world at that strange house in the red-light district and how she had come to be employed at such a trade. When Mukhtar emerged, he found the two of them talking congenially together. He was happy, because his statue had met with the unanimous approval of the judges, and the head teacher, Laplagne, had not been able to believe that Mukhtar had sculpted the statue on his own. This professor had come from France expressly to teach the art of sculpture, and it had surprised him to find a talent like Mukhtar's flourishing this way in the absence of any prior instruction. He took him into a room off to the side, set before him a slab filled with chunks of clay, and told Mukhtar to mold it, in his presence, into whatever shape occurred to him. At that moment, Mukhtar caught sight of a picture hanging on the wall of the room—it was *Venus de Milo*, the most famous statue in the Louvre: a naked woman with arms broken off. At once he imagined her stepping in front of him in all her radiant nakedness, and he began to sculpt the clay in her image. Once more the professor stroked his beard, awestruck, and agreed then and there to admit him to the school.

Aisha gave a cry of joy, and Mukhtar hugged her hard. Nabawiyya al-Mustahiya pouted. "You ought to have hugged me first, dear," she said.

All they could do then was laugh.

◆ ◆ ◆

Aisha was startled to find the Pasha himself standing before her little desk. From the time of her appointment at *al-Liwa*, it had normally been she who went to his office, and she never imagined that he even knew the way to hers. But here he stood, a man of middling height, with a sparkle in his eyes as if his body had suddenly recovered from all the illnesses to which it was prey. He wasn't coughing or breathing hard; he was stroking his moustache with an air of satisfaction.

"You're to come with me, Aisha," he said mildly.

He walked before her, his carriage erect. Aisha followed him, simultaneously surprised and bedazzled. She had thought he was going to charge her with the translation of some speech or other—she had translated many of the letters and speeches he was always sending to members of the British general assembly or to his friends who worked as writers or journalists. But the Leader did not turn toward his office; he made his way among the desks of the men in the pressroom. He and Aisha went out the door, he headed down the steps, and she followed. This was becoming odder by the minute.

In front of the building a one-horse carriage, reserved for the Pasha, stood waiting for them, and the driver sat at the ready, grasping the horse's reins. He made haste to assist the Leader into the carriage, but the Pasha indicated with a gesture that he was quite capable on his own—and, indeed, in a single motion he leapt up from the ground and seated himself in the carriage. Aisha looked at him in amazement, but he merely waved her into the seat across from him.

He tapped the driver's seat with his cane. "Take us to Station Square," he said.

Feeling the touch of the whip on its back, the horse whinnied, and the carriage set off. Now the Leader turned to Aisha, his features set in a youthful smile.

"This is a historic occasion," he said, "and you are the only one with whom it is fitting for me to share it."

The streets were thronged with people all hurrying in the same direction as the carriage. Aisha discovered the secret of the Pasha's exultant happiness when she read the news item that only *al-Liwa* had published, featuring it in the headlines. It seemed to her as if the tattoo of the horse's hooves was the Leader's heartbeat; his chest rose and fell with his easy breathing, as though everything he needed he obtained from the city air. All at once he had become livelier and more amiable.

The direct route to the station, however, was blocked off. English soldiers stood behind the barricade with weapons at the ready. The driver redirected their carriage toward the side streets, making for the city center, then Opera Square. From there the way descended into Clot Bey Street. Amidst arcades and colonnades that went on and on there were numerous wine shops and cafés, many of them festooned with decorations and hung with vividly printed signs announcing to customers that women and wine could be had at half-price this night. The crowd grew still more dense, and signs for the railway station appeared. The carriage proceeded with increasing difficulty, until it stopped altogether. Some of the milling crowd, however, recognized the Pasha, and hastened to clear a path for him. Their voices rose as they called out to him, shouting, "Today is your day, oh Leader!"

He gestured for silence, not wanting this day's events to become a demonstration or an occasion for a display of schadenfreude. He directed the driver to stop the carriage in one of the streets leading off from the square so that he could watch the main entrance to the station. There were a great many Egyptians amassed in one corner and surrounded by English soldiers. Until this moment they were silent, even though they had come to express their joy, which had been so long suppressed.

In another corner were the other Europeans, men and women, dressed in their finest attire, chatting in a relaxed fashion. In the middle of it all Aisha recognized Lord Kitchener—"hero of the Sudan," as he was called—pacing anxiously. He stared with hatred at the mob of Egyptians who had dared to come out and attend this spectacle; perhaps he was just waiting for them to speak out, so he could annihilate them all.

The Pasha beckoned to Aisha to sit beside him facing the entrance to the station. She heard him speaking as if to himself. "It is a small victory," he said. "The occupation hasn't gone anywhere, but here at least is Cromer, on his way out. Will God let me live long enough to see all the British soldiers leave?"

Lines of British soldiers appeared, headed by an honor guard. They held aloft gleaming swords, and on their heads were caps adorned with feathers. An open carriage came in sight, drawn by eight horses sporting brightly colored feathers and fitted out in lustrous brass ornaments. Lord Cromer sat with his head held haughtily, scarcely seeing all those who stood waiting for him. He had gathered all his energies for the sake of this moment, so that his departure would be a resonant occasion. The Pasha looked on wide-eyed at Cromer's advancing parade, while the sound of military music rose up from a platform beside the entrance to the station.

"Why do you hate him so much?" Aisha asked. "Is it on account of what he did at Dinshaway?"

"That is one of many reasons. This man has humiliated us quite enough. He secured the occupation, made it our destiny. He forbade our children to be educated and informed, barred us from the administration of our own country, and prohibited us from pursuing any craft or industry. His goal was simply to transform us as a people into a mass of ignoramuses, unable to function without their governance."

Lord Cromer's carriage drew nearer. The soldiers raised their weapons and stood at attention. The carriage halted in the middle of the square; Lord Cromer disembarked before a line of officers and commanders, and proceeded to shake their hands. Then the silent Egyptians began to murmur—for a long time they had held their peace, but now their moment of protest had arrived. Lord Cromer turned toward the sound, and noticed the small group of Egyptians. He seemed puzzled by their presence, and by the fact that they had a voice. It seemed to Aisha that he turned his head and looked directly at where she and the Pasha were sitting; he squinted, trying to make out their features. She knew that recently he had spent his days suffering from severe stomach pain, to the point where he couldn't manage to digest any food, even baby food, but this had had no effect upon his upturned moustache or the look of contempt that shone so coldly from his eyes. For a brief moment the murmuring stopped, and silence fell. Lord

Cromer turned to resume his farewell ceremonies, but just then a voice rose from the crowd, shouting, "Down with the murderer of Dinshaway! Down with Lord Cromer the coward!"

The cry cut through the sounds of pomp and ceremony, all the self-important swagger that had held sway over the square. Now voices rose from hundreds of throats; the space filled with the pulse of angry chants. A tremor ran through the close-packed ranks, but at a resolute nod from Lord Cromer the honor guard stood straight in two rows and raised their swords on high so that he might pass beneath them. Yet he stood hesitating, staring at the people, expecting them to fall silent.

The chanting continued. The Pasha rested his chin on his cane—it seemed that each was aware of the other's presence; the pitch of anger rose still further when the crowd saw Lord Cromer hesitate—they reckoned he must be having second thoughts about leaving, and they began to shout, "Get out! Scram! Murderer!"

Lord Kitchener drew himself up and gestured to the soldiers, who raised their rifles, leveling them at the people's hearts.

Starting up in alarm, the Pasha cried, "God have mercy, there's going to be a massacre!"

He rose to his feet in the carriage, supporting himself on his cane and struggling to stand erect, despite the slightness of his frame. All eyes turned to him, but most especially those of Lord Cromer, who saw him standing there in his black suit, his red tarbush, and his upturned moustache as if to issue a warning against making any false move. Each regarded the other with suppressed hatred, and the onlookers all held their breath, watching the two men apprehensively. Lord Cromer's face grew paler; he seemed to display signs of decrepitude, as well as the symptoms of poor digestion. In the end he decided not to draw out the challenge, and to avoid inciting a massacre at the occasion of his farewell. He turned around and proceeded in between the two lines of the honor guard. Kitchener still stood ready to spring into action, and from a distance could be heard the roar of cannon, resounding from one of the barracks in Shoubra. By the conclusion of the twenty-one-gun salute, Lord Cromer had reached the train, whose whistle sounded, signaling its departure.

All the people moved off, and in their midst the Pasha's carriage proceeded in silence. The Pasha was breathing hard—he seemed drained, and in his face were none of the signs of contentment that Aisha had expected to see.

"Sir," she said anxiously, "what's the matter? Are you all right?"

He smiled faintly. Reaching out, he touched her chin gently with his fingers. "Cromer's gone," he said. "Yes indeed . . . but with him has gone a piece of my life. We were twins, he and I, and the contest between us robbed us of our health and shortened our lives. Now that he's gone, I feel as if my own time has come as well."

Unsettled, Aisha said, "God grant you many more years, Pasha. There's still a long fight ahead."

She knew her words were empty. He was frail, his rejuvenation only temporary and already a thing of the past. Life had begun to slip away from his body. Still leaning on his cane, he gazed at the streets, the sidewalks, the passersby, through eyes filled with unshed tears. He was endeavoring to imprint upon his vision all the passing scenes, taking in all the details, before his eyes closed forever. He began to speak, his words mixing with the horse's hoofbeats, and with the voices from the street, which rose each time someone recognized him.

"Yes," he said, "a long fight indeed. It requires my lifetime and those of other men. I started this movement in my own defense, and in defense of those to whom I am connected. Do you know, when I went to study law in Europe, I discovered that they didn't know anything about us. They knew there was a country called Egypt and that it had been mentioned in the Bible, and that at a certain point the British had invaded it and appropriated it for themselves, that it was inhabited by a nameless, faceless people with no history, a herd of dumb beasts; they were astonished if we spoke French, and if we learned their civil law, this was counted no less than a miracle. All I wanted, Aisha, was to reclaim our names—for them to know that we were human beings, with individual personalities, with our own joys and sorrows. I wished for the Egyptians, as well, to get to know themselves. It is a tragedy, young lady, to look in the mirror and not see your own face, not recognize it. I wanted the Egyptians to be aware of their own presence in the world, and not to keep dying in droves—they died digging the canal, they died in Orabi's war, they died in the floods, the plagues, and other disasters, and no one cared about them, for they had been transformed from human beings to numbers. Numbers don't have destinies—there's no blood price on a number, a number doesn't even merit a moment's pause for remembrance or mourning. When Khedive Abbas called on me to form a secret party with the object of liberating Egypt from the British, I couldn't believe my ears. We thought along different lines: he wanted to free his throne from British dominion, while I wanted to free my people. Even the khedive himself didn't know we had names—he spoke Arabic haltingly, and got my name and the names of my comrades wrong every time we met. No one who ruled Egypt ever gave a day's thought to the idea that we might have names, but I didn't want the khedive to forget, or for Lord Cromer to forget the names of those he killed at Dinshaway. Everyone needs to understand that we are not weeds growing on the banks of the Nile. I simply want them to know that we are human beings with independent minds, individual characters—not mere numbers."

The carriage continued on its way. The Pasha insisted upon conducting Aisha himself to Sayyida Zaynab Square. His face was pale and grave when he bade her goodbye, and for a moment she imagined that it was the last time she would see him. Feeling profoundly sad, she entered the saint's shrine, and began to make the circuit around it. Weeping, she circled it again and again, without stopping.

She heard the news on a day when the sun scarcely showed itself and a mask of fog lay over the city, obscuring its features. She was taking the stairs at *al-Liwa*—it wasn't yet past midday, and the paper was not ready to go out. Her heart had misgiven her all day. She had seen Mukhtar in the morning, although the route they followed had changed, for she was now in the habit of accompanying him to the School of Fine Arts first, before making her way to the paper. She found Abdel Rahman al-Rafiy sitting on the steps. He was crying like a child, his round face shining with the tears that flowed without restraint. In words choked by his sobs he told her, "He's gone and left us—the Leader, he's gone and left us orphans . . ."

Leaning on his shoulder, she began to weep as well. She recalled the Pasha's last words to her, as if he'd been delivering a eulogy, both for himself and for the world that was collapsing around him. Al-Rafiy patted her shoulder, then got to his feet, preparing to go upstairs. Startled, she asked him, "Won't you go to the funeral?"

"I'll leave that to others," he said. "I must prepare the front page of the newspaper and give it its black border. Everyone must feel how great a loss we have suffered."

She walked by herself, half-blind, scarcely able to distinguish anything in the surrounding streets. Life went on in silence: buying and selling and haggling, tramway cars in the square, the madmen who hung about the shrine, and visitors to the saint, all drifting about like ghosts, as if they were living through the last moments of the world. Shouldn't everything stop, even if only for a little while? Entering the twisting, narrow lanes, she didn't hear the voices of the neighborhood's residents. With all the sorrow she held confined in her heart she hurried, ran down the few stairs to the basement, and began pounding on the door, shouting, "Mukhtar!" with no care for who might be listening. God must have loved her in this moment, for the door opened and she found him standing before her. She flung her arms around his neck and wept. He picked her up in his arms and carried her inside, where she burst out, in broken words, with the news of what had happened. He stared at her, appalled. Tears were pouring down his cheeks as well—in one way he felt guilty, because he hadn't supported the Pasha as he should have. He hadn't understood that the man was burning up, that each battle he joined robbed him of a part of his life.

Mukhtar and Aisha held each other, not speaking, and they did not notice when darkness fell upon the room. He kissed her lips, which were salty, and she clung to his neck. It was her first kiss, and she had waited a long time for it. But her heart was heavy with grief, and did not allow her body to succumb to the trembling sensations of desire. She was clinging to him for support, in the hope that the warmth of their mutual contact might ease her mind a little. He ran his fingers through her hair; she stayed where she was, held unprotesting against his chest. Doubtless Umm Abbas was expecting her back by now, but she did not move from his side.

"Light a lamp," she said. "I want to show you something."

The gaslight flared, and he brought it close to her face. She undid the buttons on her sleeve, baring her arm before him and revealing the image of the cross tattooed there—pale, just as her skin was pale. He felt it with his fingers, then looked up at her wonderingly. "Are you a Christian?" he asked.

"I had to pretend I was," she said.

She told him everything she could remember of that time, everything she had been keeping inside for all these years. She wanted him to know her more fully and genuinely. She confessed to him all the sorrows she had concealed deep within her. Everyone she had encountered had seen only one side of her life, but here she sat now in his arms, under the pressure of his gaze, which compelled her to make him see her as no one else had. She felt herself made real, with him looking at her in the lamplight while she revealed to him the various layers of her life. Tears fell from her eyes, especially when she recalled her mother, the greatest deprivation she had suffered, the separation a bitterness that cut into her heart. Finally, still weeping, she cried out in anguish, "All I want at this moment is my mother. I want to tell her how much I love you, and how badly I need her beside me. I don't want to go back to that little village, which I hate—I want her to be here with me, in this vast city, far from the fear of my uncle and of the others, the ones who threatened her life."

"I'll go to her," said Mukhtar, moved by her distress, "and bring her to you."

She looked at him, astonished and hopeful. "Would you really do this?"

"I must, so that I can ask her permission to marry you."

Her eyes, bright with tears, were fixed upon him. All at once this terrible day had been transformed into her day of good fortune. Mukhtar, the celebrated artist, under whose fingers stone melted, and for whom all the newspapers competed, was asking for her hand in marriage!

In disbelief, she said, "You really want to marry me?"

"And what else," he said, "did you think the outcome of our relationship was to be? Umm Abbas would kill me if for one moment I considered abandoning you, and so would all the saint's madmen and visitors!"

She imagined him turning up there, in the remote and isolated village of Beni Khalaf, being met by the mother who was powerless to handle her own affairs and the uncle who was ready to pounce. How, she wondered, would Mukhtar manage things? Would he be able to wrest her mother from the claws of that vicious man?

"Please," she said to him, "don't do this now . . . wait at least until I tell you."

He was taken aback. "I thought you'd be in a hurry to get married. I'm earning enough now from my drawings for the newspapers to be able to set up a household."

But she was afraid, trembling as she mounted the stairs and made her way to where Umm Abbas awaited her. She flung herself into her embrace, and the older woman patted her back. After a moment she said, "You spent a long time with him. I noticed you went to him early in the evening. That was quite a while for the two of you to sit together without touching—at such moments your body would weaken in his presence."

"I was in need of it," Aisha said through her tears. "The Leader died today, and I felt desolate. And besides, Mukhtar has asked to marry me."

"I would have killed him if he had done otherwise. Seeing as you've found your way to his lodgings, you'd best make haste and marry him."

In the morning, Mukhtar was waiting for her. All night long he had turned over in his mind the idea of marrying her until he felt absolutely certain about it. He was no longer concerned about any impediments that might be placed in his way. He wanted to find out from her more details about the village and how to get to it, but Cairo was grieving. People gathered daily around *al-Liwa*'s headquarters, coming from all over Egypt: students from the law school, crews who worked for the tramway system, sheikhs from al-'Azhar, farmers from Upper Egypt, warehouse workers from Alexandria—they all came and stood long hours in front of *al-Liwa*, eyes fixed upon the closed doors and windows, as if they expected the Leader to look out from one of them at any moment. Aisha met their questioning stares every morning, and she was powerless to offer them an answer. *Al-Liwa* itself was reeling, with death peering over its shoulder. Each day the writers and editors made their way there, thinking this day was to be the last—death was stalking the paper. Readers would not find in its pages the impassioned articles the Leader had penned, no matter how many of his old pieces they might rerun, or how much they might draw on his sayings. The radiant glow that once emanated from his pen had vanished now, and from pole to pole darkness had begun to creep across the pages of *al-Liwa*.

But before the first anniversary of the Leader's passing came Mohammad Farid who, in the pages of *al-Liwa*, called for the greatest demonstration Egypt had ever seen, with the goal of demanding independence and a constitution. The dream held by the late Leader was not dead—a new leader had come, bringing new ideas and calling for a different kind of action. He had lived long in Europe, had witnessed the movement of the oppressed classes, and seen the portents of the war to come. He understood that Egypt, in its delicate position, would be a helpless lamb upon the sacrificial altar of the great powers, and it was imperative that he seek out its secret reserves of strength. He looked for the first time at the dispersed proletariat masses and the servile peasants—would it be possible for them to organize, and to gain strength and a will of their own?

In spite of all the obstacles, he aspired to set up guilds and labor unions for them, but first he wanted them to go out into the streets—he wished to hear their voices, to free them from the malady of their deeply ingrained habitual silence. So he sent out his call for uprising through the medium of *al-Liwa*.

Three days before the time set for the demonstration, Mukhtar disappeared without saying anything to Aisha or telling her good-bye. He wasn't waiting for her in the morning, and he didn't escort her home in the evening. Amm Jumaa, the fava-bean seller, who was the first person in the neighborhood to awaken, told her that he had left early, carrying a small suitcase. Aisha's heart contracted—had he done it, then? Had he gone to her distant village? Or had he gone on an ordinary holiday to his own hamlet in the center of the Delta? Had he seized the opportunity of the end of the academic term and gone to implement his plan, the one that never left her thoughts? He should have bided his time a little—then she might have overcome her fear somewhat and gone with him. Why hadn't he told her before? Was he afraid she would hesitate, and refuse? He had left her powerless, unable to do anything but wait, pursuing thoughts that drifted in a mind half-absent. She saw the delegations assembling, the slogans being written, heard the chants being rehearsed, and tried to persuade herself that all would be well.

The night before the demonstration, Aisha didn't sleep. She stayed sitting by the window, watching the opening to the narrow lane, thinking Mukhtar might appear at any moment. But the little shops extinguished their lights and a distant moon appeared in the sky, while clouds gathered and hung there gloomily. The old muezzin climbed up the minaret of the saint's holy shrine and began the call to prayer.

Aisha heard the sound of Umm Abbas moving heavily about the apartment, making her ablutions. Getting up and going to her room, she found the old lady sitting there wrapped in her white veil, saying her prayers in a soft voice. She wiped tears from her eyes and turned to Aisha, saying, "I'm praying for you, Aisha, and for Mukhtar to come back safely to us."

Aisha swallowed uneasily and sat down across from her in silence. Umm Abbas studied her for a moment. "Are you still planning to take part in this demonstration?" she asked.

"They're counting on me to organize the female students' faction," Aisha replied. "There's a special section for them in the square where the demonstration is to be held."

The old lady sighed, perplexed. "What is the point," she said, "of this rash adventure, of putting yourselves all at risk, as long as we're stuck with the occupation and the sultan is asleep?"

Aisha remembered these words as she walked alone to Abdeen Square. The city lay quiet and watchful. The square, situated in front of the sultan's palace, was empty but for the municipal cleaning staff. She leaned against a lamppost and cast her eyes about, trying to discern the places in which security officers stationed themselves. The police did not appear in uniform, but a great many secret service officers and other government men stood ready. She knew she had come too early, but she was hoping that the noise and tumult of the demonstration would quell the strained anxiety that convulsed her from within.

People began flocking to the square. As usual, students from the law school were the first to arrive. They were a small group, wearing elegant suits and brilliantly colored tarbushes, but their strident voices were raised to rouse the somnolent and demand a constitution. Then came members of the factory workers' collective from Shoubra, in their blue work clothes; next came dockers from the warehouses, who had arrived the previous day from Alexandria and passed the night sleeping on benches at the railway station; then the first waves of schoolgirls made their appearance, dressed in black with white veils covering their faces. Aisha led them to a section of the square that was well removed from where the police were. It was her job to shield them from contact with others, and to see to it that their voices rang out resoundingly in the demonstration.

The square continued to fill up with people, with large contingents arriving en masse, carrying signs and chanting slogans. Their faces brown and gaunt, they had found their opportunity to howl their protest. Aisha looked at them as she stood amid the ranks of girls. It seemed as though there was no end to the influx of people, and that the square kept expanding to accommodate them all. Then police troops appeared in their black uniforms, as if they had been waiting for everyone to assemble before surrounding the square on all sides and blocking every exit. The demonstrators, however, were too numerous to be surrounded by any force. As was their wont, for the time being the British soldiers left matters to the Egyptian military, whose dark faces looked frightened and subdued. The square filled with the voices of revolt and rebellion, from which the plaintive, pleading tone had vanished—they were fed up with all the years of begging. Aisha watched their faces as she chanted alongside them—if only the Leader could have been present to hear them as they shouted, defending their presence here, their ownership of their own country. They occupied the realm that, in all the world, belonged to them, and breathed their share of its air. It was as if those stiff figures painted upon the walls had stirred from their places, a temporary wakefulness seeping into them. No one knew how long it would last—the police forces might attack at this very moment, casting silence over everything. But the shouting went on; all these dispersed bodies had merged into one throat. Aisha wished Mukhtar were with her—this sudden animation would move him just as he was moved when life crept into the heart of a lump of stone.

By noon the police had wearied of the protesters, and strove to press them back, away from the walls of the palace, so that other groups from the city center would not join forces with them. With the help of their metal armor and their truncheons, they kept them from advancing. Sticks came down on the heads of some, and blood flowed. They had entered the fray in earnest. The British came, mounted upon chargers that whinnied furiously. Aisha was trying to round up the girls and draw them away from the trouble spots, when all at once she was startled by Mukhtar standing before her—thin and pale, his hair disheveled—amid the milling bodies. Unable to believe her eyes, she flung her arms about his neck, and he embraced her there in the middle of the crowd. The girls clapped for joy, and paused briefly in their chanting. Even as the soldiers' clubs came down upon the front ranks, Aisha cried to Mukhtar, "I can't believe you've come back to me!"

"And I got your mother's consent to our marriage as well."

Aisha's heart pounded, her chest heaving with emotion. "Did you see her?" she cried, stricken. "Is she well? Is she . . ."

He put his arm about her shoulders. The people were growing more agitated, bodies massing and jostling around them. The chanting turned to shouts of rage. Mukhtar spoke up so she would hear him. "She's fine. She has been a little unwell, but she is all right. She wants to see you—as soon as her health is restored . . ."

The local chief of the British constabulary appeared, issuing orders. He was riding his charger and wore a blood-red tarbush upon his head, his face deeply flushed as if to match it. He looked down upon them all with contempt as he cantered about on horseback. He had not foreseen that the site of the demonstration would accommodate them so well. He gave a sign to the soldiers and they raised their clubs on high. "Strike!" he shouted hoarsely. "Hit them hard!"

Aisha turned. She had wanted to remove the girls farther out of harm's way. The crowd surged, and the girls cried out in alarm. The soldiers had managed to divide the ranks of the demonstrators, plunging in among them with their iron shields and their cudgels. Mukhtar seized Aisha's hand and tried to pull her away, but she cried, "I can't leave the girls on their own—they'll be trampled!"

She herself was about to fall, as the police chief shouted an order to the soldiers to use still more force. He turned halfway about on his horse, drew a pistol, and fired above the heads of the protestors. Nobody knew whether or not the shots had struck anyone. Mukhtar spread his arms, trying to shield Aisha and the rest of the girls from the press of demonstrators and the pushback by the police. The protestors defended themselves, converting the poles on which they had mounted their signs to clubs with which to face down their antagonists, and pulling up the stones that paved the square and throwing them at the soldiers. The battled raged on all sides. People began to fall upon the ground, and no one could be sure of their identities. The girls screamed, terrified, and the soldiers rushed toward them, discovering that their circle was the weakest. Mukhtar shouted to them to move away and seized a club. Aisha tried to push the girls away, toward a place close to the palace wall. Mukhtar pointed to the entrance of the Balaqsa Quarter, but at the same moment the police chief turned his horse about, having heard the girls' cries. All at once he made for them on his horse in a charge swift and terrifying as a bolt of lightning. Aisha shrieked in alarm as some of the girls fell to the ground. The stallion was heading for Aisha, about to run her down, when Mukhtar raised his club and brandished it in the face of the agitated horse; he didn't know whether or not he had struck the horse, but it whinnied loudly and reared, in an effort to come to a sudden stop. The police chief lost his balance and fell from the horse, his body hitting the ground hard.

Everything came to a standstill. The hands brandishing clubs in the air went quiet, and the frenzy of the protestors subsided. The soldiers' mouths fell open, and time stopped. There was an extraordinary moment of silence, in which the only person who moved was the police chief. He pushed himself up off the ground and staggered to his feet. Mukhtar drew back, finding himself completely surrounded by a ring of soldiers armed with truncheons, which they held up high, as if forming a wall of spears. The police chief rubbed his head, and found blood smeared on his fingertips. He gasped, and attempted to rally his strength.

"Animal!" he shouted, and then, to the soldiers, "Seize him at once!"

The soldiers came out of their reverie and set upon him. He tried to push them away, but they fell upon him with their clubs. Aisha screamed and tried to break through the ring of soldiers that encircled him, but they shoved her aside. The protestors snarled with rage, but more soldiers laid into them with their clubs. Some British officers appeared and began firing their weapons. Screaming, the girls rushed toward the entrance to the Balaqsa quarter, while the law school students withdrew until their backs were against the wall, and the dockworkers clashed with the soldiers. Aisha stumbled as she tried to reach Mukhtar, and felt a sudden sharp pain in her head as a cruel blow struck her. She staggered and fell to the ground, and everything went black.

She didn't know how much later it was that she regained consciousness. The square was deserted except for a few remaining protestors, some wounded and some unconscious. There were some signs left behind, along with broken clubs and paving stones that had been wrenched from their places. She rose unsteadily. Al-Rafiy was bending over her, gazing worriedly at her. He looked tired and worn. He wasn't wearing his jacket and his necktie was soiled and askew, his shirt torn and bloodstained.

"Thank God you're all right," he said with a sigh of relief. "I was afraid we'd lost you."

She gave him a distracted look. "Where is Mukhtar?" she said.

"They've arrested him. They arrested many people. We'll appoint lawyers from the party to go and secure their release."

He was trying to reassure her, but she was frantic, and completely at a loss. "I want to go to him," she said. "I want to know where he is . . ."

"They must have taken them to the police headquarters in Ataba," al-Rafiy said. "I can use my influence as a lawyer to find out exactly where they are and let you know, if you like."

Unconvinced, she was inconsolable, and he saw no alternative but to take her with him to Ataba. Dozens of people were gathered in front of the building, which was silent—all the detainees had been swallowed up within it, and it did not look as though any entreaties would be answered.

Night fell upon them all as they waited there, unmoving. Gas fires were lit around the walls of Azbakiya's garden, and activity began to subside in the square, apart from that of the food vendors. The soldiers surrounding the building stared at the people anxiously assembling. Aisha had no choice but to wait. It distressed her that she had been responsible for what happened. If she had not been there in the middle of the demonstration, Mukhtar would not have gone to her, and if not for her he wouldn't be in his present difficulties. How could she go back to Gamamiz Lane? How could she face Umm Abbas? Everything was in ruins: love, marriage, the hope of seeing her mother.

The darkness thickened, and the lights of Azbakiya began to go on. Informers circulated threateningly among the waiting crowd, and nighttime's chill settled over the square. In despair, many people left, as the police headquarters maintained its silence, but Aisha could not take her eyes off the building. She was waiting for some kind of miracle, for Mukhtar to look out at her and renew his promise to marry her and to take her to see her mother. The cold bored into her bones, and for the first time in a long while she picked up the scent of wolves. She cast all about her and saw no shadow of any wolf in the square, but behind the old houses, where the shadows were deepest, she heard dogs barking, as if they too sensed the wolves' presence. Feeling a touch on her shoulder, Aisha started in alarm, but standing before her she found Nabawiyya al-Mustahiya with her heavily painted face. Aisha was amazed that she had come.

"You can't stay here all night, love," Nabawiyya said to her. "The square is dangerous—it's going to fill up with drunkards and British soldiers. You need to get away from here now."

Aisha was not upset by Nabawiyya's coming, for she was urgently in need of someone to stand with her and keep her company in the chill of this night. Abruptly she gave way to weeping, whereupon Nabawiyya opened her arms and enfolded her. Aisha inhaled the fragrance of heavy perfume mixed with powder and sweat. "I can't go away and leave him in this place," she said through her tears.

"He won't be here long," said Nabawiyya. "Tomorrow they'll move him to Qirrat Maidan at the Citadel, which is where the interrogations will be held."

Aisha's heart contracted. She had thought matters would be sorted out here, in this place, that the business would be quickly concluded, but now she awoke to the fact that there was a legal matter involved, and interrogations, and prison. Nabawiyya was speaking from long experience of running after people who had been accused of something or were considered suspect, and she knew that political cases generally took longer than other kinds. Once more, she patted Aisha and spoke calmly to her.

"Believe me, my dear," she said, "it's no use waiting. He may not even be here to begin with. Come along now, I'll take you home. It will kill Madame Umm Abbas if neither one of you comes home tonight."

Suddenly reminded of Umm Abbas, Aisha realized she must now be sitting by the window, anxious and helpless. News would have reached her of a massacre that had taken place at the square, and doubtless her worst fears were assailing her now. Nabawiyya's logic prevailed—there was no one left in the square but soldiers and some informers—all the rest had been felled by despair and exhaustion. Aisha, too, was overcome by this day's exertions. Nabawiyya took her by the hand and led her away, one hand reassuringly on her back.

Nabawiyya hailed the driver of a carriage who was sleeping, parked next to the post office. She sat in the back next to Aisha, who, feeling a bit of warmth, realized how chilled and lonely she had been. The carriage set off, the horse's hoofbeats cleaving the silence. Nabawiyya brushed away the traces of tears from Aisha's face. "My dear," she said, "don't drown yourself in love. Your Mukhtar's nice, and all that, but men are worthless. If you break things off with them they go to the ends of the earth to keep you from escaping, but if you seduce them they get you pregnant and then they run away. They—"

Aisha stared at her, astonished at her daring and fearful that the driver would hear her, although he appeared unconcerned. The streets were virtually empty, and unusually dark. Umm Abbas, Aisha thought, would hear her out as she told her story, but she would be very angry with her. She wouldn't forgive her for what had happened to Mukhtar.

Nabawiyya kept talking, trying to stave off the dreariness of the silence and the dark. She spoke about the women at the house in the red-light district. Word of the demonstration had reached them as they were preparing to welcome their customers, and they had decided at once that this was no time for work or pleasure, but that they must all join their woes with everyone else's on that sad night. The lights of the Sayyida Zaynab Mosque appeared, and as human activity filled the square Aisha felt a little more at ease. The two women disembarked together, Nabawiyya insistent upon escorting Aisha to the entrance of the narrow alleyway. In spite of herself, Aisha felt embarrassed that anyone should see Nabawiyya walking beside her, and she wished the night were even darker. Nabawiyya must have sensed what was in her mind, for she stopped and said, "You'll be all right now—no one in the neighborhood will bother you."

Aisha turned to her, grateful for her perceptiveness. "Can you get back home on your own?"

"Nighttime," Nabawiyya said simply, "is my cover and my protection. It's the light of day that exposes me to shame."

"I needed your help badly. I don't know how to thank you."

"No need for thanks, my dear. We'll meet again—I visit the Umm Awajiz shrine at Sayyida Zaynab every Thursday."

Aisha said good-bye and stood, perplexed, watching her. Then she dragged herself home with heavy steps.

The days that followed were heavy as well. Umm Abbas grew flushed and angry, her expression reproachful, and she swore she would not speak to Aisha until Mukhtar returned. Aisha took up her vigil in Citadel Square, consumed with fear and apprehension. The buildings of the Citadel towered grimly over her, British flags fluttering atop its lofty walls. The flags, a blatant symbol of British control over a vanquished city, had been raised on the first day they arrived—the khedive himself had surrendered to them the keys to the Citadel gates—and the flags had never yet been lowered. Every day the ranks of their soldiers, with their red faces, descended from their barracks within the Citadel in a long line, parading their might from the arms bazaar to Khalifa Street.

Aisha stood amid a crowd of people. The old Ottoman prison, of pallid stone, confined all manner of prisoners behind its walls. Aisha was seized with fright on finding herself among the wives of murderers, drug smugglers, and highwaymen—what, then, must it be like inside the prison, and how would Mukhtar fare in such company? What scars would this terrible ordeal leave upon his soul?

After many long and bitter days, Mukhtar's comrades began to emerge from the low prison gate, their faces sallow and their eyes wandering, unable to tolerate the sun's glare, as if they had been kept in the pit of a dark cellar. Hope sprang to life in Aisha's heart—she expected Mukhtar to appear at any moment. He would be pale, his beard grown long, and he would be starving, but he would be as eager for their reunion as she. She would take him in her arms and kiss both his eyes, so that he would forget his travails. But he did not come out—one face after another appeared, but not his. Every day the prison shut its gates without her having seen him, and that access of hope she had felt faded from her eyes. Umm Abbas's silence went on and on.

Aisha saw al-Rafiy coming and going in a state of exhaustion, accompanied by a team of lawyers. She begged him to give her some answers, but he shook his head. "It's a very difficult situation," he said. The police chief himself has accused Mukhtar of attempting to kill him. In refuting this charge we are attempting the impossible; it will take time."

She couldn't believe that he would remain alone inside the prison, while she lingered, lost, in the middle of this forbidding square. Her days were bitter, her nights filled with nightmares. How many more days would she have to go on like this? How many weeks? How many months would pass before she could see him once more?

◆ ◆ ◆

In the middle of the night Aisha started up in fear, with a nightmare crouched upon her chest and a sound of muffled blows coming from downstairs, like a continuation of the bad dream. She got out of bed and dabbed at the sweat that had broken out on her brow. Barefoot, she went to investigate. She could hear the sound of Umm Abbas's slow and regular breathing as she stood listening for a moment on the other side of the door. The noise was coming from below—violent blows, sounds of something splintering and falling in pieces. The sounds emanated from the untenanted basement. What was happening? Was it another police raid? Or were thieves wreaking havoc among Mukhtar's irreplaceable sculptures? What should she do? It was no use rousing the elderly lady—there would be nothing she could do. Aisha picked up a small lamp and opened the door. She went downstairs, the cold steps sending shivers through her as she placed her feet on them one after another. The lamp trembled in her hand, and nearly went out, as the sounds of demolition grew louder. She took the last few stairs, which led to the basement door, shaking with fright. The hour was late, and there was no one she might call for help. There was nothing for it but to confront whatever sort of person might turn out to be within.

The door was unlocked. Aisha hesitated before pushing it open. Then she held the lamp up and stepped inside. She saw Mukhtar standing in the middle of the room, clutching a hammer, which he was about to bring down upon a sculpture of a peasant woman. When he sensed Aisha's presence, the hand holding the hammer paused, and he turned toward her. He was tall and gaunt, his visage implacably angry. A thick beard encircled his cheeks, and in his eyes was a savage gleam. She gasped with a mixture of joy and alarm. Setting the lamp down on a small table, she ran to him, embracing him with all her strength. She could feel the protruding bones of his chest pressing against her breasts. She buried her head in his neck, inhaling the smell of prison that clung to his pores. But his face was still distant from her. His arm with the hand that held the hammer was raised high, while the other arm made no move to touch her. "Thank God you've come back to us," she cried. Overcome, she burst into tears, still clinging to his neck.

She was unaware of how stiffly he stood there, silent and unyielding. She tried to hold him more tightly, to connect with his body and give it some of her own warmth, but then she heard his voice saying, "Don't touch my back. It hurts."

She drew back in alarm. She saw the look he was giving her—a stare that held nothing of either love or enmity, as though she had intruded upon a private moment and she had no right to be there. She gazed at him pleadingly, as if entreating him to shed this grim demeanor, to let her touch his face and to kiss him, and ease her mind. He turned his face away, avoiding the look in her eyes. She burst out with all her questions at once. "When did you get out? Why didn't you come upstairs? I never stopped waiting for you. What have they done to you? Why are you destroying these sculptures? Why?"

He raised his hand and gestured for her to be silent. In the same cold voice he said, "I'm tired. I can't talk."

"And yet," she replied with some asperity, "you can smash these sculptures."

He spoke sharply. "I no longer need them. I no longer need anything."

Cautiously, she approached him. She refrained from trying to embrace him, so as not to hurt him or make him pull away. She placed her hand gently on his face, and he didn't prevent her. She could see plainly in his eyes the pain he was in. She stroked his coarse beard and felt the cold sweat that covered him. She noticed little wounds, purple bruises, and she registered his deadly pallor. He couldn't bear to look at her, and closed his eyes. At once tears slid from both of them. "Mukhtar!" she cried in distress. "Mukhtar, my love—what have they done to you?"

He took her hand and removed it from his face, not roughly, but firmly. "Nothing," he said. "They made me hate myself . . . and hate everything around me. Isn't that enough?"

He shuddered, trembling all over, and she withdrew her hand fearfully. All she had to offer him was her love, but he didn't want it. She gestured toward the wrecked sculptures. "You're angry and exhausted now. You ought not to destroy your life's work at such a moment. Calm yourself, love—everything will be set to rights."

Her words only made him angrier. He waved the hammer at her, shouting, "Nothing will be set to rights! This country is rotten—I could smell the stench of its rottenness from prison, and I understood that it would never wake up, that it would continue, oblivious, under the yoke of oppression and injustice. Here there is nothing to live for; everything invokes death!"

His voice rose, his rage filling the room. Aisha drew back until her back was against the wall. She composed herself so as not to break into tears. All the feelings of humiliation he had suppressed while in prison had exploded, and he had no one on whom he could vent his rage except for the sculptures and Aisha herself. Nearly choking on her words, she said, "I beg you, Mukhtar—don't say such things. And please stop waving that hammer."

He lowered the hand with the hammer in it, and let out a breath from deep in his lungs, as if he were shifting a burden off his shoulders. "You shouldn't be here at a time like this," he said to her. "I want to be alone."

He was sending her away—he didn't need her. He held her responsible for his having gone to prison and for the outrages he had suffered. She didn't want to take offense—she was still determined to preserve the thread that bound them.

"I'll see you in the morning," she said, "won't I?"

"If morning comes," he said. His voice was cold.

She dragged herself from the room; her feet felt heavy. She leaned against the wall, breathing hard. She heard no sound of demolition, but his voice rose in sudden, harsh sobs—poor boy, they had hurt him grievously, injuring him in body and spirit. As she went into her room and sat on the bed, she attempted to reassure herself, "He'll calm down in the morning." The Mukhtar she knew would come back to her. She closed her eyes and tried to sleep. But she couldn't.

In the morning, Mukhtar was not there. Aisha went down to see whether he would come up and have breakfast with her and Umm Abbas, but the door to the room was wide open, and the half-demolished sculptures stared at her, empty-eyed. His clothes lay in a heap, bundles of paper containing his drawings were scattered about—everything was there but he himself, as if he had not yet got out of prison. She wept on Umm Abbas's shoulder, feeling as though her life had hardened into ice. Where had he gone? Had he gone home to his village? Would he be back come nighttime, or tomorrow? At what time and in what condition would he return?

She stood at the gate to the School of Fine Arts. Seeing many of his classmates on their way out, she took courage and approached one of them, a young man by the name of Ragheb Iyad, whom she knew from a previous occasion. "I heard," he told her, "that the school expelled him because of his political activism. He may not be able to finish his studies. It's a shame that they would treat a talented artist so cruelly."

Aisha wandered blindly through the alleyways. She understood what had happened, how devastating it was: not only had he been imprisoned and humiliated, but the dreams dearest to his heart had been laid waste. She went to the offices of *al-Siyaasa*, and to the café to which most of the students from the School of Fine Arts repaired, where they displayed their work. On a table in the center of the café was a sculpture he had made, of three blind men. She felt she was like them: completely blind, groping about in the streets, unable to see a thing. She went back home, to the old woman who was waiting for her. Umm Abbas wept bitterly, as if lamenting her own lost child, the child she had carried and named, but with whose living reality she had not been blessed.

He did not return until the evening of the following day. Aisha saw him entering the neighborhood, before he hurried inside the house and hid himself in the basement. He hastened his steps over the small cobblestones, as if someone were after him. He looked even more wretched now than before; his thick beard made his face look darker, but he was still pale, looking as though he might fade away. She hurried into the salon, expecting to hear his footsteps on the stairs, or his knock upon the door of the apartment, but all was quiet, and remained so. Umm Abbas stared at her questioningly.

"He's come back," she said, "but he hasn't seen fit to come to us and tell us what he intends to do. He's begun to hate me, truly."

Umm Abbas studied her for a moment. She tried to get up, struggling for breath, and Aisha went quickly to help her; she was heavy, flaccid in all her limbs. Aisha opened the double doors of the apartment all the way and helped her through the doorway, which she had not passed in years—not since she was widowed, and immobilized by both her sorrow and her stoutness. She shuffled along painfully, and Aisha, taking pity on her, entreated her to come back, but the lady was resolved to go downstairs, despite her labored breathing. She gripped the banister with one hand, clinging to Aisha's arm with the other. Aisha's eyes filled with tears, but she collected herself in the face of the old woman's determination.

They stopped in front of the door to his room. Aisha hadn't the courage to knock—she cowered behind Umm Abbas, leaving her to do the knocking and to order Mukhtar, in strident tones, to open up. He did not dare oppose this voice; he opened the door, and presented his ravaged, grieving face. Startled, he stared at Umm Abbas, who was still panting and red-faced, her heart pounding, but who, in spite of all that, raised her fist and faced him down. "Who do you think you are?" she scolded. "You think you have no family, that there's no one to worry about you or wonder what's become of you? Have you forgotten your obligation to us?"

He backed away, caught off-guard by her rebuke, and Umm Abbas stepped forward, entering that room for the first time in many years. She resumed her tirade, gesturing toward Aisha. "And this poor girl," she said, "who waited for you at the prison gate, exposed to the elements, and stayed awake nights—how can you treat her so callously?"

He looked at them both, seeming lost and pitiful, as if prison had torn him up by the roots, leaving him no place to which he could assert any connection, no one with whom he might claim any bond. He would have liked to weep, to throw himself into the old woman's arms and tell her all his woes, everything he had suffered in the cells at Qirrat Maidan, but he stood there before them and kept himself in check. The two of them were, of all people, the last ones before whom he wished to appear weak and defeated.

"I can't stay here after all that's happened," he said hoarsely. "I'm going away . . ."

Umm Abbas went abruptly quiet, staring at him in consternation. "What?" she exclaimed. "You're going to go live somewhere else?"

"Another country," he said. "Egypt has slammed its doors in my face, stripped me of everything. There's nothing left for me but to go and find a haven in another land."

Aisha gave a muted cry. He glanced at her, then quickly lowered his head. There was nothing he could do to ease the blow for her. He went on hastily, as if to unburden himself of the two of them. "I kept vigil all night long in front of Prince Yusuf Kamal's palace in Ain Shams. I didn't leave until I had met with him. He agreed to my traveling to France when he heard that the School of Fine Arts had dismissed me. This is my only recourse."

Umm Abbas sat down on the base of a broken sculpture; Aisha was still leaning against the wall, unable to speak. It was all too cruel—there were no words for it. "You did what you did," Umm Abbas said bitterly, "you made your arrangements and obtained consent, all without letting us know—without saying anything to this poor girl, whom you promised to marry?"

He did not raise his head or look in Aisha's direction. In a sharp voice he said, "Things have changed. I can no longer promise anything."

Umm Abbas struggled to her feet, supporting herself with whatever she found to hand. "Take me upstairs, child," she said. She held onto Aisha's hands, and they went out of the room. The staircase seemed endless, as the two of them mounted it in defeat, Aisha still supporting the older woman and trying to keep her moving forward, and to prevent her from falling. The only sound she could hear was that of Umm Abbas's hoarse breathing.

All was silent until the call to prayer at dawn, the muezzin's voice plangent and supplicating. Umm Abbas did not appear to have stirred from her room. Then at dawn Aisha heard the sound of her wooden clogs upon the floor as she got up to perform her ablutions, and recited the Qur'anic verse of "The Chair." No sound came from her room, and Aisha didn't dare get up to check on her. She watched the light of day gradually spreading into her room, without moving from her place, even when she saw Mukhtar leaving the quarter, in the same wretched state and wearing the same clothes as on the previous day. He proceeded in haste, as if fleeing from something, without a backward glance. He knew she was watching him, and didn't want to meet her gaze with his own.

Once the sun had drenched the earth, Umm Abbas left her room, her face pale. There was nothing to be said; they took no breakfast, but sat in silence, waiting for nothing. In the middle of the day, Aisha rose and dressed. When the old woman looked questioningly at her, she said, "I'm going to visit the shrine at Sayyida Zaynab."

She made her way through the streets with bowed head, not wanting anyone to see last night's despair in her face. She slipped in among the crowd of people weeping and begging and clinging to the shrine, which was draped in green velvet embroidered with Qur'anic verses in gold thread. The sound of prayers rose from within the ancient mosque, along with the voices of the black-clad women wailing their entreaties. Aisha felt a powerful urge to weep. She was one with the others in their weakness, their poverty, their helplessness. "Umm al-Awajiz," she cried fervently, "protector of the unfortunate—bring back to me the Mukhtar of old, whom I loved! Sow in his heart the seeds of love for me, that he may find peace and be at ease."

She would need a miracle, truly, to get him back before he was lost to her entirely. She went to a corner of the shrine and curled up there. Someone came to a stop by her, and she knew who it was without raising her head. At such moments Nabawiyya would always appear. Aisha remembered that it was Thursday, the time when Nabawiyya regularly attended, and now here she was, standing before her, swathed in black, like the dozens of other unfortunate and powerless women. Her face was free of makeup, her eyes filled with tears. She, too, sought help and redemption. Their eyes met, and their fingers entwined in sympathy. Together they left the mosque and sat in the busy, marble-paved square. All at once Aisha felt herself in need of this meeting, even though she had not intended to tell Nabawiyya a of what had happened.

Nabawiyya al-Mustahiya sat cross-legged on the ground. She looked into Aisha's face and tried to smile. "You didn't sleep last night, did you?" she said.

"Is my fatigue so obvious?" Aisha replied.

"Maybe," said Nabawiyya, "but I know the reason for everything that shows in your face."

"What is it . . . that you know?"

"I can't talk about it here, or I'll make the lady of the shrine angry. Let's move away from here."

Nabawiyya stood up briskly, held out her hand, and helped Aisha to her feet. They walked together, disregarding the beggars' hands reaching out to them. Aisha didn't mind when Nabawiyya placed a hand on her shoulder.

"I know," said Nabawiyya, "that Mukhtar loves you dearly, and that no other woman has replaced you in his eyes. Perhaps the time he spent in prison is responsible for his recent conduct. I wanted to tell you what happened, so that you would be aware, and know how to deal with him."

Aisha's heart sank—she didn't need any more troubles having to do with Mukhtar. She halted in her tracks, turned and looked at Nabawiyya in dismay. Nabawiyya swallowed hard and said, "Mukhtar came yesterday to the house in the red-light district, paid the price of admission, and asked for me. I was startled to find him at the door to my room."

"He wanted to sleep with you?"

"Naturally, I refused. I have my principles, and I don't betray a friendship. I knew he was not in his right mind. One look at him—the state he was in, the way his eyes flashed—was enough to tell me what sort of madness had hold of him. He might even have hurt me if I'd given in to his wishes. I shouted at him until I succeeded in embarrassing him, and he went away from my room."

Shocked, Aisha heard her out. Should she believe these words? Was it Mukhtar Nabawiyya was talking about, or someone else? In a faint voice, she asked, "Did he go to another woman then?"

"There's no use in lying. The truth is I can't say one way or the other—I never left my room, and I didn't ask any of the other girls. What I can say with certainty, though, is that he wasn't in a fit condition to manage anything."

Aisha walked on beside Nabawiyya, but she no longer heard anything she said. At every turn she was discovering a new and alien side to Mukhtar. She didn't really know him at all. Did he just need a warm body more than he needed love? Were her love and devotion not enough? Was this the reason he had withdrawn from her—not just what had happened to him in prison? She said goodbye to Nabawiyya and went back through the narrow lanes.

Umm Abbas was sitting in her spot, from which she had not moved since the break of day. They tried to talk to each other of trivialities, everything but Mukhtar. Aisha prepared food, as a distraction, but neither of them ate much, each with a lump in her throat. They ran out of things to say. Aisha sat by the window, waiting for nothing, as the light faded and darkness fell. She fell asleep where she was, overcome with fatigue.

She awoke, shivering, to the sound of a knock at the door. The apartment was dark; no one had lit the gas lamp. She got up and went barefoot to the lamp, while the knocking at the door continued as she tried to light the flame. The wick quivered and the apartment glowed with a pale light. Umm Abbas was asleep, open-eyed, in the place she had occupied since noon. Aisha called out to inquire who was knocking, but no one replied. Heart weary, she wanted no more surprises, but she picked up the lamp and opened the door to find Mukhtar standing before her, his eyes reflecting the light that illuminated his pale face.

Her hand shook and she took a step back. Waking, Umm Abbas gasped as if she had seen a ghost. Mukhtar stepped forward into the room. Aisha hastened to set the lamp down, lest she drop it. He remained standing close to the door, as if expecting to be sent away at any moment. Umm Abbas rose, leaning upon her cane, muttering that she would go to her room.

Mukhtar looked at Aisha and said, "I couldn't go away without speaking to you first."

She was having trouble breathing, her lungs struggling to take in air—if only he would approach her and put his arms around her, she would forgive him everything, forget the foolishness of which Nabawiyya had told her. But he stood there, tall and thin and cold. "You cannot imagine," he said, "what happened to me in prison. I, an artist and a mayor's son, found myself all at once among thieves, murderers, and brigands. All the demonstrators who had been around me were let out, while I was left there to suffer degradation in place of them all."

It seemed to Aisha that she ought not to hear all this out in silence. "They testified on your behalf," she said. "All of them said that you had not struck the police chief, and that the horse reacted to the crowd. Even those who were at the edge of the square and didn't see anything gave witness for you."

"But they got out, and they left me there alone to suffer the real torment of prison, where there are no witnesses, and where unspeakable things happen. When I left that place I had lost my faith in everything."

"You're not in prison now. We can take up our life again."

"After all that's happened, I'll never be able to forget, or submit, or be happy. If I stay here I'll march in every demonstration, put myself in the vanguard of any protest movement I can. I won't be able to draw or paint or sculpt—my anger and outrage will prevent me. I'll be at risk of arrest and humiliation all over again, and I'll lose even more of myself. This is why I must go away from here—to retrieve myself."

Fighting tears, Aisha said, "And what about me? Have you given me not even a moment's thought?"

"There is nothing you can do but wait for me—only I don't know until when."

"Such a vague promise."

"It's the best I can do!"

He spoke sharply, and held himself back, keeping his distance from her. Aisha's mouth felt dry as he spoke his last words to her, then turned away without offering so much as a touch. All at once she was angry, angry that he should treat her so, and she shouted at him. "Did you go to the red-light district? Did you try to sleep with Nabawiyya al-Mustahiya?" He turned and looked at her, confusion in his face. In an uncertain voice he said, "Perhaps I did, and perhaps I didn't. I am not myself, and this body is not mine."

Then he turned once more and went out the door, closing it behind him. Aisha stood frozen in place, hearing the sound of his footsteps descending the stairs.

7 • The Village of Beni Khalaf

A SMALL CASE BESIDE HER, Aisha stood on the railway platform, all but carried off by the cold wind. A few meters away from her the man stood, keeping a furtive eye on her. He loomed tall and massive, his *jilbaab* billowing in the gusts. A woolen scarf wound about his neck largely obscured his face, and his head was wrapped in an enormous turban. All that showed plainly was the thick moustache that divided his face in two and his cold, implacable stare, which sent shivers up her spine each time she felt it upon her. The station was not crowded; there were just a few passengers, trudging heavily along, toting bags and bundles larger than themselves. He carried only his cane. He had been confident of the success of the brief errand on which he had come: to bring her back.

Aisha was alone and apprehensive. Mukhtar had made his stealthy departure months before, without seeing her, and without bidding farewell to Umm Abbas. He left the key to the basement room with Zahran, who kept a store at the corner of the street, instructing the shopkeeper to return the key to its mistress and to tell her to dispose of the rest of his things—including the sculptures—to consign them to the rubbish heap if she wished. Umm Abbas wept bitterly on receiving the key, and vowed that she would never open the basement room. Aisha understood that, no matter how long she waited, he would not return.

The winter grew colder, and every day the rain fell in torrents, filling the alleyways with mud and making passage through them difficult. Aisha tried to resume her ordinary life, but in vain. *Al-Liwa* stopped printing, beset by relentless pressure from the British on one side, and from Sultan Hussein Kamil on the other. Mohammad Farid left Egypt, forced into exile. Everyone at *al-Liwa* was put out of work, and Aisha could not find in herself the fortitude to go and seek work with a different paper.

The ground shook as the train pulled into the station, puffing out a thick, black cloud. It must have come from the train yard, for it was empty, discharging not a single passenger. Without a word the man stepped onto the train, not waiting for her to board first—he had no doubt she would follow him. Aisha stood where she was, watching the platform fill up suddenly with people—she didn't know where they had all come from: passengers carrying baskets made of palm leaves, women clad all in black, disgruntled effendis, and one Englishman, twisting the ends of his moustache. Aisha stared at the iron girders that formed a lofty bridge, upon which the pigeons had made a nest for themselves. They could take wing and soar to the other side without anyone's being able to catch them. She lamented that she had believed the man and followed him through all these streets, from the Sayyida Zaynab quarter to the railway platform—but how could she take a chance on whether he was lying or telling the truth?

When she had arisen in the middle of the night to the sound of loud knocking at the door, she had imagined for a moment that Mukhtar, unable to bear a protracted separation from her, had come back to her. She was ready to follow him to the ends of the earth. But on opening the door she had found this man standing before her. She recognized him at once, despite the passage of years, as if he could follow her and it was no use her trying to escape. He bore no trace of a resemblance to her father; they were not full brothers. He was the black sheep of the family—as her father had used to say—causing no end of trouble. She drew a sharp breath, horrified, and tried to close the door in his face, but the man had crossed the threshold before she managed it. He had planted himself in the middle of the entryway, in his voluminous *jilbaab*, the woolen scarf wrapped around his neck, forcing his presence on her, as if she had never left his sight for an instant.

"How did you find me?" Aisha gasped.

He looked at her for a moment, as if in mockery of her flight and concealment. "Your mother," he said "sent me herself. She fears she may die without seeing you."

Aisha's heart contracted, even though she knew such sentiment was uncharacteristic of him—still, the reference to her mother made her gasp with shock. She heard the sound of Umm Abbas as she struggled to get up and make her way out of the room. She paused before the two of them, and studied the strange man. She pointed her cane at him as if to say, "Who is he?" But Aisha didn't dare speak.

He turned to Umm Abbas, placed his hand upon his chest, and said humbly, "Your servant, Omran, Aisha's paternal uncle and her mother's husband, one and the same."

Umm Abbas paid no heed to his polite gestures. At a single glance she had apprehended the state of deathly fright that gripped Aisha.

"What do you want?" she said.

Disregarding her hostile tone, he said neutrally, "The lady who is Aisha's mother, my wife, is very ill. It is she who asked me to come here and inform her daughter that she wishes to see her—this is her last wish."

Umm Abbas's hand flew to her chest, but Aisha backed away and said in a hoarse voice, "I won't go anywhere with you."

In the same neutral tone he said, "As you wish—I am only the messenger. I shall return today, at once, to the village. Her state of health does not permit me to linger here in order to persuade you. I have informed you of her condition, and no one will blame me if you never see her again . . ."

Umm Abbas interrupted. "Is she so very ill?" she asked anxiously.

"She is dying. I am here in a race against time—had she not asked me to come here, I would not have left her, with her condition so grave."

Umm Abbas looked questioningly at Aisha—what was her decision? Aisha did not know how to answer this. With half her mind she believed him, while the other half recalled her mother's warnings not to trust him under any circumstances. Umm Abbas went to her and patted her shoulder—Aisha had not told her everything, but she sensed her confusion. "Don't you want to go?" whispered Umm Abbas.

"I want to see her," replied Aisha in an unsteady voice, "but I'm frightened of him."

Omran took a step toward them, and spoke directly to the older woman. "I'll bring her back as soon as her mother has been assured that she is well. If her fate is to live, then she herself will return here with her daughter. But if her time has come and God takes her, I'll bring Aisha back myself."

He spoke in a gentle, persuasive tone, but who could guarantee her return? Who would protect her if her mother died? And who would pardon her if her mother should die alone and grief-stricken? If only Mukhtar were with her at this moment—he was the only one who could have protected her. Umm Abbas decided the matter.

"The wishes of the dying are sacred," she said. I'll help you pack your case."

Umm Abbas fought back her tears as she assisted Aisha. She bade her farewell at the door, and Aisha followed the man who proceeded in front of her without a backward glance. He struck the earth with his cane and the wind filled his *jilbaab*, as if it were the sail of a boat making ready for departure.

She stood long on the platform. From the window Omran cast his level gaze upon her and said nothing. An old man approached with doddering steps, and rang the brass bell. In response, the train whistle blew. Her stomach lurched as she bent to pick up her case and, without meeting his gaze, mounted the steps to the train. She proceeded down the aisle between the wooden seats, and sat across from him. He leaned his head upon his cane and closed his eyes. She knew he could still see her. The train whistle blew for the last time before it began to move. The houses of Giza began to recede behind them. The minarets disappeared and were replaced by palm trees. The edge of the mountain appeared, dark blue, in the distance. The shining surface of the Nile came into view, stirring in her feelings of regret and longing.

She closed her eyes and surrendered to the endless rocking, through long hours during which the train stopped occasionally for passengers to disembark and others to board. She opened her eyes and saw doum palms and Indian fig trees alongside the tracks. Behind them were plantations of palm and sycamore and lemon. The mountainside was closer, and in it appeared the openings for the tombs carved into the rock, as well as the dusty white domes of the saints' mausoleums. Vendors who worked the little stations boarded and began crying their wares—dates and tangerines—in singsong tones. Still Aisha and the man sat cloaked in silence. He opened his eyes from time to time and looked at the distant horizon, ignoring her presence. Night's shadows crept up on them and hid all the familiar landmarks around them. It seemed as though the train had entered a dark and endless tunnel.

Nightmares assailed her even though her eyes remained watchful. At last a gray light split the horizon. Green fields appeared, covered in a fine layer of mist. He was asleep with his head on his cane. Mud-brick houses came into view, huddled as if in fear, their drab color further darkened by moisture from the dew. The train stopped for three hours at a remote station to take on water and coal. They were the only ones who did not get off. They sat on in silence, face-to-face, each avoiding the glances of the other. The train resumed its journey and the scattered villages followed one after another, clustering along the riverbank until there was no more space.

Flickering gaslights, mounted on poles, illuminated nothing but a tiny area around them. She got off the train, stood outside the wooden shack, and gazed upon the village, which was wrapped in darkness. The crowns of the palm trees concealed beneath them houses that looked like faint shadows. Her father's house was outside of the village, far from the congestion of these dwellings. Passing among the sugarcane fields, they walked a narrow corridor from which rose the sound of powerful winds. The howling of wolves mingled with the noise of barking dogs that came from the direction of the village. Hearing at last the voices of the wolves, she found them oddly familiar—a sign of welcome to which she was unaccustomed. Omran walked faster—was he anxious about her mother, or unnerved by the wolves' howling? She caught the scent of her house—the emanations that rose from every house: of mud-brick walls, combined with the smells of salt bogs, of curdled milk, of the stagnant water in the irrigation ditches, of dung patties, and of the little calves just born. In spite of herself she cast back into her memory, and her eyes filled with tears of loss and longing.

The house could be clearly seen despite the darkness. It was her father who had chosen its location and overseen its construction. Behind it stretched the lands that belonged to them. She hurried up to the closed door and knocked upon it with her fist. Her mother would come out at any moment and put her arms around her—and then, whatever would be, let it be. But the door stood silent. From his pocket Omran drew a great key tied to a length of twine, and turned it in the lock. Had the door been locked from the outside against her mother for all this time?

The door opened and she rushed inside. He stayed where he was, in the courtyard, while she sprang lightly up the mud-brick staircase to where her mother's room had always been. A dim light came from the room, faint hope amid doubt and darkness. She stopped, breathing hard, before the door, and called her mother's name for the first time in many long months. The door was ajar; she pushed it open and entered the room half-shrouded in darkness. There was a gas lamp covered in a layer of soot, and an open wardrobe displaying her clothes. In the middle of the room was a brass bed draped in white mosquito netting. Aisha called out to her mother once more—her scent filled the room, but there was no answer. She pulled aside the netting—the bed was empty. She cried out, calling her again, expecting her to emerge from some corner and embrace her daughter. But all was silent.

Frightened, she sucked in her breath and backed out of the room. She stood at the top of the stairs; he stood at the bottom, immovable as a wall. "There's no one in the room!" she cried. "Where is my mother?"

"In her grave," he replied, fingering his moustache.

She leaned back against the wall, and her tears flowed freely. "Oh, God," she said, "this is what I feared . . . my God . . . I won't ever see her again." Her legs would no longer support her—she collapsed in a heap upon the floor, unaware of him as he climbed the stairs.

He stood before her, observing her, stone-faced, as she wept without relief. "There's no use crying about it now," he said. "She died ten days ago."

Aisha lifted her head. She couldn't see him clearly. He had lied to her, and succeeded in luring her here. She heard him say mockingly, "Your mother did a good job of hiding you, but that foolish effendi who came here from Cairo—he gave it all away."

If only she could be alone now, if his shadow would just move away from her a little, so that she could weep for her mother and quell the pounding of her heart. But he came closer to her, seized her shoulder, and pressed it. Through her tears, she screamed, "Don't you dare touch me!"

In the same mocking tone he replied, "But I can't help it!"

She got to her feet and went into her mother's room, her last remaining sanctuary. She locked the door behind her and threw herself onto the bed, empty of all but her mother's scent. She wept softly, so that he wouldn't hear her voice. The lamp, its fuel used up, went out and darkness fell. She had become his prisoner. Her only escape route was through the door to the room, and he was sitting in front of it.

She heard a scratching at the door, as if he were trying to dig through it with his fingernails. He muttered something in hoarse tones—although she hadn't understood the words, she was quaking with fear. She could hear howling in the distance. Was it possible that someone from the village might notice that she was held captive by him here? Was there any hope of rescue? She must think quickly—perhaps she could make a bargain with him, leave him a part of her inheritance from her parents, if he would let her go unharmed. Perhaps that was what he was after, and then he would release her to the light of day. At the very least, he would take her down to the port and register her arrival in the village, and then she might be able to get away, having paid the price of her bad judgment.

She started up in terror at a great crashing sound, and the door shook with the force of his blows. She screamed, but there was no place for her to take shelter. Everything was enveloped in darkness; he had no wish to wait until morning.

The bolt securing the room gave way, the two wooden panels of the door burst asunder, and his massive frame appeared. He approached her where she sat cowering upon her mother's bed. Would begging do her any good? Was there any point in resisting him? She felt his fingers sink into her flesh and smelled the odor of his breath, rank with alcohol and tobacco. Giving way to tears, she struggled to clamp her legs together, but he inserted his knees between them. She strained her face away from him, trying to avoid his own, so he delivered a vicious blow to her temple, shouting, "I'll have none of your tears, and it's no use struggling!" When she tried to dig her fingernails into his face, he struck her again. Her head was on fire from the blows, and the salt taste of blood was in her mouth. He put his face next to hers and bellowed, "If you value your life, do not fight me!"

He restrained her, holding her wrists away so that she could no longer push him from her, and then he crushed her beneath his body. Panting, he talked on. "There was no escape from this," he told her. "From the moment your mother was promised to me in marriage, I knew I would have you, although she, foolish woman, made me wait a long time." With his fingers he seized hold of the collar of her dress and, with a yank, ripped it efficiently down the front. She felt the cold night air against her chest. She pushed him away and sank her nails into his face, but her efforts were too feeble to have any effect on him. She felt his coarse hand seize her breasts. He held her down with one hand, and with the other tore her dress off and rent her underclothes. Fully roused now, he stripped her of everything. She lay naked, cold, and desecrated. Once again he thrust his knees between her legs, opening her up entirely. She screamed piteously as the pain shot through her—he had plunged into her very depths. She heard the sound of his panting as he rose and fell above her, and her stomach roiled with nausea. She wished she could vomit—if only she could breathe—but he would not stop. Now he was roaring like a beast, indifferent to her inert form. He groped her with his hands, doing with her as he pleased, raising her legs, changing his position, pressing upon her torso—he was heavy, so heavy. He tried to probe her mouth with his tongue, and when she pressed her lips together and turned her face away he struck her yet again: more pain, more blood filling her mouth, a nightmare without end. She felt him go rigid all at once as he reached his climax within her shattered body. He moaned feebly, as if his soul were about to depart, and then she heard his voice, triumphant, saying, "This is just the beginning. You'll get used to it before long . . . and you'll enjoy it."

He got up off of her at last and hurried out of the room, leaving Aisha like some lifeless rag tossed aside. As she lay there, too weak to move, she detected glimmers of gray light creeping in through the gaps in the shutters, while the crowing of roosters rose from the courtyard. She struggled to get up, gathering her damaged clothing about her, but her knees betrayed her and she fell to the floor. She managed to crawl, despite the bruises and lacerations that covered her, and her swollen face. She wanted to get to the door, to cry for help, in the hope that someone might hear her. But before she could reach it he startled her by opening it himself.

In came Omran once more, carrying an axe. She drew back in alarm, clutching her tattered dress to herself. Did he mean to kill her? He didn't glance in her direction, indifferent to her there on the floor. Using the blunt end of the axe-head he set about affixing the loosened hinges once more in place. She trembled at each blow of the axe as if it had fallen upon her own head. Paralyzed, she stared at him. Then, having repaired the door, he closed it again behind him, and she heard him slide the bolt, locking her in from the outside. The room had once again become a prison, and she wept silently. She wanted to get up and wash herself clean of the stickiness that fouled her body, but she stayed motionless where she was.

Sounds came to her from the village as it awoke: cattle lowing while the farmers urged them along, children calling—but the voices were far away, coming from another world. Supporting herself on the bedposts, she got to her feet and groped her way around the room until she found what she was looking for: clay vessels filled with water—she knew her mother had looked after herself fastidiously. Aisha moistened a bit of her torn dress and washed herself as best she could. Her face was hurting, inflamed where he had struck her, and her wounds stung as she cleaned away his bodily fluids as well as her own blood, with which her legs and belly were stained, and from time to time she drew a sharp breath. Then she went to her mother's wardrobe and sorted through the old dresses that hung there, from which she selected a *jilbaab* and put it on. It seemed to emanate warmth and safety, residual traces of her mother's embrace. It was this that would protect her.

She went to the door and tried rattling it, but it stood firmly locked against her. She then tried the closed window, but its wooden frame was likewise secured by large nails. He had laid the trap well before luring her into it. She was too far away from anyone for her screams to be heard. She didn't dare approach the bed;

instead she curled up in a corner of the room, her knees pressed to her chest and her arms wrapped around her legs, and fell into a deep sleep, her first since this dreadful journey had begun.

When she opened her eyes there was not a trace of light left; darkness had returned, and there was no more sound of voices. She felt cold, dehydrated, and hungry. She had eaten nothing since leaving the house of Umm Abbas when—like a fool—she had followed him and given him his chance to do to her as he wished. What did he intend to do with her now? Would he give her something to eat, or rape her again, or leave her here in the darkness to starve to death? She dared not move from her place—she expected only the worst.

Hearing the sound of his footsteps coming up the stairs, she clung harder to the wall, wishing she could make herself invisible to him. The door creaked harshly and rays of light appeared, as he walked into the room with a lamp in his hand. He turned around slowly until he discovered her whereabouts. Hanging the lamp on the wall, he sat on the edge of the bed and fixed his gaze on her, as if enjoying the sight of her wretchedness and her obvious terror. He seemed exultant at his triumph over her slight body, the unexpected ease with which he had taken possession of it.

"You must be dying of starvation," he said. "Hunger is the best sauce, as they say—there's plenty of food, but you'll not have a single bite of it until you do everything I tell you."

He stopped speaking to observe her reaction. She neither moved nor made a sound. "Don't cringe like that!" he bellowed furiously. "Get up off the floor!" He sprang from the bed and pitched himself at her—she could see he was prepared to beat her again. As she struggled to her knees in an effort to stand up and face him, she was assailed by all the pain he had already inflicted on her. He stared at the garment she was wearing. This enraged him further. "I don't want to see your mother ever again!" he shouted. "I've seen enough ghosts and demons. Take that thing off."

"Don't do this to me," Aisha sobbed. "I'm your brother's daughter!"

"My brother be damned, your mother, too—and you. All of you deprived me of what was rightfully mine. Do you know what they did to me? And all for the sake of a miserable little fool like you. My father—your accursed grandfather—disinherited me on the grounds that my mother was a Gypsy, a transient, and he gave everything to your father. Then, after your father died, they forced me to marry his widow, that dried-up old crone. Then I found out that he had left everything to you. I was bought and sold, may you all rot in hell!"

She stared at him, stunned by the savagery of his anger—his mouth was flecked with foam, his eyes bloodshot. The mention of her father had driven him into a frenzy. She backed away from him, fearful he would resume his assault on her. He reached for her, and she stiffened; then he took hold of her mother's dress and, as before, tore it off of her. She tried to shield her breasts and groin, while he, heedless of her fright, stared at her in her nakedness, his mouth agape.

"I didn't get a good look at you the first time. This is not like your mother, bony as a tree branch; this is the body I've always dreamed of possessing."

He took off his *jilbaab*. She shrank from him, crying, "My God—not again . . . ," but he advanced on her, picked her up, and flung her onto the bed. Her limbs were weak with hunger and cold; he engulfed her with his body, overcoming her struggles with ease. She could only weep helplessly. "It only hurts the first time," he sneered, seizing her breasts and swamping her with his breath. It was painful still, although to keep him from hurting her even more she made no attempt to resist him.

This time, fortunately, he finished with her quickly and got up off of her. "That body of yours won't be so lifeless for much longer." He flung this at her like a challenge. "I'll bring it to life in spite of you." Slinging his *jilbaab* over his shoulder, he strode naked from the room, and she heard the sound of him locking the door from the outside. She remained where she was, splayed naked upon the bed, not caring even to get up and wash herself: in such a state, let death come to her.

Darkness descended once more, along with a paralyzing cold. By leaving her this way he meant to break her will and subjugate her entirely. She sank into a series of nightmares without end, waking in terror at the slightest disturbance. It was strange that her body could still house any scrap of life, that life hung on and would not leave. She felt that he might descend on her at any moment.

Faint glimmers of light stole in through the locked window; she took refuge in a corner of the room, her ears alert for any sound coming from the direction of the door, but it seemed he was oblivious to her existence. He went out to carry on with daily life, secure in the knowledge that she was his hostage and would remain so. It didn't matter to him whether she was alive or dead; perhaps if she were to die that would be the best outcome as far as he was concerned.

Days—or perhaps hours—later, she heard his footsteps, the door opened, and then he stood before her holding a metal tray. She shrank back as he approached her. He set the tray down in front of her and took a step back. She couldn't help looking at the food on the tray: gleaming tomatoes, slices of cheese, and rounds of bread. Her stomach churned, but she tried to maintain her composure. Seated on the edge of the bed, he stared mockingly at her. She tried to reach for the food but he snarled at her. She stood up and lifted her eyes to him pleadingly. "You'll not eat unless you take off your clothes," he commanded. "Remove your dress before you touch the food." She backed away fearfully, shaking her head, so he stepped forward, picked up the tray, and turned to leave.

Aisha watched him in alarm as he opened the door. He was on the threshold when she cried, "Wait . . ." He turned, but stayed where he was. She lifted her hand and pulled the dress off, exposing her body to him herself. He set the tray before her and sat watching her. She was like a ravenous animal struggling beneath his feet as she tore off pieces of the bread with her teeth, devoured the cheese, and plunged her face into the tomatoes.

How much time passed between the first pale manifestations of light and utter darkness? How many days went by with her in his clutches? He would thrust himself upon her without warning, beat her for no reason, and take her without resistance. Sometimes he brought her food, but he always prolonged her intervals of starvation, and forced her to disrobe before he would permit her to eat. He bent her to his will, rousing her basic instincts—hunger, fear, and desire—always punishing her without compunction.

Then, at last, he allowed her to leave the room. He stood by the door and beckoned for her to follow him. It didn't matter what he might do—there could be nothing worse than this. She caught the scent of the damp fields; all at once she could see different colors—the crowns of the palm trees, the clouds tinged with red, the pigeons returning to their dovecote towers—and her eyes filled with tears. She descended the staircase into the courtyard.

He barked an order. "Go in and relieve yourself."

The cramped chamber beneath the stairs was familiar to her. He stood by the door, locking it after her. She made an effort to empty her bowels soundlessly, then washed herself and went out to him. He gestured for her to walk to the middle of the courtyard. She caught sight of the door leading out of the house, which was secured from the inside by an immense iron lock. An enclosure for chickens and ducks occupied one corner, as well as a shelter housing a donkey; in the middle was a pump, beside which was a metal tub—the very tub in which her mother had been accustomed to bathe her when she was small. In its center was a little wooden stool. The memory stirred her soul—the memory of that intimate ritual in which her mother would seat her on the stool and begin pouring warm water over her; suddenly all the familiar fragrances grew vivid in her mind: of the colored soap, the scented powder, and of her mother herself—it all came to her like a dream, and she forgot that he was there, staring at her. She took off her dress without shame at her nakedness, and sat cross-legged in the tub. She quivered at the sensation of hot water coursing down her body—water he fetched from a black earthenware kettle with a fire going beneath it. She felt fingers separating the strands of her hair and untangling the knots—were they his fingers or her mother's? The fingers soaped her all over and scrubbed her with a sponge, rousing every cell in her body. Aisha kept her eyes closed, leaving the fingers to pass over her breasts, her belly, her back; they stood her up in the middle of the tub to wash her thighs and her legs. She felt no rough touch as the water flowed over her like a warm cloak enfolding her in its intimate embrace. Her cuts and scrapes hurt, but heat dissolved the pain; she wept with longing, and the heat soothed her tears. A sense of new life crept into her limbs. He wrapped her in a towel soft as down and dried her flowing hair, her belly, and her legs. Then he picked her up in his arms—she made no sound, no protest. She was still lost in the world of her childhood as he carried her up the stairs, and warmth still enveloped her.

He laid her on the bed, removed the towel, and covered her with his body. He moved slowly and gently, as if the ritual of the bath were still under way. There was no pain; his fingers were not brutal, his breath was less repugnant than before. His heavy breathing above her aroused in her a strange throbbing sensation; warmth pervaded her body despite her nakedness, along with a tremor she tried to resist, suppressing her sighs; she felt that her body was no longer her own, with every fiber of her being responding to his touches. She wanted to hold onto something, but found only his shoulders. She sank her fingernails into them. The room filled with an odd smell, which drove away the previous stench—his sweat and her own, a mingling of their bodily secretions. From somewhere there came a brief flash, as if a breach had suddenly opened up to admit light from some distance source. She cried out.

He finished with her, but did not leave the bed. He stayed, stretched out beside her. She turned on her side, away from him, not daring to face him, but she felt his chest pressed against her back and she made no attempt to move away. She was fearful of finding herself alone in the gloom and the cold. He laid his massive thigh across her own small rump, while his hand came to rest below her waist, and his breathing settled into a regular rhythm. Her limbs were relaxed beneath this contact with him, as if her former body—the one that had refused him—had vanished entirely, and she had been taken over by another, stimulated by desire and driven by hunger, with no room for pity or tears spent on the old Aisha. There was nothing left to weep over.

In the middle of the night he left her, not yet trusting her enough to sleep deeply by her side, and with him went the warmth. She was back in the cycle of starvation and waiting—protracted stretches of waiting, broken only when he appeared, carrying a tray of food and demanding her body. When she saw him, she responded, in every nerve and every cell, in spite of herself. Hunger combined with cold, as there would be no food for her unless she was naked, and there would be no satiety until she got into bed. Time passed as she lay beneath him, the hours of darkness being confused in her mind with those of daylight, and one day connected to the next as if they were all one. No touch of his now failed to arouse her; her mind had grown rigid since she'd entered this room, so that she was scarcely capable of speech any longer—touch alone was the last of her faculties tethering her to life, and he regulated the rhythms even of this. He controlled her body when he left her, holding it hostage to the offerings of warmth and satiety that he alone was able to provide for it. He was her only link to the world—supposing that there was any other world outside this room.

On a certain terrifying night her need of him was greater than ever. Since midday there had been thunder and lightning without cease, and when night came flashes of light continued to flicker in through the slats of wood that blocked the window. Even the wolves were angry—perhaps the lightning had goaded them to a frenzy, rousing their instincts. Omran was not around—no doubt he was at the Greek's tavern, on the other side of the village; and here she was in this great void, the doors secured firmly against her with their enormous locks. She urgently needed him to be there, needed the contact of his warm and vital skin. If he was gone much longer she would die. She paced around the room to bring her body to life, looking for some opening that would connect her to the outside. She stood beside the window—the voices of the wolves were more distinct now. She discovered a food tray—on which were a spoon and a dirty metal plate—doubtless he had forgotten to remove it from the room. She picked up the plate and began using it to bang on the window. She inserted the spoon into the openings in the wooden slats, and tried to pry one of them up, concentrating her efforts on the weakest section, but she managed to dislodge only one small piece. A glimpse of dark sky was suddenly revealed before her. She saw the falling rain, felt the drops on her fingertips, savored its taste on the tip of her tongue.

She climbed up onto a small chair and, stretching her neck, saw the muddy earth below. The wolves were standing there, directly below her window, raising their heads toward her. Their eyes shone as if flashes of lightning had collected in them and now cut across the darkness to her. They were not howling, but gazed sorrowfully at her. Aisha stared gravely back at them. They were free, while she was helpless. They couldn't do anything for her—no one, not even these creatures of the night, could extend a helping hand to her.

She heard his footsteps mounting the stairs, and she drew back from the opening at the window, hoping he would not see it and punish her. He opened the door—she was thankful that he was there, but there was nothing she could do for him other than to run to the bed, take off her clothes and offer up her body to him, a naked sacrifice. She waited for him to come and begin touching her, but he looked at her in surprise. He had drunk a great deal, and come in this dreadful weather with the intention of having her whether she wanted it or not, but he had not expected her to catch him off-guard with so open a gesture. Trembling, she watched him move toward her—was she shivering with cold or with unwonted desire? It didn't matter—the only thing that mattered was that he get into bed and put his hands on her.

That night her body was compliant beneath him—eager and responsive as it had not been before, transformed from the coldness of isolation to the warmth of desire that precedes the brimming-over of ecstasy. He felt incapable of keeping up with her as she spun from one climax to another. He stopped, raised himself up a little, and looked at her in astonishment. She avoided his gaze, still gasping for breath and unable to master the paroxysms that convulsed her. He fingered his moustache, dazzled and bemused, as he realized that he could control this body, now and forever. He brushed aside her hair, which was damp with sweat, so that he could see the expression on her face and look deeply into her eyes. She stared dazedly back at him.

"We can't go on like this," he said, "or continue living in this place."

She said nothing. He placed his hand on her belly to stop her shaking, then spoke again. "Let's sell this accursed land," he said. "Let us leave this miserable village and go to some big city, where we may be able to live and no one will recognize us."

She had nothing to say to this. There was no place for her to take shelter in the state she was in. He pressed against her from behind, and she responded at once to the warmth he gave her. She had become his creature, his private object, no longer possessing the ability or the will to oppose him.

"We'll leave at dawn," he continued. "I'll saddle the donkey and we'll go together to the trade center to arrange matters for the sale. All you have to do is make me your agent and I'll see to the rest."

He grasped her by the waist and pulled her to him, hooking his great thigh over her. She sensed that he wanted her again, so she shifted onto her back and gave herself to him once more.

He woke her before first light. She had been sleeping deeply beside him, dreamless and free of nightmares. "Get ready," he whispered to her. "Put some clothes on while I go down to saddle the donkey. We'll leave in a little while."

He got out of bed, and she heard him descend the stairs. She got up obediently and went to the wardrobe to look for one of her mother's old dresses. She found the sheath her mother had most liked to wear when Aisha's father took her to town. Pulling it on, she paused when she heard strange noises coming from downstairs—animals snarling with fury, as close as if they were in the courtyard. She heard the sound of Omran shouting angrily, "Get out of here! Go on!" But the snarling only grew more savage. She dressed quickly, but dared not open the door. She retreated to a corner of the room and huddled there. Then she raised her head in astonishment as Omran's shouts turned to moans, and then to cries for help. She could scarcely believe she was hearing this powerful man cry out—she felt as though fangs were tearing at her own flesh as well. Then Omran went quiet, but the snarling continued; before long it became a sustained howling, like the announcement of a kind of victory. Aisha's fear turned to an uncontrollable trembling that shook her to her core, as if she had reached another climax that came from some unknown source and took her unawares. Silence fell. There was only the sound of the wind. Once more she was alone in a world in which silence prevailed.

She stayed huddled where she was, expecting him to open the door and come to her, shout at her to get ready and follow him. But the soundless minutes went on and on. She got up and went to the door, listening from behind it. Then she reached out a trembling hand and tugged at it. It was unlocked. She stepped over the threshold into the dim morning. No sun had risen, and traces of the rain made the stairs slippery. She descended several steps, to where she could see the whole courtyard: the clay oven, the chicken coop, the donkey's shed, the pump, the earthenware pitcher, the row of crockery jars that held cheese and butter—everything in its place. Omran was there too, lying in the mud, his eyes bulging, nearly naked, the only garment that had covered him now in shreds. He was as huge as ever, his moustache neatly curled, but his face was frozen. He could see her drawing near and peering at the blood that stained him, but he didn't rise up, lay her out on the ground, and have his way with her. His eyes and lips expressed his lecherous desire even now, but he was motionless. His body bore the marks of rending teeth, his flesh red and ragged. Evidently the wolves had all had a turn at him, and been powerful enough to bring him down, toppling him from that place of lofty invincibility in which he could rape and ravage at will. She looked about, seeing that the ground was covered with the tracks of claws, and the door was open. The lock, also unfastened, hung from one of its panels. Doubtless he had unlocked it in preparation for saddling the donkey, but the wolves had seized their opportunity and attacked him: he had opened the door to his own destruction.

She stood for a while by the body laid out before her, not daring to touch him or address him. She was afraid to make a move, lest the vitality seep back into him. Distant voices came to her from the village, along with the lowing of cattle as the villagers made their way to the fields. She didn't know what to do. She shut the door to the house and sat down on the staircase, facing him and studying his body, which seemed poised to rise. But he did not get up. She felt as though she needed him, as though no one would be able to gratify her senses as he had; at the same time, she felt that she was free of him—desire and disgust mingled within her, and she wept at the frailty of her body, the weakness of her will. She wanted to offer him to the wolves and let them devour him, ridding her of him once and for all. She tried to remember the body of that other Aisha, as memories of ephemeral moments from a distant past floated through her mind: of the rose that Isis's brother had given her once when he asked her to dance; of sitting in the open air with Sister Margaret; of the madman Howard Carter painting her in the guise of a pharaonic princess; of riding in a carriage beside the Leader; of receiving her first kiss from Mukhtar—fragments of memories that seemed to record events that had never occurred.

She went upstairs to the bedroom. She found the case she had brought with her tossed into a corner, untouched from the moment she had arrived with it. She searched her mother's wardrobe, looking in the secret places she knew so well, where she found some banknotes and leftover silver riyals. She tucked them into her bag, draped her mother's velvet shawl over her head, and went downstairs. There he still was, laid out in his place, but his skin had a blue tint to it now, and his expression seemed angrier, more savage. She turned her face away and went out, securing the door from outside by means of the lock. Let him stay where he was and rot.

She covered her face with the edge of the shawl as she made her way along the narrow track between the cane fields. There was no trace of the wolves. Some farmers passed by her, pulling their animals along, and she pulled the shawl more tightly across her face. The wooden building that housed the train station came into view, shrouded in mist, the exhalations of the earth. At last she ascended the gravel-strewn platform; the place was still empty, the tracks stretching into the distance, waiting. Aisha crouched in a corner—it was all she was capable of now.

The stationmaster Amm Bakri arrived. His appearance had not changed since her childhood—his olive-colored gallabiya worn at the elbows and knees, and the lantern, always lit, that he habitually carried. He hung up the lantern and rang the bell. He waited until he heard its echo resounding across the fields and then, sighing and at ease, seated himself on a bench, stretching out his legs until his feet touched the rails. His workday had begun. He did not notice Aisha huddled there.

Little by little the platform began to fill with people, some of whom she knew. She hid her face carefully. Most of the passengers were women taking village goods to the nearby port, while a few were men, who mingled with the women, strutting their specious virility. They chatted with the stationmaster, none of them noticing anything unusual afoot. Everyone in the village had passed an ordinary night—all but Aisha. They were in possession of ordinary bodies, which moved about freely and without shame, undergoing their share of cold, of morning light—all but Aisha. Her body was incapable of resistance; she possessed the body of a base animal that responded only to forbidden feelings and gratifications, dirtied with sweat and other bodily secretions—*his* secretions; contaminated by blind desires, by utter, abject degradation.

From afar came the sound of the train's whistle, and soon it appeared over the horizon, trundling along slowly, until at last came the moment of her deliverance from this place. She didn't know where she would go—she must simply get out, wrest herself away from here, and then perhaps her sense of shame would diminish a little. The train pulled into the station. Amm Bakri rang the bell with delight, as if he had not expected the train to turn up. The women swarmed, carrying their baskets. Aisha felt her stomach contract, and her mouth filled with bile, and she made haste to distance herself from the crowd. The train whistle blew shrilly, but Aisha was staggering, as a burning eruption rose up from her innards. She bent over the ground and vomited, a stream pouring from her mouth in spite of her, while the train's whistle went on urgently shrieking.

8 • The Red-Light District

NABAWIYYA AL-MUSTAHIYA struggled to open her eyes while the black serving girl kept on shaking her. Radiant light stole in through the window—it was noon: still early.

"There's a visitor who insists on seeing you," said the serving girl.

Nabawiyya al-Mustahiya turned over and tried to pull away. "No customers in the morning," she muttered. "Impossible."

The previous night had been exhausting—a pack of Australian soldiers had descended upon the house like desert rats. They were frightened of the war—of the eccentricities of the Turks, the precision of the German gunners. They suffered interminably from nightmares, even at the critical moment of their business with her. Their manner with her was rough and primitive, and she took no pleasure with them.

Yet the serving girl would not let her be. "It's not a man," she said, "it's a young girl. Poor thing—her face is covered in scratches and bruises."

Nabawiyya al-Mustahiya's own body bore its share of scratches and bruises: the tax on a night's earnings, as people called it. "Girls like this are not my concern," she grumbled. "Send her to our mistress. Send her to the Madam."

But the servant did not withdraw—she seemed to sympathize with this unknown girl. She went on shaking Nabawiyya, until Nabawiyya was obliged to get up out of bed. She proceeded barefoot across the cold tiles through the silent corridors of the house, heading for the main hall, which was overlooked by the other rooms. At first she couldn't get a good look at the girl, who was swathed in black, and hiding her head in her arms, as if acutely embarrassed to find herself in such a place. They were all like this in the beginning. Then the visitor lifted her head and Nabawiyya gasped, clapping a hand to her chest. The girl's face looked as though a whole battalion of Australians had had their way with her.

"Aisha!" she exclaimed. "Who did this to you? And where have you been all this time?"

Aisha flung herself into Nabawiyya's arms and gave way to tears. "Forgive me," she said, "but I had nowhere else to go."

Nabawiyya thought, *Can the world have shrunk so much for you that you come of your own accord to the red-light district*? Aloud, she said, "When I went to inquire about you, Umm Abbas told me you'd gone home to your village. What happened to you?"

Aisha didn't know what to say. The thing was too mortifying to mention even to Nabawiyya al-Mustahiya. She withdrew from Nabawiyya's embrace and looked at the black servant, who was standing there watching them. Nabawiyya understood the meaning of Aisha's glance, and drew her by the hand. "We'll go to my room," she said, and she led her through the silent passageways, so intricately interconnected that Aisha would not have remembered how to find her way back out of them.

The room was narrow, the largest object in it being the bed in which Nabawiyya plied her trade. A mixture of odors hung in the air: of strong perfume, of powder and tobacco and wine. There was a small cupboard, slightly open, crammed with glittering clothes, a round mirror, and a small white basin containing water muddied by a mixture of strange colors. Aisha did not sit upon the bed, but retreated to a small chair in a corner of the room.

Nabawiyya turned to her and said, "You wouldn't have come here except in the direst need. What's happened to you?"

Aisha glanced up in confusion. She didn't know whether to stay or make a run for it. She spoke. "I'm so frightened," she said, "and I don't know where to go. My belly is heavy, and every morning I feel nauseated, and . . ."

Once more Nabawiyya's hand flew to her chest. "Heaven help you," she cried, "did Master Mukhtar do this?" She remembered that Mukhtar had gone away months ago, and she stared bewildered at Aisha, who fell once more to weeping. Nabawiyya patted her shoulder and said, "No, of course it wasn't Mukhtar. Unthinkable that it should have been Mukhtar, and even more unthinkable that it can have been anyone else. Who was it?"

"It doesn't matter who it was," said Aisha. "It was done against my will and without my consent, that's all. First of all I want confirmation. This has never happened to me before, and I don't know what to do. I couldn't go to Umm Abbas. I came to you, because you would keep my secret."

Nabawiyya looked at her in perplexity. What had become of this innocent girl? Who was it that had so violently assaulted her? She said, "Of course I'd like to help you, but first we must get the Madam to agree."

“The Madam?”

“She’s the head of this house—I’m just one of the working girls in her establishment. We must seek her permission before we do anything.”

Aisha stared, at a loss. She was terrified matters might get out of hand, but Nabawiyya pushed her gently toward the bed. “Everyone is asleep now,” she said. “No one in this house wakes until afternoon. We all take breakfast together at sunset, same as in Ramadan. Rest a little—the bed is big enough for both of us.”

Aisha hesitated a moment, then lay down upon the bed. She could never have imagined that this proximity to Nabawiyya would give her such a sense of security. She removed the black shawl from her head, loosening her soft tresses, which were matted with bits of mud. Nabawiyya reached out and removed them with her fingers. “Don’t you want to unburden your heart,” she asked, “and tell me about what happened to you?”

Aisha closed her eyes. She had no desire to relive the anguish she had suffered. “It wasn’t to me that this happened,” she said. “It happened to another body that has nothing to do with me, and it’s for this reason that I’ve come to you, to restore my body’s purity.”

Nabawiyya stroked her hair, and whispered, “Sleep then, and be at ease. You’ve come to the right place.” Aisha closed her eyes once more and fell into the deep slumber of a child who has not slept for a long time.

She woke a few hours later to see the faces of several women all around her. They all knew of the young girl’s dilemma, and had come to get a look at her. It was an old and well-known story that had brought her to this house. She sat up in alarm and retreated on the bed until she was against the wall. She cast her eyes about for Nabawiyya, but couldn’t find her, and her fear rose. Yet the faces were not hostile. They were young, not much older than she was, eyes puffy from sleep and with traces of yesterday’s cosmetics still clinging to them. Their features were fresh, still unaffected by life. They didn’t try to approach her; they were all looking sadly at her, knowing that she was only a few steps away from becoming one of them.

There was a commotion behind them, the sound of footsteps and the clinking of jewelry, the tinkling of anklets. The line of girls gave way, separating to either side of the room, and an enormous woman came in, the only one not in a state of deshabille: a mask of different hues concealed the wrinkles in her face, her head was covered by a colorful kerchief sewn with gold coins, and her arms were encircled by a great many bracelets, which jingled with her every movement.

Her presence amid the silent crowd was distinctive. Behind her stood Nabawiyya al-Mustahiya—waiting and watching like the rest. *This is surely the Madam*, said Aisha to herself uneasily.

The woman approached, and said imperiously, "Get up." Aisha wound her fingers in the bedclothes, but Nabawiyya, in the background, inclined her head, indicating that she should obey the woman's orders. She straightened up and tried to climb out of the bed, but the woman gestured for her to stay where she was, then said, "Turn around." Once more Aisha obeyed her and turned all the way about. She retreated again until she was against the wall, and the woman spoke again, harshly. "Show me your legs," she said. "Pull up your dress." Aisha closed her eyes, wishing all of them would vanish from the room. She was certain it had been a mistake to come here. But the Madam was speaking again. "At any rate," she said, "this type pleases no one but the English."

The room was silent. No one knew whether this meant affirmation or refusal.

The Madam spoke again. "She can be our good deed, then. Send the 'attendant' to her."

Jingling and clinking, she left. In silence, the girls all followed her. Only Nabawiyya stayed behind. She smiled wanly at Aisha, who said in a strangled voice, "You've disgraced me."

"The walls of this house are not strong enough to hide secrets, and there are no locks on any of the doors. During the night you'll hear all the women's moans as they work. You're not at school in Asyout anymore, love—you're in the red-light district."

Once more the door opened and a woman came in, a black-skinned giantess with blunt features, her cheeks divided by long and ancient scars, her lips engorged and darker in color than the rest of her. In her long ears were ivory earrings. At the sight of her, Aisha's fear redoubled—even Nabawiyya herself seemed frightened. Attempting a fond smile, she said, "This is Umm Zaghloul, the 'attendant.' She always rescues us when we find ourselves in difficulties."

The woman paid no attention to Nabawiyya. She raised her hand and said firmly, "Leave us."

Nabawiyya stood up at once and went out, closing the door behind her. The woman turned and studied Aisha for a moment, trying to pinpoint her age. She pursed her lips and fluttered her long, thin, black fingers in the air. "Open up and let me see what you've got between your legs," she said. Aisha shrank away from her, clamping her legs together and drawing them up to her chest. The woman approached the bed, still waving her fingers.

Tears sprang from Aisha's eyes. "Please," she begged, "be gentle with me."

The woman opened her mouth and began speaking rapidly, in the accent of the south. Her teeth showed, as did her gums, tainted dark blue with zinc. "I've been a slave for many years," she said. "The slavers drove me from Atra and took me on the Forty Days Road. I've worked in all the great houses, and I've had my fingers in the private flesh of all the princesses and ladies and serving girls. Yes, these fingers saved all of them from scandal: the princesses who liked being bedded by seducers, the ladies who fell in with stable grooms, the servant girls who yielded when their masters lusted after them—I emptied all their wombs. I kept all their secrets hidden, and gave their husbands the gift of blissful ignorance. These fingers will save you, too."

Such words were not reassuring to Aisha, but it would be of no use to resist. There was no hiding that part of her body now that it had been truly defiled. It was only that she was frightened of enduring still more pain, and further disgrace. She looked pleadingly at the woman, but the scarred face remained impassive. Whatever those fingers might do to her, it couldn't be worse than what had happened to her already. The woman removed Aisha's pants and examined them as if looking for telltale stains. Then she tossed them aside and turned to Aisha, who trembled as she felt the fingers creeping about on her skin and penetrating the depths of her flesh, exploring the viscid wetness of those interior surfaces. Aisha gasped and tears streamed from her eyes. She felt degraded, defenseless against this humiliation. The woman made no attempt to make matters any easier for her, even by speaking to her. The fingers probed, and she remembered the pain of that first violation. Umm Zaghloul spoke then as if reading her mind: "It's your first time, I think," she said. "Before that you were a virgin—your muscles in there are still strong."

"Have pity on me, I beg you," Aisha implored her in a strangled voice, but the woman went on digging with her fingers until the pain was unbearable.

Suddenly the woman exclaimed, "Your cervix is hard as a rock, girl. You are pregnant—no doubt about it." She pulled her fingers out, studied the sticky wetness clinging to them, and then wiped them on a towel. Aisha closed her legs and pulled away, huddling against the wall. Her worst fears had been confirmed: the disgrace was attached to her body. Mortified, she hid her face from Umm

Zaghloul. Had this happened in the moment when her body relented and grew responsive in spite of her? Had her cells seized upon that ephemeral moment of pleasure and stored it in her viscera?

"It's still early," said Umm Zaghloul. "May God help you unburden your womb."

The procedure commenced at once. The household was always ready for such occasions, and to hesitate or delay would only complicate the pregnancy. They moved her to a room well separated from the areas in which the women worked. Umm Zaghloul brought a stove and a pot for boiling potions, in which she placed a special mixture of wild herbs—delivered regularly to her by the boats that crossed the cataract at the border of Sudan, they were reasonably fresh. To these she added dried tree leaves and some oddly tinted powders. She stayed patiently seated before the pot as it bubbled and boiled, and strange odors pervaded the room. The herbs became a dark concoction, which she poured into a clay vessel and offered to Aisha. Aisha found the smell nauseating, but she swallowed it. Umm Zaghloul produced a long scrap of fabric and wound it so tightly around Aisha's belly that it felt as though her abdomen and her back were jammed against each other. Then Umm Zaghloul left Aisha in the darkened room.

She didn't know how long she was there alone, but at some point the pains started. Her stomach convulsed as if it were being torn apart from within. She shouted for help, but no one heard her. The house was ablaze with its nighttime activity, and everyone was too busy for her. The sounds of drumming and singing, along with drunken shouts, rose up all around. The binding cloth was still taut around Aisha's midsection, constricting her breath. She tried to loosen it, without success. She got up and groped her way around the four walls of the room; then she began vomiting uncontrollably.

The girls came late, carrying candles and gas lamps. Their faces were liberally smeared with cosmetics, and their clothes barely covered them. They crowded into the narrow room, despite the stench, and knelt upon the floor, searching carefully for traces of blood amid the puddles of vomit. They shook their heads sorrowfully, and swiftly cleaned up all the mess. They settled Aisha's head upon the pillow, and left. Nabawiyya Mustahiya stayed briefly, stroked Aisha's cheek, and gazed at her with sadness in her eyes.

The business was repeated the following day: a dose of the herbal concoction, pain, vomiting. "That's how it is with bastard children," said Umm Zaghloul, "they hang on. The only way they come out of hiding is when spirit and flesh part company." Aisha writhed and gagged, and her thighs were stained with fluid, but there was not a drop of blood in it. Umm Zaghloul turned Aisha over onto her stomach and sat upon her back until she was nearly strangled, but still the fetus clung to the wall of her womb. Her face grew pale, her skin dry, and the dark-skinned woman said, "There's nothing for it but the rod. It's a whole other kind of pain, and more dangerous than anyone can know, but there's no other way." A thin iron rod, bearing traces of dried blood: the only way to open the cervix and "knock the pea loose from its pod," as Umm Zaghloul put it. Aisha lay unresisting; she had lost all hope of deliverance.

Nabawiyya brought Aisha a small flask. "This is cognac," she said. "Real cognac—not some cheap imitation. Drink all of it—it will dull your pain and warm you up." It tasted like firewater, and made Aisha's stomach hurt all the more but, to her surprise, she relaxed a little once the intoxicant spread through her veins. The room filled with strange faces: Mukhtar was gazing at her in vexation, pain, and sorrow; there, too, was Omran's face, with its bloodstains and teeth marks. The music of singing and dancing seeped in from somewhere; she was dizzy, floating in a place of infinite shadows. She did not sense the women as they entered the room all in a group, but she felt them descend upon her. She tried feebly to resist them, but the black woman warned her not to make any sudden movements, lest the rod puncture her womb. She was assailed all at once by violent pain—she felt as though her head would explode with it. She cried out, and then everything faded away, and she was engulfed by the limitless dark.

She woke from a darkness that was like death to find herself lying beneath many blankets, in spite of which all her limbs felt cold. Unable to summon the strength to move, she watched the chilly light creeping in upon her from the window. Strange that she was still alive, in this room, which was like a grave, surrounded by such a ghastly stench. She felt thirsty—dehydrated—but she couldn't move. She sank once again beneath a wave of recurring nightmares.

At last Nabawiyya al-Mustahiya came, along with the other girls—she heard their voices filling up the room, and a draft of fresh air entered with them. They approached her, fear stamped upon their pale faces, and drew aside the blankets that covered her. A quantity of blood stained her belly and thighs, as well as the bed in which she lay. With a collective gasp, they drew back and gathered in a knot against the wall. One of them, near tears, cried, "Another child lost!"

Then they got to work. They brought a basin, cold water, some oily soap, and black palm husks for scrubbing. They set to removing all the blood—still fresh and rank-smelling. They took off all of Aisha's clothes and washed her all over, then dried her, sprinkled talcum powder on her, and wrapped her in white terrycloth toweling. They wrapped her in dry cotton garments, like a creature lately reborn. They changed the bedsheets, cleaned the floor, and took away the soiled clothes and blankets. They performed all these tasks in silence and in harmony—as if carrying out a ritual to which they were habituated—without complaint or resentment, but also without any delight in the conclusion of events: they knew that what they were doing was eradicating the traces of a life that had been terminated.

They brought her a hot meal, of which she ate little—the empty space in her belly still pained her. Umm Zaghloul made no further appearance, knowing that after performing such an operation she would encounter only hard glances, and that the bitterness always continued to stare out from the girls' eyes for some while, even though she had delivered them from scandal and shame. At last Aisha slept calmly beneath the warm blankets, until the pain and the nightmares caught up with her. Then she dreamed of Mukhtar for the first time—he was far, far away, and yet she felt that it was possible for her to reclaim some part of the life she had lost.

Gradually she recovered. With Nabawiyya's assistance she left her bed. No one asked how long she would stay. Perhaps it was invariably the case that whoever came to that house in such straits did not leave it. She got into the habit of walking by herself in the morning, when the house was quiet and still, and empty of strangers. She meandered through the capacious halls and interconnected corridors, past windows of fitted glass and rooms in which the girls slept alone, exhausted. She could hear the sound of their deep breathing, and smell their perfume mixed with men's sweat. A wearisome profession, truly—how could these women endure those creatures, who were so brutish? This place was a maze that was like a seduction, pervaded by invisible particles of lust. She walked on until she came to the main hall of the house, where the girls would seat the customers who came to this establishment: one way or another, all the corridors in the building led to this hall, whose walls were high and encircled by windows covered with fine latticework. In the ceiling was a squared-off dome, through whose stained-glass panes soft, clear light penetrated. Tucked into the corners of the hall were couches and cushions; great mirrors hung upon the walls, each one reflecting the opposite side of the hall, so that everyone present could see everyone else, all at the same time. Here were leftover bits of food, empty bottles, and pieces of the girls' underclothes, colorful and flimsy, scattered carelessly about like dead butterflies. The vastness of the hall, with the light shining directly into it, made her feel afraid, and she always preferred to return to the dimness of the corridors. On rare occasions she went down into the cellar, which was very dark, its air stagnant. She would walk among the larders, the strings of onions and garlic, the shelves stacked with bottles of drink and vials of aphrodisiac that came from India and Malay. She would walk until she tired of walking, when she would find herself suddenly before the door to her room—it was the house itself that had directed her steps. It opened its arteries for her, then closed them again at the right moment.

On a certain night, although the house was not hers to wander, Aisha could not bear to confine herself for long in her room. Barefoot, she went and hid behind one of the latticed windows, through which she breathlessly watched the goings-on below. The main hall was brilliantly lit up with candles—hundreds of them, distributed throughout the room, in a blaze of light and warmth whose intensity felt to Aisha like hot exhalations. A small group of instrumentalists was seated there, continuously playing music to which it seemed no one was listening. She observed the interplay of colors: the girls' shimmering garments; the flushed faces of the men; a dancing girl with an immense candelabrum on her head, loaded with lit candles, under which she moved in the midst of the cheering throng. She was being accompanied by a skinny young man who wore a *jilbaab* made of silk and a belt around his waist. He moved with more agility than the girl weighed down by the candelabrum, striking the cymbals he held in his hands.

The clientele, scattered all about the room, never left off cheering. They shouted drunkenly, smoking their hubble-bubbles and gulping their glasses of drink, while tendrils of smoke rose from the heat of the candles and enveloped everything and everyone, making them all resemble colorful ghosts, on the border between fantasy and reality. An extraordinary night, laden with desires freely expressed, and with insatiable lusts.

"Do you like what you see?"

Aisha turned, startled. It was the Madam, who stood in the shadowy corridor. Aisha had not seen her since that first day, when she entered the house. The woman moved toward her, with her ponderous frame, and stared searchingly at her. "You're still pale," she told Aisha, "and not very strong. Your body needs to fill out a bit. Then we'll be able to train you, and you'll be ready to begin working."

Aisha felt her throat go dry. She tried to speak without betraying the tremor in her voice. "I can't do that," she said. "I want to thank you for all you've done to help me . . . but I can't . . ."

"Nonsense. I know you're an educated girl, that you speak the language of the English, and that you used to work for the Leader. Nabawiyya has told me a great deal about you. But in your present circumstances, you're better off with this kind of work. And who knows? Perhaps one day you'll be a madam, like me."

A stabbing pain flooded Aisha through and through. "Impossible," she said, "I could never touch a man or let a man come near me. It would kill me."

The Madam came closer to her and put her hand on her shoulder in an attempt to still the tremors that rocked her. Aisha could smell the fragrance of her heavy perfume and hear the whisper of her trinkets. "The first time," said the Madam, "you were the weaker party. It's different here—you'll always be the stronger one: a benefit that a woman can enjoy only in our profession. Men come to us submissively. They leave their arrogance and pride at the door, pay us their money, and then disport themselves before us like buffoons. They do what we tell them to do, and at the end of the night they weep upon our shoulders and beg us to keep their secrets and conceal their failures. You are not the first to fall prey to their treachery—all these girls have shed their blood in that little spare room, but that was their redemption: never again would they be controlled by members of that sex, with its filthy ways. Perhaps you will not be able to avenge yourself upon the man who wronged you, but you will exact your revenge upon *every* sort of man."

She paused, breathing hard with the effort of so much talking. Aisha bit her lip. She did not want to seem rude or ungrateful; she had not yet given thought to where else she might go but, be that as it might, she knew there was something waiting for her other than simply to become one of the working girls of this house, a pale point of light at the end of this dim corridor. With a shudder, she exclaimed once more, "I can't—I can't!"

The woman drew Aisha into her arms; all at once she seemed to her to be an artless little girl—the girl she herself had failed to raise and protect. "I won't force you," she said. "In order to take any pleasure in this exhausting profession, you must choose it for yourself."

Releasing her, she took Aisha's hand and led her to a small couch. She seated her there and sat down opposite her. She reached up and brushed away the tears that had sprung from her eyes.

"Listen to me," she said. "You won't be like these girls. You're different from other girls. All of them are of peasant stock, or were ignorant servant girls. They can't read or write. But you—you can help me. You can intercede in the conflicts that arise between the girls and the soldiers at arms who frequent this house—the English, the Australians, even the Indians. You won't have to lay hands on a man, and no man will touch you unless you want him to."

Aisha could not speak. She threw her arms around the Madam and embraced her once more. "You've been so kind to me!" she said.

"It's nothing. It's just that you remind me of the daughter I lost. Her father took her, and brought her somewhere far away from me. You'll be free. I won't press you, after all you've been through."

◆ ◆ ◆

Slowly, and without pressure from anyone, Aisha entered the world of the red-light district. Her days passed one upon the other within the walls of the house until her memories of the outside world paled. She did not become one of the girls, but she became part of the web of their life. She knew that moments of joy were few, and days of grief were long. From behind the barrier of the latticed windows she followed the women's nightly revels, their temporary intoxication with the men's lust for them. But once the colors adorning their faces had run together, their individual features would vanish, and they would take on a kind of uniformity. During the few daylight hours, they seemed like individuals, poor and rootless, each with her own misery, her own wound that refused to heal.

The Madam inducted her into the system of primitive interdependencies that she had devised. She knew men from the police station near the house, who would pick no quarrel with the customers, and would disregard complaints and charges brought against those customers; she knew how much she must give them each week, what was the price of a high-ranking officer and that of a patrolman who loitered about the walls each night. She also knew the protection fees exacted by the neighborhood strong men; she knew who was admitted to the house at no charge and for whom the prettiest girls were reserved. She dealt with wagon drivers, food and drink vendors, drug dealers, and sellers of medical supplies, perfumes, cosmetics, and antidotes for syphilis and gonorrhea. It was astounding that the

Madam could manage on her own to keep all these things in order, relying only on her memory, without the aid of written records. She could not read or write well, but her inborn talent enabled her to deal effectively with Pashas and cabmen alike. With practice she had come to realize that her customers were of different types and classes; they might share the same woman or pass through the same bed, but it was impossible that they should sit together to socialize or exchange pleasantries. For this reason she set up a schedule for every type of customer.

There was a night for the strong men, who came to the house in their finespun clothes made of cotton and silk, carrying sticks and cudgels and were accustomed to smoking sweet tobacco and hashish, and to drinking barley beer; their designated night was always a raucous one, a meeting of all the strong men who were constantly kicking up rows in the narrow lanes, but came to agreements within the house about dividing up shares and levying protection fees; the girls sealed these deals with their bodies.

There was a night for soldiers at arms. They would arrive thirsty, and drink great quantities of whiskey and cognac; they would be ravenous to bed any woman, and would wander the house naked all night long.

There was a night for effendis and dignitaries, during which there would be little sex, little wine, and much lassitude—a dull night, on which the Madam took care to engage a singer from the entertainment centers of the Rod-el-Farag marketplace. The singer would moan away, repeating the same words over and over, until everyone grew dizzy with the monotony of her voice and the effects of cheap wine.

Out of all the days of the week, only on Friday did the house open its doors at noon, to receive students from the upper-division schools. It was a pleasant day, on which the only drink to be had was mild beer, and the girls were offered at a discount. But the clientele inspired a great deal of merriment and frivolity, as well as disputes, for they all thought they had fallen in love on their first sexual encounter. The girls liked this day. They wandered among the students, strutting like queens, enjoying the dazzled expressions in the eyes of those young men. Even Aisha herself would come down to the main hall and sit with the girls. It was all a bit childish and silly; the students would climax before even attaining the edge of the bed, and return to sit with the crowd, hiding their embarrassment amid the girls' reassurances that what had happened was quite normal, and they would do better the next time.

One strange day—noon on a Friday—she saw Mukhtar sitting among them. It was not the Mukhtar who had come to hate her and his country and resolved to go away after he came out of prison, but the Mukhtar she had first met on the steps of *al-Liwa*: quiet, dreamy, and confident, as if he grasped in his fist the mud of first creation. He was a slender youth and tall, like the real Mukhtar, of a rather dark complexion. His hair was thick and a bit coarse, and he had the same thin little beard and long, supple fingers—and he was a student at the School of Fine Arts. His name, though, was not Mukhtar, and he showed no sign of recognition on seeing her face. All the same, she kept staring at him in fascination and longing. Why had time not stopped at that long-ago moment? Why had her infatuation not been consummated with the first kiss he gave her?

The youth was talking to her, while she gazed at him with her eyes misted over. She let him hold her hand and entwine his fingers with hers—his grip was gentle and warm. The girls watched her from a distance, and whispered under their breath. They grew still, so as not to rouse her from her trance. The young man's touch had sent her to some other, distant world, bygone days never to be retrieved. She came to herself when she felt his lips upon her face. He had pulled her to him in a bold move, so that she was fully in his embrace, but when she smelled his breath she realized that this was not Mukhtar. Her whole body convulsed, and was overtaken by stabbing pain. She pushed him away so forcefully that he fell to the floor. She stood up in a panic and fled across the hall, not regaining her composure until she was back in her room and had shut the door behind her.

The house itself was no longer a secure place to hide. It could not keep at a distance the tumultuous events of the outside world. The dream disappeared, the one that had been inspired by the glow of the candles and the exhalations of desire. It was the night designated for the neighborhood strong men, and the house was preparing for it with mounds of hashish and bottles of barley beer mixed with orange-flower water, while the girls readied themselves for the candelabrum dance. The men came, with their vanity and their curled moustaches, leaving their clubs and cudgels at the door. They removed slippers and shoes, and sat like sultans at their ease. Aisha, as usual, was in her room off to the side, updating the account books and sorting out which girls would go with which men, so as to forestall any sort of dispute. She had become familiar with each girl's stamina; there were some who could manage only one round a night, and others who pressed for extra appointments. The sound of drumbeats and cymbals rose, and it seemed as though no one realized that the Great War, which had engulfed all of creation for long years, had come to an end, and that there were thousands of soldiers who had been awaiting this moment.

The war had begun with an abundance of sentiment. Poets and young men dreamed of a war that would last only a few weeks, and lead everyone to better days, a finer world. But the war had devolved into a grisly bloodbath, savagery such as the soldiers had never seen. Not since the Stone Age had humankind known anything like it. The slaughter continued, without achieving anything, for some fourteen hundred days, during which millions of men huddled in trenches filled with mud and snow and rats; they ate pig meat and smelled like pigs. Poison gas was used for the first time; hundreds of bodies were left to rot, strung on barbed wire, and no one dared to risk getting near them so as to bury them. The great guns fired thousands of shells, reducing cultivated land and small villages to immense pits resembling the craters of volcanoes, destroying bridges and dams, and turning vast areas into mires flooded with putrid water. Every side killed its hostages and imposed blockades on entire cities, until their inhabitants starved to death. The war went on until no one was dreaming of victory any longer. Whispers of a call to retreat and a concession of defeat turned to shouts of anger, and in the end millions fell and died, while all the vultures that had run the world also fell—those who had arrogated to themselves the divine right to rule. Shamed, these instruments of war withdrew, leaving all the rest to their own devices.

The soldiers had been waiting for the moment in which the bells would ring, signaling an end to the butchery, so that they could plunge into that ultimate refuge, that house situated in the red-light district—they craved release; they wanted to make certain that traces of the will to live still resided within them. They poured into the network of corridors and arrived at the main hall, and the strong men stationed at the door could not stop them. They entered the hall, panting, desert sand still clinging to their garments. They had not seen active duty, because the real war had not reached them, but the long days of waiting and of sleeping in foul trenches amid the desert rats had stirred up the water of life in their veins. The strong men had smoked all the hashish, drunk all the bottles of barley beer and orange-blossom water, only to find themselves suddenly surrounded by all these dusty faces—and there were not enough girls to go around. One of the solders stepped forward and picked out the first girl he happened upon, taking her arm and pulling her to himself. In protest, the girl screamed more loudly than she needed to; she was the spark that inflamed the crowd. The British soldiers' insults and their crushing of the demonstrations awoke in the strong men's minds, and they felt the bitterness of occupation, of oppression, of the wait for an independence that never came.

The soldiers advanced with the swagger of victory in all those battles in which they had taken no part. All the men lost their heads and set upon one another in a battle as dreadful as if it were a still-unresolved conflict from the war itself. No one heeded the shouts of the Madam begging for calm and promising them that she would satisfy everyone, that she would request reinforcements in the form of girls from neighboring houses. Aisha ran to one of the men to ask him to make haste in summoning the police; meanwhile, the battle intensified. Besides sticks and clubs, tables, chairs, musical instruments, and trays of food were pressed into service, as well as slippers and shoes. The great mirrors that hung upon the walls shattered, the candelabra were smashed, and food and drink were scattered about, as were the candles. The only light remaining was the faint illumination of the hanging lanterns.

At last came the sound of police whistles, but even then they didn't stop fighting until an officer fired a volley of shots in the air and struck one of the lanterns. Then, breathing hard, they all stopped what they were doing. Their features, bathed in blood, had become indistinguishable, and the police rounded them all up, but once they were in the middle of the road an officer discerned the presence of English soldiery. They were exhausted and compliant, but the officer, quaking, released them at once, before what had happened should become known. He took all the strong men to the police station.

Work at the house had come to a standstill and the girls seemed lost and melancholy, having no other refuge. Not one of them was in a position to return to the poverty of the family she had left years before. Workers came to make repairs, and the Madam left to spend a few days in Alexandria, without giving a reason for the journey. Aisha sequestered herself in her room.

◆ ◆ ◆

She did not open the door to her room until late in the night. Nabawiyya kept knocking insistently, until Aisha got out of bed, dizzy and sad. Nabawiyya came in and they sat together in the light of the little nighttime oil-burning lamp. Nabawiyya studied Aisha for a little while. Of all the girls in the house, she was the only one who knew the secret of what had happened to Aisha. She kept silent for a moment, then said, "He's here, and he asked about you." Aisha knew at once whom she meant, and was shaken to the core, understanding now why her friend had come at such a late hour. "It's Thursday," Nabawiyya continued. "I went to Sayyida's shrine and visited Umm Abbas. It was she who told me that Mukhtar had come for a brief visit to Cairo, once the roads opened up. He was exhausted. Things didn't go so well for him in Europe, especially during the war years. But he went to the basement room to have a look at his sculptures, and then he went to your village."

Aisha drew a sharp breath. "He went to Beni Khalaf?" she exclaimed.

"Umm Abbas told me he returned without any real news of you. He knew your mother had died, that the wolves had torn your uncle limb from limb, and that the house had been abandoned and taken over by some Gypsies, who are living there now. He came back, despairing and downcast. Now he's preparing to return to Europe once more."

Struggling to hold back her tears, Aisha said, "Oh, God—why do you torment me by telling me these things?"

"He still thinks of you, and he misses you, Aisha."

"I miss him, too, but what's the use of any of this? How can I see him, with my ruined body and my shame? The look of contempt in his eyes would kill me!"

"Men, as a rule, are stupid, it's true. But perhaps he would understand . . ."

Mukhtar was part of another life—a distant dream there was no longer any possibility of fulfilling. To think of consigning it to oblivion was painful, but to recall it was even more so.

"He'll take the train to Alexandria tomorrow, and from there he'll go by boat to Europe. He could be away for many years. You may never see him again."

With that, Nabawiyya went off to bed, leaving Aisha sleepless, roused by her longing to see Mukhtar. What had become of him, in all this time? Were his wounds as deep as hers? Perhaps she could find a way to see him from a distance—she would be able to bear that, in spite of the sorrow it would invoke. She watched as day broke outside her window. There was no movement. The girls were all asleep, and the repairmen had not come yet. Aisha dressed and went out into the corridors. As she passed Nabawiyya's room she thought of waking her, but it seemed to her that this was her own private moment, which she needed to experience in solitude. She went out into the empty streets, where the winter wind assailed her, catching up refuse and fallen leaves in its gusts. The city was slowly awakening, with vendors pulling their wooden carts, street cleaners preparing to commence the day's work, and the military policemen casting sleepy glances at the passersby. The streetlights in Station Square were still lit, although it was daytime now. Aisha looked warily about, not wishing to find herself suddenly face-to-face with Mukhtar when she was not ready for him. She hid her face carefully, and made her way into the station, hiding behind light poles as she went. She found the platform for the Alexandria train, which was still empty, but for a few travelers who wandered about silently. Mukhtar was not among them. She kept watch, concealing herself behind a column, while the annihilating cold overtook her. She wished the train would never come, that Mukhtar would never come, but that he would stay in Egypt—perhaps there was some hope. This savage world would not be so bad with him in it. He would provide her with an incentive to come out from behind the walls of the house in the red-light district, even if there were no means of attaching herself to him. She would live as a servant at his feet, if he wished it. Would she ever be able to overcome her profound sense of defilement? The train pulled smoothly into the station in a puff of smoke, emitting a whistle that gradually faded out. The people waiting on the platform bustled around, boarding the train, but Mukhtar did not appear. She hoped the train would pull out and be gone before he should come, but then she saw the driver emerge from the engine and go into the little café beside the platform.

He was still there when at last she saw Mukhtar coming, walking with the same long stride she had never been able to keep up with. He looked thinner and taller; his hair had grown longer, his beard thicker. He moved like a ghost treading upon an unearthly surface. Her heart pounded. She wished she could rush over to him and throw her arms about his neck. There was no one there to see him off—he was solitary, just as he had been when she saw him the first time. She was his last farewell. He stood upon the platform, in no hurry to board the train. He stood there looking at his ticket, casting glances around the platform, at a loss. Then he took a deep breath. She sensed how alone he was—this was her moment to approach. She would have to tell him everything, and he would have to bear his share of guilt with her: he had left her alone and defenseless—it was he who had cracked open the secret of her hiding place, where she had been protected, enabling Omran to penetrate it. If Mukhtar had stayed by her side, none of this would have happened. But now he climbed aboard the train and disappeared all at once from view. She hadn't imagined that such would be her final moments with him. She saw the driver and his assistant rise from their seats in the café and head for the train. The time had come. She moved a few paces forward on the platform, wanting to touch the outside of the train that contained him, but she drew back when he surprised her by looking out of a window. He glanced to the right and to the left, studying the empty platform, and his expression grew still sadder. Was he looking for her?

There was a young girl walking along the platform. She wore a school uniform—perhaps she was a student at one of the French schools. She was clutching her satchel of books, her expression one of fear and confusion. Doubtless she had not told her family she was going to the station. Her face lit up when she spotted Mukhtar looking out of the window, and she began to hurry across the platform. Aisha's heart fell—she would never have imagined that a new girl could come into his life so quickly, or that she would be so young. Was she his sweetheart, or merely an admirer? She stopped in front of his window, tossing her satchel onto the ground. Reaching up as high as she could, she clung to his neck and pulled him toward her, so that he nearly lost his balance. Weeping, she pressed her face against him, while Mukhtar caressed her back. He seemed very tender toward her, and did not attempt to extricate himself from her embrace. The train whistle sounded. The girl stood back a little and now they rapidly exchanged a few words. The train began to move, and the girl ran to try to keep up with it, but he had to content himself with waving to her. He wiped his face, and Aisha could not tell whether he was brushing away his own tears or traces of the girl's. The train gathered speed, bearing Mukhtar away. Aisha and the schoolgirl remained behind, alone on the platform. The girl watched for a little while, through her tears. Standing only a slight distance apart from each other, Aisha and the girl wept over the same man. With a passing glance at Aisha, the girl picked up her school satchel, and each of them went her way, neither making any attempt to speak to the other.

◆ ◆ ◆

Aisha's heart quaked when she caught sight of the minaret of the Sayyida Zaynab Mosque. Her steps grew heavy as she walked along Khalig Street. She hadn't imagined that she would ever dare to set foot in the shrine again. Nabawiyya took her arm, urging her along. Aisha remembered every paving stone of the way, the whinnying as the horse-drawn buses passed, the signs for shops selling sweets—such as the one where they were standing now—and the smells emanating from al-Rakib's restaurant. All her bygone moments with Mukhtar came to life again within her. The sight of the station still pained her, throwing her into confusion, the yearning she'd harbored not yet extinguished. But the closer they got to the mosque, the more agitated she became. She felt unclean, as if filth and shame remained a part of her and it was unseemly for her to enter the inviolate shrine.

When Nabawiyya asked her to accompany her on this visit, she had flatly refused. She wanted to stay within the walls of the house—she could no longer bear to lay herself open to further trauma. But Nabawiyya had insisted. She said, "It's the only way the saint can cleanse us of some portion of our sins."

Aisha maintained her composure until they crossed the noisy square, but stood hesitating at the entrance to the shrine. Nabawiyya, however, began whispering to her, "The lady receives everyone. She makes no distinction between sinners and penitents."

Aisha stumbled forward until she grasped the links of silvery metalwork encasing the shrine. There were dozens of black-clad women ceaselessly circumambulating the tomb of the saint, and the fragrance of incense rose up everywhere. She was startled to find that Nabawiyya had prostrated herself and was weeping piteously. Her sobs wracked her body, and her fingers clutched at the reeds in the mats spread upon the floor. Through her tears, she uttered indistinct prayers; the effect of her inconsolable weeping was contagious and spread among them all. Everyone there bore the weight of a particular sin. Aisha removed herself to a corner and began reciting the al-Fatiha, but her mind was unfocused. Nabawiyya crept toward her until she was sitting beside her, and the two of them went on reciting verses from the Qur'an, their voices muted, not daring to speak to each other. Aisha was tormented, for the saint had not answered her prayers, had not kept Mukhtar for her, nor granted her the strength to keep her body untainted.

Nabawiyya sat now, breathing hard, her tears were all but spent. Aisha said to her, "Let's go," for the narrow confines of the place pressed heavily upon her. They sat in front of the mosque, in the plaza overlooking the square, amidst dozens of men and women. All at once, Nabawiyya spoke. "I've been intending to leave the house," she said. "After what happened, it's no longer a safe place. I want to get married and have a child." Aisha looked at her in astonishment, and tried to hold back her questions, but Nabawiyya read them in her face. "I know what you'll say," she went on. "But 'every Majnoun has his Layla,' as the proverb tells us. Well then—there's a man who may be content with me. He knows all about me. He used to work as a carpenter in Ansiya Lane. I've known him for years. Like me, he wants to make a new start. He happened to run into a little trouble, lost his shop, and went to prison for a while. We can help each other. I have some money, and he has his profession—together we'll start over."

Aisha did not reply at first. What should she say? Nabawiyya's words seemed to reveal a possible hidden agenda. Was there really a reciprocal advantage here? Or could one side be exploiting the other? "You're taking a risk," she said at last. "You're going to give him everything you have. Can you really trust him so far as that?"

"I have no choice but to trust him. I just need half a chance—all the girls in the house need it. Don't be fooled by the dancing and singing, or the men's lust for us. The Madam is merciless—she wants her girls to be ever young. There are pimps who provide her with young girls from the countryside, and she is always replacing her inventory. She'll evict us without pity when we get a little older—the day when she drives us from her door will come, without fail."

Aisha let her gaze wander, so that Nabawiyya would not see her eyes brimming with tears. She pretended to be absorbed in the crowd milling about the square. She, too, needed half a chance—but where was it to be found?

From the far side of the square a loud commotion erupted: a group of students and men in Western attire, coming from Mubtadayan Street, shouting energetically and carrying signs. "It's a demonstration," Aisha murmured wistfully. "History always repeats itself, without hope, without change. They're still calling for independence, the right to self-determination, the right to attend the League of Nations conference in Paris—new words and slogans have been added, but the half-chance hasn't come yet. It's always the police, with their billy clubs and their viciousness, that come instead." Aisha felt she ought to get up now and join them, but still she sat there, immobile, clinging to the edge of the worn marble step upon which she sat. The rhythm of the demonstration changed abruptly—the students stopped chanting and stood fixed in place. Only one of them still called out, pointing to the middle of the square.

"Englishmen!"

Everyone turned and looked for them—Aisha was astounded that they could have come so quickly. And, indeed, the English were there, but only in the form of a solitary man who stood at the far side of the tramway station, before the booksellers with their old volumes for sale. He was absorbed in leafing through one of their books, oblivious to the demonstration, deaf to the shouting directed against him—and yet he had become the enemy. A contingent of the younger demonstrators made for him, while the rest stood still, neither taking part in the attack nor preventing it. At last the man, belatedly sensing what was going on around him, raised his head, and Aisha got a good look at his face. She cried out, and hastily sprang up from the stairs before the mosque. But the students were faster than she was. They picked up stones from the street and began pelting him with them. The man raised the book to shield his face. The booksellers shouted, trying to drive the attackers off, and became in their turn targets for the stones. Then a large rock sailed through the air and scored a direct hit against the man. He staggered and lost his balance, as the force of the blow knocked him to the ground. Aisha screamed and ran toward him. The students, alarmed, ran away and hid themselves among the ranks of demonstrators.

Aisha leaned over the man and raised his head, which was bleeding. His eyes were closed; she didn't know whether he was dead, or whether he had merely lost consciousness. One of the booksellers said, "There is no strength or power, except in God. He was a good customer."

Nabawiyya approached and tried to draw Aisha away. "Aisha," she said, "let's be off now. We mustn't involve ourselves in this affair. The police will charge us with having had something to do with it."

"Get a carriage, quickly," Aisha said to her. "We've got to get him away from here."

But it was one of the booksellers who hastened to summon a carriage, while the others picked up the man and carried him to it. They set him down on the leather seat, and Aisha climbed up and sat beside him. She could feel a pulse in his neck, and hear his faint breathing. Nabawiyya sat on the opposite seat. One of the booksellers brought a bundle of books tied with a length of twine and held it up, saying, "These are his books, miss. He paid for them before he was struck."

The carriage set off. Aisha studied the man's face, which looked tired and sad—as always. "Mr. Carter," she said, "are you all right?"

"Let's take him to hospital," said Nabawiyya anxiously.

"There's none near here," replied Aisha, "apart from al-Houd al-Marsoud, and we'll be interrogated if we go there. We're taking him to the house."

Nabawiyya beat her breast. "This is a disaster!" she cried. "The Madam will kill us!"

"She's not there," said Aisha. "Had you forgotten?"

They managed to get him to her room. Umm Zaghloul saw that his wound didn't require sutures, merely a coffee poultice. Aisha kept watch by him, observing his face in repose, and the wrinkles that had begun to find their way into his features. He was tired to the point of exhaustion, his beard growing in, his moustache limp, and his hair beginning to go grey. What sort of hardships had the passing years dealt him? No doubt Lord Cromer had seen to it that all the doors were closed against him. This was visible in his appearance, for he had lost his former elegance—nothing remained of the gentleman of old but a shabby ghost with grains of desert sand still clinging to it. She pitied him, and herself—these years had been hard on everyone.

As the shadows grew longer, she lit the lantern and hung it upon the wall, then returned to her vigil. He had opened his eyes, and was looking at her in amazement, unable to tell whether what he beheld was real or a dream. He couldn't get up, but he reached out his hand to her, entreating her to help him be sure of what he was seeing. She gave him her hand, and he gripped it firmly. Feeling the touch of her fingers, he was reassured of her actual presence, and his face lit up.

"Why it's you—my princess!" he said.

She smiled ruefully at him. "I'm no longer a princess," she replied. "And it's plain that you are no longer a king."

He tried to get up, but he got dizzy. She gestured for him to stay where he was. He looked about wonderingly. "Where am I, anyway?" he inquired. "Is this your house?"

She didn't know what to tell him. She felt she would be unable to manage a lie. Abruptly she said, "This is one of the pleasure-houses in the red-light district."

The smile faded from his face; it seemed clear enough that these few words had dealt him a shock. In a faltering voice he said, "Do you work here?"

"Certainly not," she replied. "But I live here all the same."

"I have no right to question you. I myself lived in the home of Abdel Rasul. The former director of the Antiquities Commission lives under the protection of the most notorious smuggler of artifacts. Sometimes circumstances compel us to throw ourselves upon the mercy of those we cannot abide."

Softly, without letting go of his hand, Aisha said, "Perhaps one day I'll explain my reasons to you. But I want to know what's become of you all these years. Why did you stay here—why didn't you return to your country?"

He stared at the ceiling, his face twitching with agitation. "I tried to go back," he said. "I actually boarded the ship at Alexandria. As the ship gave its first whistle and its first puff of steam, I managed to hop ashore just before they pulled up the gangplank. I couldn't leave behind my formative years; I had to complete the journey I commenced in this place at the age of eighteen. I returned once more to Luxor, to make it clear to everyone that I hadn't been driven off. I had more freedom than before, and I settled in the Valley of the Kings, at Thebes, for there was no other place I so loved. I went back to painting, and produced a great many pictures of pharaonic civilization, most of them inventions of my own imagination. I began selling them to the wealthy people who live along the riverbank, in their ships. I was also a party to deals in the sale of artifacts, whether stolen or acquired legitimately, genuine pieces or forgeries—it didn't matter anymore. These were long and discouraging years, during which my sole object was to avoid being sent away. I endeavored to keep out of sight of Cromer's men. I crossed the river and lived in al-Qurna Village with Abdel Rasul, my former enemy. I knew this would damage my reputation, that they'd all think me a thief like him, or his accomplice at the very least. It wasn't my reputation I was concerned about preserving, though, but rather my presence there."

He fell silent, exhausted. The dizziness seemed to have overtaken him again. He touched the bandage that was wrapped around his head, murmuring, "What did you put on this beastly wound?"

Aisha smiled. She could not tell him, and so she held back. She wished she could speak the way he did, to unburden herself of the grief that pressed upon her heart. "Are you still a fugitive?" she said.

"Not exactly," he replied. "The terms of my banishment have been lightened somewhat. I was able to cross to the east bank and make the acquaintance of Lord Carnarvon. He's one of the foremost among England's wealthy citizens. He's a real Ariel—he was the victim of a car accident in Germany a number of years ago, and his health continued poor afterward. He makes a habit of coming to Egypt every year for the warm, dry weather, and his condition has actually improved, but he fell in love with Egyptian antiquities, and wanted to dig for them himself. It was a failed venture—he found nothing of any value, but he hasn't given up. He has searched assiduously for someone with expertise in the field. This is how my former employer, Maspero, came to recommend me to him, and I was able to breathe easier again: I began working with a powerful man who could protect me from the tyranny of the authorities. More importantly, I resumed my real work—I acquired the right to do excavations once more, and to pursue the discovery I'd been dreaming of my whole life. You could say that my wandering days are over."

Aisha smiled again. He had regained some of his former charm and charisma. She tried to withdraw her hand from his, but he wouldn't allow it. Discomfited, she said, "Well, you're a bit better, at any rate."

"Indeed. But up to now I haven't discovered anything of importance, and my chances grow slimmer with the passing years. I'm still waiting for the magic touch that will lead me to the place I seek. There's something missing—I know what I'm looking for, but I don't know how to get to it."

At last he let go her hand. His head was clearer now, and he was able to raise himself up onto the pillow and lean back against the wall, facing her. Hollow-eyed, he gazed at her. "Do you know," he said slowly, "it's no mere accident that we've met again this way—it's fate. I don't know what's happened to you, but evidently it was terrible enough to have led you to this place. You need a new beginning, and I need inspiration. We need each other."

The lamplight dimmed, and soot began to creep up the glass chimney. The shadows deepened until they hid his face and nothing could be seen but the gleam of his eyes. Uncertain whether she understood precisely what he was trying to say, she continued to gaze at him in silence, until he resumed speaking. "Come with me to Thebes," he said. "Stay by my side while I pursue this mad digging. I need you to impart to me the lucky touch that has altogether deserted me. You are the pharaonic totem I've been looking for."

Drained of energy, he fell silent. She heard him draw breath with difficulty. It was strange to hear such words from him so soon after their meeting again. There were no promises here: merely a half-chance in a darkened room. "I don't know whether I can," she said hesitantly. "We are from two different worlds, united by nothing more than three blind coincidences. How can we join together? I couldn't endure another cruel ordeal."

"And I, likewise, would not be able to stand another failure. Come with me to the Valley of Thebes, and I'll guard you with my life."

A vague, rhetorical promise he offered her—nothing more than that. It had grown late, and neither of them could see the other clearly any longer. She rose and said, "You'd better get some sleep. I'll go to bed as well—I'll share quarters with the other girls."

"You haven't given me an answer."

"Just now you are suffering the effects of a blow to the head. Let us talk in the morning."

She went out into the hall, and went to Nabawiyya's room. The house was quiet, and the hanging lamps were about to go out. She felt her way to the bed, then squeezed in beside Nabawiyya, who turned over, muttering, "Did you sleep with him? Was he strong enough for that?"

Aisha gave her a kick, and did not answer, but turned her back. Remembering his pale face and hollow eyes, she let out the breath she had been holding back in her chest. Nabawiyya spoke again. "You're in love with him, then?"

"He is a man I've met only twice before—this is the third time. And in spite of that, he's asking me to follow him to the other side of the country."

9 • Thebes

EVER SINCE THE FIRST TIME he had come to the station at Luxor, Howard Carter had hated the facsimiles of pharaonic art displayed on its walls. He always hoped he might be given the chance to do them over, but this had never come to pass. He reminded himself each time he alighted from the train there, but this time he had someone else he could tell. She was walking beside him, an elderly porter behind them gasping hoarsely under their baggage.

They found their transportation waiting for them before the entrance to the station: four whitish-gray donkeys, two of them with saddles upon their backs, made of decoratively incised leather, and each of the four with a red rose on its head. Abdel Aal, who was also waiting for them, hastened to take their cases and load them onto the donkeys that were not saddled, but Howard insisted upon carrying the metal cage in which was a yellow canary. Preoccupied though Abdel Aal was, he did not neglect to throw Aisha a searching glance. She wore a hijab that concealed her face, not daring to go unveiled before either the glare of Luxor's sun or the eyes of its people. Howard helped her onto her donkey and the procession made its way to the banks of the Nile, where a felucca was moored, which would convey them to the western shore.

It seemed to Aisha that she had been transported suddenly to an alien world, whereas Howard behaved with the zeal and spontaneity of someone who had returned at long last to a place that belonged to him. The mud-brick houses concealed among the palms reminded her of Beni Khalaf, but here rose the stone columns of the temples, deep yellow, and the more awe-inspiring for the dust that coated them. In the distance the Nile appeared, tranquil and crimson the way it was when it was about to flood. It occurred to Aisha that, having allowed herself to come so far, if she now crossed the river there would be no turning back.

In the street parallel to the river appeared ranks of shops selling antiquities and relics—narrow, dark little places, crammed with merchandise. The shopkeepers emerged from them on spotting a procession of donkeys approaching, squinting as their eyes adjusted to the sunlight. All of them gave off an odor of decay. They exclaimed in jubilation when they saw that it was Howard who was coming. They were a mixture of nationalities: Egyptians, clad in gallabiyas and turbans; and foreigners—Greeks, for the most part—wearing short pants and straw hats. They surrounded Howard, shaking his hand and clapping him jovially on the shoulder. They had been waiting for him, as if his arrival marked the beginning of the season for them. They all exclaimed over the canary he was carrying, saying, "You've brought a golden bird—you'll have good luck, and find a treasure of gold!" He smiled in reply. No one seemed to notice Aisha, cloaked in black and sitting upon her donkey: an anonymous and featureless shape.

The merchants vied for attention, exhibiting to Howard the latest acquisitions added to their wares: marble vessels, greenish-colored brass figurines, damaged plates, and little broken scarabs. They crowded around him, asking him to examine the pieces. He offered a few words of commentary, but rejected many of the pieces with brusque gestures. Aisha watched him, wide-eyed with surprise. Certainly he wasn't putting on this performance to impress her—he was behaving quite naturally. She heard a voice beside her say, "See how clever he is—he can tell in a single glance whether a piece is genuine or counterfeit."

It was Abdel Aal who spoke. He was studying her, trying to penetrate with his gaze the veil concealing her face. "And you, miss?" he continued. "Who are you, and where do you come from?"

She turned her face away. Why did she think no one saw her or was aware of her presence? Her unexplained appearance must have stirred up everyone's curiosity, but they were ignoring her for now—it was only this man who openly questioned her. Howard was trying to back up and extricate himself from the circle of tradesmen without letting go of his smile. He waved to them, promising he'd be back, and he and Aisha once more resumed their progress toward the riverbank. The river was thronged with small craft and boats with white sails. Tied up along the beach were the grand dahabeahs in which the wealthy spent the winter, each dahabeah displaying the flag of the country from which its owner hailed. The whole city was celebrating the new winter season. Howard stopped, and gazed upon the long row of dahabeahs.

◆ ◆ ◆

I saw the American flag fluttering above the dahabeah I used to know so well. I turned to Abdel Aal and inquired, "Has Mr. Theodore Davis returned?" He replied offhandedly, "He's been here at least a month." My heart pounded. Here was my old rival, come back early—a full month before the start of the season. Would he take up digging once more? He had appropriated for himself the right to the choicest sites in the valley for twelve whole years, never giving a chance to anyone else. Only when at last he got bored with it had Lord Carnarvon and I managed to find a way in. Had he come now aiming to reclaim his prerogative? Would he engage someone to compete with me—there in that narrow strip of land—someone who would claim a share of my final opportunity? Perhaps he had heard about my failures over the years. Did he know something of Rosa? News of her no longer reached me.

I remembered those painful moments that had taken me by storm and knocked me off balance. I looked at Aisha, who sat astride her donkey, noting with surprise my confusion and hesitation. I felt that Davis's presence had punctured the joy of my return to the valley, and it was essential that I confirm my doubts and misgivings. "Wait for me here," I told her. "I'll be back shortly." I hastened away, without waiting for her reply. I climbed the stairs leading to the opulent dahabeah. Its deck was covered with a dusty plum-colored carpet. I passed among the cabins and along the corridors without encountering anyone. As I expected, I found him on the side of the ship directly overlooking the western shore, stretched out on a bench, sunbathing. The thick hair upon his chest had gone gray, but his wrinkles were still disguised by the mask of his suntan. He wore short pants and appeared so relaxed and at ease that he didn't move when he saw me, but only smiled. I couldn't tell whether it was an ironic smile or a welcoming one. Emilia was not by his side as she had ordinarily used to be. Which of them, I wondered, had left the other?

"Hello, Carter," he said. "You're just the same as you ever were—you never give up hope."

I stood there before him, at a loss. It always confounded me, dealing with this wealthy American. "Have you come to take up digging again?" I asked bluntly.

He raised his eyebrows in astonishment. "My God," he said. "Certainly not—this valley is worn out from all the digging, my boy. It's useless for you to keep searching."

Trying to maintain my composure, I replied, "So said Belzoni, some hundred years ago, and yet the discovery of at least half the valley was undertaken afterward. That Italian vagabond was the first beneficiary of this valley. He got permission to dig from the great Pasha, Muhammad Ali, but he was really a thief—he plundered the virgin valley of everything he happened upon. He shipped off to Europe many tons of artifacts, which the great Pasha thought were nothing but worthless rocks. In the meantime, the markets of Europe were rapacious consumers of such treasures, while the Pasha was captivated by the plates of spaghetti and the gold nargilehs that Belzoni presented to him."

Davis chuckled. "That man," he said, "was so greedy he didn't really take the trouble to look. We, on the other hand, have done everything in our power. Go on, son—try searching again. I, for my part, shall enjoy this magnificent sunshine, and anything you discover I'll buy from you."

He treated me with such casual indifference that all at once I was furious with myself. He left me bewildered, as if I was back where I had started from—just standing there.

◆ ◆ ◆

The felucca bore its cargo of people and donkeys to the other side of the river, while water birds circled repeatedly overhead, as if trying to discover who the newcomers were. The boat furled its sails as it approached the beach, and mooring lines were cast ashore, where people hurried to haul them in and secure them. Aisha gazed uneasily at the rocky shore, which struck her as inordinately dry and inhospitable; Howard, on the other hand, quivered with anticipation, scenting the hot wind that blew down from the sandy hills. He drew a full breath and sighed deeply, as if he wished he could draw the whole valley into his lungs. Taking her by the hand, he led her across the sand, to where emptiness and silence surrounded them on all sides. One thing was certain: there was no comparison between this and the red-light district. They stopped before two massive statues of Agamemnon. Hearing the sound of the wind as it penetrated the crevices among the rocks, Aisha felt afraid.

Why had she followed him to such a place? Had she really been that desperate? Or had she been taken in by his urgent insistence? He had left the house in the red-light district after that first night, but returned once more, and again after that. He became a constant "customer," even though work had come to a standstill. The return of the Madam from her travels did not stop him from coming. He gave her whatever money she demanded in exchange for the privilege of sitting with Aisha at his leisure. He continued to press her: "Why do you stay here? Your very scent is different from theirs. All the women of the night, the world over, smell the same, wear the same colors on their faces, and even have the same way of talking, no matter the language. None of this is true of you . . ."

She had listened to him, her expression grave and sad, knowing that, however she might try to resist, she would not for much longer be able to keep herself separate from the business of that house. The moment would come when she would lose her footing, and the fragile refuge she had once more constructed for herself would collapse in ruins. But the alternative he offered her was no less perilous: a venture into the unknown. Long hours he had continued to urge his cause with her, delaying his return to Luxor day after day. He was afraid of failure, and afraid to face it alone—or perhaps he wanted to draw solace from another's defeat. "Don't go with him," said the Madam. "Those foreigners have never done anything for us but lie to us and laugh in our faces."

One morning Nabawiyya had left the house, carrying a bundle of clothes, happy and full of hope. She swore to them all that she would return only when she held her child in her arms. Not ten days passed, though, before she came back, battered, humiliated, and penniless. The husband had stolen her money and spent it on hashish, then reviled her for being nothing but a whore. Aisha had wiped away her tears, as well as the traces of blood that mingled with them on her face. She was more and more fearful of Howard's honeyed words. And yet, truly, she did not want to be one of the girls.

At this moment someone appeared from between the two statues: a fellah, tall and thin, wearing only a pair of under trousers, a vest with its buttons undone, and a turban on his head. He had a thick, white moustache, and huge bare feet that planted themselves in the sand; in his hand was a great staff, with which he struck the earth. He had a penetrating stare, but he did not trouble to look at Howard—rather he bent upon Aisha an unsettling gaze, as if he were perturbed by her presence here. For a moment, Aisha imagined that the peculiar noises that filled the valley had issued from his own chest. Exchanging not a single word with the man, Howard took her arm and drew her away from there. They met up with Abdel Aal, who was coming from the direction of the shore, driving his donkey. He followed them at a distance.

"Who was that man?" said Aisha, shivering. "He frightened me."

"That's Abdel Rasul," Howard replied. "I told you about him."

"I thought the two of you were friends."

"So we were. But since I returned to the valley and took up digging once more, he has come to hate me."

They made their way across a flat expanse filled with heaps of rocks and tomb-openings. The heat of the day had subsided, and they were assailed by drafts of cool air from the hills. They came to a broad, open space, more pocked with trenches and strewn with rock piles than any other. Howard beckoned to Aisha. "This," he told her, "is the area designated to me. It is called Dar Abu al-Naja. I've turned over every stone here and stirred up every grain of sand, without achieving my dream. Luck is still against me."

Aisha turned and studied the place. It was full of worthless rocks. How could he have wasted so many years of his life in such a desolate spot? How was it that his passion for this was not yet spent? She was exhausted from the long journey, while he, in his exuberance, did not feel the distance at all. A great stone building rose up before them, protected by a long, thick wall.

"This," he said, "is Medinet Habu. Our little house is right next to its walls—Carter's Fortress."

She looked at the spot he was indicating. There was a modest, whitewashed house, surmounted by a small dome, like an isolated saint's shrine. With fond enthusiasm, he began telling her about the house. "It was I who designed it," he said. "The breeze penetrates it from all sides, and its balconies open out onto Medinet Habu. You can sit there and contemplate the river. It has four rooms . . ."

He went on rapturously as they approached the house. He felt the house was what would establish him in the valley, without anyone's being able to uproot him. He didn't usher her inside right away, but took her hand and led her around the outside of it. He pointed out the stones that formed the exterior wall, and she examined them closely. Each stone had an inscription: Latin letters altered in such a way as to create an impression of hieroglyphic writing. Aisha read, "Made in Bretby, England, at the behest of Howard Carter, Thebes, Egypt." She looked at him questioningly, and he laughed with delight.

"Indeed," he said, "these stones were manufactured in Bretby, in Derbyshire, at a brick factory owned by Lord Carnarvon. They were created and shipped especially for me. Now I, too, have inscriptions bearing my name in this valley, just like the Pharaohs of old!"

She smiled—what could she do but join him in his childish glee? Abdel Aal began removing their baggage from the donkeys' backs and taking it into the house, all the while casting furtive glances at her, unable to contain his curiosity.

Inside, the house did seem altogether splendid, with its windows looking out on the fat columns of the temple, and the dome that crowned it, which facilitated the circulation of air and kept it constantly moist. Then there was the capacious balcony, liberally endowed with wicker chairs, and commanding a view of the Nile, which flowed in front of it.

"Take whichever room you like," said Howard. "All the doors lock from the inside, so you'll be quite safe."

Aisha sighed with relief. So far, he had been no bother to her. Of more immediate concern was Abdel Aal, who was all ears. He stood at the ready until she pointed to one of the rooms, and then he picked up her case and conveyed it there. Entering and locking the door behind her, she felt somewhat secure.

She woke to the sound of an insistent rapping on the door. For a moment she thought she was still at the house in the red-light district—a sudden darkness had engulfed everything. She was still wearing the same dusty clothes, and the whole house was sunk in shadow. Various sounds came to her from outside: drumbeats, singing, and laughter, and light entered the house from out of doors. She peeped out through the window, which was secured, to see that a bonfire had been built in the forecourt of the house. Howard was there, sitting in the midst of a number of fellahin—she couldn't tell how many. Some of them had set up drums in a circle around the fire, and were testing them to see whether the skins had become taut. Presently, they took them up and beat upon them with joyful enthusiasm. The rest stood in a line before them, in their long trousers, colorful little skullcaps upon their heads, and laughter lighting up their brown faces. In the middle of them stood Howard. He placed his hand on the shoulder of one man, while another put his own hand on Howard's shoulder, and so on until they formed a single contiguous line. The first man in line raised his arm high, snapped his fingers, and cried, "Begin!" At once they all began to move in time to the rhythm of the drums, their bare feet treading lightly upon the sand. As Howard tripped and stumbled, unable to keep up with them, they called out to him, laughing, to bring him into step with them. He was befuddled and happy as a child. Gradually he managed to co-ordinate his feet with theirs. They all raised their heads and breathed in deep draughts of air, dancing in a circle around the drummers. They sang boisterous songs Aisha was unable to recognize, as the atmosphere grew saturated with a certain kind of masculine merriment, and the sweat poured down their faces.

When they were finished dancing, they all reseated themselves cheerfully around the fire, continuing their laughing banter in raucous voices. Listening to Howard's strangely accented Arabic, they clapped him on the shoulder, and he returned the gesture. In the middle of the fire was a sooty tin kettle. One of the men picked it up by using a piece of bent wire, and from it he poured tea into small glasses, raising the kettle up high to make sure that each glass received its complement of bubbles. Howard drank, along with the rest of them, one glass after another, just as if he were on his own turf, with his own people. How did he manage it? How could he extend his own roots this way—he, a stranger in this land—when she herself had no roots in any place?

Tea was no longer being served, but the fire burned on. Aisha was seized by a sudden tremor when she caught a flash of light at the wall of the temple, which was deep in shadow: the glimmer of eyes she knew well, observing the group ranged around the fire, then slipping swiftly into hiding once more. It was the wolves. They had not yet given up the chase.

At last the men left. Howard made his way back to the house, still humming in time to the rhythm of the dance. When he saw Aisha sitting in the shadows, he exclaimed cheerfully, "Why hello, princess! I thought you were going to sleep until morning." He lit a lantern and sat beside her. His face, still flushed, was bathed in perspiration.

"Why the festivities?" she asked.

"They're celebrating my return and the fact that work will commence soon," he replied. "Even more importantly, they think I've gotten married."

She smiled wanly at him. How should she behave? She didn't know. Would it be to her advantage to let them persist in their assumptions, or not? It didn't matter—she was a stranger on unfamiliar terrain. From afar rose the voices of the wolves—they had all awoken. Howard noticed the fear in her face, yet even so he took her by the hand and drew her out onto the balcony. He pointed at the fire, which still burned, "This fire will stop the wolves from coming any closer—and it will keep off the insects, too."

She tried retreat, crying, "But I'm so frightened!"

Not letting go of her arm, he said, "The wolves are my friends. They've followed me from the forests of Swaffham all the way to the tombs of Beni Hassan.

They guarded my door when I was living in Deir al-Bahri. They are my shadows, never apart from me."

The howling continued, and apparitions of their concealed bodies could be seen in the depths of the night. It seemed as if they were staring directly at Howard and Aisha, and she trembled more violently. When he held out his hand and drew her toward him, she did not protest—she needed a human touch. "You know the call of the wolves," he said. "They are not angry or preparing to attack. They are rejoicing in the arrival of nighttime, their domain. And perhaps they are happy because you're here. He encircled her waist with his arm—she was as close to him as she could be, feeling the heat of his body. She rested her head on his shoulder. Sparks flew up from the burning branches, and still the wolves stared fixedly at the two of them. She felt his lips upon her face as the bristles of his moustache crept across her skin. His lips found hers, and she shivered, struck by a wave of pain, the blood running cold in her veins. All at once she broke into tears, pushing him away despite her need for contact, crying, "Don't touch me!"

He withdrew his hands from her. "Calm down," he said. "Nothing will happen to you against your will."

◆ ◆ ◆

I've taken up digging once more. I had just about exhausted the area designated to me. I had divided it into squares and excavated every square with minute care, investigating each stone and every grain of sand. I came across many small things, which I gave to Lord Carnarvon to add to his collection. I tried to keep the flame of hope burning within me—I was racing against time, for this nobleman, with his ill health, could die at any moment; indeed, throughout the war years he had been on the brink of death. I never supposed he would revive, and I was certain that his exalted daughter, Lady Evelyn, would not carry on digging after him. I tried to get close to her, but she rejected me, never forgetting that I was her father's employee. Perhaps she thought I was exploiting his passion for collecting artifacts to my own personal advantage. Be that as it may, time is not on my side. Arthur Weigall, who deprived me of my position as director of antiquities, is waiting for his chance to evict me from the valley. How would my luck have to turn to help me out of these difficulties? I would need a miracle.

At noontime, after I had distributed the workers around the excavation site, I saw him coming from deep in the valley, carrying a basket on his shoulder. The sun was behind him, and I couldn't distinguish his features clearly, so I took him for one of the fellahin who come to the site in search of work. But he stopped in front of me and said, "I've got something important to tell you." I brought him into the tent I use to take shelter from the sun. He closed the tent flap so that no one would see him there. I knew his name was Ali Hassaan, like so many of the fellahin from al-Qurna Village. He wanted me to buy the basket from him: a bunch of worthless stones, some of them with inscriptions that were incomplete or indecipherable—their pickaxes always strike the wrong spot. There were fragments of pottery, a broken marble vessel, a crushed scarab—all evidence that these were grave goods, and that they had not merely been plundered, but had been brutally destroyed. But then I began turning over the stones in perplexity—it seemed as though I recognized in them symbols from a partial cartouche. I couldn't believe my eyes—they referred specifically to Amenhotep IV, the old name of the heretic Pharaoh, Akhenaten. My head felt suddenly clouded—I could not connect these artifacts to the valley in which we were digging. Times and places had got muddled all in an instant.

"Where did you get these pieces?" I asked him.

"That's none of your concern," he replied. "I came to sell this basket, and if you don't buy it, I'll find some other foreigner who will."

"I'll pay more for it if you'll show me where these articles came from."

"You'll be wasting your money. If there'd been anything else I'd have brought it to you."

"Let me be the judge of that."

"Why do you insist? It doesn't make sense."

"Perhaps I can see what you can't."

He was silent for a moment, rubbing his chin. There was a shrewd gleam in his eye. Finally he said, "I'll take the two donkeys and ten pounds."

The man was greedy, and his demands exorbitant—the pair of donkeys and the canary were the only animals I owned. But he knew I was desperate, and so, reluctantly, I agreed. He held out his hand, and I gave him the money as an advance: a single note bearing the image of the new king, Fouad I, with his twisted moustaches. An astonished Abdel Aal brought us the donkeys, and the fellah permitted me to ride one of them, while he mounted the other. Abdel Aal attempted to follow us, but I ordered him to stay and oversee the excavations.

We proceeded across the valley, leaving behind Dar Abu al-Naja and entering a "trackless" valley. The columns of Deir al-Bahri appeared in the distance. I know this region like the back of my hand—I gave it the best years of my life, but now here was this fellah leading me into a maze of rock and sand I had never seen before. He spurred his donkey on confidently. He turned aside before we reached Deir al-Bahri, but entered a narrow, rocky passage that ran parallel to its wall. How could I not have known about the existence of this passage before?

We came to a stop before a huge rock that looked as though it was suspended in midair and about to fall on us. Pointing to a spot underneath it he said, "This is the place."

I reckoned he was making fun of me, but I dismounted and, after a moment's hesitation, passed beneath the rock. I heard the wind keening shrilly, as if it had made up its mind to bring the rock down. I shivered, seeing a long crack in the middle of the rock face. There was an opening there, stuffed with fallen rocks—just a crack in a heap of stones, but it had been opened by means of chisels and pickaxes. I knew I was standing before the opening to a tomb I had not seen before, and it was clear that this fellah had not entered it, either. He had satisfied himself with gathering a little heap of things into the basket he had brought me. This was a tomb that had been far from my speculations, and a long way from where I was excavating. I had no right to set to work on it—but who was to know? Perhaps this was the dream I had been awaiting for so long.

◆ ◆ ◆

Howard did not sleep that night. Aisha stayed up with him as he paced distractedly around the main room of the house. He got out a number of old drawings he had done of the region while living at Deir al-Bahri, and traced the perimeter of the valley, the jagged rock formations, and the undulations of the hills, trying to discover where the unfamiliar tomb began and ended. At daybreak he had dark circles around his eyes. Aisha heard the racket made by the men, who arrived at an early hour. Fog still shrouded the surface of the river and surrounded the ancient city. The men were standing ready, in front of the house, holding pickaxes and other implements, Abdel Aal at the head of them. Howard had put on his khakis early in the morning, and donned a felt hat. "You'll come with us," he told her.

"But what can I do in the midst of all those men?" she protested.

He pointed to some khaki garments, similar to the ones he had on, which were piled on a little table. "You can put on these clothes," he said. "Abdel Aal purchased them in Luxor last night, specially for you."

She looked at him wonderingly—he wasn't joking. He returned her gaze, resolute. "But why?" she insisted. "All these years you've been digging on your own."

"Today is different," he replied. "I'm at the threshold of a new discovery, and it could be the tomb of which I've been dreaming. I want you by my side—I want to ensure that luck won't abandon me this time."

She had no way of putting on a veil to hide her face, although at least the trousers were fairly long. Still, she gathered her hair on top of her head and pressed the felt hat down over it. There was no donkey, so everyone went on foot. The men, amazed, lagged behind, following her the whole way, but they ducked their heads each time she looked at any of them—none dared venture any questions. They made good headway on the dew-moistened sand. As the waters of the river took on a reddish hue, Aisha filled her lungs with the morning air. She walked beside Howard, having regained her self-possession—from now on, there would be no need for her to hide.

The columns of Deir al-Bahri came into view, congregating sleepily in the lap of the mountain. The group turned aside and proceeded into the rocky passage, which was not wide enough to accommodate two men walking abreast. Howard took hold of Aisha's hand to help her across the slippery stones. The party came to a halt before the hanging rock.

The men divided themselves up at once, some to dig and others to haul away the rocks. The two youngest, meanwhile, were charged with carrying flasks of water. The men went in beneath the hanging rock and without further ado began to dig. The sounds rose of pickaxes striking stone, with no voices raised in song this time. The task demanded steadiness and efficiency—such was Howard's agreement with the men. Looking at the hanging rock, Aisha felt deeply uneasy; no one else seemed concerned about it. One of the boys offered her a cup of water, but although her throat was dry she couldn't take it. She whispered to Howard, "Is this the tomb you were looking for?"

"I don't know," he said doubtfully. "It seems too easy to be real."

The men worked on tirelessly, racing against sunrise, when the custodian of antiquities at Deir al-Bahri might discover what was going on, and Weigall come and accuse Carter of violating the terms of the permit he'd been granted. No one stopped even to ask for food or water, while Howard remained rigid at the opening of the tomb as it began to manifest itself, freed of rocky protrusions.

Only when the sun had reached its zenith was the cleanup of the passageway leading to the interior of the tomb complete. Then the men, exhausted, threw themselves down in the shade of the rock, which still hung in its place. Now it was Howard's turn to bestir himself. He picked up a small electric torch—a flashlight—sent to him specially by Lord Carnarvon from England; it was no longer necessary to use burning torches. He took Aisha's hand and they began the descent. They were accompanied by al-Raïs Gregor, the workers' foreman, who undertook to move aside the remaining stones from the passageway. Aisha felt the air grow heavy and stagnant. She could not catch her breath, but Howard kept pulling her farther inside, sweeping in all directions with the flashlight. To his surprise, the walls were smooth and unembellished with reliefs or paintings. They had been washed, smoothed down, and coated with a layer of plaster and lime, but the operation had stopped short of the artist's placing his first stroke on the wall—the magic touch that would animate a gloomy void with the pulse of life. He swung the flashlight, looking for some kind of sign, anything that would guide him through this unknown corridor. There was nothing but more rocks. Panting, the workers carried these outside—there was no air, and the smell of their sweat was stifling. Aisha leaned against the wall to rest a little, and then the corridor opened before them onto a fairly spacious room, strewn with piles of nothing but ruined objects—pots, figurines, wooden boats, and sarcophagi—everything ruthlessly demolished. No one had tried to steal these things or to profit by them. They looked like the remains of a great fire—the plaster walls were begrimed with a layer of soot, and there were charred remnants of wooden figurines and statues, as if a battle had taken place in this confined space.

"Did thieves do all this?" asked Aisha fearfully.

"Thieves don't wreck things this way," said Howard miserably. "They know that these remains are the source of their livelihood. Whatever happens, they don't destroy them or try to burn them. There's something here that I don't understand."

Not wanting to leave empty-handed, he ordered the workers to take along such objects as might be useful. The fellah had been right, though: he had warned him, before depriving him of his donkeys. But he had clung to the obstinate hope of a desperate man.

The men all went out; only Aisha was left, standing before him, gazing at him in sympathy. He kept pointing the torch in every direction, until it began to grow dim. Its light faded gradually, and the darkness closed in. It seemed as though he had no intention of going back outside, of leaving this spot. Aisha also stayed where she was, scarcely breathing. She had not provided him with the touch of good fortune he'd been hoping for, any more than she had been able to do for herself.

She heard his voice, as if he were thinking out loud. "It's an unfinished tomb," he said. "They dug it in the heart of the mountain, then abandoned it. They tried to desecrate it as well. They set about burning it, and they left unseemly rubbish in it. Thieves didn't do this—rather the builders of the tomb did it all . . . but *why*?"

There was nothing she could say. There was no air for her to breathe. She felt the sweat soaking her face and body. At last she heard him say, "It's no use staying here. Let us go . . ."

In the forecourt of the house the workers assembled what they had gleaned from the piles in the tomb, then took their leave. Night began to descend upon the valley, and Howard sat silent on the balcony. The news of his failed venture would spread in the morning. The employees at the Antiquities Service would mock him, as would the traders in artifacts, the occupants of the great dahabeahs, the international consuls, and the delegates from the museums. Davies would laugh at him, Weigall would gloat, and it would be disastrous when the news reached Carnarvon. A day lost, another dream laid waste—ought he to give up?

He ordered Abdel Aal to light a fire. He went into the forecourt and Aisha sat with him there, where she was conscious of the heat from the flames touching them. They tried to separate the piles and sort their contents: bits of marble in one heap, fragmentary cartouches in another, remains of plates and pieces of pottery and wood in a third. Howard rearranged pieces in the hope of being able to assemble a complete inscription or chance upon a name. It was a long night, with the wolves keeping vigil on the other side of the expanse of level ground, staring at them. He got up to fetch the basket the fellah had sold him the day before, and rearranged its contents once more, assembling them in an attempt to make something out of nothing. He fingered the engravings, then suddenly exclaimed, with what sounded like inspiration, "It's his tomb! They were preparing it for him before he rebelled against it all and slipped their grasp!"

"Who is it you're talking about?" she asked.

"Amenhotep IV," he replied. The heretic Pharaoh Akhenaten, when he was a youth, and reigned over Thebes. They were readying this tomb for him, but when he rebelled against them and left their city they destroyed it and tried to burn it. They desecrated it and put bits of stuff from other tombs in it. This is the inscription that bears his name and his device, but in fact he is buried somewhere else, in a place no one knows anything about."

He was up and prancing around her, irrepressible. At last he located some similar pieces, bits of black basalt, and he knew that this discovery was worthless, nothing more than manifestations of unconfirmed historical accounts.

The night grew colder. On hands and knees, Aisha gathered for him a larger collection of stones, so that he could see whether they contained any of the missing inscriptions. He went quickly to the house, then came back carrying a large magnifying glass. He brought some of the stone fragments close together and examined them. "It's a tablet," he said. "Before the tomb was destroyed, the tablet was meant to be hung upon its door. The phrases are broken up—'he who is most righteous . . . shall be interred here . . . the victorious one . . . Amun . . .' It's certain the tomb was made ready for him before they changed their minds about him—my God! Here is Akhenaten, emerging before me once again, like a nightmare I can't get free of."

"But," said Aisha, "he's not buried here!"

"Who knows?" said Howard. "Perhaps he was buried in the north, and perhaps his body was smuggled here. The valley around me is full of him. He doesn't appear, but he keeps sending me signs."

He got to his feet and walked across the sand toward the shadowy temple, where the wolves were tracking his every step.

At the top of his lungs he cried into the silence, "I know you're here, somewhere near me! Why won't you show yourself?"

10 • Tel al-Amarna

WHO DRAWS ASIDE THE MASKS OF TIME? Who lifts the linen wrappings from truth's riddles? Who possesses the wisdom to comprehend the secret of death, the breath of resurrection, or the limitlessness of eternity?

On a certain night a tiny glimpse of the true nature of existence was revealed to Akhenaten. It was a night on which the wolves never left off howling with hunger and yearning. Before him there appeared a ragged-edged moon and unimaginably distant stars. He kept a solitary vigil, feeling the night's chill like a fine needle pricking at his skin. He stood naked, defenseless, and hungry; beseeching the gods that had forsaken him and refused to give him any sign. There was no more food or drink—all that remained to him were a few papyrus scrolls, with some hymns and prayers inscribed upon them, before Atun abandoned him and disappeared beyond the horizon. Why do the gods suddenly desert us just when we are in the greatest need of them? Even the moon had begun to set behind the trees, at the precise time when his spirit required a glimmer of light. He fixed his gaze upon the silvery forest that surrounded him—these dew-spangled trees were his last comfort, this was the place that had granted him solitude in a world where enemies proliferated and friends were few. How might it be possible to expel from people's souls the bitter resentments of the bygone days of their enslavement—enslavement by many-faced gods and all-powerful priests? He suddenly understood how difficult it was to bear the burden of bringing change to a world so profoundly vast and eternal.

He knew that his body, chilled and solitary, could be warmed only by the touch of Nefertiti—his wife, his beloved—and that nothing would fill this desolate silence but the laughter of his daughters. He rose, despite the pain in his desiccated joints. He stood straight, in all the strangeness of his aspect—his belly distended like a waterskin, his bulgy knees looking as if they had been put together wrong. The sun had tanned his exposed skin, and beneath it his ribs protruded, prominent and sharp. The sun had risen and set upon his naked body seven continuous days, each of them like the first day of creation, his undefended hide the first to drink up its rays and the last to be deprived of its heat. In these moments the sun is for the new god alone, that it might impart to him some of its secrets, or even give them all to him.

He descended the hill. Waiting for him at the bottom was a detachment of guards who had been stationed there for a whole week, anticipating that he might appear at any moment—or perhaps not at all. The soldiers averted their eyes so that none of them would glimpse any part of the sacred Pharaoh's naked flesh. The greatest of Atun's priests hurried forward, carrying a white abaya embroidered with threads of gold forming the disc of the sun, whose rays took the shape of outspread arms. He draped this over the Pharaoh's shoulders. The guards surrounded him; ordinarily, on seeing him they would fling themselves upon the ground and rub their faces in the dust, but the Pharaoh had forbidden this practice. It was enough for him that they bow slightly, and he permitted them to come so close to him that they could smell the fragrance of the camphor that anointed his body. Not far from them stood his own winged chariot, with white horses harnessed to it, white being the color reserved to the Pharaoh alone.

The hill overlooked a wide lake, Lake Bayim, from which had come the clay of first creation, and whose bottom still preserved earth's memory. In its waters the god bathed before rising. The heads of crocodiles protruded from it, and herons glided upon its surface, awaiting the moment of sunrise and awakening. Traced upon its ripples were the paths of the sun, moon, clouds, and stars. Beyond the lake a basin of clay stretched all the way to the edge of the silver forest, the place Akhenaten had chosen for his seclusion—here was the realm of Atun, the place he came from, although it was a dangerous region, thorny and filled with the dens of wolves and jackals. But in this way are gods normally born.

The Pharaoh shivered, feeling the touch of the cloth upon his skin. He did not wish for anything to divide him from the world's air, but he pulled the abaya about himself and made his way to the chariot. The guards mounted their stallions and formed ranks behind him, so as to follow the chariot, which he himself was accustomed to drive. He took the lead, feeling that he had returned suddenly to the real world. Awaiting him was a far-flung and profoundly unsettled nation: to the south were the rebellious priests of Thebes who would not support him or follow his religion, while to the north, on the fringes of the desert, his enemies from the tribes of Asia stood poised, demanding of him their revenge now that his father was dead—his father, who had relentlessly oppressed them and laid waste their cities. He had more enemies than one person could absorb, but happily his wife and daughters were constant, always awaiting him: droplets of love united in a tidal wave of hostility—was it really necessary that the people love him? He remembered the words that his mother, Queen Tiye, had repeated to him again and again: "Don't aspire to their love—it is a waste of time. Make them fear you, that they may obey you blindly."

But who held such power as hers? His father, Amenhotep himself, who had subdued the Hittites and the Nubians, stood trembling in awe of her, stripped of divinity. Tiye was a true goddess, possessed by the spirit of Isis. The guards of the palace used to whisper that on moonlit nights she changed into a hungry wolf, swiftly traversing the palace corridors and howling with insatiable appetite. He had continued to be afraid of her even after he became a young man. When he chose Nefertiti as his wife, Tiye did not conceal her distaste for Nefertiti's strange appearance—her pale skin, long neck, and her wide eyes, which held a trace of sadness. She always said to him, "She doesn't look properly Egyptian. What sort of blood runs in her veins?"

His father satisfied himself with giving him a look of sympathy. The old conqueror of Asia was swiftly declining toward the infirmity of age, and he had no faith in the abilities of the heir who would follow him to the throne to hold the reins of control—with his crooked legs, distended belly, and protuberant features. A king such as this—how would he be able to rule so vast an empire?

Without thinking about it, Akhenaten tightened the reins in one hand while wielding the whip he bore in the other. The chariot passed through the shadowy forest, and the guards could not keep up with him. It was as if the cares of the world, from which he had been fleeing all this time, had begun pursuing him in earnest.

All at once a wolf blocked his way. A huge animal, such as he had never seen before, it stood right in the middle of the path, indifferent to the hooves of the horses thundering toward it. It bared its teeth and bent upon him its luminous eyes—perhaps it was Queen Tiye, risen to warn him about something. The wolf let out a strange howl. Akhenaten tugged hard enough at the reins nearly to choke the horses, and they reared up on their hind legs, their hooves digging tracks in the earth. He felt himself flung high into the air and falling into the middle of a thicket of trees. He did not lose consciousness, but his whole body ached. He was pierced by thorns on all sides. It was then he saw the little points of light that approached him like tiny embers; moonlight filtered in through the tree branches and revealed their bodies—they drew so close to him that he could detect their rank odor. He lay there unable to rise, or to move at all. They formed a half circle around him, ceaselessly panting, mouths agape and tongues hanging out, as if they were deliberating, considering whether this meager meal was worth the trouble of attacking it.

One of the wolves howled shrilly, as if calling upon the whole pack to pounce—he felt their claws tearing into his flesh. He closed his eyes and waited for their jaws to close upon him—what was the point of immortality? Useless! Then there was a cry—not a wolf's howl, but a muffled shout, a tremor, and a jet of some sort of hot liquid. The claws froze and the teeth did not come. The howling voices rose, but still the warm body held fast to him where he lay trembling. He opened his eyes to find that a viscous liquid covered his face, and the body of a wolf clung to him, still struggling, with an arrow piercing its belly.

He pushed the wolf's corpse off of him and tried to raise his head. The rest of the wolves had fled, but he caught sight of something else: an apparition, white as a wisp of fog. The Pharaoh focused his eyes upon it as the phantom came closer. The characteristics of its body began to take shape: a tall, broad-shouldered figure, wearing a white abaya and carrying a bow in one hand, a quiver full of arrows in the other. It extended its powerful arm and lifted the Pharaoh's slight body out of the briars.

"As ever," said Akhenaten, "you've come just in time, Horemheb!"

Before Akhenaten could collapse upon the ground, Horemheb offered his hand and supported the Pharaoh's body, naked now that his abaya had been torn to shreds. Horemheb took off his own abaya and wrapped Akhenaten in it, revealing a pleasingly muscular body. Effortlessly, he picked up the Pharaoh, slung him over his shoulder, and bore him through the forest.

The Pharaoh regained consciousness only after two days. At first he thought he had been plunged into a ghastly nightmare, but his face was covered with wounds and his body ached with bruises. Nefertiti's lovely face was looking down at him, her wide eyes full of fear. "Atun," she said, "we were afraid you would depart, and leave us."

He attempted a smile and replied, "The time has not yet come."

Taking his words as a sign of encouragement, his six daughters burst in all at once, rushing over to his bed and surrounding him on all sides. These were moments of ease and peace in his life, when he felt that he was not pursued and threatened. He stroked the girls' curly hair—they bore many of their mother's characteristics: Nefertiti with her concave belly, delicate features, and narrow frame suitable only for bearing girls. He would have liked them to acquire from her some of the beauty with which she was abundantly endowed, but she had not given much of it to her daughters. He embraced the eldest, Ankhesen. He always felt secretly apologetic toward her for wishing that she had been a boy, so as to put an end to any anticipated rivalry for the throne. Then, too, Ankhesen, first in a line of female offspring, had inherited her mother's graceful height, but she was stronger, as if she had been about to be born male but had changed her sex at the last moment.

They brought him newly baked bread, fruit, and fresh milk. He ate a little and then, feeling that he had regained some of his strength, he rose from his bed and stood on the balcony, which overlooked the new city, Akhetaten. He had chosen this site carefully, so that it would be central to his kingdom, which extended far to the north and south, and so that it would be far from Thebes (that city of hostilities and evil gods). Before him was a plain that stretched as far as the eye could see, raised slightly above the banks of the Nile, so that it would not be vulnerable to the perils of flooding. To the west his city was bounded by the Nile, while the east was enclosed by rocky slopes in such a way as to defend it from sudden attack and to supply the stone necessary for construction of its buildings. There was also, on its periphery, a deep valley that could serve as a burial ground for all the kings when they were made ready for immortality. Indeed, workers and builders had begun constructing a new tomb for him in this valley. This was the city of light, as he had dreamed it would be—its limestone sparkled every morning when Atun's sun rose upon it. It was a divine city, with no room for darkness or treachery. Within a few years, the people would recognize how important was the call he had issued—everyone, whether here in the Nile Valley or in faraway lands, would realize that they shared a single god.

A guard entered, bowed, and announced the arrival of Commander Horemheb. He was among the few people who were permitted to enter the inner quarters of the palace and to see the Pharaoh without his throne and other regal appurtenances. A man of towering height, he entered, clad in his warrior's garb fashioned from leather strips and pieces of metal, as if he were ready to go into battle at once. The Pharaoh did not care for these ostentatious military uniforms, but he loved Horemheb. From the time they were small they had never been apart, and it was Horemheb who always intervened at the right moment and guaranteed his safety. He stopped before the Pharaoh, head bowed.

"Greetings, bold leader," said Akhenaten. "Once more you have saved my life, and I am obliged to you yet again. Ask of me what you wish!"

Horemheb took a step forward and stood up straight, to emphasize his words. "My lord, I wish to go to war."

Hearing the determination in Horemheb's voice, Akhenaten grew pale. So it was war again, was it? The word by which his father had lived his life, repeating it over and over. He died before resolving his battles. Akhenaten was silent. He was on the point of refusing the commander's request—a request set in the balance against his own rescue from certain death. At last he spoke. "I do not want Akhetaten to be a city of war and killing," he said. "I want to dedicate her to life—to sowing and planting and reaping, to dancing and singing and love. That is her true mark of distinction."

With the same resolve as before, Horemheb said, "If this city does not go to war, then war will come to her streets. Your enemies believe that when you left Thebes you were running away—that you were weak. They think your armies are riven with internal disputes, and they are picking quarrels with the Egyptian garrison at the northern borders. If we do not go to them, they will cross the land of Canaan, our ally, and then they will enter our own lands at the Valley of Turquoise and attack us."

Akhenaten held his breath. Horemheb had changed abruptly from a human being to a figure made of bronze, likewise hard and unyielding. He didn't know whether he would be able to reach him with his words, but he said, "Atun is not a god of war, and I will not dishonor his name with fighting. We are no longer at Thebes, with its wicked god, Amun. He was a primitive god who would not be sated but with blood, and who knew nothing but the language of war. Therefore, no one believed in him, but rather feared him. We must give those foreigners a god they can understand and love, and then they, too, will leave off warmongering and slaughter."

"My lord," said Horemheb, "they are barbarian tribes, and their thinking has not risen to this level—such ideas will not put an end to their insatiable thirst for killing and plundering. Our confederate in Canaan has sent a message warning us of their continual assaults upon his garrison. When our enemies have advanced so far, we must wage war to defend Egypt's gateways. Even the god of peace, my lord, needs strength."

Once more the Pharaoh shook his head in refusal. Horemheb fell to his knees. He knew better than anyone the perils that beset the country. As a warrior he had crossed the desert; he had grown to manhood and risen in the ranks, amid bloodshed and the clash of swords. But enemies were thousand-headed beasts—each time you lopped off one head, another grew in its place. And now here were these foes rising up once again, demanding revenge for all their past defeats. He again took up his pleas, speaking as if reciting an incantation, "They are like locusts, my lord. Once they have descended upon our valley, not a temple, not a village, not a city will be left: the green earth will turn to wasteland and the river will fill with blood. The only thing they believe in is the power of fire, and they leave behind them nothing but the ashes of conflagration. Before they set upon us we must go to them and engage them in the final battle."

Horemheb's eloquence was great—greater than the powers of a grim-faced soldier. Yet the Pharaoh appeared all but unmoved. "There is no such thing as a final battle, Horemheb. When war begins, it never ends. Seek a different resolution, other than bloodshed—negotiate, conciliate . . ."

Horemheb rose from the floor, his face dark with anger. He strode rapidly to one of the guards and snatched the sword from his hand. For a moment Akhenaten drew back in fear, but Horemheb turned the blade, pointed it toward his own chest and cried, "I am a man of war! I have no skill with negotiation and conciliation! Let me fight, or I shall kill myself now, before your eyes!"

They stood face-to-face, both of them shaking. In such a moment was the fate of a vast nation determined. On what power should it rely? The light of the sun, or the spark that flashes at the point of a sword? It was up to the Pharaoh to choose, but it was not within his power. He did not want to lose the commander, his friend, and he did not know where the truth lay: in his heart or in Horemheb's sword. "Give me some time, then, to reach a decision," he said weakly, sitting down on a chair. "It is not easy to pray for life while at the same time sending out armies of death."

Horemheb turned and left, his brow still clouded. Akhenaten sat on alone. Then he heard the sound of a footfall so light it barely touched the ground. He could smell her perfume as she drew near to him—she, the one person who could rouse him from his reverie. She knelt upon the floor before him and leaned toward him. He gazed into her wide eyes, which were filled with yearning and sorrow. He brushed her neck with his lips, as he loved to do, and felt a tremor in his body as she responded to him. She was responsive, too, in bed, but without tiring him or overtaxing his virility. Her desire was always proportional to his own, their appetites compatible. She was content with his satiety, and he needed only her body, no concubine's, despite his pressing need for a male heir to his throne—he could imagine none coming from any womb but hers.

Lifting to him a face wet with tears, she said softly, "A letter has come to you from Thebes."

He looked at her in astonishment. Letters for the Pharaoh never entered the women's quarters of the palace, but she explained, "It is from Ramouz. He sent it with his son, whom he charged with delivering it to you personally, or, if he could not do so, to bring it to me. No one knows of it—not even the chief minister."

Then, lightly as a butterfly, she left the room. He sat immobile, his heart pounding with anxiety, until she returned with the papyrus scroll. It was rolled up and stamped with Ramouz's seal. Surprised, he said, "You didn't open it!"

"I did not dare. But I think I know what it contains."

He opened it quickly and stared at the row of cartouches Ramouz had written with his own hand, not wishing to entrust the document to any of the scribes. His voice muted, he said, "She is still alive, but her condition is grave. The temple doctors say she cannot recover from her illness, and she has reached her final moments."

His voice shook. Hoping to lighten his burden, Nefertiti said, "Is there no way to bring her here?"

"It is too late for that," he replied. "It is I who must go to her."

"You must not return to Thebes, my lord!" she cried in alarm, "the city of the evil god Amun! The priests lie in ambush there, waiting for just such an opportunity!"

Her precautions were all that was needed to fix his resolve. Why did everyone keep reminding him that he had left Thebes a fugitive? Why did they think he was afraid to return to that heathen city? He was still Pharaoh! He could lead his army there rather than go to the north. Then none of the priests would dare try to stand in the face of his power . . . although he did not wish to use it, did not wish to foul the waters of the river at Thebes with blood. Yet he understood the extent of the danger that awaited him there.

"I shall go in disguise," he said. "No one will know me."

Nefertiti sighed—she did not agree. "Impossible," she said. You are a king—if you wish to go to your city, then go as a king. Take Horemheb, and bring an army."

"Horemheb is busy with greater battles. My battles are small ones, my wishes are pitifully simple—all I want is to bid farewell to my mother before she departs for the world beyond."

"I am afraid. Each time you leave me, I am frightened to death—the girls and I."

"I shan't be gone long. My journey will be a secret. Say that I have gone into seclusion in order to compose new prayers to Atun. I don't want my mother to see me in my kingly aspect—rather, I want her to remember the little child I once was . . ."

He saw her eyes shining with tears, and her hair piled on the top of her head—the arrangement she preferred, as it showed off the beauty of her neck. He entwined his fingers in its strands and began to undo the gold pins that held it. He felt a desire that spread from the tips of his fingers to the rest of his body. There was a tremor in their voices as they spoke, and they went together to the bed, there to calm themselves.

None knew of the journey but two of his most loyal guards. Nefertiti accompanied him tearfully through the subterranean chambers at the back of the palace. She stood and embraced him ardently, hoping he might yet change his mind, but he gently disengaged himself from her and proceeded on foot to the ferry slip, along with the two guards. He had ordered the guards, who had disguised themselves as servants, to treat him with the barest minimum of respect. He trusted them to negotiate with the ferryman as to the cost of the journey, without betraying his identity. He had taken care to drape his abaya over his head so that it covered most of his face. The boat was filled with earthenware vessels, as it transported honey and dates from the south, returning from the north with jugs of wine, as well as shipments of wheat and flax. One of his companions pointed to him and announced to the ship's crew, "This is a great merchant on his way to Thebes to buy large quantities of onions. He will sleep upon a bed belowdecks, for his health cannot withstand the cold air coming off the river."

The ship set out in the middle of the night, when the wind from the north filled its sails. The prow plunged into the middle of the dark waters, like an adder loosed from captivity. The sailors burst into song as they hauled the ropes, and their rough voices filled the night. He sat upon the ship's rail, watching the landmarks of Akhetaten recede. His nose lost the scent of lime and mortar—the city had not yet taken on the smell of humans; it did not know their crowding, their moments of love, or their daily quarrels--a clean city, lacking the elements of life, memories to be described. The muddy shoreline began to rise like a shadowy dam built to conceal everything behind it. All at once he remembered that he had not given Horemheb the answer he was waiting for. Perhaps this journey was an evasion.

He could not sleep the first night. The oppressive odors of the ship's bowels stifled him, as well as the sounds of mice ceaselessly chewing. He went up on deck, where everyone snored in cacophonous chorus.

Only a single sailor stayed awake at the helm, keeping the ship on course between the banks. All the lands were in need of someone to steer a course for them. Ought he to change his thinking and forsake his god? Should he relent and yield to Horemheb, let him prosecute his wars against everyone? In the final days of the reign of his father, Amenhotep, when he was at his weakest, in the moments of his enfeeblement, the nation was at the pinnacle of its strength. Emissaries of foreign nations poured in, bearing tribute and seeking to secure peace treaties. No one knew that the old lion was growing weak and powerless—toothless. The palace scribes spoke Akkadian, Aramaic, and Greek. Akhenaten, as heir to this throne, was always solitary, watching in thoughtful silence all that happened. He would go down to the markets of Thebes and sit there in disguise in the shops, which were crowded with foreigners. He kept company with traders and travelers who roamed the world, talking with them about the leaders of the Far East, who had been reincarnated over many lifetimes, and about the mighty warriors of the north, who lived and breathed for war alone. His mind stored away all these new ideas as he explored his old city, realizing that its powers were false, its glory a passing thing that would not long endure. It was essential that Thebes desist a little from making war on others, that it listen to their ideas instead. The priests stood firm against all this new thinking, and would be bent upon perpetuating the war, because all the profits from invasions and conquests poured into their temples.

When day broke, he was still awake. He passed the remaining days of the journey between states of wakefulness and insomnia. The complexion of the river, meanwhile, was changing, the brown water becoming denser, while on shore mountain chains appeared continuously, brilliantly colored beneath the sun, cloaked in crimson shadows at sunset. The river narrowed at times, when the mountains on both sides closed in upon it and the ship drew near to shelves of rock, and it was possible to see the mouths of the tombs and caves that sheltered fugitives. Absolute silence fell, and even the birds stopped following the boat, not to reappear until the mountains drew back, a green expanse spread out on either side, and palms and sycamores came into view. The boat stopped beside mud-brick villages presided over by pigeon towers, and the sailors disembarked to buy bread, vegetables, and fruits from the farmers.

Toward the end of the journey, the winds picked up, and the boat began to glide along easily, even though it was sailing against the current. The north winds bore it like an impetuous bird, but the sailors trimmed the sails and changed the direction of the rudder so that the ship came sharply about and tied up by the shore.

"We draw near to Thebes," said the ferryman, "and we must prepare ourselves before we enter the city. We must offer the required greeting—Thebes is the master of all the world's cities."

Akhenaten remained standing at the prow, his heart pounding. There was no turning back now: here he was, come once more, in disguise and fearful, to the city whose god he was—was it possible that they might detect his presence? Did they still remember his face? The boat sailed on through the night until, as day broke, it arrived at Thebes. The ship was adorned with palm fronds, sycamore limbs, and wildflowers, a tradition observed by mariners whenever they approached the master of all the world's cities. They brought out drums and tambourines and began to sing as the boat slipped through the mist that lay upon the surface of the water.

Before them appeared a flat expanse, profusely green and studded with palms, behind which rose a chain of grey hills. There, too, were the walls of stone, which began at the edge of the beach, and formed a circle, to separate the city from the perimeter of the desert. The palaces overlooking the shore, with their thick columns, could also be seen, as well as the tops of the obelisks and the temples. There was the smell of the city, so familiar to Akhenaten—how it had lingered in his senses: the fragrance of the jasmine trees, the breweries, the lime-kilns, the tanneries, and the perfumeries. The moment the prow of the boat made contact with the shore, everyone entered into the city's hubbub and commotion. They were beset by porters, beggars, and children leading donkeys. Akhenaten adjusted the hood of the abaya covering his face before preparing to disembark. He would have preferred to arrive, and to leave, by night, but it was the flow of the Nile alone that dictated the times of arrival and departure. He must look for a place to stay, and to take his meals, until evening.

He went ahead, the guards following a few steps behind him but never out of sight. The city was more crowded than usual, boisterously enlivened by a special celebration. The sound of drums and singing rose from a great many tents, which had been set up in the middle of the street. The temple squares were filled with people, and everywhere there were tables laden with food and drink, but what surprised him most of all was the large number of slaves who were strutting around, flaunting their oiled black skin and leading by the hand women of various colors. Akhenaten probed his memory, trying to recall which great occasions were so noisily celebrated by the city, but all he could think of was the festival associated with the succession of a new Pharaoh following the death of the previous one. Were they, then, celebrating his departure?

He stopped in front of a tavern. The voices of men and women rose stridently from within it, and it occurred to him suddenly that this was the right place—the place he had been looking for. He would go in and mingle with the inebriated crowd. He would sit quietly in a corner and spend the rest of the day there, until the shadows fell upon the city. There was nothing else for him to do, so he signaled to his attendants to stand near the door, so that they could warn him of any approaching danger. It was a dimly lit establishment, oppressively smelly, set upon stilts formed of palm trunks and thatched with their fronds so as to repel the sun's heat. He made his way among the scattered tables and couches, around which the drinkers were seated. Set before them were great flagons of beer topped with white foam, as well as plates of green onions, fava beans, and lupine seeds. Akhenaten did not care much for beer, for it was Amun's preferred libation, and the priests filled his temples with casks of the stuff at times of celebration. Now he must sit and make a pretense of partaking with everyone else of drink and its heady effects. Indeed, the proprietor of the shop came forward at once and set a full cup before him.

He sharpened his ears to listen to the diffuse conversations, which were being conducted in all manner of languages and dialects. There were peasants from places all along the valley, from Nubia in the south to Memphis in the north; Akkadians who had crossed the desert to come from the countries between the Tigris and Euphrates; sailors from the northerly isles; fishermen from the coasts; shepherds from the open country; and the Bedouins of the desert. They conversed intimately, alcohol having dispelled any barriers between them. He tasted the beer, which was sour and disgusting. He closed his eyes, wishing that he was not in this city, that he was sitting at home, surrounded by his wife and daughters, in a city fresh and blooming, unencumbered by the sins of the old world. He lifted his eyes and found, seated before him, a black-skinned woman, naked from the waist up. She leaned toward him until her breasts were directly beneath his nose. She was one of those in-house prostitutes, so common in these taverns—they would take customers to houses specially assigned to them around the perimeters of the temples. In a hoarse voice she asked him whether he might like to take his ease at her lodgings for a little while. He declined, his face reddening; she looked away in annoyance, then went off to join a group of women, who whispered, then laughed obstreperously. He looked the other way; the place was filled with women, a great many of them, of various sorts and different colors, but no sooner did he turn his head again than he found himself face-to-face with a bare-chested black male slave who began showing off the muscles of his chest and arms. He offered his services. "What kind of services?" Akhenaten asked in a strangled voice. "My god—no!" And raucous laughter burst from the women's table. The slave shook an angry fist at him. The tavern was in a state of such tumultuous agitation he could not stand it—and yet he could not leave. From the corner of his eye he noticed another woman, who sat by herself not drinking beer with the rest. Before her, however, was a glass of high-priced grape wine. She was beautiful, and wore a splendid gown. She seemed to be affiliated with this place. He knew her face, despite the cosmetics that masked it—he was sure he had met her on several occasions, perhaps within the palace or at temple celebrations: an important woman, or at least the wife of an important man. His memory had retained the impression of her features even after he left the city, but he could not remember her name. What had brought her here? Might she recognize him? He ought to get up and move away from her, but now he found that in fact the woman had seen him, and her gaze commanded him, as she stared at him quizzically. He groped in his pocket for a coin to leave for the tavern keeper, but she had risen from her place and begun to move toward him, blocking his exit. Had she recognized him and decided to confront him? She approached his table and leaned toward him, her breasts all but spilling from her gown.

"There's no need," he heard her say, "for you to sit by yourself on such a day as this."

She went around the table and sat down next to him, pressing herself against him so that he felt one of her breasts resting against his arm. Despite the odd situation in which he found himself, he breathed a sigh of relief: she had not recognized him, perhaps because of his beard, which had grown out during his river voyage, or because she couldn't imagine that the Pharaoh of Egypt would be sitting in a stuffy hole like this one.

She spoke again, pressing him, "You're new here, aren't you?"

"Indeed," said Akhenaten.

The woman pushed her breast still harder into his arm. In a voice husky with louche desire, she said, "Don't tell me your name or where you're from. All I want is for us to take advantage of this opportunity together, before things get back to normal. Right now all cravings are permitted, nothing is forbidden. Come, let's seize the day before it's too late!"

Boldly she reached out and placed her hand on his thigh. His whole frame convulsed with a shudder, but he couldn't resist asking, "What *is* this riotous holiday that the city is celebrating?"

Surprised, the woman said, "You really are a stranger in town, then—what luck! I adore strangers."

She took his hand and placed it on her bosom, which was soft and warm. He felt himself drenched in cold sweat. "We're enjoying the inter-annum holiday," she said. "The old year has finished, and there are three days before the new year begins. So now we're all living outside of time, outside of all regulations and proscriptions. Everything is allowed—you've come to the city at just the right time!"

She tried to sit on his lap and put her tongue in his mouth, but he pushed her gently aside. He needed to hear more from her—it enraged him that the feasts of Amun still held sway over the populace. "Don't be afraid of me, my dear," she said. "I'm not doing this professionally—I'm a respectable married woman, and from the high-ranking classes of this city, too. But this is a chance for me to gratify my appetites. As soon as the new year comes everyone will forget all about what happened!"

"And where is your husband?"

"Oh, don't be dull. He's somewhere or other, doing the same thing I'm doing. Look around you. Everyone in the tavern—even respectable wives like me—is looking for strangers for some unconditional fun. Just give me a little piece of silver so Amun will be pleased with me . . ."

The mention of Amun was enough to bring him abruptly to his feet. She clutched his hand and tried to pull him toward her. "You don't know what you're missing," she said.

He snatched his hand away and started to weave among the tables, until he found his way out. He could scarcely believe he had made it out into the fresh air once more. He wandered the streets blindly, watched over by the two attendants. This was not his city. Even during the wildest of celebrations he had never seen it in such a state. Evening was falling, and torches were being lit everywhere, filling the air with the smell of pitch. There rose a general clamor, women's cries mixed with the sounds of dancing and singing, as the city passed through these unruly moments of abandon, in which there was no time and the gods had no power. The streets were crowded with vendors, whose wares were spread upon the ground: spices, strong-smelling perfumes, necklaces of beads and African ivory, soft carpets, herbs and potions from Asia. Tents, shacks, and huts had been erected and were clustered around one another, women's sharp cries issuing from within them. There were wooden tables laden with all sorts of food. Gypsies told fortunes; African women danced naked around a blazing fire, digging their heels into the mud and whirling in the air like black butterflies; noblewomen came leading slaves by the neck into reed huts. A woman stood beside the road, advertising her price on a sheet of papyrus—and a low price it was, because sex was allowed and virtually free. He walked along the walls of the Temple of Karnak, from inside of which he heard the chanting of the priests and the clanging of cymbals, while the outside wall teemed with prostitutes and gigolos, and virgins offering their virginity for sale in exchange for a piece of silver.

At last he came to the old royal palace, which was not far from the Temple of Karnak. The palace was cloaked in shadow, and bats swooped around it. The trees surrounding it had grown into a forest, which screened it entirely from the city. There was no one in the vicinity—as if everyone feared the palace, although his mother, the queen, had not left it, nor had she declared any antipathy for Amun. She had little faith in his new god; she had refused to leave Thebes and join him.

She remained in her accustomed wing of the palace, keeping none by her but a few faithful servants. She could not have imagined living far from the city that had seen her in her glory.

He looked about before advancing along the avenue bordered on either side by palms. The palace came into view, with its columns and its walls of stone: dark, secluded, inaccessible except by a wooden bridge that passed over an embankment of mud. In times past this was where the guards had stood, barring entry to strangers; now, however, there was no one. He ordered the attendants to stand at the access to the bridge, and proceeded alone toward the entrance. The wooden planks of the bridge creaked beneath his feet, as if threatening to give way. The air had grown cold—everything around him had taken on an aspect of wildness and desolation. Tendrils of hyacinth bean, bougainvillea, and wild brambles grew around the entryway to the palace, while on either side rose broken statuary, in whose gaping holes bats had taken up residence. On hearing his footsteps, the startled creatures burst out in a black cloud. He climbed the dirty steps and entered the palace at last.

There was a shrill cry—of a tormented woman, in desperate pain. Could this be the voice of the queen? Had he come too late?

He hurried on into the palace's stony recesses. He could smell Queen Tiye's fragrance everywhere, for she still had not given up her habit of spraying perfume all around her wherever she was; she had her own special and distinctive mixture, which came from Nubia, and she left traces of it everywhere she went. Some slave girls appeared, and were astonished at the sight of him. He did not pause, however, as the fragrance led him toward her room. He saw someone coming from the inner chambers of the palace, panting with the effort of animating his corpulent body. Catching sight of him, Akhenaten stopped at once—even in dim light, he recognized him: it was Ramouz, the governor of Thebes, who had maintained his loyalty to Akhenaten, despite pressure from Amun's priests. Ramouz fell to his knees before him, but Akhenaten raised him up and said urgently, "How is she?"

"The sight of you will bring her back to life, my lord," Ramouz replied.

This was not true. The smell of death mingled with the scent of her perfume, and the cries rose up once more. This time there was no doubt that it was she. They both shivered, and Ramouz said, "She is suffering from terrible bouts of delirium, as if the spirit of Sekhmet had taken possession of her. She destroys anything within reach, and digs her fingernails into the faces of the slave girls and servants. It's got to where everyone fears to approach her."

He started walking again through the palace's dusky corridors. When he caught sight of the door to her room, his pace slackened. He took in his surroundings: torches almost guttering out; a row of black-clad women sitting and leaning against the walls of stone; bats colliding with the walls like souls that had lost their way, and leaving traces of blood upon the stones; torn curtains and broken pottery; the air stagnant with the mixed odors of vomit and burnt pitch; the sound of things being shattered. A slave girl emerged from the room in headlong flight. He went forward hesitantly, and went in.

It was a spacious room, lit by dozens of candles emplaced along the walls. Moonlight was reflected back from the balcony, which opened onto the Nile. He saw her bed on one side of the room; the diaphanous curtains draped around it stirred. It was the same bed in which his father had died. With trembling fingers he parted the curtains, and saw her stretched out there, her eyes closed, her body desiccated and emaciated, thin as a reed; her skull was hairless, her skin darker than he had ever seen it. Feeling his legs give way beneath him, he sat down on the edge of the bed. Her face, sallow and wrinkled though it was, retained its gravitas, its awe-inspiring dignity.

All at once her features convulsed—was it a spasm of pain, or was she dreaming? Or had she caught his own rank odor? She opened her eyes and stared at him in astonishment. Hollow-eyed, she tried to work out who he was: this exhausted and bedraggled man, the Pharaoh of Egypt, scion of the gods, son of the most powerful of kings on earth . . . a dreary ghost such as appears only in a nightmare. Nevertheless, a sorrowful light dawned in her face, and she smiled feebly. She recognized him, even though she had dismissed him. She reached out with her fingers and clutched his hand. Frail though she was, she clung to him, not wanting to be parted from him, not now.

"Stranger that you are," she said faintly, "you no longer much resemble him whom I once knew."

In silence, he held her gaze. Neither of them, any longer, looked the same as before. She attempted to rise, but could not. Catching her breath with difficulty, she said, "Are you not a rather lowly Pharaoh? Creeping back into your city in disguise. I expected you to come with your army and burn it down!"

"I wished to come only to see you," he replied, "not . . . not to start a war."

A spasm went through her body. "Are you in pain?" he asked gently.

She tried to smile, but her voice came weak and gasping. "Pain no longer has any meaning, my son," she said. "I've endured all kinds. More pain or less—it makes no difference."

Next to her bed was a large table covered with vials of medicine and jars of ointment and herbal powders—none of them of use anymore. She studied his face earnestly. "Isn't it strange?" she said. "You, who at one time did not resemble your father—suddenly, just in this very moment, you've come to look like him. So long ago . . . how youthful and strong he was, especially when he came to me at Akhmim to take me away, as his bride, to his regal palace—ah, but this palace is not so regal without him."

At this moment he felt as though he ought to bend over her, take her frail body in his arms, and lay his head upon her breast for a few moments, as he had been used to do when he was small. But they stayed as they were, apart. Tiye did not feel the need to draw any nearer to him or touch him more than she had done already. She was looking at him sharply, with a searching gaze. "Why have you done all this to us?" she said suddenly. "Why did you turn the world upside down? Weren't you strong enough to let it be?"

In her sunken eyes was all the vitality that remained to her. So intently did she fix her gaze on him that she communicated her own fears to him. This question had long consumed her—doubtless she had deferred her own death, waiting for an answer. His throat felt dry. He had come to bid her farewell, not for a reckoning. He turned his face away and in a low voice said, "Because I hated Amun. Not for one day did I ever believe in him."

"Liar!" she said, her voice shaking. "You believed in him just as your father did—it was he who made Amun lord of the gods, and you yourself were about to build a great temple to him. What was it that changed you so suddenly?"

What happened had not been sudden. For a long time he had struggled with himself and suffered from the impediments thrown up by the priests, but the moment had come when he could bear it no more—he had reached his limit—he hated Amun, and this caused him to hate them all. He said, "Why do you insist on knowing this?"

She spoke once more, her voice still unsteady. "Because it would release me from the pain of thinking about it," she said. "It would ease my mind a little to know that there was a reason. Everything pales beside the charge of heresy which they attach to you. Speak to me truly and tell me something that will heal my spirit."

She took on her queenly aspect, and the candlelight reflected in her eyes turned them to a pair of glowing coals. She would not believe anything he might say to her—she would detect the lie in his face. He did not wish to speak of his private reasons—the deep anguish that had beset him from the time he was a child, right up to this moment. Hesitatingly, in sorrow both for her and for himself, he said, "You wouldn't like to hear what I have to say."

"Whatever it may be," she said firmly, "I shall bear it."

He spoke haltingly, uncertain of what he should say. Yet his breast was heavy with its burden—he had not dared to reveal his secret to anyone, even his new god. From the depths of his soul he summoned up the difficult words, remembering that long-ago night.

It was the night of the full moon, when all who dwelt at Thebes turned into animals. Sirius, the Dog Star, had reached the middle of the sky and the rising waters of the Nile had surged so wildly at its banks that the bulwarks had burst, sending through the veins of the earth the first potent gush, which would fertilize the fields and rouse the dormant waterwheels. At such times all the spirits of black magic would awaken to partake of the special festivals that were mounted for Amun's sake. At that time Akhenaten stood upon the threshold of young manhood, his veins throbbing with his own potency, with urgency, with desire. He was not yet permitted to attend the festivities being held inside the temple. His father had left off warmongering, and his powers had waned—he kept to his bed most of the time; it was Amun who relentlessly ran the city of Thebes, the priests having vanished beneath their masks. And it was his father, the king, who had elevated Amun above the rest of the country's deities, making him the god who subsumed the characteristics of all the others combined. He made everyone in Thebes understand that he was an absolute god, and without equal. Among the priests he had a dark and hidden place in the Holy of Holies, but little was known as to what sort of rituals went on within it.

It was Nephru, his attendant and friend, who had given him the inspiration for the idea. Nephru was the son of Ramouz, Thebes's administrative chief, and it had fallen to him, out of all the noblemen's sons, to serve as companion to the Pharaoh from childhood, sitting with him at his lessons and accompanying him on hunting trips. They had remained close, growing up together, learning to read and write, going out to hunt, sometimes even wearing the same clothes. It was Nephru who had awakened him on that moonlit night and suggested that they sneak into the temple to observe the fertility rites that were being held for Amun. Nephru was brimming with restless vitality. The palace slave girls pursued him relentlessly—unlike the young Pharaoh, solitary and severe, who avoided everyone. Nephru knew the location of the secret passageway that connected the palace with the Temple of Karnak—in a moment of passion, one of the slave girls had told him.

He followed Nephru nervously, fearfully—but Nephru was eager and excited, precocious in his physical maturity and possessed by a craving to learn the secret of these rites. They went down to the garden, where the moon flooded the lawns with light and everything was touched with magic, and a sense of anticipation. They entered the dark tunnel, where the air was close and hot. They dared not carry a torch, but set off groping their way along. The tunnel was clean, paved in stone, and spacious enough to accommodate a man on horseback, or a woman borne in a sedan chair. It sloped downward, as if leading them to another world.

At the end of the tunnel a faint light appeared, and when they emerged from its mouth they found themselves right in the temple's central hall, which opened before them as if inviting them to proceed still further. They passed among dozens of torches, watched by the eyes of immense stone statues. The sacred lake came into view, its surface stirred by the night breezes. There were no priests, and guards were not allowed this far into the temple. They circled the obelisks, which stood like drawn swords, and stole into the marble-tiled inner corridors. They observed a statue of Amun with a ram's head and curved horns, which stared at them as if in collusion with them. The young Pharaoh's heart beat rapidly, but on he went, following Nephru.

The sound of music and drumbeats rose from somewhere within the temple. The two youths advanced, hiding behind columns, until before them stood the inner chamber of the Holy of Holies, the deepest and most secret realm of the temple. The hall was blazing with torchlight and redolent with incense. The wooden ceiling, inlaid with sculpted patterns and perched upon towering columns, had the design of a lotus blossom. The space was teeming with men and women, but no one noticed the two of them—the rites had reached a frenzied climax. There were nude women, their bodies gleaming in the torchlight, performing a circular dance to the rhythm of the boisterous music under the gaze of dozens of priests, who stood in a line next to the wall feverishly ogling them.

He stared at the women, shocked—he knew all of them, although he had never seen them naked before. Still, he knew their faces well—they frequented the palace, where they would spend long hours in the queen's wing and the Pharaoh's garden. They were the wives of Thebes's luminaries, its dignitaries and leaders—respectable, influential women. Who had stripped them of their clothing and exposed them this way? Amid the din, they kept turning. Then a very tall woman stepped forward and stopped in front of the altar. She was draped in a gown of sheer linen. She stood there in silence, motionless, until a new group of priests entered. They themselves were bare-chested, with short garments below. They were driving a fat ram that had been raised inside the temple—it evoked the head of Amun. They lifted it onto the high altar, constructed of marble. As they set it down they bound its legs. The high priest came forward—a man well-known to the young Pharaoh. Grasping a sharp knife, he stood before the ram and began to recite prayers. Then he brought the knife down upon its neck, taking its head off in one stroke, as a fountain of blood gushed forth. The woman now stepped forward, removed the gown that clothed her, and poured blood over her naked body. Nephru drew back with a gasp, not daring to continue watching the spectacle. He sensed that he had got in over his head, and seen more than was fitting. He turned his back and hurried away, vanishing even as the young Pharaoh stood on, transfixed, incapable of movement.

◆ ◆ ◆

The queen sat up—a strange animation had come over her. She stared at him, a peculiar expression on her face. "You sneaked in and saw me naked?" she exclaimed.

But she was unable to get out of bed. She floundered weakly, waving her hand at him. "Stop," she said. "No more."

But he could not have stopped now, even if the words were to freeze on his tongue. He was helpless to stop the flow of images that were passing through his memory. The secret his mind had striven for all these years to erase had awoken, as if a hole had opened up in the wall of his memory and everything had begun to spill out of it. Without any conscious desire on his part, the horrifying details of that night had come back to assail him.

◆ ◆ ◆

Her body, covered with blood, lay across the altar, red and gleaming and inflamed with desire. The high priest removed his clothing as well; he appeared huge in his nakedness. He wore a mask resembling the face of the ram—accursed symbol of Amun. As the priest approached the altar, she made ready for him, parting her legs. The young Pharaoh was on the point of losing consciousness. He could never have imagined his mother—a Pharaoh of Egypt who terrified everyone, offspring of the sacred gods and wife of the Pharaoh who had conquered half the earth—laid out like a common prostitute before a man with the head of a ram. He set upon her, and she, bloodied as she was, welcomed him with an urgency that mounted together with her cries, as they moved together to a single rhythm. The priests' voices rose in a hoarse cacophony, as if in a summons to the other naked women, who now all hastened to anoint themselves with the bloody residue. Trembling with desire, they lay down beneath the feet of the younger, shaven-headed priests.

Akhenaten's tears fell as he watched his mother crushed beneath the weight of the enormous priest, who now turned her over onto her stomach, and continued ravishing her without a pause. Akhenaten sobbed out loud, but no one noticed him, the sound of his anguish overwhelmed by the orgy of bodies in their feverish revels. He retreated back into the long, desolate tunnel, and sat there for the rest of the night, weeping and shivering. He would never be able to look any of them in the face again—not the high priest who had lain with the woman who held the throne, nor the younger priests, who had violated the noblewomen of Thebes.

◆ ◆ ◆

His tears flowed: before Queen Tiye's eyes the Pharaoh was weeping, as the memories of his youth—corrupted and lost—awoke within him.

"That was a sacred rite," she said bleakly. "We had to perform it each time the Nile flooded. I regarded my body as not my own. Once it was covered in blood, it became a body that belonged to the goddess Yamout, and he was her husband, the god Amun."

"No!" he replied, shaking. "It was a rite borne of Amun's debauched priests! I hated him from that moment, and I hated Thebes, and I hated . . ."

He fell silent, not finishing his thought, but the queen got up, her limbs overtaken by an extraordinary energy. She tried to get as far away from him as possible, coming to a halt at the wall of the balcony overlooking the river. She leaned against it and wept. It was the first time he had ever seen her weep. "Woe to you, Tiye!" she moaned. "You'll die with your son hating you, you'll pass into the shadows of the other realm wrapped in the bitterest kind of hatred . . ."

Silence fell between them. The only sound he could hear was her struggle for breath. All at once she realized that he had done what he did because he was ashamed of her: he was trying to salvage his own throne from the fiasco that had been ordained for it. It was not simply to prove his authority that he opposed priests who were stronger than he was; it was also that they harbored a secret contempt for him. He had begun his reign in fear of them, had decided to build a temple to Amun—easily the greatest temple ever built—and had chosen a location far from Karnak, in the hope that it would be relatively unsullied. A great portion of the construction was completed as he tried to persuade himself that he was more devoted to Amun than all the rest of them, but when the builders began construction of the Holy of Holies, with all its gloomy rooms and tortuous vaults and hidden altars, the odor of blood rose to his nostrils, and he knew that he could go no further. He could not deceive himself by establishing yet another place for the enactment of ritual orgies. He halted the construction, so that he might reconsider. But the priests wouldn't hear of it—they spoke to him in soft, sorrowful tones: he must resume construction, appropriate more land to cover expenses, and guarantee them a greater portion of the spoils from the wars he would wage in the future. He did not want war, nor did he want to acquiesce in robbing the innocent, or to be half a Pharaoh, fit only to be the son of a dishonored mother. It was then he came to his decision, then that he stood up to them. No matter what it cost him, he would not finish building this temple.

He was alone, in his lowest, his weakest moments. His wife was expecting her second child, and he could see that her narrow frame would produce only more girls, which would weaken him and his throne still further. It was essential that he look for someone who would help him, but the priests launched a surprise offensive against him. They set a mob upon the house of Ramouz, the governor of Thebes. They looted it, and surrounded the rest of the Pharaoh's men. It was an unambiguous message to him, a warning to him to recognize who held the reins of power.

He found himself picking up an axe and taking the secret passageway between the palace and the temple. He stood solitary before the immense statue of Amun, with its bloodstained ram's head: the god that had violated his mother. He raised the axe and brought it down, but its blade left not a scratch. The statue held solid, issuing its challenge to him. The priests emerged then from their hiding places in the temple and surrounded him. He had no means of retreat; it was up to the priests to defy the laws of nature, and kill the god's son. At this moment Horemheb entered—Horemheb: his totem and his redemption, who always appeared just in time to rescue him when he stood on the brink of death. In standing by the Pharaoh's side Horemheb was obeying his father Amenhotep's last command. It was he who intervened at this moment to wrest him from the hands of the priests and bring him back safely to his palace, and it was he who stood beside him as he spoke unsteadily, saying, "This city won't hold the two of us. Either Amun goes, or I do."

Then came Horemheb's reply, succinct and resolute. "A Pharaoh," he said, "does not leave his throne." But Horemheb, as a true military man, despised the priests through and through, seeing them as no better than worms, bloodsuckers good for nothing but robbing the farmers of their harvest, the soldiers of their spoils, the river of its water, the earth of its salt.

The Pharaoh went to bed that night believing he had been defeated, but he woke in the morning to the screaming of the priests as Horemheb's soldiers pursued them, stormed their temples, and broke statues of Amun over their heads. It was a lightning strike, leaving chaos in its wake, but the victory was incomplete. The priests gathered their adherents—the fanatical agitators and the idle unemployed—and then it was war in the streets of Thebes. The harvest was still a long way off, and the city filled up with people who crowded around the feet of the demolished statues and wept. It was not possible for the army to engage a street war on a daily basis, or to batter people who hadn't done anything other than weep and beg. The Pharaoh, meanwhile, had passed the point of no return: Thebes was no longer fit to live in. As if all the odors of filth and decay had not been sufficient, added to these now was the smell of blood.

Tiye stood shivering in the cold that came off of the river. He could see that her legs would not long support her, so he went to her and lifted her trembling body in his arms. She was very light, as if she had been hollowed out from the core. He tucked her into bed. Unable to speak, she gazed at him. This was all she had wanted from him—this gentle touch, imperfect though it be.

"Queen Tiye," he said, "Mother. I could never hate you. May I die before such a thing should come to be. But I love my new god, Atun—it was he who rescued me on that bloody morning, and commanded me to leave Thebes. He revealed himself to me in my distress, when I was alone, and he saved my life. It was he who gave me the strength to go to Akhetaten."

She lay with eyes closed, exhausted as never before. The silence of death had begun to impose itself—yet it is difficult for the spirit to leave the body. It struggles to escape from the smallest toe of the left foot, in the form of invisible particles, each carrying a part of life, of memory. The particles representing luminous deeds depart lightly and easily, those of darker deeds with a dying cry. She held onto his hand, lest she be swept away by the winds of death. The slave girls who had fled now began to come back into the room, where they stood close to the wall. They carried candles to light the way to the afterlife, all of them sensing the presence of death.

But the one who was approaching now was Ramouz. Panting and agitated, he paid no attention to the queen laid out upon her bed, or to the atmosphere of mourning that pervaded the room. Addressing the Pharaoh, he cried, "They've learned of your arrival, my lord!"

"What? So soon?" Akhenaten replied.

"There was some woman who saw you in a tavern, and she recognized you. She went and informed the priests."

The sometime whore of Amun had done it, then. He knew it was only a matter of time until they arrived—certainly they had spies in every palace, no matter whether it was the palace of the queen mother. "I won't leave my mother," said Akhenaten. "Let them come."

His mother pressed his hand, opened her eyes, and said weakly, "Save yourself, my son. It would pain me the more to see you come to harm on my account."

"Come with me, then," he replied.

"Let me die in peace—in my own house, and my own bed."

There was a commotion outside the palace, and the sound of savage yells. She heard the sound of stones striking the palace walls, and the nighttime calm gave way to shouts of rage.

"They've occupied the embankment," said Ramouz. "They killed the two guards who were with you. The slaves and the guards won't be able to hold them off for long. Come, my lord, let us go!"

He kissed her brow. She smiled weakly at him, lifting a finger to signal that he should make haste and go. The slave girls watched all this fearfully, not knowing what fate awaited them. He followed Ramouz, whose great bulk jogged along the passageways in the direction of the rear quarters of the palace with their prospect of the Nile. They descended the stone staircase leading to the tenebrous waters. "You are a good swimmer, my lord," said Ramouz. "It is your only means of escape."

"And she?" Akhenaten said, hesitating.

"I shall defend her with my life," replied the other. "All these years they have not dared to touch her, nor will they now."

Akhenaten flung himself into the water, feeling that his humiliation was complete. The shore seethed with an agitated mob carrying torches and swords. He struck against the current with his arms, fleeing yet again. It would have been a worthier thing for him to stand against them and die like a Pharaoh, but he was not about to relinquish his chance at revenge on this corrupt city. He would not stop, would not surrender to them. He would live so as to accomplish his vengeance. If they harmed his mother, he would return and burn down their city. He forged on through the water toward the western shore—it was distant, gloomy, and desolate, but they wouldn't dare pursue him to such a place by night. They feared the spirits of the dead that awoke in the night. Tiye must be dying at this very moment—he had lost her before he could properly forgive her, and he had lost Thebes before acquiring the skill of dealing with it. From a Pharaoh he had become a fugitive. On the point of being sucked down into the depths of the cold water, he pleaded with his body to grant him the strength to resist. He clutched at the reeds, which cut his hands, and struggled toward the beach. At last the uproar from the mob subsided, and only the glow of their torches remained. They moved off, and he entered a different world, dragging himself from the chill waters to the stickiness of the mud.

The wind moaned as it blew down from the hills where the dead lay. He found himself weeping, feeling the extent of his mortification. It wasn't merely that he had become a fugitive, but that the light of day might not fall upon him except as a rigid corpse. Even now the priests were surely organizing search parties. He studied the opposite shore and the frenzied agitation of the torches as they moved over it. Were they readying boats, so as to cross over to him? Would not the sacrosanct silence of the other world hold them back? He staggered forward, groping his way among rocks and stumbling into holes. From afar he heard the howling of wolves—no doubt they, too, awaited his demise. Hearing a noise behind him, the rustle of footsteps, he crouched upon the ground and took hold of his knife. Raising it on high he stood up, poised for action—but the wolf he was expecting did not appear. Standing upright upon a rock he spied an apparition—had the spirits in truth awoken? It seemed to be a skinny sort of ghost, wearing nothing but a ragged bit of linen and holding a tree-branch in its hand. Akhenaten held his breath, but then he heard the ghost speak.

"You must have committed a great sin, or they would not be pursuing you so fiercely."

A human being, then, just like him: one of those who dwelt among the tombs, or perhaps an outlaw. It made no difference—he could be no worse than those on the opposite bank. The figure sprang down off the rocks and came toward him. Striking the earth with his cane, he said, "Follow me, before they cross the river to get you."

Akhenaten roused himself and followed. They moved away from the river, climbing into the hills and plunging in among the rocks. He saw the river from above, boats beginning to mass upon it, his pursuers on board and the light from their torches reflected upon the surface of the water. The man, however, did not trouble to look behind him. There was nothing Akhenaten could do but follow him. The wet garments clinging to him grew colder. He was panting, but he must not stop, so they continued their breathless ascent, as if the hills had no end. Then the man gestured for him to halt. The boats had reached the bank, and soldiers bearing torches were leaping ashore. He and the man stood behind a rock, holding their breath, while the soldiers went to and fro along the river's sandy shoreline—it did not occur to them to make a foray into the hills where the dead lay in their tombs.

"We'll keep going, to a place where they'll never reach us."

After a laborious trek, they came at last to a cave hollowed out among the rocks, an unfinished tomb. The man proceeded into the darkness as if his feet knew the way by heart. Akhenaten stayed by the entrance, while the man squatted upon the ground and began to beat rocks against one another. He continued this operation until sparks flew, igniting a pile of straw. He quickly blew on this to fan the flames. Akhenaten came forward, entering with a sigh of relief. He had been about to freeze. He surveyed the contents of the cave: a bed of straw, stone implements, and clay pots. He seated himself before the fire. Thick smoke rose from it, and the man went on feeding the fire with kindling.

"Are you the guardian of the tombs," Akhenaten inquired, "or a fugitive like me?"

"I'm a dead man," came the reply. "Or, more to the point, I've come back from the dead."

In the firelight it was only just possible to make out his features. He was pale and desiccated as the surrounding rock. He picked up one of the clay pots and from it produced some ears of dried corn, which he placed upon the fire. The firewood began to crackle and give off sparks.

"I was just a slave," said the man, "a body without life or a soul. When my master died I was supposed to be buried with him, so that I could serve him in the hereafter, but he had been a cruel master. Unwillingly, I endured my servitude under him in this world, so why should I care about him for all eternity?"

"And did they bury you with him?" Akhenaten inquired.

"They placed his coffin in the tomb, put me in there with him over my protests, and then they blocked the opening with stones and mortar. There was a container full of food, and I was resigned to my fate, but the air was stifling, and I found dying slowly hard to bear. He had not treated me so as to deserve my dying for his sake, and I could not reconcile myself to the idea of a living death. I was caught in the jaws of death—I had to escape. And so I began searching frantically for a way out. To my good fortune, a collection of my master's weapons had been buried with him. He was a merchant, and a coward—never in his life had he taken up arms, and yet he collected them zealously. I selected from among them a sturdy sword and began removing the mortar that blocked the passageway—it was still fresh, and I was afraid the air inside the tomb might run out before I could find my way outside.

"I would have liked to tear away my master's shroud and make him face eternity bare-boned, but there was no time for that, so I went on clearing the mortar and rattling the stones. Whenever I got tired I sat down and cheered myself up by spitting on my master's coffin. Sand began to rain down on me, and each time I moved one rock another one confronted me. Then the moment came when I was trying to move a stone and it startled me by tumbling off into space. I was plunged into painful darkness, my body aching with weakness and fatigue. When I opened my eyes I could see a distant sky and glittering stars: I had won back my life. I cleared away the rest of the mortar and moved through the opening, exultant, gulping in the fresh air. It was fortunate that I had come out at night, for if they had seen me by day they'd have seized me and killed me. The only thing I could do was to stay here, amongst the dead, but at least I'm alive!"

The fire had warmed the whole place, and the corn was about to burn. They ate together. His stomach contracting, Akhenaten realized that he had not tasted food in quite some time.

"I need to travel north," he said at last.

"It's a long way," said the man, "and unsafe."

"If you were to accompany me, you'd become the richest man in Egypt. I want no more than a friend I can turn to throughout the journey."

The man lowered his head and thought for a moment. Then he said, "Never mind your promises of wealth. You're in no position to fulfill any such promises, but I do indeed need to get away from the danger that lurks in this place."

His name was Ka, meaning soul. He had given himself this name after liberating his soul from the death trap. He was well accustomed to hardship and the life of a fugitive, so he slept deeply, while Akhenaten remained tense and uneasy throughout the night. He could not believe all that had happened in the course of a single day. They hadn't the time to waste in this place, with each of them a hunted man—the hunters would come and search every hole in these hills. He did not sleep at all that night; he was still awake after the fire went out and the wolves howled with hunger. As soon as the darkness had receded a little, he woke Ka. They began their travels at dawn. They descended the hills on the other side of where they had come up, well away from where the hunters might expect to find him, and continued the journey far from the banks of the Nile.

They walked all that first day amid blank valleys, the Nile appearing in the distance like a silver ribbon, unmoving among the desolate mountains that enclosed it on all sides. On they went, quickly, hoping to be able to pass through this wasteland alive. The man did not ask him a great deal about himself or why they were after him, and Akhenaten kept silent. Even if he had spoken, it would have been impossible for Ka to believe that he was in the company of the Pharaoh of Egypt. Exhausted, they slept beneath the shade of an acacia that stood alone in the emptiness. They cooled themselves with river water. Hunger beset them cruelly, but the leaves of the acacia were bitter.

They took care all the while not to be spotted by anyone who might be watching from a boat out on the river. They found some Indian figs growing among the rocks, and Ka proved to be an expert in extracting their prickly sweetness. After two days of walking, the mountains began to draw back a little from the Nile, and green earth came into view. They could not believe their eyes, as they beheld the verdure that extended all the way to the river's edge. They saw some men standing in the shade of the palm trees, using their feet to knead mud mixed with silt, to produce the material necessary for manufacturing pottery and mud bricks.

Before the men stood a woman holding a small whip in her hand, as if she were their supervisor. Akhenaten and Ka felt as though they had escaped from the valley of death and come back to life. The woman turned toward them and studied them for a moment without fear or surprise. Signaling to the men to keep working, she approached the two of them and peered boldly into their faces.

"You are in the village of Naqada," she said. "Seldom does anyone come here through the wilderness. Are you runaways?"

It was nothing unusual—this remote village was well accustomed to desperate strangers turning up there. Ordinarily the residents would provide them with food, while not allowing them to stay, but nothing was done without the village matriarch's consent. The woman called to the men, warning them not to neglect their work in her absence. Then she led her two visitors into the village. The fields were packed with men working tirelessly, while women stood at the end of each field, some of them holding canes.

"What an odd place this village is," whispered Ka. "Here the women rule the men."

They passed through a stone gate into the village lanes, where there were houses carved into the rock. The villagers' faces seemed to reflect the irregular features of the mountains themselves. Neither in its composition nor in its architecture did this village resemble any of the mud-brick settlements scattered along the river's edge. As they proceeded, a group of curious women gathered around them, reaching out with their hands and touching them, palpating their skin, and sniffing at the odor they gave off. Then these women sullenly withdrew. Akhenaten glanced about in surprise. All of the village houses bore the features of Set, god of murk—perhaps it was for this reason that its inhabitants saw nothing wrong in receiving any fugitive or exile who came their way. Set was the killer of light, who cut the body of Osiris into pieces. He left the cultivated fields to the peasants and people of no consequence, appropriating for himself the desert and the wide-open spaces. This village, situated at the edge of the desert, was annexed to it, and so there were statues and reliefs of Set to be seen everywhere. The most important of them depicted a strange animal, incorporating a sort of donkey's body which nevertheless wore a crown and held a scepter.

The village matriarch was a woman well advanced in years, who lived in a space carved out of the belly of the mountain. She said to them, "This is a village of temporary refuge—we won't turn you over to any guards or soldiers or priests, for we hate them all, and we answer to no Pharaoh or god, other than Set, who has been generous with us, and who killed all the other gods. But you must not stay long—we do not wish to mix with other folk."

"We cannot proceed by way of the river," said Akhenaten.

"Everyone watches the river," said the old woman, "especially if there are fugitives at large. Your only choice is to move from village to village, until you vanish into the northern reaches."

"And how can we do that?"

"Why don't you purchase a couple of mules? Have you got the money for that?"

Akhenaten was silent. He looked questioningly at Ka.

"Well, then," said the woman, "you'll continue your journey on foot."

Ka got to his feet. He reached into his belt and drew out a little bundle of worn cloth. It contained a few small nuggets—they were dirty, but their yellow color announced of what metal they were made. He offered them to the woman. "Will this suffice?" he asked.

The woman's eyes flashed. "But they are stained with dried blood!" she said.

"Be that as it may," Ka replied, "they are gold. Meat of the gods."

The following day, as they were loading food supplies onto two donkeys and preparing to resume their journey, Akhenaten asked about the bloodstained gold pieces. "They are my master's teeth," replied Ka indifferently. "I extracted them from his mouth—he had no need of them anyway."

The days of traveling continued, night blending into day, the unending cycle of existence: each evening the sun boats departed from the sky and left it empty for the glittering stars who were the daughters of Tuut. At this time the cold winds set in motion by the wings of the falcon Horus blew upon them.

The farther they got from Thebes, the safer Akhenaten felt. They made stops in small villages. Sometimes they plucked unripe fruit from the fields; sometimes farmers took pity on them and provided a loaf of wheat or barley bread. This was the meal they always expected, for bread is the food of farmers, Pharaohs, and gods alike. Akhenaten recalled how, when he became Pharaoh, among the most important acts in the ceremony of his enthronement had been the distribution of bread to everyone, followed by a visit to the temple to divide a loaf of bread with the goddess Hathor, for a bridge between the world of men and that of the gods was formed when the two entities shared morsels of the same loaf. But now their moments of satiety were rare. Especially as the mountain drew in from the edge of the river and the wastelands closed around them, hunger was constant.

The mountains of Ament, rocky formations evocative of sorrow, came into view. Their foothills had borne witness to the clash of the gods; behind these rocks the sun first hid its face, and then there was no more light until Osiris was sent forth. Boats ceaselessly plied the river, transporting guards and angry priests who watched the riverbanks with their searching eyes. Akhenaten and Ka stayed hidden for days before resuming their journey. Now small islands appeared in the middle of the river, each of them a submerged part of Osiris's body, around which silt and water moss had collected—in this way had the perennially fertile islands been formed. Around them circled the crocodiles that devour sinful hearts, and hippopotamuses, with their huge, yawning maws.

Where the watchful mountain receded a bit, papyrus plants grew at higher elevations, a sign of life in the face of waste and desolation. The land was swathed in green, and the lowing of the sacred cows could be heard—a gift of the gods. The body of the goddess Hathor had been transformed into a cow, and the gods had sent cows down from the heavens, distributing them generously to the farmers who toiled throughout the valley.

The two travelers did not always depend on donations of food—rather they would recompense the farmers by setting to work with them—digging small canals, building dams, and clearing the irrigation ditches of plant matter that sucked away the water. In the moments before sunset Akhenaten would observe the herons as, invariably, they turned northward toward the mouth of the river, like unsettled spirits seeking a place of permanent rest.

When they had collected enough food, they would move on. They passed heaps of mud brick, limestone quarries, and pottery workshops. They would not sleep anywhere but beneath the shade of a sycamore: the tree of life, which gave shelter to all fugitives and kept beasts of prey at a distance. No dreams came, but there were unremitting nightmares. Akhenaten learned not to fear the wolves, but to be at ease with their voices in the dark of night. The long journey had left them scruffy and dirty, obscuring their features to the point where no one troubled to look at their faces anymore. Gypsies seized the mules, and outlaws robbed them of whatever food they had. For long days they were tormented by hunger, but they managed to reach Dendera, where the god Ptah formed the first pottery clay. At one of the mud-brick dumps they found a place to work in exchange for enough food to stay alive, and shelter to keep them from the cold. Akhenaten was happy at this trade, for this mud was composed of all the constituents necessary for the formation of life, and could be transformed so as to take on the shapes of all creatures. He learned to mold the rough clay before firing it, and to paint it after it had been baked. The artisans were confined to the colors applied by the ancient god—green, like the verdant fields, background for a picture of the snake Uto, who suckled Horus in his infancy; and red—like the color of the Nile when it surged in readiness for the flood. Akhenaten realized, as he mingled with all the people amongst whom they passed—farmers, shepherds, builders, carpenters, and even Gypsies and bandits—that he was, like them, made of clay, and not from the light of Osiris, as he had once been wrongly taught. Time lost its rhythm for him, as the trades in which he engaged blended into one another—he thought he might walk the road forever. He was changing, his hands growing both rougher and more dexterous. His fingers grew broader, clever at grasping implements, like all craftsmen. Now he recognized the value of the hand depicted by artists upon the temples, and why the sun's rays were represented as the fingers of a human hand. His protruding belly had withdrawn into itself and grown firmer; his legs were straighter. He had become proficient at working in various handicrafts, and at negotiating the balance between days of hunger and days of satiety, as well as sleeping in the open, or else in the shadow of a boulder.

When they reached the city of Abydos, Akhenaten knew he was near the end of his travels. He entered the city's enormous temple, presided over by statues of the jackal-headed god, guardian of the dead. Jackals had cavorted around him throughout the journey; now a young priest assured him that the actual head of Osiris was buried in this place, that a jackal served as its protector from the gods of wickedness, and that people by the hundreds made pilgrimages here on every special occasion. Akhenaten approached the spot the priest had pointed out to him, and seated himself before it, trembling.

"I do not hate you," he whispered. "I am not powerful enough for that. You are not the evil god, Amun—you have suffered greatly and paid a high price for your godliness, with all the parts of your body scattered far and wide throughout Egypt. What sort of country demands the dismemberment of its gods before it can calm itself?"

On they went, and suddenly the forest of silver leaves emerged from the shadows and stood before them, as well as the vast lake, still as a solitary heart. Akhenaten could smell Akhetaten before he saw it: the lime and mortar that had lingered in his nostrils before . . . he didn't know how many days ago. He was confident that if he walked the streets of the city now, no one would recognize him, with his tanned skin, the heavy beard obscuring his features, and the lamentable state of his clothing. He would have to reassemble the fragments of himself.

The stone wall of the city appeared in the distance, surmounted by torches whose flames flickered in the night breeze. Akhenaten signaled to his companion to halt, feeling that he dared not enter the city now. He must recover his breath, which seemed spent, after such a long time on the run.

"The city has surely locked its gates," he said. "Let us spend the night beneath its walls."

Ka, who did not see the use of waiting, said, "I don't believe you are fleeing this city as well!"

Akhenaten leaned against a tree and calm began to settle over him. He studied his roughened hands and his broad feet with their fissured skin. He felt he no longer needed any god. He had been right when he believed in the sun that engulfed him as it did everyone else, but he would not allow anything to enslave him.

"Throughout this journey," said Akhenaten, "you have not asked me who I am. Neither did I tell you, for I knew you would not believe me. I am the Pharaoh of this city, Pharaoh of this whole country!"

Ka stared at him, astonished. He didn't know whether Akhenaten spoke in earnest or whether he was teasing him. "I knew," he said, "that you were a person of some rank, for I did not see the brand of slavery upon you, or the ruggedness of a farmer. But now you go too far—the Pharaoh is a god, not a helpless human, a fugitive!"

"Perhaps you are right about that, but it will not be much longer before you know that I speak the truth."

"If you are truly Pharaoh, then let us approach the gates of the city, so that you can call to the guards to open them for us."

"I'll not enter my city in such a state. All I ask of you is that you follow me for what is left of this journey. It is the last gamble you will risk: to remain a slave fleeing death, or to become the faithful subject of a Pharaoh."

Ka looked at him, his eyes flashing. There was no gamble, for he had nothing to lose. They would go forward, together to the end.

They walked on, toward the city walls. Akhenaten trembled with longing, imagining himself pressing his lips at last to Nefertiti's long neck, clasping his daughters in his embrace and burying his face in their hair. He would be the first person to enter the city, with the earliest light of day, amid vendors, farmers, construction workers, and servants. He would go at once, before anyone saw him, to her wing of the palace, and take her and the girls in his arms, concluding this episode of his life without rancor or vengefulness.

Suddenly, they stood still, hearing the sound of heavy breathing penetrate the quiet of the night. They turned about, each grasping his staff—having lived together through such moments as this many a time, they had learned well to stand back-to-back and resist whatever came. A little spot of light glowed, a twinkling of false stars; a rancid smell arose and there was a faint roaring sound, but the wolves did not appear. Still, the travelers had entered the wolves' domain, and they must leave it at once. They began to walk away, but saw a tiny creature huddled beneath a tree—the diminutive ghost of a strange animal. It moved, rose, and stood upon its feet: another illusion from the mirage of the forest. A sound came from it, not a bestial howl, but something between a whimper and an entreaty, weak and feeble, containing nothing of that animal tension. They exchanged glances, mystified. It was a small child, naked, frail and emaciated, with a dirty face from which none of its features could be discerned but two gleaming eyes. He stood holding out his arms pleadingly, still making that odd cry. What had brought him to this place? And why hadn't the wolves devoured him? Was he a wolf under enchantment?

Before they could resolve to be on their way, the light of the moon revealed the shapes of the wolves surrounding them in a great circle, mouths gaping and tongues lolling. They stayed where they were, standing back-to-back, fearful that any movement on their part might rouse the creatures, but the wolves, in any case, closed in on them slowly, until they could see their wide eyes and their sharp teeth. Akhenaten and Ka brandished their sticks, and as the beasts howled and charged, Akhenaten wielded his stick and struck one of them on the head—he had grown skilled at aiming blows, at maneuvers, at defending himself. The wolves, however, did not retreat, but took up the attack once more. He felt one of them sink its claws into his leg, and he struck at it without mercy. Then he heard Ka's voice saying faintly, "My staff's broken."

"Look for a tree branch, quickly!" he shouted, as the circle of wolves closed in. He realized that his back was now unprotected—Ka had fallen to the ground, and at once two wolves had pounced upon him. He cried out, trying to fend off their teeth, as Akhenaten turned and began striking his two assailants. But all the wolves set upon the fallen man, raking him with their claws and teeth. They held fast, unwilling to relinquish their prey without a fight. Akhenaten, however, was striking out at them in a frenzy of blows, and so they redirected some of their ferocity toward him, swift and agile in their assault. He was no longer that pampered Pharaoh, who withdrew and fled—he did not withdraw—it was the wolves who withdrew. They left the prostrate form, turned tail, and fled. It was his first victory, but it came very dear, for here was the body of Ka, flung down upon the ground and covered in blood. Akhenaten placed his hand upon him—he was shuddering and gasping for breath, and Akhenaten did not know what to do. He drew aside the rags that covered Ka's chest; there were wounds and teeth marks all over him. "You'll be all right, my friend," he said gently, "and we'll go to my city."

Ka smiled through his pallor, but still his body shuddered in unbearable pain. He closed his eyes. Akhenaten waited for him to open them again, but this he did not do; he shook his friend cautiously, but there was no response. Death had pursued him all the way from Thebes, and in this spot it had overtaken him at last.

Akhenaten heard a whimper beside him: the little creature was staring at him. He gazed back at him until he was certain that it really was a human child. Then he brushed away the dirt that obscured his features, and his fingers encountered a bit of spittle smeared around his mouth. It was still sticky—could the child have been nursing? Could it be that the wolves had been suckling him? How long had he been here, and how old was he now?

He looked at the still form that lay upon the ground. Had he surrendered his spirit? And had Atun sent another in its place?

Akhenaten stood up and began gathering fallen leaves, which he spread over Ka's body, laid out lifeless at his feet, until it was completely covered. Then he sat beside Ka for a while. The creature sat down, too, and silence fell over everything. Moments from that strange journey passed before Akhenaten's eyes—the fear, the hunger, the constant wariness. How was it possible that they had slept side by side, and eaten from the same bowl—the slave returned from the dead and the heretic Pharaoh?

The horizon grew pale, and the torches atop the city walls were extinguished. He stood up, and with a final farewell glance he took the hand of the strange little being, who murmured contentedly, closing his little fingers around the Pharaoh's hand. Akhenaten soon discovered that the child could not walk normally, so he picked him up and carried him toward Akhetaten's walls.

They entered the city with the first light of dawn, amid a group of construction workers, street cleaners, and farm women from the villages, who were carrying vegetables, eggs, and fowl. There was nothing in the Pharaoh's appearance, nor in that of the skinny, naked child, to arouse suspicion. Akhenaten carried the child through the nearly empty city streets, through stillness without color or life, in the hours before the sun intensified. Why was the city waking up so late? There were many black-clad women sitting beside the wall, as if in a state of perpetual waiting. Some old women leaned feebly upon canes; few guards kept watch over the walls, and still fewer were stationed before the Pharaoh's palace. Everything was mournful. The little boy rested upon his shoulder, overcome by sleep; it seemed he was mute, incapable of any human speech. The Pharaoh attempted to climb the marble stairs, but he was stopped by a guard, who looked him over with obvious disgust. He would allow no beggars near the palace. In an effort to get the guard to recognize him, he made him scrutinize his face, but he was odd-looking and he smelled bad, and the guard pointed a spear at his chest and told him to be off. So he withdrew, and seated himself beside the old women and beggars, who were waiting for charity from the luminaries who entered the Pharaoh's palace. The sun rose higher. The child awoke hungry and looked at him beseechingly, then stuck his fingers in his mouth. Akhenaten looked back at him—what could he do?

A group of servants emerged from the palace carrying a large tray laden with loaves of bread. The beggars and old women surged forward, as the servants tried to establish order amid the jostling crowd, so that each person would receive his share. But the mendicants knew that the number of loaves was always smaller than that of the hungry. Akhenaten spied the minister by the name of Ai, standing at some distance and watching as the bread was distributed. He remembered putting Ai in charge of this task. His chance had come at last. Taking hold of the child, the Pharaoh rose to his full height, thrust out his chest, and advanced confidently toward the minister, ignoring the spears of the guards, which were pointed at him. Alarmed, Ai stared at him. Then he peered into his face, stunned, his mouth open in astonishment as he heard the Pharaoh say imperiously, "Make way for me to enter my palace, Ai."

◆ ◆ ◆

Nefertiti wept as she had never wept before, and the girls clung to his neck, but when they saw the little boy they drew back, and stood ill at ease, watching him warily. Even after he had been cleaned up and his body clothed in a garment of linen, he resembled more than anything a wild animal. He ate voraciously, stared at them with hostility, and seemed prepared to bolt whenever anyone tried to approach him.

"Who is he?" said Nefertiti.

"A gift from Atun," Akhenaten replied. "We have not been blessed with a boy child, and so he has sent us this gift."

"But he is a wild animal, no tame creature," she said. "He does not even know how to speak. I'm frightened to have him among us."

"He shall learn and become human," said her husband. "He is Tut . . . Tutankhatun . . . because it was Atun who sent him to us."

The boy's features, once revealed, were fine. He was very thin, his skin stretched taut across his ribs. The most alarming thing about him was his sharp teeth and long nails, as well as his preference for uncooked food. It fell to Nefertiti to care for him, to designate a servant to feed him, and to appoint a tutor to teach him how to speak.

Akhenaten looked into her small, delicate face, her wide, anxious eyes. "What happened to you on your journey?" she asked.

He countered with a question of his own: "What happened to my city? Why does it seem so grief-stricken, so despairing?"

"It is the war. Horemheb has gone to war!"

"What's this? I did not authorize it! How did this happen?"

Feeling himself betrayed, he gave a cry of wrath. This, then, was why the city seemed fearful and tense, so full of women and old crones, the walls defended by so few guards. Ai came, trembling, and with him the chief guards, the high-ranking officers, and the men who saw to the preparation of matériel, horses, and weapons; Horemheb had assembled all he could command, and headed north. "How," Akhenaten shouted at the assembled men, "could you follow his orders? How could you yield to him?"

"We were unable to stop him," said Ai. "Emissaries came from the north to inform us that the Hittite tribes were approaching from their own borders. They had crossed the land of Canaan, and . . ."

"Then you were a party to these war games!" the Pharaoh interrupted, still more enraged. "What possessed you to believe those emissaries with their false messages? From the beginning Horemheb has been driving us toward a needless war. What made you so sure we were in danger?"

"My lord, he is our military commander, and he knows what needs to be done . . ."

"And I am your Pharaoh, and I too know what needs to be done. Begone, all of you—leave me."

To a man, they were trembling; they had never imagined that he would grow so angry. Horemheb had taken all the men, matériel, and weapons that he could, had readied an army very quickly and without anyone's blessing, and had left Akhetaten defenseless against the priests from the south, who might attack at any moment. Akhenaten had thought he could take the initiative and go after them, but now he feared that it might be they who would come to him and attack him right there in his own city. He must now gather more guards and soldiers. He no longer wished for revenge—he wished only to salvage his dream, newly threatened with annihilation.

That night the household was heavily perfumed with incense. Feeling the pressure mounting in his chest, all at once he craved the outside air, redolent with the smells of crops, of manure, of mud and of herbs that grew wild.

"My lord," cried Nefertiti, "be gentle with me, or my ribs will break!"

Her body, too, was fragrant with scent, soft and pale and fragile. He was not making love to her so much as he was pouring into her all the rage, frustration, and hunger that seethed within him. He got out of bed and looked out over the city walls. There were more guards now, and hundreds of torches glowed. It was his wish that the city be kept lit all night long, that the constant illumination might give him a sense of security. Nefertiti rose and stood behind him. Sensing her naked body, he clung to it, seeking its warmth.

"You are shivering, my lord," she said.

"I feel as if I had not yet returned home," he replied. "That I am still lost in the wilderness."

"Was it an arduous journey?"

"It was terrifying. I saw people of whom we know nothing. We rule over them, and compel them to worship us, to speak of us with reverence, without troubling to look at their faces. We belittle their struggles, the brief lives they live in the service of ridiculous things—those farmers who are so proficient at planting and reaping; the builders so skilled in measuring length and height; the quarrymen; the dye makers; the workmen; the painters, sculptors, and engravers . . . all the knowledge they have acquired has availed them nothing. For long years we have drained away their lives and demeaned them, for the sake of building our monstrous pyramids, while we leave behind us nothing useful! What is the point of burying in a pyramid a foolish king like me? During my travels I saw those mountainous installations, the huge temples, the obelisks, the monuments to kings and gods. Wasted lives, squandered efforts! Why do we do this to them? Why do we not leave them be, to plant and reap as they are accustomed to do, why are we not content with our portion of the yield and revenues? All those stones they cut from the mountains, leveling them—why did we not allow them the chance to build dams with the stones, to supply them with water and protect them from drowning in the floods? Or even to make them into walls for their mud-brick houses, which are always falling down? Why after all this do we beat them with whips and drive them into war?"

Taking pity on him, Nefertiti said, "They are slaves. They have no souls."

"But what became clear to me during the flight from my enemies is that they do have souls, and names by which they are called, and destinies. Destinies," he added bitterly, "of which we take no notice!"

"But at least," she said, trying to ease his mind, "you've done none of this. You've built no pyramids or temples. And you haven't sent anyone to war—that was done without your knowledge!"

"My father did such things," he said, "and my grandfather before him. I feel as though I were carrying the weight of them all."

It took many days for the Pharaoh to reunite properly with his city once more. He brought in members of the peasantry in greater numbers, and appointed them as guards. Then, when news was brought to him that Queen Tiye had died on the very night of his attendance upon her, that her palace had not been stormed, and that she had been buried in the family vault beside her husband, his ire was soothed, and he decided to leave Thebes to its fate—he would not go to war with it—and yet he feared that Thebes would come to him, and so he summoned the sons of all the distinguished houses and set them to guard the walls on a twenty-four-hour watch.

It was long months before Horemheb returned to stand before him. He wore his military garb, his broad chest encased in a shield of bronze, bearing traces of the blood of battle and dust from the road. The sun had colored his skin and his features had grown harsher. According to the Pharaoh's source, he had left all his forces outside the gates and entered the city on foot, without his war chariot. He stood before his Pharaoh, out of breath.

"News of your defeat has reached me," said Akhenaten.

Horemheb hung his head. Akhenaten detested war, and yet to be vanquished in war was always cruel, and even if fully expected it was not to be endured: his only option at such a moment was to order the execution of the commander who had disobeyed his orders from the outset, only to meet with defeat in the end.

Horemheb, though, was unsettled, the taste of desert salt still in his mouth, the residue of overheated blood still running in his veins. "Everyone has forsaken me," he said. "You promised me support and assistance, and then you left me and disappeared. I needed you, needed your authority, so that I might assemble an army fit for fighting, so that the intransigent provincial leaders and tight-fisted tax collectors would obey me. The outcome was that I went out only half-prepared, more like an adventurer than a military commander."

"No one asked you to embark on such an adventure."

"It was not for my own glory. I went to save the northern borders. The enemy was about to invade by way of the Valley of Turquoise. Had I not gone, they would have come all the way here."

"Had you not gone, the war would have subsided. This way it will never end. Any time we assemble our forces we are bound to attack our enemies, and any time they regather their own strength they are bound to attack us. The conflict continues endlessly, pointlessly. There is no absolute victory, no decisive defeat. We could have looked for another way—not this."

"I am a military leader, and my job is fighting, not conciliating enemies."

"You are a military leader no longer. Leave your weapons and insignia. Henceforth you are no longer commander of Egypt's armies."

Horemheb stood stock-still, in stunned disbelief that the Pharaoh could dismiss him in this manner. He should have ordered his execution, or consigned him to a distant prison whose whereabouts no one knew—any other decision was foolhardy or mad. No one could guarantee the conduct of an old warrior or keep weapons long out of his hands, and a leader such as Horemheb must be either at the head of his soldiers or in the grave. But the Pharaoh was incapable of killing him, for not only had he been his friend and savior at his times of greatest need, but he had been Egypt's war leader since the time of Akhenaten's father, beside whom he had waged every war, and defeated all the primitive tribes that had opposed Egypt.

"It is best that you kill me, my lord," Horemheb said calmly.

Akhenaten preferred not to understand the meaning of his words. "I am aware," he said, "that no Pharaoh besides me has ever done otherwise. But I could not, in my position, put to death an old friend."

Still, Horemheb stood before him, as if inviting him to change his mind, but Akhenaten turned his back, so as not to confront his wrathful glare.

The Pharaoh's men could scarcely believe their eyes when they saw Horemheb walk out of the palace alive. They stared as he passed through the city streets and made his way to his own palace. But they all knew that he would not spend the night in the city—not for one more day would he remain here.

That evening Nefertiti said sadly to her husband, "You've made us a new enemy. You should have put him to death."

"What a gracious executioner you are," he said, with an attempt at a smile. "I wanted only to prevent Horemheb from killing, not to become a killer myself."

He was dreaming, as was his wont, thought Nefertiti, closing her eyes in sorrow. And when the alarm was raised, it was Ai, the minister, who brought the news to the Pharaoh as soon as he could. One of the guards on night duty had seen Horemheb leaving, with his treasures, his weapons, and his women, and no one had dared to prevent him—there had been no standing orders to stop him in any case. It was said that he was on his way to Thebes, that depraved city.

Akhenaten received the news grim-faced. It was he who had laid open the way for Horemheb to flee; he had not wanted a confrontation with him in this very place, within the precincts of the city itself. Ai, however, could not conceal his astonishment, or resist counseling the Pharaoh. "What remains of our army is still outside the city—we could pursue him, my lord, and cut off his access to the south."

"There is no army," replied Akhenaten quietly, "that would hunt down its own leader. More likely they would join forces with him. Take these soldiers, feed them, clothe them, and treat their wounds. Then dismiss half of them and set the rest to guard our city walls."

Baffled, Ai withdrew. The Pharaoh was resolved to squander his own forces on every front and thus advance the strength of his adversaries. Nevertheless, Ai carried out his orders, and calm descended upon the city. Half the soldiers left, pleased with their lot. Those who remained behind grumbled, but they knew that their wages would be doubled, and that houses would be assigned to them to live in, as well as brides—all these amenities within the city, rather than in some narrow trench outside of it. It fell also to Ai to carry out still more bizarre orders: to prohibit, henceforth, the construction of any sort of temple, obelisk, or pyramid. Moreover, he was to assemble the artists and command them not to portray kings or gods on the city walls, but rather to depict farmers sowing seed, driving cattle, and gathering in the stalks of wheat each season; to represent blacksmiths, fishermen, and builders; to engrave pictures of singers, dancers, drummers, and all manner of entertainers—bringers of joy and delight. Above all they were to eschew the use of gold—the color of supernatural phenomena and miracles—as well as black—the color of grief and mourning; instead they were to take their colors from the verdure of the grasses, the blue of the sky, and the redness of the river when it brimmed with life and fertility.

Truly the strangest order of all, though, still awaited Ai, when he made his way to the palace on a certain morning and found the main hall filled with the city's luminaries—all those who had embraced the Pharaoh's new creed and followed him to this place. Nefertiti was seated beside Akhenaten on the throne—a thing that happened only on the most momentous occasions.

"I wish," the Pharaoh announced, "to put an end to war between us and the Hittite tribes to the north."

The crowd cheered wildly—they had been expecting this—that the harvest season should complete its course, after which the young farmers would be summoned, the revenues collected, the foundry furnaces ignited, and a vast army assembled, the likes of which Egypt had never seen, able to launch a ferocious and decisive battle against the barbarian tribes. The Pharaoh, however, was quiet for a long time, until the uproar subsided and all the mingled voices fell silent.

"I had nothing so complicated in mind," he said. "If it were war that I wanted, I should have retained Horemheb—he is the most qualified, despite his recent defeat. What I was thinking of was to dispatch a delegation of high-ranking Egyptians to negotiate a truce between us and them."

The babble in the hall turned to muted but angry protest, the faces of the people registering disappointment. "My lord," said Ai, "divine Pharaoh, it has never been our custom to send a conciliatory delegation. These are primitive tribes, and they recognize no contract or treaty. The great Pharaoh, your father, first subdued them, until they capitulated—if we ask them to make peace, they will think us weak—indeed they already do. It is impossible that we should ask them to make peace when we have just been defeated—it would be the surrender of the vanquished!"

"I do not want war," insisted the Pharaoh. "I dismissed Horemheb because he would talk of nothing else. We shall form a high-ranking delegation composed of noble Egyptians. They will go to the barbarian lands and speak in earnest of our desire for peace. We must make them understand that we are entirely sincere—we shall tell them about our new god, and once they become believers we will all be followers of one god, and from that day forward we shall not wage war."

It was difficult to argue with him when he was so intent upon his convictions, so certain he was right. His advisors were all older than he was, and they knew the true character of these tribes, their long and bloody history. Nevertheless, the nobles came together in spite of themselves, and let the Pharaoh choose from among them who should be members of the delegation. He selected ten of them, and then one who could read and write fluent Hittite. He wished to have a treaty drawn up in two languages, which should not merely be written upon papyrus sheets, but also engraved upon tablets of solid granite.

The whole city turned out to bid farewell to the delegation of nobles as they boarded boats in which the river would carry them northward. Thereafter they would travel by horse and carriage, crossing the desert to the Valley of Turquoise, and from there to Canaan (thence to where the Hittites dwelt). They were laden with gifts of gold, bearing the symbols of the sun with outstretched hands, as well as palm fronds and ears of grain, as an expression of the desire for peace. The Pharaoh saw them off, smiling radiantly; they gave back strained smiles of their own.

Was it possible that his taking this step might bring a period of peace and tranquility? That he might savor his life, far from violence and menace? He had long striven to transform this little city into a peaceful paradise, hidden away from the world's hellfire. Such were Akhenaten's thoughts as he sat quietly on the balcony overlooking the palace garden. From a distance came the sound of pure laughter such as had not been heard within the palace walls for a long time. It issued from a place where no outsider found admittance: the garden in which the palace residents took their rest and repose. He got up and moved toward the source of the laughter, then stood contemplating the scene before him: a fountain from which water bubbled and rose high, and his five daughters running about with no clothes on, nothing concealing their slight bodies. Among them the wild child ran naked as well. His complexion was somewhat darker than theirs, his body more muscular, maturing. The girls' chests, with their small breasts, rose and fell, and the boy ran after them, with the beginnings of an erection. They converged, collapsed in a heap, and lay upon the grass. Droplets of water spangled the girls' skin, refracting the colors of the sun's rays. It was an atmosphere full of the pulse of sensual awareness, with shouting, merriment, and laughter, with teasing and touching. The youth had lost some part of his feral nature, allowing the girls to roll on top of him, and permitting his own hand to touch them lightly. Akhenaten felt no resentment or indignation, either toward the hand that brushed their breasts in passing or of their little rumps colliding with the boy's body. The air was full, more with the irrepressible life that coursed through these little limbs than with anything sordid, and the spray of water washed away any base desires. He ought to go to them and put a stop to their play, but he didn't dare: in such an atmosphere of openness, there upon the fresh grass and beneath this blazing sun, there was no trespass—that was possible only in secret rooms and in the chambers of temples and the Holy of Holies.

Then he heard Nefertiti's voice behind him. "They are growing quickly, and he is growing up in their midst. You must do something."

The following day he took the boy hunting with him. They rode together in one war chariot, and he let the child take the horses' reins. He taught him how to steer, how to drive the horses gently and firmly. He noticed that the boy's voice had begun to deepen, a sign of his approaching maturity. They went slowly around the perimeter of the far-reaching lake, and plunged into the forest where the wolves had suckled him at their teats. Akhenaten watched the boy, expecting memories of the wild forest to awaken in him and rouse his yearning for it. But he went on driving the chariot as if he were now of another world. Akhenaten tried to teach him to throw a spear and shoot arrows, but he himself was not a skilled hunter to begin with.

He waited a little, until the time came to rest at the edge of the shimmering lake. Then he said, "From now on you must not see the girls except when they are clothed, nor let them see you naked. Then you won't lust after them, nor they after you."

The boy nodded his head obediently; in general he did not speak much. "Just one of them," Akhenaten continued, "is destined for you. It is she who will reveal her body to you and make you king of Egypt, so do not betray her, or show your own body to any other."

The Pharaoh rose and went to the chariot, the boy following him, speechless. From the time he had entered the palace and understood his inferior position, he had never imagined that he should be a king. Akhenaten himself had not thought to mix his royal blood with a child fostered by wolves, but what alternative did he have? At last he said to him as the city walls came into view, "Tomorrow we shall perform your ritual circumcision."

This was the beginning—circumcision distinguished Egyptians from all the primitive tribes. This, then, was the beginning, the boy's inauguration into the realm of maturity and legitimacy—a rite of purification through which he must pass in order to become a Pharaoh—it was essential that his manhood be apparent to all, with nothing obscuring it. Akhenaten had happened upon the heir he sought, and his daughters would not now be vulnerable to opportunists and adventurers. The city was decorated with palm fronds and branches of holm oak, while torches blazed atop the walls and in the center of every square. Drumbeats sounded and the air was heavy with incense, as the priests advanced, their heads shaven as was required of all who practiced medicinal arts of this kind. They bore their instruments, keen-edged, polished and gleaming, wrapped in linen cloths, as well as a box of pharmacopoeia, containing narcotic herbal compounds to alleviate pain.

The boy, however, appeared frightened and pale, and too small to be fit to take the throne. Tut came forward, having been bathed and perfumed, and dressed in pure white garments. Once the foreskin was cut and drops of blood had been spattered upon the cloth, the garment would be preserved as evidence of young Tut's having achieved manhood, proof that he could now stand proud before the gods, who decreed that all of their followers, Pharaohs and priests, must be circumcised. The hall was crowded with members of the city's nobility, while the Pharaoh, upon his throne, presided. They seated Tut on a little bench and placed between his feet a basin made of gold. He was terrified, his knees knocking, but the priests gripped his hands and forced his knees apart. At the sound of his shrill cries the drumbeats started up again, and the nobles approached the Pharaoh, bowing before him and offering their congratulations. No one paid any attention to the boy, who had lost consciousness and whose wound the priests were busy bandaging. They all knew it was enough that Tut should marry one of the Pharaoh's daughters for him to ascend the throne—but was this wild child truly fit for the throne of the gods?

The drums beat on, and the dancers swayed. Nefertiti watched it all with sadness in her eyes. She wished that the king to be were a child of her womb rather than a mere vagrant raised by wolves, but Akhenaten was besotted, drinking wine that had been brought specially for him from the city of Buto at Tel al-Faraina and made after the fashion of the goddess Hathor, when she pressed the grapes with her bare feet so as to stoke the warmth in her lovers' souls . . . but now, suddenly, all grew quiet. The drums fell silent and the dancers stood still. The slave girls shrank back and the nobles rose from their seats in alarm. A queer-looking man stood in the middle of the hall, dust-covered and unkempt, dressed in torn clothing, wounds all over his body: a pitiable wretch. No one knew how he could have got into the palace. Akhenaten rose to his feet—it seemed to him that he knew this face.

The man spoke loudly enough for all to hear. "The noble delegation," he said, "has returned, my lord."

Without waiting for an answer, he turned and staggered, exhausted, out of the palace. Akhenaten dared not raise his voice or issue an order. Already on his feet, he started after the man; Nefertiti rose and followed, trying to catch up with him. Without a sound, everyone went, no one daring even to breathe. Darkness had descended utterly; the torches flickered, casting their light upon a wagon standing in the palace courtyard: a crude thing made of untrimmed tree branches bound together with plant fibers and drawn by a single broken-down horse. An intolerably putrid stench issued from the wagon. Nefertiti shrank from it, as did the other women and the slave girls, nearly asphyxiated by the smell. Akhenaten, however, kept going. And he saw his noble delegation—or, rather, what was left of it. It had been transformed into an undifferentiated heap at the bottom of the wagon, covered by bloodstained cloaks. The strange man stepped forward and drew back the coverings from the heap: severed heads with staring eyes starting from their sockets; severed arms with fingers contorted in supplication—a futile attempt at self-defense; dismembered legs; bellies slashed and eviscerated—the delegation had been transformed altogether into fragments of amputated limbs, flayed skin, broken bones, and the smell of rot. The Pharaoh stood appalled. He had offered up ten of the most eminent of Egypt's noblemen—those who always wore white cloaks embroidered with gold thread, who perfumed themselves with sandalwood and ambergris, who gave good counsel and were skilled at reciting poetry and recounting ancestral tales, at telling jokes, and at describing the indiscretions of the ancient gods—had offered them up as easy prey to the northern tribes.

Crows came to life and spread suddenly across the city skies, croaking raucously, announcing their hunger. The ragged man pointed at them and said, "They never stopped pursuing us. They've followed me from the land of Canaan—now occupied by the Hittites—all the way here."

The cawing of the crows roused Akhenaten. This must be a nightmare—what else could it be? But the scene before him was real, in all its horror and sorrow. Some of the women gasped and then began to weep: solitary wives made widows, mourning the last remains of their husbands. Panicked, Akhenaten turned and looked about—he wanted someone to explain to him what had happened, but all the men near him were ashen-faced and struggling for breath as if the battered corpses lay upon their chests. He turned to the man in the tattered clothing and said, "Who are you?"

"I am the last witness of their death, sir—the only one the Hittites left alive. I was of no account—the only thing I was good for was to bring back the bodies of the noblemen and give an accounting of their tragedy."

Akhenaten turned to Ai, his minister, and commanded, "Prepare these worthy men for burial, and arrange ceremonies for them befitting their station." Then he signaled to the man in rags. "Follow me, and tell me what happened."

Inside the palace, Tut lay upon the floor, bleeding and moaning. The servants fled before the ragged man, as if he were an emissary of the dead, and they hesitated long before they would reenter the hall and carry the bleeding boy away to tend to his wound.

He who had come back from the dead was the scribe who had accompanied the delegation, having gone with them because he could write and speak Hittite fluently. He had witnessed the slaughter, and endured the degradation that preceded it. When the Hittite kings, who had taken Canaan by storm and then assumed control of it, learned that an elite delegation had come from Egypt to make a truce with them, they listened, sneering, to the proposal. They were not pleased to know that a new god had been born from nothingness. They all believed in Set, the god of murk, and they were not about to change their ways. They bound the ten noblemen by their necks with ropes and paraded them through the dusty streets, between the leather tents and the houses of thatch, proclaiming their triumph. They beat the faces of the nobles with the soles of their shoes and branded their skins with the tokens of prisoners and slaves: such was their revenge upon Amenhotep's army, which had relentlessly humiliated them. Now victory had come to them easily and resoundingly. They assembled all the city's residents in the main square and lit a great bonfire, in which they burned all the gifts the delegation had brought. Then they began to revel in butchering the noblemen and severing their limbs. They ate their victims' livers and smeared their chests with their blood, dancing all the while to the beat of their war drums.

The man stopped speaking and waited for further questions, but the Pharaoh was silent, his face pale—the pile of severed limbs answered all questions, not merely heralding the abject collapse of his dream but also putting him on notice that he was perched upon a dangerous precipice. Worse still, Horemheb was aggrieved, and it was his own fault. Atun had forsaken him and failed to set him on the right road. And if he himself had begun to doubt Atun, then how were others to believe in him?

Symbols of mourning were hung throughout the city. The locked crypts were quickly opened and made ready. The embalmers confronted the problem of the dismembered bodies, and the reunification of each severed limb with its owner, lest a body enter the afterlife in an incomplete state. The Pharaoh did not sleep that night. Tut's fever was high, his little member swollen, and the girls surrounded him, mocking and teasing him. Akhenaten looked at his flushed face and felt that all was lost, that it was up to him to redeem his throne.

Ai came precisely on time. "We must go to war," Akhenaten said at once. "There is no help for it—you must assemble the army and resume their training. We shall make haste to recall Horemheb—he is the only one capable of engaging this battle."

Ai stared at him, but made no reply—he had not expected such a reaction. But the northern tribes had declared war, and the Pharaoh must face a war whether he believed in it or not. Hesitantly, the minister replied, "I am afraid this will not be possible, my lord. We do not have the necessary funds to ready such an army."

The Pharaoh looked at him in disbelief. Once, no one would have opposed him—nothing could have stood in the way of what he willed. He glared at his minister, who prevaricated, "The tax revenues were not good this year—the priests from the south withheld their share, and their sting is more potent now, since the renegade leader Horemheb joined forces with them."

Had he lost the war before it even began? Had he forfeited, in a single stroke, both the required moneys and the most capable of leaders?

"I shall open my grain-storage facilities," he said, "and I shall offer up all the gold in my possession."

"And from where shall the men come?" replied the minister. "In this regard, Horemheb is one step ahead of us—he is preparing to attack us."

Why had he known nothing of all this? Why had all these disasters been concealed from him? Was everyone, in fact, awaiting his downfall? "Why did you not inform me of all this in a timely fashion?" he demanded.

"We thought we would be able to overcome these difficulties without troubling you about them, but calamities have accumulated in a way that could not have been foreseen."

Akhenaten roamed the palace like a madman. He looked into Nefertiti's eyes and saw that they were sadder than before; he saw that the faces of his girls had grown pale with fear, and that the swelling persisted at the site of Tut's wound. He ascended to the upper floors of the palace, from which he turned about, now toward the north, now toward the south. Who would come for him first, the barbarians of the north or his erstwhile allies? Who would be the first to spill his blood?

"The boy," he said to his wife, "shall recover in a day or two. I wish to prepare him for marriage to Ankhesen."

"Why such haste?" whispered Nefertiti uneasily. "She is older than he, and he is still weak and ill."

"I want the new Pharaoh to be ready."

She did not understand what he meant, but he was not in a fit state for her to debate matters with him. She knew that their whole world might collapse at any moment. The girl herself, however, Ankhesen, lost no time in voicing her protest. "How can I marry that foundling, with his swollen thing? I want a husband who is actually a man!"

Nefertiti gazed at the girl. Her body was beginning to bud out, and she gave every evidence of having a sensuous nature such as no one could mistake. She showed a distinct preference for going without the benefit of clothing and had filled her room with mirrors. She followed the Pharaoh's guards with a misty-eyed gaze in which desire and apprehension mingled. But now she was expressing her wishes in no uncertain terms.

"Your father," said Nefertiti, "has chosen him to be the Pharaoh who shall sit at your side upon the throne."

Furious, the girl cried rudely, "Shall sit at my side upon the throne! But who will lie beside me in bed?"

"Such words, my young miss," her mother replied angrily, "are fit not for the queen of Egypt, but for the whores who walk the streets!"

Ankhesen stormed out, casting a contemptuous glance at Tut as she passed by his room. She took to watching the palace guards hungrily.

◆ ◆ ◆

"Why have you distanced yourself from me this way? And why have you caused my enemies to move in so close to me?"

More alone than he had ever been before, Akhenaten contemplated the sun disc as it sank slowly behind the horizon. Torches by the dozen would not serve, however brightly they blazed, to deliver his heart from the darkness that was creeping over it. The colors were draining away from the clouds, and the light upon the horizon was blinking out. Was it possible he could see the first of the torches carried by the invaders as they approached? He would stand long in expectation of them, and just when he tired of waiting they would come suddenly. How many Pharaohs had stood as he did, waiting for the blow to fall? He alone had lost his weapons and been forsaken by the gods.

The youth recovered, and the priests removed the bandages from his wound, but Ankhesen's anger was not appeased. The date of the wedding must be arranged, but it was not a propitious time for any kind of celebration. The Pharaoh himself paced the walls, fortifying the city. He drilled the soldiers and inspected the weapons. Everywhere he went, the chieftains and builders followed. He ordered that all points of entry be sealed and the thickness of the inadequate walls be doubled; everything was poised, everyone feeling the tension that gripped the city. But Akhenaten kept asking himself, "How long can we hold out?"

He felt the need to breathe freely in the open air—perhaps Atun would be pleased with him, take him up once more, and inspire in him some means of extricating himself from this mortal chaos. Nefertiti gazed fearfully at him on hearing what he had to say.

"You would venture out again? All these fortifications around the city, and yet you'd leave it and go out into the open? Will you not be risking your life?"

"It is what I need at this moment," replied the Pharaoh. "I shall go and return in secret." She could not oppose him—he had become an anguished spirit, unquiet the whole night through, wandering furtively about the city, subject to accidents and insults. Might the open country be good for him?

He sneaked out by way of one of the rear gates to the city, with no one the wiser but a few trustworthy guards, who smeared their faces with dust as they begged him to allow them to accompany him and keep watch over him through the night. Nevertheless, he went forth alone, as was his fate. He removed his shoes and his feet sank into the mud. Feeling the cold and the sharpness of the gravel, he proceeded by the routes that had not been cut off. He traversed the interlinked irrigation ditches and drainage canals, then removed his cloak and stood naked beneath the stars. He was conscious of the nighttime chill as it touched his skin, imparting to him the sense of peace he had been missing. How feeble he seemed! And how infinitely old the world appeared to him. He panted as he ascended the ancient hill. He would remain there, naked, until his pores opened and the first rays of the sun burst forth. It would be a long night, but he must endure it until the world began to awaken. As he started to shiver, he recited the prayers he had not uttered for a long time. He understood that his moment had come as his stomach roiled and he could not repress the moan that escaped his lips against his will, and he vomited some dark liquid. Exhausted, he sat upon the ground, held fast to the grass and pebbles. Nothing was secure here anymore; everything was too slack to get hold of, nothing could be relied upon. His face bathed in cold sweat, he curled up on the ground, spent. He knew he would not be able to rise again, would never more grasp the scepter, or sit upon the throne.

From a long way away, he heard a voice asking, "Are you all right, my lord?" The inflection was neutral, evincing neither malice nor sympathy, but it was that voice and none other, deep and gravelly, resounding in the silence of the empty air, with nothing that could give back an echo. The man advanced and stood before him, towering in his massive height, with his white cloak and the spear that was ever in his hand, gazing impassively down at him. There was the Pharaoh, naked, prostrate upon the earth, his body smeared with dew-moistened dust.

With an effort to compose himself, Akhenaten said, "As always, Horemheb, you have come just in time. How long have you been watching this place?"

"For days," Horemheb replied. "I was hoping I might meet you before I was forced to storm the city and invoke a bloodbath."

"Your army is ready, then?"

"Of course. We have had the city surrounded for some time. The guards on the walls see us every day, as do the farmers and the workmen who pass through the gates each day. Yet no one has said anything."

"It seems that everyone is collaborating in the downfall of my city, with no word spoken to me. What were you going to do with me? Storm the palace and kill me?"

Horemheb replied, in some distress, "I should not have dared to do that."

"But I left you no way around it. So that's the way it is . . ."

"The country is in a state of collapse, my lord. I must hasten northward to face the enemy there, and your city stands in my way. I've got to get through it first, whatever the price."

"And it is I who am the price . . . a negligible price for an honorable mission—is this not what you tell yourself every morning?"

Horemheb was silent for a little while, glancing about as if in an effort to restrain his agitation—and it was strange that emotion should be evident in a man who was never moved. At last he said, "I had hoped to find a solution."

The Pharaoh was gasping, as another wave of pain seized him. He clutched at the dust and the grass, trying not to shift his position. His face was drenched in cold sweat. Horemheb moved forward to offer him a helping hand, but Akhenaten gestured for him to stay where he was. Trying to speak strongly and clearly, he said, “And did you think you would find such a solution?”

Horemheb hesitated a moment, gazing into the silent blankness of the night, at the tranquil lake, the lifeless moon. Then he spoke. “Of course. We must cover this country’s exposed bones, give up this god that has corrupted everyone, and return, all of us, to Thebes.”

Akhenaten regarded him steadily and calmly, doing his best to conceal the pain within him. “What an exceedingly cruel solution,” he said. “You ought to have stormed my palace and killed me first.”

Suddenly, Horemheb went slack, casting aside his spear, and from his great height he fell to his knees before the Pharaoh, crying hoarsely, “My lord, I beg of you . . .”

“By Atun—such a show of weakness! How can you defeat the enemy if you fall down this way before a helpless and ailing Pharaoh? Do you not see what you are doing to yourself?”

“My lord . . . your whole body is perspiring and giving off a foul odor—are you ill?”

“I am dying.”

“What!”

“I have taken poison. I bought it from an apothecary in the city who did not recognize me. I told him that I was going to administer it to my wife’s lover and I . . .”

His words were cut off as a spasm of nausea assailed him, and he began to writhe upon the ground, rolling in the dust. He was as emaciated as if he were about to vanish. “My god,” thought Horemheb, “what a wretched and tormented soul I see before me.” He felt tears starting in his eyes. So much anguish, with eternity still seemingly so distant and unattainable. Was there any chance of rescuing him, or was he altogether too late? His face beneath the light of the moon was deathly pale. “My lord,” said Horemheb, “I can carry you, and . . .”

“Don’t. But hear what I say. Marry my daughter Ankhesen to that boy, Tut. Make him Pharaoh. And build me a secret tomb, so that those scoundrel priests of Amun cannot disinter my coffin.”

"I shall, my lord, I swear it."

Akhenaten's body convulsed once more, and his breath came rapidly. He clutched Horemheb's hand, as if fearful he would go away. Yet he was a king, dying there in the mud and dust, with nothing to soothe his pain and grief. Weakness pervaded his body, and his fingers grew slack, as he faded slowly from existence, sinking further into the dust. The sound of his breathing gradually ceased, and his body grew still, but his eyes remained open. Horemheb waited long before closing them with his own hand.

11 • Thebes

At Last

AISHA STOOD IN THE SHADOW OF THE STONE GATES. She had walked a long time among the barley fields, hearing the stalks of grain whispering to her beneath the wind, as if warning her. She paid no heed to this; the valley seemed familiar and benign in the light of day. She wore the same khaki garments Howard had brought her, which made her feel more connected to this place. Today she was alone, Howard having left her early in the morning, taking Abdel Aal with him and crossing the river to the opposite bank. He had said that he might be gone all day, but that she could wander freely, without risk. She knew this—she saw the meekness in the eyes of the fellahin as they pulled up the noxious weeds, bending over stalks of barley and giving thanks for the ears of grain. She was one of them. They might have abused her body and broken her spirit, but still she was one of them. Her route brought her to the gate of Medinet Habu. Depicted on the front of the structure she saw the snake staring at her, and she hesitated a moment, then went on into the temple.

She was surrounded by walls of stone whose antiquity lent them a kind of dignity and solidity. Atop the walls she saw extensive platforms, which had been constructed for the soldiers who were positioned there to defend the city. She passed through a series of little rooms, to which sunlight penetrated through small apertures. The building resembled an old castle in which kings dwelt—perhaps the kings had used to come here seeking protection when their enemies swept the eastern shore. She entered a broad atrium, and suddenly the walls were full of brilliantly colored paintings: pictures of a great king—Howard had told her on his first visit here with her that this was Ramses II. He reclined lazily amidst his favorite concubines, who offered him flowers and perfumes and things to drink, and gazed rapturously at him, while he smiled in contentment. But contentment did not last long. As Aisha walked on she found that the drawings changed: the Pharaoh left his comfortable bed and mounted his war chariot.

The concubines had vanished, and enemies had appeared before him, carrying swords and lances. All signs of felicity were gone from his face, replaced by a pitilessly cold expression.

The corridors and rows of columns intersected; she spied a statue of greenish basalt, and beside it another that had fallen to the ground: the same king, in a moment of intoxication, and the moment of his collapse. Aisha reached the interior courtyard. It was darker here, but the paintings were still vivid. At last the king appeared in the act of offering his sacrifices to the gods, his head bowed and his posture one of extreme humility. Was he giving thanks for a victory, or asking forgiveness for a defeat?

She heard a noise like the rustle of wings, and something that sounded like faint cries. She turned in alarm, but saw no one. The noises grew louder, and when she lifted her face and gazed upward she found that the ceiling was filled with bats, flitting about, colliding with the unyielding walls, and falling, broken-winged, like sightless ghosts. She drew back and tried to retrace her steps, but the bats descended and began to whirl around her. All at once the light failed; the place went startlingly dark, and she lost her way to the exit. She began to hurry—it seemed to her that she spied the shadows of other animals, animals that darted among the columns, as if the wolves, too, had awoken. She hastened her steps still more, and found that she was lost in a colonnaded maze, the bats still in pursuit. She stopped in consternation when she caught sight of someone at the end of the colonnades. He was seated beside a column, before him a built-up fire and a tin pot for making tea. He watched her approach with a penetrating stare, as if he had known that the bats would lead her to him.

He spoke in a voice made frightening by the silence of the temple. "Come forth, woman who has roused the creatures of the night!"

It was Abdel Rasul, the man she had seen on the day she first set foot upon the western shore: he wore the same clothing and the same turban, his large feet bare. She stopped where she was, rigid, afraid to move and cause the bats to attack her. The man did not get up, but spoke again. "These bats have not pursued you without cause," he said. "They are the guardians of the temple, prohibiting all whom they perceive as a threat to this place from passing the gates or wandering the corridors."

Shaking, she replied, "I am no threat. I came here before, and nothing happened . . ."

With unmistakable scorn, the man said, "You came with the foreigner—I know that. I also know that he brought you here after the gateways to the valley had been shut in his face—he wants you to open up its secrets to him."

Aisha was frightened—this man knew a lot about her. "I haven't told him anything," she said. "Besides, I don't know anything about this place to begin with."

"It is not for nothing that the creatures of the night have awoken, woman. You stand now in the heart of the temple where the gods receive their sacrifices and reveal their secrets, and the wolves troubled you from the first moment you entered this valley until you arrived here."

His voice resounded throughout the temple. He made no move from his place—he had no intention of hurting her, or so it seemed—but the knowledge that he had watched her every step so carefully made her fear him. Her throat dry, she said, "The wolves have always followed me—but that means nothing."

"Our ancestors knew that wolves were capable of opening locked doors. Their luminous eyes can pierce the veils of darkness. Everyone in the valley knows that they are bringers of light. Anyone who reads the inscriptions on the temple walls knows that they watched over Horus when he was young. Perhaps you yourself were one of these creatures."

He spoke in riddles—she couldn't tell whether he was warning her or threatening her, but one thing for certain was that he could not have been more mistaken about her.

"Perhaps you have me confused with someone else," she said. "I'd better go now."

His voice rose in anger, startling her. "You shall see what you shall see," he said, "and you know what you know, whatever you may say about it. What I fear is that you may pass along what you know to that pale-eyed foreigner. The valley is full of them, and if we give our secrets away to them they will pull the land out from under us and cast us into the river."

Aisha shuddered. Somehow this man made her feel that she was guilty of something. He spoke more softly, and held out a glass of hot tea to her, but she shook her head. He took up his staff again and pointed at a block of stone. "Rest a little here on this stone," he said. "I won't hurt you. Have some tea if you like—only listen to me."

She sat down facing him, but she dared not reach out and take the proffered tea. Now he spoke calmly. "Those foreigners," he told her, "believe that they alone are able to read the inscriptions. But we also read them, and we understand their meaning better than those men do—because they are ours. But we don't tell them that. We let them believe in our ignorance and lack of insight. I shall tell you a tale that is inscribed upon the wall of this temple. I don't believe this foreigner you came with knows anything about it. When the war was waged between Horus and Set, god of darkness, Set managed to pluck out one of Horus's eyes. It was a sacred eye, which saw what no human could see. To this day that eye is still lost. Many people have possessed it for a moment in time, and assumed the power to pierce through the veils, but they lost it for not understanding how to wield it properly."

Aisha, unwilling to believe such fables, said, "I have nothing to do with any of this."

"Who knows?" he replied. "All I wish to tell you is that you must be careful of this stranger—otherwise, you will be punished. That is all I have to say. And now you may go."

She got up and turned away from him, amazed, despite his assurances, that he had not harmed her. It was odd that she found her way now easily, and that the bats no longer followed her. The air outside was still warm, the foliage brilliant in its greenness, the river pure blue, and she had woken at last from a murky nightmare. She hastened her steps until she reached the house and shut all the doors and windows behind her. She sat upon her bed and pulled the mosquito netting around herself, as if to conceal herself from the penetrating eyes of the old man—indeed, from the eyes of all who spied upon her.

◆ ◆ ◆

The days of waiting and of madness will not end! That old man, Lord Carnarvon, has left his chilly lair in the north and is coming to Luxor, requesting a meeting with me in all haste. Up to this point, our relations have been excellent. I haven't forgotten that he rescued me from that time of wandering and aimlessness, nor do I think he has forgotten that I added to his collection of artifacts pieces that were rare beyond what any museum dreams of owning. But the years are passing by, while my desperate search continues unabated. Ever since I discovered that empty tomb, I have labored in the valley like one possessed, a team of diggers behind me, baffled, not knowing what it is exactly that I want—I myself haven't known. All the rocks and caves and empty trenches mocked me. I've had to calm down a little in order to meet Lord Carnarvon, who has come expressly for me.

We disembarked from the felucca on the eastern shore, Abdel Aal and I, and the new donkey I bought at the village market—he wasn't a good one: he was dirt-stained and, try as we might to wash him, there was no restoring him to his original color. But he was what was available. It was an inauspicious thing to take him across the river, but I needed a conveyance for the sack in which we carry our provisions. The luxurious dahabeahs moored along the shore had multiplied, along with the variety of flags flown over them: English, Americans, French—even the Germans, defeated and bankrupted though they were in the last war, had a small dahabeah. Naturally, Davis's dahabeah was in its place—perhaps he was even now lying at ease, his gray-haired chest bare beneath the winter sun, while I hurried off to the hellish scene that awaited me in the Winter Palace.

I left Abdel Aal and the donkey. The hotel's terrace—whose design was modeled after English gardens—was full of activity, rosy-faced people sitting companionably drinking lemonade and cold beer and contemplating the white sails plying the river. They exchanged chitchat and showed off the fake artifacts they'd just bought. All of them appeared to be strangers—it was as if they wore skillfully crafted masks. Lord Carnarvon was not among them—perhaps he had swallowed a handful of his various medications and way lying in bed, gazing toward the sun from behind the blinds and imagining his cells warming up.

I crossed the crowded reception area, exchanging a few words of greeting with the hotel employees, and studied the pharaonic art that filled the walls, reaching all the way to the ceiling. Some of the frescoes were based upon my own paintings, but they'd been crudely executed. I climbed the stairs leading to the wing Carnarvon occupied, pausing briefly to catch my breath. I knocked at the door, which was opened by Lady Evelyn. A few months before, I had thought her the most beautiful woman alive—all I needed was one touch of her fingertips. But now she looked like an animate wax effigy, her movements calculated, her steps constrained. She gave me a half-handshake and the ghost of a smile, and offered me a martini garnished with a cherry—I had not known that she began drinking so early. Then, abruptly, she left me alone.

After a while I heard Lord Carnarvon coughing as he approached, wearing a dressing gown of English wool. He was looking pale. Permitting me to take his elbow and lead him to a chair, he sat down across from me and fixed his eyes on me, waiting for me to begin talking, stating my modest achievements until he should shake his head, vaguely derisive. I did not speak. He stared at me with weary eyes, then said suddenly, "I hear you discovered a tomb that was entirely empty."

I hadn't expected the conversation to begin this way, with a mocking, faintly pitying inquiry. The news had spread quickly, but such was always the case: diggers would pass the news along to smugglers, and from there it would travel to the buyers and other traders, until it reached the occupants of the dahabeahs, and the old gentleman himself, who would receive it along with his morning coffee.

"Not quite. Rather . . ."

He didn't permit me to finish. Obviously bored, he said, "Perhaps others had got there before you. This valley is no longer of any use—every stone in it has been turned over by at least two or three people."

He took a draft from a glass of water that sat beside him. I left my own glass untouched.

"There have been some disappointments, perhaps," I said, "but this tomb has filled a gap in the historical record. I found there a broken tablet upon which the name of the king who succeeded Akhenaten is mentioned. It is surely a reference to Tutankhamun. No one had discovered this tomb, nor had anyone robbed it."

He lifted his hand to silence me. He looked unconvinced by all I had said. I observed that his long fingers had grown skinny and wrinkled, so that they looked rather like bird claws. "That will do, sir," he said. "It is time we concluded this business—we can't keep dreaming forever."

In despair, stricken all at once with defeat by his words, I replied, "We can keep digging a while longer. I'll reduce the workers' expenses—reduce my own wages if you wish."

The old man shook his head stubbornly. He was more displeased than I had imagined. "The problem is not the expenses," he said. "I know that prices went up after that dreadful war, so that a single day now costs us a full five pounds. The real difficulty, however, is that the years are passing by, and death hovers by my bedside. I have become convinced that I shall not live to see this discovery. Let us have done with this whole affair, Howard."

"But," I said hoarsely, "you did promise me a few more months—you promised that we might carry on with the work until the end of the season."

"And can you guarantee me that death will wait?"

It enraged me that he was taking this self-pitying line of argument, this false surrender, this trumped-up expectation of personal annihilation. The bitter war years had passed him by and he had lived through them, even as millions in their prime had perished. I tossed him the latest document, in the hope that it might stir his interest. "In this tomb, which everyone thinks was empty, I discovered a number of intriguing things."

Once more he lifted his claw-like fingers and said in that same all too familiar tone of British world-weariness, "No more of these endless documents. You have one month from today to wrap up this whole operation."

As he got to his feet, I protested, "I just need a bit of time."

He did not reply, but only held me in his dull-eyed gaze. I could hear nothing but the sound of his breathing. "In that case," I said defiantly, "I shall continue the work at my own expense."

"For how long? A month? Two? A year? Believe me, Howard—it's all used up, this valley."

Where had I heard this sort of talk before? Who had been repeating it in the old man's ear until he believed it? Lady Evelyn appeared at the door of the room and stared at me in cold silence, accusing me in her own way of being about to drain off the last dregs of her father's strength. Why did she maintain such a cold demeanor toward me when for all these years she had not even noticed me? I had no alternative but to rise, nod my head at the two of them, and take my leave, without even having touched my drink—not that I'd been about to drink anything in any case. I descended the stairs, breathing hard, feeling that no one gave a damn about me. I sat on the terrace, thinking. Would there be any point in going back to him one more time, to make him see how great was the loss he was setting us both up for? Would it do any good to beg him? I was certain that I was very near to my discovery, so certain that I was not going to plead with anyone—I would keep digging at my own expense. I would not go back to those vagabond days again.

The felucca took us, casualties of a lost battle, back to the western shore. The donkey was the only happy one among us, for he had eaten a satisfying meal of fresh clover. Abdel Aal was miserable, for I had refused to purchase many of the things we needed—tea and sugar in particular—the very stuff of life, as far as he was concerned. I was wretched, and the tedious minutiae of shopping would have made me feel still worse. On the other side of the river I saw Abdel Rasul making his way along, leaning upon his staff and leaving the prints of his bare feet upon the sand. He didn't turn in my direction, but I knew he saw me. He was watching for the moment when I would leave the valley. I walked beside the skinny donkey—perhaps walking would help me to relax. I saw the holes I had dug, the rocks I had turned over, and the valley that continued to withhold its secrets from me. They knew more of such secrets than I did—I might go on slaving over my excavations for years on end, while they would discover all the hidden sites with devastating ease. They could read the symbols and decipher the coded mysteries by some means we had not yet achieved. How could I possibly keep pace with them and evade Abdel Rasul's control over this valley?

◆ ◆ ◆

Aisha stood waiting for him on the balcony, looking pale. This was the last refuge for both of them alike. As Abdel Aal led the donkey to the annex at the back of the house, she found herself hurrying toward Howard. She embraced him and gave him a sisterly kiss, sprung from an access of fearfulness and need. Then she drew back quickly. Howard took off his hat and threw himself wearily into a chair. She sat before him on the floor and fixed her honey-colored eyes upon him. Her long lashes fluttered like a butterfly's wings, and as he looked into her eyes he found that he felt quite passionate toward her—there was no one else left for him in all the wide world.

"What is it?" she said. "You look so sad."

Feeling sorry for himself as he did, he was unable to conceal the furious anger he harbored. "It's all over," he said. "That old man, Lord Carnarvon, has given me only one month's reprieve. After that, there will be no more funding."

She drew a sharp breath, dismayed. "And what is to become of us?" she asked.

They knew their destinies were interdependent, and that the end of his work in the valley would mean the end of their relationship, the end of his connection to this strange country. In an effort to reassure her, he said, "I won't give up, Aisha. I'll keep digging at my own expense . . . I'll find some other funding, I'll . . ."

He didn't know how he would accomplish any of this, but he sensed that she badly needed to hear these words and the false comfort they offered. He could have wept. Aisha got up from the floor and sat beside him. She cradled his face between her hands and wiped away a tear that had escaped his eye. They stayed like that, sitting close together, hands clasped.

This, in truth, was the first of the days of madness. Howard barely slept at night, waking at the first light of dawn and leading his group of diggers, with a load of baskets and waterskins, aimlessly over the rocky, hilly, debris-strewn terrain, penetrating the uncharted reaches of Dar Abu al-Naja, which had taken on a brittle, corrugated appearance. No sooner would they begin to dig than he would change his mind, dashing about over rocks and trenches, only to repeat the same routine at another site. He no longer attached any importance to completing diagrams of the trenches he had made, nor did he distinguish among any of the places where he had already dug. Where he saw a spot still untouched by the mattock, he shouted at the workers. They could not understand him, and did not carry out his instructions. They always went on digging in the wrong place, producing nothing for him but more lifeless rocks, when what he wanted was stones that spoke in glyphs, revealing their secrets. The workers stared stupidly at him, not knowing which of his contradictory orders to obey.

The search had become a nightmare that pursued him waking and sleeping. He scarcely touched any food, and for long hours, day and night, left Aisha not knowing where he had gone, always returning weary, listless, and begrimed with black dust. And all the while, Abdel Rasul traversed the valley, appearing before her leaning on his staff, a constant warning of she knew not what. She craved Howard's help, but she had no idea how to get it, for she knew that if matters went on in this way he would collapse. He grew thinner and thinner, his moustache was bedraggled, and he no longer troubled to wash away the dirt that covered him. She wished then that this ghastly month would come to an end, and they could go away from here—perhaps they could have a new start in some other place.

One morning she awoke to find him already up. He was a new person, the aura of lunacy suddenly gone. He was calm, clean-shaven, washed, and animated. From the way he was dressed, it appeared that he did not intend to pursue the digging on this day. "We'll go together to Luxor today," was all he told her.

She didn't know what to say. He gazed at her, making her understand how badly he needed her presence. She was afraid to face the ever-watchful eyes always fixed upon the eastern shore, but now he began urging her to put on those peculiar garments he'd had her wear before, and go out with him, her face uncovered. In some way or other, he wanted to acknowledge her publicly, wanted everyone to see her at his side. And she could not deny her pleasure at his having regained his ease and composure, or his taking her out in public, unveiled.

Abdel Aal was waiting for them with the odd-colored donkey. Aisha rode, and Howard walked beside her. At the riverside, a felucca came and collected all the passengers. Abdel Aal was carrying a sack carefully over his shoulder. Aisha observed that it was partially filled, and Howard looked insouciantly happy. She didn't know precisely what he had in mind, but she noted the conspiratorial glances that passed between him and Abdel Aal. As soon as the boat reached the eastern shore, he asked Abdel Aal to take the donkey and go far from the curious eyes of the onlookers inside the hotel, and to settle the animal down with a large helping of clover. He led Aisha to the Winter Palace's terrace, which was crowded with the morning's customers. She looked fearfully about her, irresolute. The men were dressed with impeccable elegance, while the women were all in white and protected from the sun by wide-brimmed hats. A waiter set cold drinks before Howard and Aisha, and Howard asked him to bring all the available newspapers, English and Egyptian. The waiter placed a pile of them on the table.

"Wait for me here," Howard said to Aisha. "I shan't be gone long. You can amuse yourself by leafing through the papers and watching these fools—I shall return directly."

He left her then and went out to the street. She watched him until he vanished from sight. She was ill at ease, looking anxiously at the waiters in expectation of being asked to leave, since Howard had departed. She dared not even browse through the pile of newspapers, although no one approached her.

◆ ◆ ◆

I left Aisha and went to the road that extended along the riverbank, where Abdel Aal was still waiting for me beside the donkey, which was absorbed in its meal of clover. I gave him all my instructions, pointing out to him the dahabeah with the American flag raised above it. He was to take the sack with him, pretending to be a vegetable seller, and board the dahabeah. There he was to wait for me without speaking to anyone. After he'd gone, I stood rooted in place, peering all along the street, in case I should catch sight of any of Weigall's men—I knew them all, for they had previously been my own men. Once I had made certain that the coast was clear, I set off myself. The Nubian servant lowered his head before me as he informed me that Mr. Davis was still asleep. No doubt he had staged one of his boisterous parties, which never ended before dawn, and had drunk a lot of bad American whiskey. I enjoined the servant in no uncertain terms to rouse his master, for I hadn't time to wait. I took the sack from Abdel Aal and told him to return to the donkey.

It was some time before Davis appeared, rubbing his eyes, reeking of wine and cigarettes. He was surprised to see me at such an early hour, puzzled at my tense and rigid aspect. He gestured for me to sit down facing him, ordered the servant to bring cold beer, and bade me make myself comfortable until he had a chance to come more fully awake.

I spoke at once. "I've come to sell you something," I said directly.

He raised his eyebrows quizzically. "Don't tell me you've found something in that empty tomb," he murmured.

"It was inevitable that I would find something—I can't bear all the ridicule I've been getting from everyone on this subject."

I didn't mention that I had not been content to accept my initial defeat. I had been determined to go on my own to examine anew the empty tomb, feverishly intent upon challenging both my own disposition and the luck that had forsaken me. Davis sensed that I was onto something, that the earnestness I evinced was not without substance, and that it behooved him to refrain from further sarcasm. Suddenly amiable, he held out a bottle of beer and offered it to me. I declined, although I could have used it. I knew what a wealthy man Davis was—perhaps the very wealthiest of men—but he was aware that, despite the ill luck that had clung to me, I was always one step ahead of him.

"And what," he said, "have you brought me now?"

"Are you sure you wish to make a purchase?" I asked him.

"I'll buy anything you care to sell me," he replied.

I emptied out the contents of the sack and spread them before him. I had to shake off the sand that still clung to them, but for all that the gold sandal had not lost its luster; there was a green cosmetics pot that still held the remains of fine powdered kohl; a scarab of bluish quartz that, although scratched and cracked, was nevertheless whole and magnificent; and a shining amber necklace missing only two of its beads. I saw the amazement plainly in Davis's eyes—he would not have imagined that I could have happened upon this treasure and kept silent about it, without anyone's finding out.

"What is all this?" he said. "In which tomb did you come across these objects?"

Confidently and without hesitation, I replied, "They belonged to an Asiatic wife of Ramses II."

He didn't bat an eye. He just kept staring, openmouthed, unable to contradict me. Then he asked uncertainly, "Have you told Lord Carnarvon about this?"

"It's nothing to do with him. All you need to know is that I discovered these things in an area outside his jurisdiction, and by rights they are mine alone."

In this I was sincere. I had put my life on the line for the sake of these objects, returning on my own to the empty tomb several times. I had thrust my hand into every crack, risking snakebite and the scorpion's sting, and sat for long hours heedless of the wolves. What else could a desperate man such as I do? And at last I had happened upon this cache—it was in one of the deeper cracks, bundled in linen wrappings—maybe some priest, or perhaps thieves, had shoved it in there and forgotten where it was.

"Naturally, I shall take these things," said Davis, "but you do understand . . . I'll have to contact the Metropolitan Museum."

"I'll wait while you place the call."

I knew that all means of overseas communication were available on this dahabeah. I wrote down my asking price. It wouldn't take long, and it was not in his interest to delay matters. He left the room. I gave him the opportunity to look over the pieces and make certain they were genuine; the most important thing was that he would not be able to come up with anything corresponding to a tale of Asiatic wives. After this it was necessary that I get back to Aisha: she was the talisman bearing the luck I had at last encountered.

◆ ◆ ◆

Howard came back, dashed up the stairs and made his way among the tables, then sat down across from her. He was in a good mood, although sadness lingered in his eyes. "I've made a little bargain," he said, "and now I can carry on digging for a while."

The waiter brought breakfast—white cheese, toast, butter, and eggs, with plenty of fruit juices and milk. Howard pushed aside the bundle of newspapers. "Tomorrow," he said, "there will be talk of me in all of these papers."

Aisha smiled at him. She was growing accustomed to her surroundings. As they ate, the dining area filled up with people. A number of them clapped Howard on the shoulder and congratulated him. An elderly *rebaba* player sat on the steps outside and began to sing a dreadful song about a brother who killed his sister for the sake of honor—the waiter hurried over and drove him off, but he kept coming back. A cool breeze wafted in off the river, and Howard took a deep breath, expanding his chest as if he wanted to contain the breeze inside it.

"Why are you so attached to this place?" Aisha asked him, puzzled. "I long to get away from it."

"I feel," Howard replied, "as if my arteries had filled up with this country's sand. When I go to Swaffham, and the fog there surrounds me, the air is so saturated with the smell of rain that it nearly strangles me. The only way for me to go on with life is to stay here."

An elderly man and a pale-faced woman passed by their table. The man stopped, overcome with astonishment, but the woman shot them a venomous look and proceeded on her way. Howard rose and extended his hand to the old man, unhurriedly and with no show of eagerness, as if he had been expecting this moment.

"Good morning, my lord," he said. "Lovely to see you enjoying this warm weather."

Aisha observed that the woman, who had stopped a short distance away, was still glowering hatefully at them. The "lord" gestured toward Aisha and said, "Lovely to see you enjoying yourself as well, Howard. Won't you introduce me to your pretty friend?"

"She is a pharaonic princess," said Howard. "I discovered her on the western shore."

The man laughed, then said succinctly, "Then all these years haven't been in vain. This is perhaps the most splendid of your discoveries."

With that he nodded and went on to join the angry-looking lady. Aisha needed no explanation—she knew that these were Lord Carnarvon and his daughter. A bitter taste rose in her throat. "Was it so that those two would see me with you that you brought me here?" she asked.

"Of course," Howard replied bluntly. "I wanted to show them that I have a stake in this place I won't easily forgo."

She looked at him in consternation. Had he really brought her here to defend his presence in the country, or had it been to provoke the jealousy of that pallid woman? "His daughter . . ." she said. "Were you hoping to make her jealous?"

"I doubt she sees anything but her own face in the mirror, anyhow."

Aisha realized that it was she who felt jealous, and the feeling had spilled over, trespassing on the neutral zone she had set up in self-defense, which she had forbidden herself to approach.

"Well," she said, "you succeeded conveying your message to them: you're not alone."

They walked together through the city, conversing with the Saïdis they met in the streets. They drank fruit juices—sugarcane and pomegranate. He bought her a red velvet shawl, and she put it over her shoulders, fingering its soft fringe. Howard saw her face, how it had bloomed, and insisted upon buying her a gold necklace that looked exactly like the one worn by Hatshepsut. He placed it around her neck, and she laughed, feeling actually happy. No one had ever indulged her this way, and she felt like a true queen. They sat in a little restaurant, where they ate hot kebabs and lentil soup made with marrowbones and sipped strong tea. They walked between two rows of statues depicting rams, until they entered the maze of columns at the Temple of Karnak. They proceeded among the columns, which towered loftily above them, numbering 122 in all, then on through the rest of the temple—the altars, the Holy of Holies. He read the inscriptions to her and interpreted the kings' cartouches. She had begun to learn from him how to read the vocabulary of this strange language. They sat by the edge of the sacred lake. On the other side of the river, the façade of the Temple of Deir al-Bahri could be seen, surrounded by an aura that made him melancholy. With a hand on her shoulder, he drew her a little closer. She shivered, but gave herself over to his touch. She felt possessed by a rare moment of heart's ease, of freedom from fear. Her spirit, long since broken, craved healing. She wanted to unburden herself of all the weary secrets she harbored.

In a tremulous voice, she talked to him, revealing for the first time all the sufferings she had endured for so long, omitting no hidden detail. She remembered the night on which she had told Mukhtar the beginning of the tale, how he had kissed her eyes and clasped her to him. But that had been an innocent time, when she had not felt such bodily shame. She drew back her sleeve and showed him the mark of the cross. She explained that her mother had tried to ensure that she would elude the trap set by her uncle, but she had fallen into it anyway—had her own volition taken any part in this? It was mortifying to admit the desires that dwelt deep within. But her uncle had raped her and broken her spirit, robbed her of her original body and left her the one Howard now saw before him. Her cells had quickened in spite of her, carrying the residue of that violation. She felt utterly defiled, and this in the end had led her to the house in the red-light district.

Howard held onto her hand, as she wept and trembled. He felt himself the unluckiest person in the world, and yet here was this pharaonic princess, who had emerged from her painting to tell him her horrifying tale. He drew her into his arms, stroked her back, and said, "We all pay a price, one way or another. This has been a cruel passage for us both."

She walked by his side, leaning against him, the earth still soft and the horizon pale. She wiped away her tears, to hide them from Abdel Aal, who was waiting for them by the riverbank, the donkey beside him. As the felucca bore them upon the surface of the river, a rough song could be heard coming from one of the fishing boats—a lone fisherman seemed to be serenading Aisha and Howard. The opposite bank loomed nearer, desolate and familiar. She leapt ashore, and the silence enveloped her from every side. She declined to ride the skinny donkey, but walked with Howard along a sandy path, Abdel Aal following behind them at some distance, and with him the donkey. She saw the fellahin coming from their fields, together with their livestock, ghost-like, engulfed by a haze of dust stirred up by their feet, heading for al-Qurna. Then the valley was empty, and the clouds changed from purple to gray.

Howard began to speak, pointing out the rocks and the deep trenches amidst the undulations of the hills: stories and anecdotes about each spot—she had already heard them, but he talked on cheerfully. His voice lost its gaiety, however, as they approached Dar Abu al-Naja, the area on which he had expended so much effort, searching and delving, all to no avail. The rocks were grim and sharp-edged, as if they had emerged only reluctantly from the earth, the holes so deep that it seemed they must penetrate to the other side of the world. And all of it in vain.

With a shudder he exclaimed, "I have dug here . . . and here . . . and here . . . until there was no place left to dig but under my own skin!"

She reached out and brushed his face, hoping to soothe him as he had done for her. They were about to lose the last place left to them under the sun. The brief day's happiness dissipated; a great heap of rocks was blocking their way, and there was nothing for it but to go around it and make their way to the house. In amazement, Aisha pointed to the rocks and asked, "Was it you who made this pile?"

"I and everyone who came before me—all those who tried to dig, and came up empty-handed."

"Why did you not move it aside and dig beneath it?"

"I could not—it was beyond my capacity." He gestured toward a place obscured by shadows. "Here is the entrance to the tomb of Ramses II, which is visited daily by dozens of people. If I were to begin dropping rocks upon them, Weigall's men would whet their talons and drive me from the valley."

"You should have driven them out first."

"It is a small, worthless triangle of ground, particularly as it lies close to a tomb that has in fact already been explored."

The words were hardly out of his mouth when Aisha startled him by setting off, up the pile of rocks. Darkness had fallen upon them, and she wanted to look at the lights on the other side of the river. Before he knew it, Howard found himself following her. Abdel Aal sighed in exasperation, having no choice but to sit down and wait beside the donkey. Aisha kept climbing until she reached a level expanse composed of dust, pebbles, and little rocks, which covered the roof of the ancient tomb. The lights could be seen reflecting off the surface of the river: a tiny glimmer of hope amid the gathering darkness. Stepping up beside her, Howard put his arm about her waist, and they stood together as the evening chill descended.

She slipped the velvet shawl off her shoulders and laid it upon the ground, and they sat down side by side. It looked like a clear night, now that the clouds had dispersed. The sky seemed more rich with stars than she had ever seen it.

"I was hoping," he whispered, "for a discovery that would ensure we could root ourselves here together . . . but I promise you, I won't part from you wherever we are."

"Lord Carnarvon's reprieve is not up yet," she said, smiling. "And no one can tell what this land may hold in store for you."

Everything receded into the distance, leaving behind only the quiet of this moment. Painful memories, too, grew less acute, the sense of shame at having been raped. The night breathed upon them, combining heat from the sand and cold from the river. He reached out to cup her face in his palms, and she shivered, but tried not to pull away. His lips gently brushed hers, and there was no alarm or repugnance, but a warmth that pervaded her. His moustache was bristly against her nose; all fear had dissipated, replaced by a hungry passion. She could feel the pebbles pressing against her back through the fabric of the shawl, and it was painful at first, but the pain melted away when she felt herself enclosed within his embrace. His fingers found their way beneath her clothing, and she thought to herself, amazed, "My God—my body does not refuse him." She wound her arms about his neck and drew his head down until she could feel the heat of his breath between her breasts. Warm through and through, she turned her head and sought his lips, pressing her own between them. She could feel the night breeze slip between her legs, and now she tried to restrain him, to prevent him from reaching the center of pain in her body, but to her astonishment there was no pain. She felt herself grow light as he moved rhythmically within her, and with an effort to fix her position on the ground she sank her nails into his back, holding back her cries, lest the wind carry them to the foot of the hill. Behind the horn of the mountain she spied a hesitant yellow moon looking down upon them. She had no need of it—a light had been born within her, as if the stars had found their way into her, driven out the darkness, and extinguished her thirst.

From the base of the hill came Abdel Aal's voice, shouting, "Hey, Englishman! Wolves!"

Aisha started and extricated herself from his body's warmth, gathering her clothing together and wrapping it around herself. They heard no howling, but the scrawny donkey had begun to bray in alarm. Once more Abdel Aal shouted, in mounting terror.

"They've caught our scent—it's too dangerous to stay here!"

Howard gave her his hand and helped her to her feet, but her knees were too weak to support her. Breathlessly, they made their way down the hill. The moon spread its light across the sand to the edge of the river, but Abdel Aal pointed toward the dense shadows at the temple gates. "There they are," he said, "keeping watch. They could attack us at any moment."

Aisha felt the warmth drain from her limbs. "They are behaving strangely," said Howard. "They are not howling or making any movement—there is something out of the ordinary here."

"Be that as it may," said Abdel Aal, "they could set upon us at any time." He began to loosen the large cloth that was wrapped around his head, a long, odd-looking piece of fabric. From his pocket he drew a box of matches with which he began trying to set the edge of the cloth alight. His attempts were unsuccessful at first, but he went on striking matches until a flame ignited the hem of the fabric.

Abdel Aal took the lead, waving the cloth in a circular motion, while the burning edge of the cloth began to blaze, and to scatter bits of itself, still alight, like luminous butterflies. "Follow me," he cried, and they followed, clinging to each other. Still Abdel Aal waved the cloth in circles. "It is in case of situations like this one," he told them, "that we wear these enormous turbans." From afar, the wolves' eyes glowed brightly, piercing the veils of darkness, guarding the gates of the dead.

Howard and Aisha found it unbelievable that they had reached the house before the turban was entirely consumed. Abdel Aal refrained from looking them in the eye. He merely tossed what was left of the fabric onto the ground and quickly led the donkey toward the annex, without pausing to hear a word of thanks. The wolves took up a frenzied howling, which went on all through the night, until morning.

◆ ◆ ◆

I awoke early. I heard the voice of the muezzin coming from the direction of the temple. There was a cold wind, and the river birds circled ceaselessly, seeking their livelihood. Aisha was asleep, the door to her room locked. It did not suit her that I should share her bed this night, despite all that had happened between us. She preferred to be alone, even though she was shivering, and the howling of the wolves would not let up. I saw Abdel Aal standing upright, facing the direction of the sunrise as he prayed upon the dew-moistened sand. The light was spreading slowly from behind the horn of the mountain—everything came from this direction, so why could my dream not be fulfilled in this place?

I waited until Abdel Aal had finished praying—I could tell he was done when he turned his face first right, then left. I approached him and said, "Go and gather the men. We shall start our work early today."

"We haven't had breakfast yet," he replied in his gruff fashion, so familiar to me.

"There isn't time," I told him. "Go, before they leave for the fields, or cross to the other side of the river."

I stood there until I saw him take the donkey out of its pen, straddle the beast, and head toward the village. I didn't wait—I went on ahead of the rest and proceeded to the site where the rock pile was. It didn't seem as grim as I had always been accustomed to finding it. It was taking on colors, absorbing all the tones of the light, as if new life were seeping into it. At that moment I realized that I had not waited in vain, that this king who had eluded me for so long was about to reveal himself. I climbed the rocks, as I had done the day before when following Aisha. The red shawl was still spread out upon the gravel. I picked it up in both hands and buried my nose in it—it bore her scent, and that of the lovemaking we had experienced together: a clear and unmistakable sign to me that I should begin in this spot.

When I descended once more, the men had gathered at the bottom of the rocky slope, and were looking curiously at me. It was strange that we should gather in this place we had so long avoided. It was a massive heap of rocks, and it would be difficult to get through it, but it was our last chance.

"We shall remove this pile and dig beneath it," I said. They regarded me. I saw their eyes gleaming, their faces upon which the skin always appeared to be stretched taut, with no flesh to spare. They were accustomed to obeying orders, no matter how bizarre they might seem, knowing that our ways were often tortuous, even as the earth yielded up its riches to them as easily as if the treasures themselves had called out to them. They exchanged uncertain glances—it was a hard task—the rocks were heavy, their edges cuttingly sharp; their shoulders would crumple, their backs break.

"What is the matter with you?" I shouted at them. "Why are you just standing there?"

Al-Raïs Gregor stepped forward. Not daring to look me in the eye, he said, "We want a daily wage of five piasters for each of the men, and two for each of the boys."

"That is too much!" I exclaimed, surprised and incredulous. The war had driven prices up, to be sure, but not to this extent. "You are trying to take advantage of my position."

"Look at what you are asking of us, Englishman. These rocks will be the ruin of us. They've lain here so long they've fused together. It will be difficult, if not impossible, to dislodge them."

He was right. But I didn't want to look like a soft touch, especially since I didn't know how many days the operation would take. "I'll pay four piasters," I said.

He turned to his men, who looked stonily back at him. Clearly they had entrusted him with speaking for them, and were reluctant to interfere.

"That is too little, Englishman," he said. "This could be the last work we ever do, and only a fool would risk his life for nothing!"

He backed up until he stood with the men, as if he drew from them the strength to confront me. I was speechless with amazement at the stance they were taking. All these years I had counted upon the familiar bond I shared with them, but it seemed I had been mistaken—or perhaps I was closer to my goal than I knew, and all that stood between me and this king I sought was a few piasters. I could see the gleam in their eyes as they watched me—they were afraid, too, that I might refuse. In a matter of just a few minutes we had reached the point of no return. The men picked up their pickaxes, and the youngest among them took up the baskets, while the youths took the waterskins; I carried only my desperate dream, and an unexpected moment of love. I had to find a way to save face.

"Very well," I said. "Five piasters it is, then, but we'll work without stopping until the call to evening prayer."

They breathed a sigh of relief, the crisis averted, and began to distribute themselves about the site according to their manner, so well-known to me—a method deeply ingrained in them, which they followed whether they were sowing seed, gathering the harvest, digging irrigation ditches, or building a house. It was the same process by which they had constructed these massive temples and forbidding pyramids, for the same trifling wages. The strongest among them began shaking the rocks loose, using only their hands, while the weaker availed themselves of the pickaxes' blades. The shortest men carried baskets woven of palm leaves, and the boys filled the waterskins. They erected a tent for me beside the rocky hill, and some of their female relatives from the village came, set up a hearth, and began preparing bread. They brought tall earthenware jars filled with hunks of aged cheese and pickled turnips. The site came fully to life, and I knew that the rock pile would be removed, that nothing now would prevent this.

The morning hours were passed in work without surcease. The antiquities inspectors came, glanced at us in passing, and went away again, feeling some malicious satisfaction, no doubt, that I had taken upon myself the removal of this pile. The way to the tomb of Ramses II would be cleared, and they would take all the credit for themselves, while I myself would succeed only in running up against the walls of an old gravesite.

When the sun reached its apex, the men stopped work and took their first meal—perhaps the last as well, for this day. They broke the light, freshly baked loaves, laughing, slapping onion bulbs against their huge palms and devouring them with pleasure. They had aged cheese and pickled vegetables. They were experts in compensating for the salt they lost through sweating by consuming mineral salt. I could not share the food with them; I did not touch even the light meal Abdel Aal had brought for me.

After eating, they went back to hauling rocks and digging in the dirt, and kept it up for the rest of the day. The hill did not look as if it had been diminished in the slightest, or that it would be possible to remove it.

I returned to her at the end of the day, exhausted. She allowed me to kiss and caress her, but did not respond in kind. Did she regret having made love with me the night before, or was it the wretched Eastern taboo against forbidden things that had awoken in her? Would she feel less guilty if it had been rape, rather than a matter of mutual desire? I pointed out the pile of rocks lying in the forecourt of the house—I had tasked Abdel Aal with bringing the first of the rocks to be brought down by the men from the top of the hill, and these they had piled up in the shape of a small pyramid. I gave her the red shawl she had forgotten to pick up, and she smiled—a sad, distracted smile. I kissed her neck and her lips—she was unresisting, but not warm. At last she said, as if in apology, that the angry howling of the wolves had disturbed her all through the night, rousing terror in her heart. I sensed that the barriers between us had not yet fallen.

The stack of newspapers we had brought from the eastern shore had not been touched. Some of my old paintings were spread out upon the table—had she spent her time in contemplation of them? Amidst the papers I spied a picture of a pharaonic cartouche, on which I had written in hieroglyphics the name of cold Lady Evelyn—could it be that Aisha had recognized the name? It did not matter. I tried to draw her toward my room for more lovemaking—I was certain that if we made love at leisure, in an intimate moment behind a locked door, much of this tension would dissipate. But she could not do it—her eyes filled with tears, and I was afraid she might turn away from me once more. I went to my room, frustrated—although thoroughly weary, I could not sleep. The howling of the wolves was still at an angry pitch, coming from the direction of the temple. It was as if all the valley's wolves had converged upon this spot near our house. What could have roused them so? After a few minutes, as I hovered between sleep and waking, I became aware that the door to my room was opening. Aisha entered and flung herself down beside me in the bed. I took her in my arms—she was in a state, her limbs trembling violently and her teeth chattering.

"They're watching me!" she whispered.

"Who?" I asked, bewildered.

"The wolves! For a moment it seemed to me that they would attack us . . . then they began fighting with one another, and they are still at it."

Was she imagining things? And yet their noise could still be heard. They did not sleep, and they upset my sleep as well.

The days passed, long and wearisome: dry sand, burning sun, and endless layers of heaped-up rocks, ranks of workers who toiled without respite. The stones were transported from that stubborn hill to out-of-the-way places, so as not to impede the passage of visitors and inspectors. We filled up the holes we had dug before, and still the original surface of the ground was reluctant to show itself.

Aisha's sadness did not recede, nor did the wolves' fury abate. As she wept upon my chest, I said to her, "It is just the howling that has followed you all your life, without doing you any harm."

"It isn't only the wolves," she replied. "It's him I'm most frightened of—he comes here every day. He keeps his distance from the house, but he stares in my direction, standing there holding his staff."

"Who?" I asked her.

"The one called Abdel Rasul."

Exasperated, I exclaimed, "He's nothing but a thief who steals artifacts. I shall bar his way here!"

"You can't," Aisha replied with a shudder. "He is one of the spirits who occupy this valley. This place is dreadful—it is haunted!"

Things went on in this tiresome fashion—by day I was exhausted by the raising of the stone, and at night the wolves' furious howling kept me awake. I could see the men staggering with strain and exhaustion; meanwhile their expressions, the malevolent look in their eyes, made it clear they were getting fed up. They felt they were exerting themselves in a pointless cause. We were all of us in thrall to these stones. The men were ready to sacrifice those accursed five piasters just to have done with the stones and with me, but I could not stop. I was unsteady beneath the sun's glare. My whole life had come to a standstill over the excavation of this little patch of earth.

◆ ◆ ◆

Aisha sat up—she had awoken feeling as if she were choking—the nightmares were unremitting, until she could no longer distinguish between waking and sleeping. She could find in herself no appetite for food or desire to go out. She knew that in the outer courtyard she would discover wolf tracks, together with

Abdel Rasul's footprints. On the table she found the bundle of old newspapers—he had put them into a sack and brought them back when they returned from the east bank all those days ago. On the first page was an image resembling her own face—puzzled, she studied it. Of course it was not a picture of her. It was a sketch of a stone statue, whose face bore all the same characteristics of her own: an Egyptian peasant woman, raising one hand as if to welcome the sun, while the other rested upon the head of a scaled-down figure of the Sphinx. Mukhtar had returned from his years away in France. His face looked tired, but the faded photograph could not conceal the sparkle that shone from his eyes. He was talking about his plan to erect an immense statue symbolizing the awakening, the new renaissance. It was a distant reminder of another world. Even now he had not forgotten what she looked like—the problem was that it was no longer her face, no longer her body. Her spirit had dissolved, everything was distorted, her path a fateful road taken, on which there could be no turning back.

From outside she heard a moaning that was not the wind, but an actual wail, coming from the direction of the temple. She hesitated a moment, then walked slowly out of the house. She spied them by the stone wall, a long line of black-clad women, their heads likewise covered in black, beating their breasts and weeping without cease, leaning like a black sand dune disturbed by the wind. At first Aisha took them to be part of a funeral procession on its way to the tombs, but there were no men, nor was there a body. She really could not tell what had set them weeping so, but the incessant lamentation added to her own distress. All at once she felt that they must have come for her, to bewail her fate. She tried to retreat, to conceal herself inside the house, but one of the women turned toward her and fixed her with a hard look. Aisha drew in her breath sharply, for the woman had her mother's face, as if she had risen once more from death and come to mourn the wretched pass to which her daughter had come. Aisha shut all the windows and locked all the doors. And still she was beset by the sound of wailing.

◆ ◆ ◆

Like a miracle came the magical moment in which the men succeeded in removing the last of the rocks. At last the surface of the ground appeared, dark and moist after being so long hidden from the sun. We all collapsed, overcome with weariness. The men prostrated themselves upon the earth, thanking their distant God. Yet there were still more days of toil ahead of us, for now we must prepare to excavate the hard soil, uncertain all the while of achieving any result.

I tried to tell Aisha about what had happened, but she seemed to droop, her expression full of confusion and pain. All at once she said to me tearfully, "Why won't you leave off digging? Why can't we go away from this dreadful place?"

I looked at her, taken aback. I had never imagined she might try to stop my endeavor, after I had expended so much effort and got this close. It was she who had designated the place for me, laying out her red shawl as a sign no one could mistake. Voices had been calling to me, and the king awaited me in the hollow ground. How could I now break my appointment with him after waiting so long? But she would not be silent.

"This place will destroy us both," she said. "I've seen a terrible vision. Those wolves—they are not angry without reason!"

Enraged, I shouted at her, "And where do you wish us to go? Shall we go back to the house in the red-light district?"

She stared at me, stunned. I had wounded her cruelly.

I rose at dawn, so as to slip away without having to face her, but I found her awake, sitting on the front balcony, gazing at the fog-shrouded temple. The courtyard was full of wolf tracks, as if they had spent the night there. The rock pile I had fashioned into a small pyramid now lay scattered all about. I studied her face. Her eyes were hooded, and ringed by dark circles. Her lips moved, but her words were inaudible; perhaps she was praying to some unknown god to prevent me from pursuing my goal. I had no time for such foolishness—if she wanted to go away, let her go alone. I was not about to sacrifice the dream of a lifetime on account of a woman's superstitions.

The women were preparing to make bread, while the men arranged baskets and repaired shovels, and the boys filled waterskins with river water. It was another day, and it would be strenuous, but it was different now—or such at least was my dream. First I must put Aisha's sorrowful face out of my mind. I drank a glass of strong tea with the men, invoking with them the name of God before they applied themselves to the earth with their pickaxes, turning over the black soil. Looking as though until this moment it had never been touched, it was redolent of the air of ancient times, of death without resurrection. The men hefted their shovels and filled the baskets, squaring the sides of the trench so that they would not fall inward. They worked on, delving into layers of earth without stopping, the air seeming to pulsate in a curious way—we were all waiting for something extraordinary to turn up. I saw an ancient clay cat, a marble vessel, a broken bottle, and fragmentary bits of inscription—rich soil such as any excavator might dream of, but it wasn't what I was after—I was waiting for the king on whose existence my fate depended.

At noon the fragrance of fresh bread filled the air, mingling with that of the earth's depths, but I didn't permit anyone to stop working; I pressed them to keep digging. The sun, however, was brutal, and exhaustion had overtaken us all, with the king still well out of reach. At last I signaled to them to stop, to take their rest and their lunch. One of the youths, though—the ones who carried the waterskins—shouted suddenly. "I see the edge of a staircase!" he cried. "There are stairs!"

We all rushed over, leaping into the chamber, our bodies tumbling over one another. Dust rose up in a cloud, and we could no longer see anything. We turned about, scrabbling in the dirt, shouting when a part of the sand wall collapsed. But there was the top of a staircase. With our hands we moved aside the dirt and the pebbles, unearthing the first step, the second, and the third, all leading down into the bowels of the earth. We forgot about food, forgot the burning sun and our weariness. Dust rained down on us, but we uncovered more steps. I wept, but no one took any notice of my tears. Our faces were all coated with dust. The men cried out in the name of God as each step was revealed, and with them I plunged into a different era. As darkness, like destiny, crept upon us, we lit the torches and kept digging, reaching all the way to the twenty-fifth step. I took up a torch and approached the wall that rose before the final step. There was a stone in the way, chipped and sharp-edged, beneath which was a door, or the entrance to a vault, and there were inscriptions on it. Raising the torch, I was able to read the hieroglyphics easily. There was one cartouche, bearing one name: Tutankhamun. "Oh, king, you who eluded me so long! I've found your resting place at last!"

◆ ◆ ◆

They wanted him back at Thebes. But he knew it only as a terrifying city. They wanted to marry him to a girl he hated, who regarded him as a wild animal; they wanted to set a heavy crown upon his head and give him a scepter to clutch against his chest; they wanted to weigh his body down with gilded clothing, leaving his spirit no opportunity to roam the wilderness he so loved. They had even taken his old name from him and given him a different one, along with a new god. No one paid any heed to the question of what he himself wanted. How could he express himself in the face of their antagonism, or address himself to Horemheb's unyielding determination?

Tut was hiding within the palace, hoping they would not find him and force him to do all these things. He only wanted to postpone the affair so that he might mourn his late father, but they would not permit him even this final chance to say farewell.

Akhetaten had changed since Horemheb's soldiers had assumed control of the city, virtually without opposition. The minister Ai had been the first victim, even though he, too, had surrendered. The warriors of the south had raised on high the banners of the god Amun as they overran the streets of the unresisting city. In the vanguard was a rank of priests, with their shaven heads and those implacable looks they cast upon the crowd. The city's sentinels threw down their weapons and went out to greet the warriors, but these looked on them with contempt. Horemheb brought to the palace the news of the Pharaoh's death, entering for the first time Queen Nefertiti's private wing. He breathed her fragrance; he saw her bed. She surprised him by receiving the news unflinchingly. She was grief-stricken, but not shocked, for she knew intuitively that her husband had left seeking death. Horemheb wished that at such a moment as this he could shed the soldier's stern aspect and fall to his knees at her feet, confess to her the intensity of his desire to warm her bed, now grown cold. But the daughters were weeping inconsolably. Tut, meanwhile, attempted tried to slip away into a corner, but Horemheb spoke to him severely.

"When the days of mourning are over," he said, "the marriage rites shall be held. You are to marry the eldest daughter, Ankhesen, and become Pharaoh of Egypt. Such was the decree of the late Pharaoh, which I promised to carry out."

Couldn't they have chosen another of the girls? Why must the throne come at such a cost? And yet who would dare oppose Horemheb? His soldiers had secured their grasp on every part of the city, while his priests had shut the temples of Atun and arrested the priests of the fallen god. No one dared ask what had become of the Pharaoh Akhenaten. How had he died? Where was he buried? What ceremonies had been undertaken to ensure that his spirit should proceed safely to the afterlife? None dared: not the vanquished city—the very sun hid its face—nor the nobles who came in droves to declare their allegiance to Horemheb and their deference to the god restored, Amun. They feared for their lives, trembling at the thought of the priests' vengeance. Who would pay any heed to a heretic Pharaoh, when no one even knew to what end the paths of eternity had led him?

Horemheb's orders were abrupt and peremptory: "You have one week to leave this city, Akhetaten. Thereafter, it stands no more."

The city's end came swiftly, but inevitably. It had been a passing fancy, in a land that lived and breathed only nightmarish visions. The soldiers spread out, and the smell of pitch wafted from everywhere. The residents came to the fearful realization that Horemheb's threat was to be carried out: he would burn the city as soon as the grace period ended. The tradesmen began emptying their shops and storehouses of goods. Ships and smaller vessels drew near to the beach and stood ready, while their crews prepared for unremitting days of labor. The houses began to expel their contents: heaps of furniture; of clothing; of pots and pans; a few memories, some regrets. Objects from the houses filled the bowels of the sailing vessels. Hundreds of people without means descended upon the streets, seeking a way to escape.

Meanwhile, the priests began working savagely to efface all images of the sun with extended arms. Tut stood alone on the balcony of the palace watching the city in its death throes. Atun rose weakly from behind the horizon, hastening each day to hide himself once more. The Pharaoh's daughters were afraid of being snatched or raped, but the soldiers surrounded the outside of the palace, guarding it from the common rabble, and from the priests, and no one dared approach the palace walks. The royal ship stood in the river, awaiting the departure of the Pharaoh's family. Nefertiti, though, did not stir from her room—it was as if she was insensible to what was going on around her, did not smell the odor of pitch that permeated the atmosphere.

Soon the final day was upon them. Horemheb himself came to the palace to help them make their way to Thebes, that frightful city, but the Pharaoh's daughters greeted him with terror in their eyes. Their old friend was no longer a friend, but a cruel man determined that none should defy him or stand in his way. "Our mother," said Ankhesen, the eldest, "does not wish to leave the city. None of us wishes to return to Thebes."

He had no time for such maneuvers, the ploys of women. He went to Nefertiti's quarters, the slave girls retreating before him. He found the queen seated before the window, impassively surveying the horizon. Hearing his footsteps, she turned to him as if unseeing.

"My lady," he said, "this is the last day. We must all leave."

"It is you and your soldiers," she replied, "who designated this day. I shall not leave my city. I will not go to that hostile city my husband deplored, the city that hated him."

He found himself at a loss. He dared not force her to leave. He dared not even approach her, or touch her with so much as the tips of his fingers. "The city will burn," he said.

"I shall burn with it then," she said. "Here my husband died, and here I shall die."

Just so had Queen Tiye acted, and all the foolish queens before her. He stood there a while before her, hoping she might yield. It seemed to him that she saw him, and saw how afraid for her he was. But her face remained set, her staring eyes weary: gone from them was that captivating gleam, ephemeral enchantment, conveying vague promises. They had become two dull metal orbs. Did she despise him? Had she despised him all along?

There would be no point in speaking further. He turned and left her. The exodus from the palace had begun—ranks of slave girls, male slaves, and servants who had never imagined that the queen would sit on alone in a city about to be put to the torch. Once more he faced the girls with their frightened eyes.

"We will not leave this city," said Ankhesen, "so long as our mother does not leave."

"You in particular, little princess," he said between clenched teeth, "must come with me. I shall carry you to the ship against your will if you put up any resistance. Your sisters may stay behind if they wish."

"And you will burn them all?"

"The city will not burn," he said. "For Queen Nefertiti's sake, I grant it life. But ruin lies beyond the walls. None shall remain here but the vipers, the crows, and the wolves. All shall follow me, willingly or not."

Ankhesen fought them vigorously when they picked her up and carried her to the ship. She struck the guards with her fists and clawed at their faces. She looked at Tut with hatred as he walked beside her, head bowed. Horemheb led the throng as if the spirit of Amun—that evil god—had taken possession of him. The ships and other craft—small rowing boats, too—crept along the surface of the river, while onshore another creeping procession kept pace with them, of horses, mules, donkeys, water buffaloes, and cattle, heavily laden with goods, all heading south.

The city walls appeared, pale and silent. The light within them had died, and with them would die the most beautiful woman on earth. Horemheb thought of her, sitting submerged in terminal silence. She had not given him a chance, nor herself the chance to awaken from her sorrows and begin to move toward a rapprochement. How could she not have sensed his desire for her all these years?

The river bore everyone, willing or not, to Thebes. It was the priests who received them all with baleful glances—but this was no time for reprisals. The new god was dead, along with the alternate city and the heretic Pharaoh, and there was nothing for the priests of Thebes to do but celebrate their dominion over all the valley's cities, without exception.

The old pharaonic palace was reopened. Ankhesen sat in one corner of it, while Tut crouched in another part. They did not meet or exchange any conversation whatsoever. All the same, preparations for the wedding continued. Thebes was lavishly decorated. It was announced that the new Pharaoh had changed his name to accord with the god Amun, and that the first of his deeds would be the construction of a new temple in the center of Karnak, by which means he would establish his obedience and reverence for the venerable deity. Tut, afraid and isolated, knew nothing of what was happening around him. He didn't know who had changed his name, or who had ordered a temple for this unfamiliar god. The whole city was blazing with activity, celebrating its easy victory. Tut alone felt vanquished, and missed Akhenaten, the man who had given him his new life—and now here was Tut, taking Akhenaten's throne, marrying his daughter, and repudiating his god. He was a traitor—he knew it in his heart—but he wasn't strong enough to do anything about it.

On the day of the wedding, the palace filled up with people: priests and chiefs, the luminaries of Thebes, those who had never left it and those who had gone away and come back, the penitent and the servile. Horemheb directed them all with stern exactitude. This wedding was the inauguration he must complete before undertaking to change everything.

Ankhesen appeared wearing a black robe—she had not yet relinquished her mourning clothes. Tut was seated on the throne, his head bare and his hand empty; he had acquired none of the splendor of a king—he looked like a terrified boy, searching for a means of escape. He was afraid to go near Ankhesen. She sat next to him, disdainful as ever. She was remembering her mother and sisters, from whose midst she had been plucked for the sake of this dismal marriage. She looked at the priests, who were seeing to the completion of the wedding rites—she was ready to explode. The high priest of Amun was offering the two of them a beaker full of milk mixed with honey.

"This honey," he said, "is the nectar of the sun, the milk that of the moon. They are combined just like your sacred conjoined lives. Each of you completes the other: you are the goddess Isis, who offers the throne to her husband, and he it is who shall be born anew by your grace, to be as Osiris, and you shall remain together until time completes its circuit, until Sirius the Dog Star appears, the seasons of the flood succeed one another, and Amun grants you both power and dominion over all creatures in this land beloved of the gods. I bless your marriage and proclaim you the new Pharaoh, Tutankhamun."

Ankhesen was about to refuse, but at a sharp glance from Horemheb she took a sip, just enough to wet her lips. Then Tut, nauseated, drank as well. The high priest drew near and set the crown in place, a huge thing compared to Tut's small head. It consisted of two colors: red for Upper Egypt and white for Lower Egypt; it was bisected by the guardian serpent, from which rose two feathers, representing truth and justice. The eye of Horus, with its distinctive tapered corners, looked out from the middle of the crown. Tut's aspect changed once he was wearing the crown: he grew taller and more striking, seated there upon the throne. But Ankhesen grew still more furious with him. She would have liked to get up and leave him sitting there alone, this vagrant who had stolen her father's throne and bound his destiny to her against her wishes. But the ceremonies had not been concluded yet. The priest was handing him the scepter—the scepter of Amun, who was responsible for repelling enemies. It was made of sycamore wood, and had the head of a wolf. It was covered with a layer of gold, to give light to the world of the hereafter.

Slaves entered, bearing large wooden platters, on which were fresh loaves of bread, the steam still rising off of them. The slaves approached the throne and halted before it. The Pharaoh rose, took the loaves, and handed them out to everyone. The first loaf went to Horemheb, the second to the high priest, and the rest of the nobles and luminaries followed. Then Tut turned to Ankhesen. She glared at him, and he shrank back. Only Horemheb observed this, for at this time the ceremonies were over. As the sound of drumbeats rose and grew louder, dozens of dancers made their way into the center of the hall, where they began swaying to the rhythm. Outside, the assembled masses, in their thousands, cheered as platters of bread and jugs of beer were brought down from the palace, and servants began dispensing them at no charge. The city was suffused with an atmosphere of gaiety it had not known for some time, the men bedding the women indiscriminately, as if the energy ignited in the wanton city streets might engender strength in the loins of the new Pharaoh.

The Pharaoh himself, however, stood helpless before his bride as the night ended. Everyone had left, and Ankhesen stood there quite naked, challenging him with her body, resplendent in its budding womanhood. She had inherited her mother's coloring, as well as her willowy frame and bewitching eyes.

"You'll not touch me," she said to him. "I won't let a wolf child into my bed."

Her voice rose high and shrill; the palace had ears, all attentively pricked. Tut had no choice but to go away and leave her. He went looking for a room in a faraway corner in which to retreat, the moans of the lecherous and unbridled crowd ringing in his ears.

In the morning he attempted to salvage some sort of victory in the alien streets. The attendants dressed him in his gilded robe and placed the crown upon his head. He ascended his war chariot, drawn by eight horses, and his lavish entourage made a thorough tour of the city. Horemheb followed him in another carriage, a little way behind. When he reached the Temple of Karnak, the priests gathered around them, holding fragrant censers, and the temple virgins emerged, scattering flowers at their feet. None of this alleviated Tut's feeling of estrangement: not the chanting of the crowds, the façades of the houses, the emblems of the gods, or the droning of the priests. He was alone, with no remedy for his loneliness.

Afterward, he sat upon the throne for hours on end, people coming and going before him. They knelt to convey their reverence, told him their names and their many soubriquets, although he was incapable of remembering anything. They laid gifts at his feet: golden vessels, jeweled necklaces, and costly robes, in constantly replenished piles of goods brought in by his followers. He had no idea what he was supposed to do with all of it. At last Horemheb clapped his hands, and everyone filed out. Tut was exhausted and trembling, but Horemheb stood at attention before him, unyielding and grim as ever.

"Beginning tomorrow," he said, "you shall give the order for the peasants to leave their fields and the workers their tasks. We must assemble the greatest army this land has ever known. The enemy has overrun the Valley of Turquoise, and will soon reach the fertile lands. We must not merely drive them back—we must pursue them to their own lands and lay waste their cities."

It was always war, one begetting another. Tut, though, was frightened. All those who were providing him with protection would now leave him and go far away. Horemheb seemed to know what he was thinking.

"I shall leave guards with you, chosen from the most faithful of my men. They will carry out orders at your command. They will kill without hesitation anyone you wish done away with—you have only to say the word."

"Say the word . . . ?" Tut echoed in a hoarse whisper.

"Be resolute in issuing all your orders, and do not repeat yourself. Even the queen—expect from her nothing less than total submission. In truth she gave up the throne to you, but it has become yours now. You must fill her womb quickly—this is what I have found when it comes to women. Use any method you wish, and think nothing of resistance or pain or cruelty—be as cruel as you like as often as you like. The Pharaoh must be harsh, always."

Horemheb began preparing the country for war once more. The peasants took off their blue overgarments, and harvested reeds from the riverbanks, which would be transformed into shafts for spears. Iron and bronze were combined to be forged into swords and spearheads; grain silos, jugs of oil, and linen thread were requisitioned; women gathered in the temples to weave soldiers' uniforms. Peace and quiet had withdrawn from the valley, and tomorrow the warriors would call out their entreaties to the gods for help, before they turned and made their way northward.

The army left the city—thousands of peasants, transformed into soldiers. They had taken up their spears and their armor; the professional soldiers had mounted their war chariots. They all passed before him as he stood upon the balcony of the palace, Queen Ankhesen beside him.

He was frightened of her, and of everything else in this city. He thought he would die if he so much as raised his voice just a little. How could he assert his authority over those priests, who had their way in everything? How could he be safe, lost in the dim corridors of this palace, laid end-to-end with traps to ensnare him? Lurking in every passageway was a hidden enemy, but the greatest foe of them all was in the bedroom—the room in which he had found no place until now, and here he must make a beginning.

She sat upon her bed, surrounded by slave girls, who anointed her body with oils, perfumes, and honey—the same recipe Queen Tiye had used. She'd paid no attention when he entered and stood in the middle of the room, so she was startled when he spoke up and ordered the slave girls to leave. They hurried out.

He approached her and took her by the arm, but she clawed at his face with her nails like an angry cat. When he pushed her roughly back to the bed she struck his chest with her fists. He forced open her legs, and she pulled his hair, so he yanked off the fabric that covered her chest. She tried to repel him, but he pressed himself between her thighs. They struggled in silence, their agitated breathing the only sound. She looked him straight in the eye, then gave up the fight. Her exposed chest heaved, and her pale belly rose and fell. She let him do as he wished. He gasped and perspired, groping aimlessly with his hand. Her scowl vanished, replaced by a sneer. She neither resisted nor assisted him. He struggled on, clutching at her legs and pressing himself to her torso. His breath became the snorting of a beast. All the while she fixed him with the same mocking stare and faint smile.

When at last his efforts ceased, she said, "Now get up off of me, valiant Pharaoh."

He was choking—the corridors of the palace were stifling and endless. He increased his haste, seeking the river, a fresh breeze to dry his sweat, but he stumbled on, through the side passages, until the face of the river appeared, black and silent, without a breath of air. He sat upon the steps leading down to the water. The opposite shore seemed far away, dark and desolate—if only he could escape to it. There he might give way to his tears with no one to see him. He heard footfalls, and turned to find a detachment of four guards standing behind him, protecting his back. They left him only when he went to the queen's quarters, but no sooner did he reappear in the open than he came once more under their direct scrutiny, precisely in accordance with Horemheb's orders.

"I want to cross to the other shore," he cried.

"We'll fetch the royal bark at once," one of them replied.

The oars beat upon the surface of the river, slicing the dark waves. His heart was heavy and the opposite bank seemed unwilling to come any closer. Behind him were the lights of the palace, refusing to disappear. All he wanted was darkness to hide the emotions that showed on his face. The boat kept rocking, rocking on the face of the water until it made contact with the mud of the riverbank. The oarsman stood up quickly, got out of the boat, and bent over before him, so that the Pharaoh might step upon his back and thus reach the sand. Tut was trembling, but the earth here was solid, perhaps more than in any other place. Here was more silence, more darkness than anywhere else. He motioned to the guards, who stayed by the riverbank, watching for any movement on the water. Only the elderly oarsman stayed with him, following, at a certain distance.

"What is this place?" said Tut.

"It is the Valley of the Kings, my lord," the old oarsman replied, surprised. "Here lie all the great kings who make their way to the afterlife."

In the distance rose the howling of wolves; the sound pierced him to the marrow. He remembered the taste from long ago, of milk running into his mouth. The memory woke within him hunger, desire, the need for warmth, driving out the torpor of palaces and lazy familial comforts. The voices rose as if the wolves had caught his scent.

"Let us go, my lord," the oarsman said fearfully. "There are a great many of them."

He made no move. He saw their eyes gleaming in the darkness and their nimble shadows flitting among the rocks of the mountain that loomed over them like a great beast's horn. He laid hold of his garments and removed all the finery and jewelry that weighed him down, at the same time releasing a great cry—he had returned once more to their world—he must surrender his body to their fangs and claws. He moved toward them, trying to make contact with their bodies, but the oarsman began to weep, and called for the guards. No one dared touch him, so the four guards moved quickly to form a line between him and the rocks. One of them held up his hand and said, pleading, "My lord . . ."

Tut drew breath with difficulty, also nearly weeping. There they stood, forming a barrier between him and the freedom he sought, keeping him on a throne he did not like, with a wife he could only detest. There was nothing to do but turn and stumble back through the sand, ready to collapse with every step, the rest of them behind him not daring to place a hand on him, until he heaved himself at last into the boat.

Later he went back again to the western shore, but in daylight it appeared less forbidding, despite the scowling rocks, heavy with the sarcophagi of the dead. The guards accompanied him, along with the priests of Amun, walking behind him as he cast about in the sand, in an effort to recall the place in which he had stood during the night. He tried to familiarize himself with the features of the rocky terrain, to discover the imprint of claws upon the ground, to sniff out the scent of urine always left behind in places where the wolves had been. At last he pointed out the spot, addressing himself to the high priest.

"Here I wish to build my tomb," he said.

The priest stared. "Your tomb!" he exclaimed. "Is this not rather premature?"

"Work begins tomorrow," Tut replied sharply.

Work indeed commenced the following day. There were few men—most of the houses had been emptied of adult males, leaving the women alone, their beds cold. Yet workers must be found, in deference to the Pharaoh's orders. The first tunnel penetrating the depths of the earth was begun. He stood and watched the laborers as they scooped out soil and cut through stone. This supplied a pretext for him to spend as much of his time as possible on the other shore. The work proceeded all through the day, and at night by torchlight.

News came regularly of the war being waged in the north. Every fifteen days a messenger came, sand-coated and blood-soiled. The battles raged on—they might flare up and subside, but the casualties never abated, nor did the ships cease their plying of the waters, bearing matériel northward, where they sailed laden with wheat, barley, salt, honey, onions, and with them northbound passengers. While the messages kept coming, the northern tribes had retreated to their own side of Egypt's borders and the struggle had moved into Canaan, but it would not stop unless and until the Hittite enemy was driven back behind the northern river, which as far as Egypt was concerned was the line of safety.

One way or another, matters of state were carried out. Ranks of clerks and other employees skilled in many languages took on all assignments. The young Pharaoh knew virtually nothing of what went on, and if he asked the answers he received were at once vague and incomprehensibly detailed. The tomb, though, kept expanding beneath the surface of the earth, a black hole with walls of jutting rock. When he peered into its murky depths, he felt them calling to him. He got into the habit of keeping a solitary vigil, in order to listen to the howling of the wolves, while the torches stayed lit all night long.

He would steal back to the dark palace and go to bed alone, where he would lie with his eyes open, hoping to keep the nightmares at bay. Meanwhile, the keening of the wolves never stopped resounding in his head. He imagined his skin covered in fur, his canines grown into fangs, his nails sharpened into claws. One night he opened his eyes in alarm to find the light of dawn peeping through the curtains. He could see clearly Ankhesen's face regarding him. She was not angry or poised for a fight. Her hair hung loose, its locks wreathing her face, and she wore a thin gown through which her breasts were plainly visible—she took no trouble to hide them. He heard her whisper very softly, sounding the way she had in her long-ago childhood.

"What is troubling you?" she said to him. "Why do you seek death so eagerly?"

He stared at her in astonishment. She spoke with a gentle kindness to which he was in no way accustomed—nor would he ever have imagined her leaning over him in this intimate way—she was all but clinging to him, fearless and unguarded. She spoke again. "Am I the cause of all this?"

In a strained voice he said, "I used to think so . . ."

"What is it, then?"

"The man they have defamed, the god we have abandoned . . . this is the cause I did not perceive before. This is the curse that has befallen both me and you."

"But the throne is ours!" She was staring at him, mystified.

"For the sake of that throne," he replied, "we have forsaken everything. And so we have been ashamed of things that should not have shamed us."

He spoke sadly, painfully, but his words were true. Perhaps she had been averse not to him, but in some way to herself—both of them had recoiled from themselves.

Now for the first time she attached herself to him, trembling. "Be all that as it may," she said, "don't leave me alone. This city frightens me!"

He caressed her, and she flung her arms around him. They were too close to permit either the clawing of each other's faces, as in their first encounter, or even an exchange of words. They were both trembling, and her hair hung down around his face.

"Make love to me now," she whispered in his ear. "Do as you will with me—I am content."

The following morning the rising sun found them warmly asleep in each other's arms—the cold that had beset them since their arrival in the city had dissipated. Although she was hungry for more, she contented herself with this measure of warmth and affection, for there was no preventing him from crossing the river every day to follow the progress of work on the tomb. It extended well into the earth, with rooms and corridors, a hidden cavern designed for the resurrection of the dead. The dreary walls of sand disappeared behind a layer of white plaster: a smooth and gleaming surface that mitigated the gloom of the lightless burial chamber. Next would come the artists to paint the walls of the tomb.

But the army stayed away longer and longer, while households made up of only women grew more and more oppressed. The flood season drew near, but there was no one to sow seed in the earth, so when the waters engulfed it and then receded, nothing grew but grass and weeds. The army would have had to return earlier, before the floods, to ward off the specter of famine, but the soldiers stayed away, beyond the horizon, while the number of messengers reporting from the north dwindled, and such news as they brought was contradictory. The army had advanced considerably upon the barbarian tribes—but had it reached the river that was its goal?

At last the army returned, Horemheb raging like a cyclone, begrimed with sand and bearing many wounds, some of them still bleeding. His army was exhausted, its numbers reduced nearly by half. They looked around, their eyes wandering in their heads, reeling with hunger and fatigue. Horemheb, though, when he stood before the Pharaoh, appeared strong and confident, as was always his way. Tut sat upon the throne, the queen at his side. They trembled when they heard Horemheb's booming voice—all these months they had fancied they were true monarchs, but here came Horemheb to put them in their place, like the two little children they were.

"I come," he said, "to announce our victory, my lord."

This was not evident from his appearance, and if such a victory had indeed been achieved, then it had been very costly. Tut dared not say a word, or ask for details. He simply stared fixedly at Horemheb.

"We destroyed their settlements," Horemheb continued. "We evicted them from Canaan and drove them back beyond the river. The Hittite king has pledged not to attempt to antagonize us further, and he sent his son as hostage, to ensure that he keeps his promise." Horemheb gestured and said, "Come forward, Tayfour."

A slender youth advanced, bare-chested and tousle-headed. He stood trembling before them. Tut looked him over uneasily. His hair was dark blond, his eyes disquietingly pale. He was trying to disguise his primitive ill nature with a mask of servility, and he kept his mouth closed to conceal his fangs. His nails were long and filthy, his bare feet broad, ill-suited to his wiry frame, as if he had walked a journey of many miles. Ankhesen studied him as well, equally ill at ease: those strange eyes, blue as if they contained a miniature sea; his disheveled locks straggling upon his wide shoulders. His legs were strong, like those of a wrestler—he could have lifted her up onto his shoulders if he had wished, and carried her off. There was a protracted silence, while Tut tried to find his voice.

"I congratulate you, brave warrior," he told Horemheb at last, "but what are we to do with this hostage? Are we to kill him or imprison him?"

"My lord," Horemheb said, "he is our hostage. Should any harm come to him, it would mean a renewal of war. We must play host to him, and guard his life."

"Very well," Tut replied casually. "Let him be housed in one of the lodgings adjacent to the palace, then. We have no wish to provoke the barbarians' wrath."

The servants led the youth away. Ankhesen followed him with her eyes until he disappeared from view. Then Horemheb began to tell them of his deeds and offer up the spoils. It was plain enough that he really had been victorious. From the enemy's temples he had seized statues of Set, the god of darkness, whom they worshipped. He had got hold of their flags, fashioned from dyed animal hide, and made off with their leaders' iron coats of mail. He had appropriated gold from their treasuries. Not only that, but he had ordered the rape of all the women, so that they would bear children of Egyptian blood, who would declare no more wars upon the land in which their fathers dwelt.

With Horemheb back, there was virtually no need for the Pharaoh who sat upon the throne. The ranks of those seeking favors, the beggars, and the sycophants, dwindled. The country seemed enervated, as if it were trying to recover its breath. To begin with, Horemheb dissolved the army and paid off the soldiers. They were required to surrender their lances and swords, and to return once more to their starving villages. Axes were raised and brought down upon the earth, tilling it and clearing it of dead matter. The waterwheels turned, lifting water from the river's edge and depositing it into the irrigation canals, which had become clogged with weeds. The fields drew breath once more, the dust shivered as it received the new plantings. But the war that had grown distant still raged within the palace, whose chief inhabitant seemed to be laboring under a curse. Tut had been seized by a sudden weakness, and one night he found himself unable to rise. Ankhesen's moans and her efforts to rouse him were of no avail—he was simply too feeble to accommodate her. Horemheb's footfalls resounded through the palace corridors at all times, without cause. Tut made no further attempt to return to her bed, while his longing to cross to the opposite shore increased.

The tomb continued to grow, the way a viper creeps along below the earth. Ankhesen sat alone all day long, and for many hours of the night as well, amid the slave girls' silly chatter and the toadying of Thebes's upper-class women. Her friends from the city in which she had grown up no longer came; abashed, they kept to their own homes. Ankhesen felt desperately lonely.

On hearing her slave girl, Amnet, remark, "What a gorgeous creature he is!" she rose and went to the girl's side. It was then that she saw him pacing about the palace garden, like a captive animal. He was lean, but muscular. His skin shone with perspiration, for he had not yet adjusted to Thebes's hot weather. With a gasp, he lifted his hand as if groping for a breath of fresh air. Quivering, she gazed at him, feeling herself at one with him—just like him, she had been snatched away from her family, her people, leaving behind her mother and sisters, as well as her father's grave, whose whereabouts she did not even know. She had become a prisoner within this stifling palace. She wished she could go down to him and touch him, offer him some sort of kindness, let him know he was not alone in this strange land. Standing beside her, Amnet gave off her own distinct fragrance. She was a pretty girl, from one of the noble houses of Thebes, and her scent was that of Ankhesen's grandmother Tiye. All the women of Thebes had insisted upon wearing it after the queen's passing.

"He is not a 'creature,'" said Ankhesen.

"He is wild and dangerous. My mother always warned me about men with pale eyes—everyone fears them."

"Perhaps it is he who fears everyone else," Ankhesen replied. "If Horemheb should become angry with him, he might kill him in an instant."

Ankhesen felt her heart fill with pity for the young man, a despairing hostage in a strange country whose language he did not know, threatened with death at any moment. In Amnet's voice she could sense her hunger; the girl could not suppress a tremor of desire. Unwittingly, she had drawn attention to the youth, and now Ankhesen saw an escape from the tedium of the vacant days her husband spent on the other side of the river.

She made sure she was alone. She took to dismissing Amnet before the hour at which he made his daily appearance in the garden. She stood behind the curtains, so the she could watch him intently. She did not know whether he had sensed her presence or not; while in the garden he was never still—it was as if he were keeping up a regimen of military exercises, battling imaginary adversaries and hurling spears at nonexistent targets. He kept up his savage routines, so as not to grow soft, to give way to a life of ease. For long hours she watched him, unable to take her eyes off him, her body tensed as if she had reached the summit of a mountain that had no other side.

She had been observing him for more days than she could count, when one day he startled her by approaching her window. She was expecting him to turn around and walk away again, but he didn't. He stopped below her window and lifted his head to confront her. She felt her breath coming faster—it was no use trying to hide behind the curtains—he knew she was there—no doubt he had caught sight of her some time ago. She opened the curtains and stood facing him, feeling her chest expand and contract. She could smell his sweat, distinctly a scent of the wild, and all the while he stood regarding her with his strange eyes, an arresting, indeterminate blue color. She did not speak—but then he addressed her in broken Egyptian.

"You are the queen, yes? I still remember your face."

With a start of surprise she said, "You're speaking Egyptian!"

"Yes. I learned it from the slave girls and attendants."

As astonished as before, she said, naïvely, "The slave girls? When did this happen?"

"All the time. They sneak into my room every night."

She gasped, staring at his body, his pale skin. He had taken some color from the sun, but it had not dispelled his whiteness. He looked powerful, overflowing with the potent juices of his youth. Those whoring slave girls—they had learned the way to his bed and not one of them had told her. Had they conspired together, or had each sought her own pleasure in her own particular way?

"Why are you always watching me?" he said now. "Why don't you come talk to me? I, too, am royalty—a prince, and my father is a king . . ."

Three guards began making their way toward him, coming from the other end of the garden. She saw them walking in his direction, their weapons unsheathed. "They'll kill you," she said, frightened.

He turned and looked behind him. Seeing them, he showed no fear, nor did he move from his place in front of her window. "They wouldn't dare," he said. "I am a hostage." The soldiers, looking no less menacing, were getting closer.

"They will kill you," she said in alarm, "because you dared to speak to me." The guards moved in, circled him, and pointed their spears at his neck. It appeared to Ankhesen as though their pointed tips had actually pierced his skin. "Stop!" she shrieked. "Get away from him!"

The guards lowered their spears and bowed their heads. She was trembling, and still he gazed at her, looking her in the eye, indifferent to the guards and their spears. "Go!" she shouted at him, but still he stood there, defiantly. This pleased her, but she glared at him and he began to move off, without turning his back to her. She stood watching him, following every step with her eyes, afraid that the guards would go after him and do him some harm. She turned to them—their heads were still bowed—and she said with undisguised fury, "Do not provoke him again. Now go!"

For the rest of the day she was unable to regain her composure—she felt as though she was burning up inside. The Pharaoh, meanwhile, stayed away all day and all night. When Amnet came, Ankhesen turned on her wrathfully. "That hostage," she cried, "the prince. Do you know where his room is?"

Amnet gave her a frightened look and colored deeply. Taking a step backward, she said, "My lady, I . . ."

But Ankhesen was apoplectic. "Wretched girl!" she shrieked. "Don't try to tell me that you don't go to him!"

The girl could not understand why Ankhesen was so angry with her.

On the other side of the river, work on the tomb proceeded, and Horemheb could only admire its workmanship and the way in which it continued to expand beneath the earth. He had gone in person to see it, going down with the Pharaoh as he descended the passageway leading underground. They entered the anteroom, the largest of all, in which everything belonging to the Pharaoh would be placed, all the things that would be useful to him in the afterlife. Then they passed through the doorway leading to the burial chamber, which was a little smaller. Here was where the coffin would go, along with the rest of the king's treasures. Horemheb followed him into each section, including the small annex in which the king's weapons would be placed.

His face expressionless, he said, "This shall be a tomb surpassing all those of the great Pharaohs."

They both knew he did not merit such a tomb, but Horemheb ordered that the national treasuries be opened, and that the gold needed for the construction of his coffin, his death mask, and the royal chariot be taken out: as if he were offering compensation for his betrayal of the fallen god and the late Pharaoh.

Ankhesen, meanwhile, still stood in her room, oppressed by a sense of bitter cold and silence. She sat down upon the empty bed, but she could neither sit still nor sleep. She got up again and hurried down the stairs. She stepped out into the wet grass. The guards would see her, certainly, but they would not dare approach her. She entered a stone building hidden in a stand of trees and dashed along the corridor, out of breath, heedless of the slaves who prostrated themselves upon the ground when they saw her. Her body was in revolt, and nothing could have stopped it.

At last she came to the place where he slept. He was naked beneath the moonlight, deeply asleep. She wrapped herself around him. He had become accustomed to these nocturnal advances, the pressure of women's bodies, trembling with desire, none of his visitors bothering to identify themselves. This time, though, he recognized the face in the moonlight and understood the enormity of the predicament in which he found himself. But she pulled him closer, growling like some famished creature. His bed was permeated with a multitude of aromas, those of other women—including even Amnet's scent. This goaded her further, and she moaned, finding his body so different from what she had known: youthful, strong, and muscular, as it moved above hers, knowing and confident. He knew where to find the key to her pleasure—the most subtle and sensitive places. A cry of ecstasy escaped her as she was engulfed by a wave of intense feeling such as she had never known. Again and again, unceasingly, her body rose up responsively, not even allowing her a moment to stop and catch her breath.

A little later, Ankhesen sat beside the window, gasping for breath, the moonlight reflected in her face, which shone with perspiration. The boy, bewildered, exclaimed, "I never imagined you coming to me on your own two feet!"

She contemplated his body, gleaming in the light of the moon. No other body had given her this pleasure, rapture such as she had never before experienced—not with the wolves' whelp, not with any of the dozens of slaves and guards. No one had given her, as he had, the sensation that her limbs were dissolving.

"If you had given me a sign," he said, "I would have slipped past the guards and soldiers to kneel at your feet."

She took his head in her hands, gazed into his pale eyes, and pressed his face to her breasts, into which, trembling, she felt him sink his teeth. She cried out in pain. "I don't want you to kneel at my feet," she said. "I want you to be king—my king."

It was a crazy idea, and yet, from the first night on, she could not stop thinking about it. She felt more certain each time she crossed the patch of damp grass, ravenous for him; each time she lay bathed in sweat on his narrow wooden bed; each time she returned, drunk and sated with pleasure. She could no longer detect any scent but her own in his bed. She would envision the details of how it might be accomplished, each time Tut lay beside her, with his slight frame and dark complexion, starting up from time to time as if relentlessly beset by nightmares. But it was an idea so outlandish as to render Tayfour impotent with fear. He got up out of bed and covered the beautiful, naked body that was his glory.

"I am a foreigner here," he said. "No one would accept me."

"When I choose you, they will accept you. It was I who gave the throne to my husband, and I can still give it to you. I am the daughter of Isis. He who sits upon my lap shall be Pharaoh."

She spoke with a keen resolve, a firmness of mind so different from the ungovernable appetites of her body. Truly she was a goddess, with her wide eyes and delicate lashes—no one could check her desires or break her will. Everyone knew of their relationship—her nightly forays were observed, her moans overheard. But his being the instrument of her pleasure was one thing; for him to attempt to ascend the throne would be quite another.

"What about the present Pharaoh?" he said. "The one who still lives—your husband?"

"This is what we must arrange between us. He is no good for this life. Every night he goes across the river—to the land of the dead. And it is there he must stay."

That night with him she gave herself over to violent passion, and did not leave off even after he had grown shaky. She had found the bodily release she had sought for so long—she had come to this point in the same crazed and outlandish way in which her father had conceived his decision to destroy the old gods and follow a new one.

In her bid to achieve her ends before revealing to all the true state of affairs, time was her adversary; she must exploit her power as queen and make all arrangements out of everyone's sight, well concealed from the Pharaoh and Horemheb—especially Horemheb. She would need enough gold to persuade the guards who watched Tayfour's every move to look the other way, and to expedite the task of the river guards in crossing to the other shore, and of the ferrymen in finding anchorage that would not be discovered by the night watchmen. No one knew the truth of her scheme—or its intended outcome. Each participant was apprised only of that small part in the proceedings for which he would be paid.

She waited for a night when the moon would be full, when the ancient wolf spirits would awaken and they would call to one another, howling all through the night, in a communication between two worlds: that of the living, and that of the dead. Seeing Tut preparing to cross to the western shore of the river, she shrank for a moment in fear of the deed she was contemplating. She clung to his neck. He felt the quivering tension in her body as she pressed herself to him.

"Don't leave me this night!" she cried desperately. "Lie here beside me and do with my body what you will—or do nothing. Only stay with me!"

But he too was gripped by a sense of urgency, every cell of his being straining toward the moment in which his senses, his former instincts, would reawaken. He saw the moon through the window, looking down upon him, pale and round, encircled by a nimbus composed of the spirits of his ancestors—they were calling on him to join them. He left her and hurried down to where the boat awaited him. The river was dark and cold.

The affair was proceeding like a destiny foretold. Had she been trying to prevent him from going, or to hasten him on his way? Then she heard footsteps approaching her room—had Tut suddenly changed his mind, and come back? But it was Horemheb who entered the room, not waiting for permission, before she could cover herself—who but he would dare to do such a thing? He stood before her, his face dark with anger, and she felt a cold apprehensiveness clutch at her heart. She shrank from his grimace, and said, "My lord Pharaoh is not here."

"Indeed," he said, his voice booming. "I am aware of that. It is you I've come to speak to, to learn what is going on between you and the hostage."

She turned sharply toward him, shaking off her fear. "You wouldn't dare touch him," she said.

"I shall remove this man and send him far away," he replied. "I shall imprison him . . . if necessary I shall kill him."

Now she spoke her mind. "This man," she said, "is the one I deserve. From the beginning that wild child has been of no use to me. He is too weak to be the king who rules my body!"

He stared at her in consternation—it seemed to him he was seeing, once again, Akhenaten announcing his rebellion against the whole establishment. "I do not understand what you mean, oh queen," he said.

It was over, she knew. "It was I who gave Pharaoh the throne," she said, "and I can give to this other man."

Through gritted teeth, Horemheb muttered, "Such a thing shall never happen. I will not vanquish the barbarians in the north only to permit them to vanquish me at Thebes. It cannot be . . ."

He left her then. She saw him crossing the wet grass, heading for where Tayfour was lodged. Would he be able to stop him? Was it possible that any harm should come to him?

◆ ◆ ◆

That morning, Howard appeared looking elegant, and happier than usual. He paid no attention to her grave expression or the effects of sleeplessness that showed in her face.

"Lord Carnarvon arrives today. He and his daughter will cross from the east side of the river, so that we may open up the tomb. I don't suppose you can meet anyone, in the state you're in."

She did not look at him. She felt her heart was breaking. Ever since he had discovered that wretched stairway he had been ignoring her. All he cared about was telling the elderly Lord Carnarvon that he had found something that might turn out to be astonishing. He had gone no farther than the outer door and the vault beyond it—he did not yet know whether the tomb, hidden behind a wall of clay, was empty or whether a king awaited him within it. He resisted his own curiosity, setting a guard over the site day and night, and enjoining his men not to speak of the matter. Throughout those days he did not see her. So anxious was he that he saw none but himself.

Aisha refrained from questioning him; she could see that she had fallen into a trap. She had thrown him a life ring—to her cost, for now here he was, back to ingratiating himself with the elderly Lord Carnarvon and his sallow-faced daughter. Henceforth he would never see Aisha, nor would he perceive the danger besetting her, closed in as she was by this angry valley.

As she stared into space, all at once the sun went behind the clouds, and the river grew dark. Before her she saw the wolves, in their dusty pelts, mouths open and tongues lolling, eyes gleaming brighter than ever by the light of day. Lord

Carnarvon and his pallid daughter must be alighting on the shore even now, making for the tomb, broadcasting the death of a king, the death of everything. The wolves moved toward her. Afraid of nothing, unstoppable, they surrounded the house on every side. She remembered the harsh expression upon her mother's face, and knew it would be useless to scream. There was no escape.

◆ ◆ ◆

Tut advanced, while the wolves howled—they were spreading out across the land, bounding over the hills, and now they were nearly upon him. He could see them clearly, and they could smell his scent. The four guards stood well away from him, close to the riverbank, trembling. The old Tut had awoken once more—there was no need for him to be in this city, or to worship this god. He must stand against Horemheb, put a stop to the inscriptions that were filling up the walls of his tomb against his will, efface the images of these gods he detested, not let them take over his destiny, his life in the other world. The howling of the wolves rose, pulsing, alive, endowing his body with extra energy. He must reclaim his rightful place, make it clear to everyone that he was not a traitor, no partisan of Amun, and not beholden to Horemheb. He would announce his repudiation of all of it, and so, perhaps, reclaim his lost manhood.

He spied the shadow of some phantom, stirring near the doorway to the tomb, then disappearing behind a rock. Was it one of the guards, or a tomb robber? He was no longer afraid—at this moment he could have faced them all—no one would dare to harm the Pharaoh of Egypt! But he felt the force of a great blow as it struck the back of his head. He heard the sound of something shattering, the rocks were spinning, the stars growing distant, and the pain was beyond endurance. Then, all at once, darkness fell.

◆ ◆ ◆

I wouldn't have believed Lord Carnarvon could manage all the steps leading to the mouth of the tomb. The lady held fast to his arm as they stepped over the rubble. Then they paused to look at me, breathing hard. They did not believe that I had anything worthwhile to offer them. I approached the old man, held out my hand, and took his arm to help him keep his balance as we descended along the passageway. The lady stood where she was, hesitating, and when I approached her she raised her eyes as if seeing me for the first time, and held her hand out to me. Incredulous, I took it, and slowly escorted her down the passage. Still she was altogether cold, casting openly doubtful glances at me. The men who had done the excavation were looking down at us from above, smelling of sweat, their faces coated with dust. But their part in the proceedings was finished. She held her delicate nose with one hand, but left the other hand in mine until she stood beside her father. She had relinquished some of her pallor, her face flushed with exertion.

I pointed out the cartouche bearing the name of the king, explaining to them the meaning of the hieroglyphic inscription. Then we proceeded on into the tomb. The air grew hot and stifling, and Lord Carnarvon paused several times to catch his breath. We came to a halt before the blocked-off wall that stood between us and another epoch, with all its secrets and illusions. The breathing of the men watching from above could be heard resounding in the passageway, but none of them dared come any closer. From a distance a faint sound reached us, like that of wolves howling, although we were in broad daylight. I took up a small pickaxe I had placed there specially, next to the wall, and struck the first blow . . . then the second. The wall was no more than a barrier of brittle clay, with space behind it: the as-yet-undiscovered tomb of a king. A small crack opened before us, emitting thickly musty air, laden with the odor of decay, and of pitch and camphor—ancient air, which had lain dormant for so many eons. Lord Carnarvon clutched his chest and began to cough violently. The lady seized his hand and patted it, glaring at me once again. At last the air grew still. Flying insects, grayish in color, swarmed about, but dispersed on encountering the outer air. Lord Carnarvon, recovering, stood up straight. I wanted him to take a look through the crack, but he indicated that he would not be able to manage it, and I dared not ask the lady. I lit the electric lamp, and directed the beam through the opening, into the interior chamber. What I glimpsed was like a dream: the shimmer of a golden mirage, glowing despite the darkness that had accumulated since the beginning of time. With an effort, Lord Carnarvon spoke to me.

"Can you see anything?" he said.

"Yes," I replied. "Wonderful things."

Historical Figures Featured in the Novel

Glossary

Historical Figures Featured in the Novel

Abbas, Khedive (Abbas II Hilmi Bey [1874–1944]). Last Ottoman viceroy (khedive) of Egypt and Sudan (1892–1914), deposed by the British in 1914.

Ali, Muhammad (1769–1849). Commander in the Ottoman army, originally from Albania; a political reformer who declared himself viceroy of Egypt and Sudan in 1805 and served in that capacity until 1848; he is widely considered the founder of modern Egypt.

Amherst, Lord (William Amhurst Tyssen-Amherst [1835–1909]). British politician remembered primarily as a collector of antiquities.

Andrews, Emma. Mistress of Theodore Davis (s.v.); in the novel she is called Emilia.

el-Baroudy, Mahmoud Sami (1839–1904). Nationalist poet and political figure, who also briefly served as prime minister of Egypt in 1882.

Baybars, al-Zahir (ca. 1223–77). A Mamluk (see glossary) sultan of Egypt, of Turkic origin; in 1254 he defeated the Seventh Crusade of France's King Louis IX, and in 1260 scored a major victory over the Mongols.

Belzoni, Giovanni Battista (1778–1823). Italian explorer and excavator of Egyptian antiquities.

Blunt, Wilfrid Scawen (1840–1922). English poet, translator, and political commentator; anti-imperialist.

Carnarvon, Lord (George Edward Stanhope Molyneux Herbert [1866–1923]). English aristocrat best remembered as an amateur Egyptologist who bankrolled various excavations, most notably Howard Carter's discovery of Tutankhamun's tomb in 1922.

Carter, Howard (1874–1939). British artist and Egyptologist renowned for discovering Tutankhamun's tomb in 1922; although a great part of Carter's portrayal in *A Cloudy Day on the Western Shore* is essentially factual, much has been fictionalized; in addition to the invention of his relationship with Aisha (herself an invention) and numerous lesser episodes, aspects of Carter's family background are only loosely depicted. Accounts differ, for example, as to whether he was one of eight or eleven children (most say eleven), but seem to agree that he did not actually have any younger siblings.

Cromer, Lord (Evelyn Baring [1841–1917]). British consul general in Egypt from 1883 to 1907; much resented among Egyptians for his repressive policies. Britain's draconian response to the Dinshaway incident (see glossary) may be seen as effectively his undoing as an administrator in Egypt.

Davis, Theodore (1838–1915). American lawyer and amateur Egyptologist; his wealth financed some of the excavations in Upper Egypt.

Fahmi, Mustafa (1840–1914). Egyptian politician who served variously as cabinet member and prime minister, accused of subservience to the British; it is not clear whether or not the incident relating to illegal ownership of slaves actually occurred.

Farid, Mohammed (1868–1919). Egyptian nationalist and reformer, of Turkish background; backer of Mustafa Kamil (s.v.), and second president of the Egyptian National Party.

Fazil, Zainab Nazli (1853–1913). Egyptian princess of Turkish origin; well-educated and vocal, she may have wielded some influence with the leading politicians of the day, both Egyptian and British.

Ismaïl Pasha (1830–95). Khedive of Egypt and Sudan from 1863 to 1879, who followed much of the reformist agenda of his grandfather Muhammad Ali, but mismanaged Egypt's finances and was eventually dismissed by the Ottoman sultan.

Kamal, Yusuf (1882–1966). Founded Egypt's first art academy, the Egyptian School of Fine Arts, in 1908, and sponsored Mahmoud Mukhtar (s.v.) in 1912, when Mukhtar undertook his studies in France.

Kamil, Hussein (1853–1917). Sultan of Egypt, 1914–17, so appointed under the newly declared British protectorate, selected for his sympathy to British interests, to replace Khedive Abbas II (q.v.).

Kamil, Mustafa (1874–1908). Egyptian lawyer and nationalist, founder, in 1900, of the newspaper *al-Liwa* (see glossary), and of the Egyptian National Party in 1907.

Kitchener, Lord (Horatio Herbert Kitchener [1850–1916]). Senior officer in the British Army and colonial administrator in Egypt and Sudan; succeeded Lord Cromer (q.v.) as consul general of Egypt, succeeded by Eldon Gorst (1861–1911).

Laplagne, Guillaume (1894–1927). French sculptor, first director of the Egyptian School of Fine Arts (see Yusuf Kamal, q.v.), who counted Mahmoud Mukhtar (s.v.) among his protégés.

Mahdi, the (Muhammad Ahmad bin Abd Allah [1844–85]). Son of a Sudanese boat builder and charismatic religious leader (member of the Samaniyyah Sufi order), who in 1881 proclaimed himself the divinely appointed harbinger of the last days (the Mahdi); he assumed military command of a force called the Ansar (helpers), and led several successful campaigns against the Egyptians and the British.

Mariette, François Auguste Ferdinand (1821–81). French scholar and Egyptologist, founder of the Egyptian Department of Antiquities. He is thought to have devised, at the behest of Khedive Ismaïl Pasha (q.v.), the plot of Giuseppe Verdi's opera *Aida*, which premiered in Cairo in 1871.

Maspero, Gaston (1846–1916). French Egyptologist who twice served as director of the Department of Antiquities; he was not in fact its director in 1891, when Howard Carter (q.v.) first arrived in Egypt. Maspero was dedicated to combating the illegal trade in artifacts, and he helped found the Egyptian Museum, in Cairo, in 1902.

Mukhtar, Mahmoud (1891–1934). Son of a peasant family, from the village of Tanbara in the Egyptian Delta. Mukhtar was one of the first students to attend the Egyptian School of Fine Arts upon its opening in 1908, but he was not actually dismissed from the school—he graduated, and went on scholarship (in either 1911 or 1912; accounts differ) to study at École des Beaux-Arts in Paris. He is best known for his sculpture *Egypt Awakened* (located in Cairo's Ramses Square in 1928), which expresses nationalist sentiment, and now stands by the avenue leading to Cairo University.

Naville, Henri Édouard (1844–1926). Swiss archaeologist and Egyptologist.

Newberry, Percy (1869–1949). British Egyptologist who travelled to Egypt with Howard Carter in 1891, having selected Carter to train as a tracer of ancient wall art.

Orabi, Ahmed (1841–1911). Egyptian military leader of peasant stock who founded the Egyptian Nationalist Party in 1879. In 1882 he led an unsuccessful rebellion against Khedive Tawfiq as part of the Egyptian resistance against Ottoman rule; Tawfiq called for reinforcements against the uprising, resulting in the British bombardment of Alexandria, which culminated in the occupation of Egypt.

Paget, Rosalind Frances Emily (1844–1925). Artist in Egypt who produced watercolor paintings of art from various sites in Upper Egypt; she is mentioned in a letter penned by Edouard Naville.

Petrie, William Matthew Flinders (1853–1942). British Egyptologist and pioneer of archaeological methodology and conservation.

al-Rafiy, Abdel Rahman (1889–1966). Egyptian historian of Levantine origin; he joined the Egyptian National Party in 1907.

al-Sayyid, Ahmed Lutfi (1872–1963). Egyptian intellectual, activist, and founder, in 1907, of Egypt's first political party, Hezb al-Umma, as a direct response to the Dinshaway incident (see glossary) in 1906. The founding of the Egyptian National Party by Mustafa Kamil (q.v.) followed soon thereafter.

Weigall, Arthur (1880–1934). British Egyptologist and author. When Howard Carter was dismissed from his post as chief inspector of antiquities for Upper Egypt in 1905 following an incident involving a group of French tourists, Weigall was appointed in his place; historical accounts suggest that the rivalry between Weigall and Carter was, at times, as bitter as the novel's narrative suggests.

Wolseley, Garnet (1833–1913). Anglo-Irish officer in the British Army and commander of the British forces assisting Khedive Tawfiq at the time of the rebellion staged by Orabi (q.v.), whom Wolseley defeated in the Battle of Tel-el-Kebir, near Suez in the Egyptian Delta.

Glossary

abaya. A cloak-like wrap, frequently made of wool, but may be composed of other fabric.

bey. Traditionally a title of prestigious social rank, achieved either by merit or through bribes and awarded by the ruler of Egypt; it may also be used more loosely as a term of respectful address.

dahabeah. A type of wind-propelled houseboat specifically associated with the Nile, and often with nineteenth-century tourism, although this type of vessel, in one form or another, has existed since pharaonic times.

dhikr. A practice, Sufi in origin, of repetitive chanting in praise of God; may be accompanied by music and dance, or dance-like ritual movements.

Dinshaway. A village in the Egyptian Delta, iconic in the history of Egypt as one of imperialist Britain's most egregious atrocities in the region (1906); the novel's description of this episode hews substantially to historical accounts.

effendi. A gentleman, specifically a non-European clothed in Western garb, except for the distinctive cylindrical hat (usually red, with a tassel) known as a *tarbush*; also used as a postpositive title, and sometimes as a proper name.

al-Fatiha. Opening chapter of the Qur'an, often recited on ceremonial occasions, but also under relatively informal circumstances.

felucca. A sailboat of traditional Egyptian design; similar to a sloop, except that, unlike a sloop, it may have two sails rather than just one.

fellah (pl. fellahin). A peasant farmer.

gallabiya. A long, robe-like garment, traditionally worn by male Egyptian and Sudanese peasants (although its use has expanded); especially in cold weather, other clothing, such as long underpants, may be worn underneath.

hajj. The Muslim pilgrimage to Mecca, specifically performed during Dhu al-Hijja, the last month of the lunar Islamic calendar; pilgrimages performed at other times of year are known as *'Umra*.

hanim. Lady; originally a Turkish term referring to an aristocratic woman, it came to be applied postpositively to the names of high-class Egyptian women.

Helmiya al-Gadida. A district of Cairo; notably more prosperous than that of Gamamiz Lane.

jilbaab. A long, flowing outer garment; similar to a gallabiya (q.v.), worn by either men or women.

khamsin. A hot southerly Egyptian wind usually carrying sand.

khedive. An official of the Ottoman court, roughly equivalent to viceroy; the khedivate of Egypt was a tributary state of the Ottoman empire, lasting from 1867 until 1914 and substantially overlapping with the British occupation of Egypt (1882–1914).

kuttab. Traditional primary school at which, in addition to religious teachings, reading, writing, and grammar are taught, with the Qur'an as the basis for instruction.

al-Liwa. Nationalist Egyptian newspaper founded in 1900 by Mustafa Kamil; the word *liwaa'* means banner.

Maghreb. The region of North Africa generally associated with modern-day Morocco, Algeria, and Tunisia.

Majnoun and Layla. The principal characters in a well-known traditional story, dating to pre-Islamic times, of star-crossed lovers.

Mamluks. Muslim rulers between the tenth and nineteenth centuries, who were originally slaves conscripted into military service; accorded privileges denied ordinary slaves, they were ultimately able to seize power in their own right and establish a series of dynasties in Persia, Egypt, and elsewhere.

mastaba. A specific type of ancient Egyptian tomb, consisting of a rectangular superstructure and one or more subterranean chambers.

mizmar. A single-reed musical instrument producing a sound somewhat similar to that of an oboe.

nargileh. A device for smoking tobacco (or sometimes hashish) consisting of a flexible or bamboo pipe attached to a bottle-like receptacle filled with water, through which smoke is drawn to filter and cool it; also known as hubble-bubble, hookah, *gouza*, or *shisha*.

Pasha. An upper rank in the Ottoman political and military system; also an honorary title similar to that accorded a peer or knight in the British system.

piaster. A small coin, equivalent to one one-hundredth of an Egyptian pound.

rebaba **(also rebab).** A traditional instrument with a small sound box, a long neck, and two or three strings, played with a bow.

riyal. A small coin (no longer used in Egypt) worth twenty piasters. (q.v.).

Saïd. Upper Egypt, generally considered to be the regions of Egypt extending south from Fayoum; the term *Saïdi* refers to an Upper Egyptian.

Sea of Shadows. An ancient name for the Atlantic Ocean.

al-Siyaasa. Fictional name of a turn-of-the-century (early 1900s) Egyptian newspaper more sympathetic to British occupation than *al-Liwa* (q.v.); the word *siyaasa* also means politics. The actual name of the newspaper founded by Lutfi al-Sayyid (see Historical Figures Featured in the Novel) was *al-Jarida*, and it was not, in reality, sympathetic to colonial interests; on the contrary, it was nationalist in character.

Born in 1946, **Mohamed Mansi Qandil** is an Egyptian writer of novels and short stories. He studied medicine and, following his graduation in 1975, practiced medicine for a few years before devoting himself to writing full time. He is the author of several novels and short-story collections.

Barbara Romaine has been teaching and translating Arabic since the early 1990s. In 2011 she placed second for the Saif Ghobash Banipal Prize for Arabic Literary Translation, and she has held two fellowships in translation from the National Endowment for the Arts, the second of which supported her translation of *A Cloudy Day on the Western Shore.*